FRITZ LEIBER'S
LANKHMAR

Praise for
SWORDS AGAINST THE SHADOWLAND

"Full of humor and gripping adventure, *Swords Against the Shadowland* is a wonderful tribute to Fritz Leiber, for Robin has splendidly captured the quintessential spirit of Fafhrd and the Gray Mouser. Somewhere in Lankhmar, Fritz is smiling."
—Dennis L. McKiernan, author of the Hel's Crucible duology

"Sword and Sorcery like Mama used to make, if your mama happens to be Fritz Leiber."**—Esther Friesner**

"Before I started reading Bailey's book, I reread some of Leiber's original work. Robin Wayne Bailey's tale captures both the feel of Leiber's language, and the larger emotional overtones of our two heroes and their world. Congratulations to Robin for such an excellent return to a world fondly remembered."
—Rachel Holmen, publisher of *Marion Zimmer Bradley's Fantasy Magazine*

"Fafhrd and the Gray Mouser live! Robin Wayne Bailey captures the essence of Leiber's classic heroes with wit and style. *Swords Against the Shadowland* is a fast-paced adventure spiced with pathos, dark humor, and banter worthy of Leiber himself. A great read."**—Lynn Flewelling**

"In *Swords Against the Shadowland,* Robin Wayne Bailey attempts, and succeeds, in re-creating Fritz Leiber's style with a new adventure of Fafhrd and the Gray Mouser. Where Bailey most fully succeeds is capturing Leiber's ability for atmospheric descriptions."**—Steven Silver's On-line Reviews**

LANKHMAR
FROM DARK HORSE BOOKS

By Fritz Leiber

Swords and Deviltry
Swords Against Death
Swords in the Mist
Swords Against Wizardry
The Swords of Lankhmar
Swords and Ice Magic
The Knight and Knave of Swords

*By Fritz Leiber
and Robin Wayne Bailey*

Swords Against the Shadowland

FRITZ LEIBER'S
LANKHMAR

SWORDS AGAINST THE SHADOWLAND

BOOK EIGHT IN THE ADVENTURES OF FAFHRD AND THE GRAY MOUSER

ROBIN WAYNE BAILEY

DARK HORSE BOOKS®
MILWAUKIE

Book design by HRoberts Design
Cover design by Heidi Whitcomb
Map art and design by Ryan Hill

Published by Dark Horse Books
A division of Dark Horse Comics
10956 SE Main Street
Milwaukie, OR 97222

darkhorse.com

First Dark Horse Books Edition: April 2009
ISBN 978-1-59582-077-8

Printed in the United States of America

1 3 5 7 9 10 8 6 4 2

ACKNOWLEDGMENTS

For Fritz Leiber, whose work I so admire, with the hope that I've done his creation some small justice.

For Richard Curtis and Patrick Neilson Hayden, with deepest gratitude for giving me this chance to walk where a giant went before.

And always for Diana.

CONTENTS

ONE

THE MOUSER'S DREAM

Deep underground, beneath the busiest streets of fabled Lankhmar City, in a shadowed corner of the secret Temple of Hates, the wizard Malygris wiped heat-sweat from his brow, leaned slender hands on his worktable, and laughed.

The triumphantly evil sound of his mirth echoed on the blackened stone walls of the narrow, rectangular chamber and among the many squat columns that supported its claustrophobically low ceiling before it drifted up the carefully concealed ventilation shafts, through the sewers and the sewer gratings, to touch the ears of a throng of celebrants who wandered through the Festival District on the first night of Midsummer's Moon, but the only one who noticed tilted his head and dismissed the sound as an amusing trick of the wind and gave his attention once more to the pretty harlot he had rented for the evening.

The yellow light from a pair of half-melted candles glimmered on the cucurbits and alembics assembled on the worktable. A stack of dusty books cluttered one corner of the scarred, wooden surface. Powder-filled vials, beakers of strangely colored liquids, and small bowls of pungent herbs, along with metal instruments, some gleaming, some scorched black by flame, were scattered about in seemingly haphazard fashion.

With two sweeps of his voluminously sleeved arms, Malygris swept the table clear, leaving only the candles and a single alembic. Glass shattered and books fluttered through the air like terrorized birds unable to take flight.

Pushing back the hood of his robe to reveal a shaved head, he bent close, dark eyes glittering, to stare at the blood-red vapor that slowly swirled inside the bulbous vessel. As he watched, a tendril of that unholy mist rose up through the vessel's tapering neck, pushed and prodded at the unyielding stopper, retreated, then probed the stopper again.

Malygris ran the tip of one unnaturally long finger around and around the outside of the stopper. There was no more laughter in him. His face contorted into a mask of jealousy and rage.

"I have you now, Sadaster, my enemy," he hissed in a whisper that was more serpentine than human. "Thief of my one, true love. Often have I struck at thee, and always have you thwarted my revenge. Nevermore, Sadaster, nevermore."

Malygris picked up the alembic with the red vapor, caressed it in his hands, ran the cool glass down the soft tissue of his throat as he sighed an almost erotic sigh, then pressed it to his breast. Closing his browless eyes, he felt the beat of his heart against the delicate vessel.

With an almost imperceptible subtlety, the vapor began to pulse, matching his heart rhythm for rhythm.

Malygris drew back the hand that clutched the fruit of his vile researches. A silken sleeve slithered down his bony, hairless arm as some faint doubt made him pause. Then, breath held, he dashed the alembic to the floor.

The glass exploded, but without so much as a hint of sound. For a moment, the red vapor pooled among the glistening shards before it began to float upward, writhing gracefully, like a ribbon on an updrafting wind.

The candles sputtered in sudden fury, spitting hot wax across the table and upon one of Malygris's blue-veined hands, eliciting from the wizard a sharp cry of pain and surprise. Without seeming cause, the flames extinguished themselves, leaving Malygris in the subterranean dark.

The wisp rose up through the roof of the Temple of Hates, up through layers of earth, through the smooth granite paving that made Festival Street. The celebrants of Midsummer's Moon, well on their way to drunkenness, took no notice as it climbed higher and higher into the night, caught a current of breeze, and wafted across unsuspecting Lankhmar, becoming more and more tenuous, then finally invisible, to a mansion on Nun Street in the River District.

The home of the mage, Sadaster, was the envy of the city's nobles. Within its gates and high walls, orange and lemon groves poured out their heady perfume, and every flower known to the world of Nehwon, no matter the season, that was not poisonous blossomed. A fountain of purest white stone created a pleasant, soothing trickle while wind chimes made random music.

In the master bedroom of this wondrous house, Sadaster lay with his beautiful wife, Laurian, asleep on his arm with only a sheet of thin red silk to cover them. Midsummer's Moon floated at zenith, but the glow of the bright star, Shadah, suspended on the horizon, spilled straight through the window. In its radiance, he admired Laurian's sweet face and felt his heart fill with love. The first signs of age marked the corners of her eyes and her lips, and gleaming in the starlight, he spied a single silver hair. Yet he loved those eyes and lips and that softly textured hair more than life.

The mist, no longer a ribbon, filtered down around the mansion, undetected by wizardly wards or protections, and waited.

Sadaster moved ever so gently so as not to awaken his wife as he kissed her hair. All traces of silver vanished from those beloved locks. With the tip of his little finger, he brushed the outer corners of her eyes and her mouth, erasing the evidence of time.

Even as he completed these simple magicks, he wept quietly, for he knew that his spells could only hide the effects of aging and that someday, Laurian, the great blessing of his life, would go to the Shadowland, as all mortals did, leaving him, with his wizard's lifespan, lonely and alone.

Drying his tears, Sadaster hugged his wife closer, and put away such thoughts. Beyond the sill, Shadah twinkled hypnotically like a rare jewel, and the nightwind played a gentle lullaby. Inhaling the fragrances that rose from the garden, Sadaster at last surrendered to sleep.

The mist waited no more. It entered the room through the walls and the roof, through the floor and through the window. Unseeable tendrils seeped toward the bed, flowed upon the silken sheets, and touching the nostrils of the sleeping mage, wormed their way into his body.

Without waking, Sadaster gave a small cough.

The Gray Mouser woke from a troubling dream and sat slowly up on the thin blanket that made his pallet. The campfire he had made to keep away the mountain leopards had burned down to red-glowing embers. Only a few tiny flames flickered here and there among the coals.

On the other side of the fire, Fafhrd, his companion, lay stretched out under a blanket too small to cover his huge frame, his bare feet and legs sticking out from one end. A strangely troubled expression creased Fafhrd's sleeping face, and without waking, he closed one giant hand slowly around the leather sheath of the great sword he called Graywand and clutched it to his body.

Unable to shake the perplexing dream from his mind, the Mouser rose slowly to his feet. The wind blew cool and moist against his face and down the unlaced neck of his rumpled gray silk tunic as he turned his gaze up toward the stars. In the north the seven-starred constellation called the Targe shone serenely, and directly above it, bright Shadah. The Mouser scratched his head.

A low moan drew his attention back to Fafhrd as his friend sat up, rubbed a hand through the tangled locks of his red-gold hair, and shook himself. Fafhrd looked toward the Mouser with an expression that said he was still not quite awake. "Little friend," Fafhrd grumbled, "the strangest dream has come to me."

The Mouser's frown deepened. "And to me," he answered, bending toward his pallet to retrieve his weapon belt, from which depended a slender sword and dagger.

"I dreamed of a jealous wizard . . ." Fafhrd started to explain. Then, as if for the first time, he took note of the Mouser's actions and came fully alert. His voice dropped to the barest whisper, and one hand closed about the hilt of the great sword. "Have I been a sleepy-eyed, dull-eared slaggard? Does some danger steal upon us?" His eyes suddenly widened. "I was on watch!"

"You fell asleep," the Mouser said, keeping his voice low. "Later, I'll poke merciless fun of you for it. For now, though, I spy no immediate threat." Fastening the sword belt around his waist, he turned back to his partner. "It is no small matter, however, this dream you've had. Were there two wizards and a woman?"

Fafhrd's eyes widened yet again, and he rose cautiously to stand beside the fire. The dim light glowed on his powerfully muscled form. Nearly seven feet tall, the Northerner towered over his much smaller companion. "Aye," he answered, "and one of them died a horrible, wasting death."

The Mouser shrugged. "I woke up before that part," he said, "But if your wizard died in Lankhmar on Midsummer's Moon, then I've had this same dream."

"In Lankhmar, yes, curse that wretched city's name," Fafhrd said with a scowl. "And there was a festival, but Sadaster didn't die until nearly the Eve of the Frost Moon." His brow wrinkled with sudden concern. "What thievery is this?" he said with an air of offense. "Must we now split and share our dreams as we share our booty?"

Bending toward his pallet once again, the Mouser retrieved the cloak that, wadded, had served his head for a pillow. It was made of the same coarse gray silk as his tunic, and he tossed it around his shoulders and fastened it at his throat. "You are still half-asleep, Fafhrd," he said. "Use those innocent-seeming green eyes of yours for something besides bait to attract pretty girls and the wives of aristocrats."

Fafhrd seemed momentarily confused. Then he stared around their small camp. "The booty!" he cried in dismay, forgetting to lower his voice. "It's gone. Lord Hristo's jewels—all our hard work!"

The Mouser raised one eyebrow and smirked. "Hard work, yes," he muttered. "You spent a whole night boffing the lord's wife until she finally lost consciousness . . ."

Fafhrd shrugged sheepishly under his partner's scolding.

". . . while I pilfered every bauble in the house."

Again, Fafhrd shrugged. "Someone had to distract her," he replied.

"You might have distracted a few of her servants or her guardsmen, too, while you were in the business of distracting."

The Northerner snorted. "I distracted her husband well enough when he returned unexpectedly to find you clutching every star in that firmament he called a strongroom."

A brief smile flickered over the Mouser's lips as he remembered the glimmering wealth in Lord Hristo's treasure chests and the comforting weight of the saddlebags on his shoulders once he had quietly transferred that wealth.

"And a merry chase into the Mountains we led him, too," Fafhrd continued, "with his soldiers hot on our heels. Damn clever of you, little man, to spill one of the bags in our wake. Hristo's soldiers fairly flew out of their saddles to snatch the sparklies from the dust." He came around the fire and dealt the Mouser a congratulatory slap on the back. "But where—tell me now and tease me no more—is the remaining treasure?"

"With our horses, I suppose," the Mouser answered simply. "Still in the Mountains of the Elder Ones."

Fafhrd glared at his companion before turning his gaze to follow the Mouser's. Abruptly, he rubbed his eyes again to make sure all sleep was gone from them. Then he dived for his boots and began pulling them on. "The Mountains!" he exclaimed. "They're gone, too!"

Shaking his head, the Mouser stared once more upward at the night sky, noting familiar constellations and the positions of the stars. "I suspect the mountains are right where they've always been," he said with a nervous calm. "It is we who are gone from the mountains, shifted somehow across the world in our sleep—a sleep no doubt forced upon you as you kept watch."

"The dream . . ." Fafhrd started, rising again and pacing about.

"Aye, the dream," the Mouser agreed in an uneasy grumble as the images came tumbling once again into his head. "We have been snatched up by some god or wizard, Fafhrd, and transported here." He stirred the outer ashes of their dwindling campfire with the toe of one mouseskin boot. "Nice of them to bring our warmth along," he said caustically.

"Pity they couldn't have brought along my jewels," Fafhrd pouted. He quickly changed the subject. "I think I know where we are, Mouser," he announced, making a show of sniffing as he paced. "There's a familiarity about the air."

"You mean about the reek?" the Mouser corrected, wrinkling his nose as he, too, sniffed. The odor of weed-rot hung in the night. Like his partner, he too had made a guess about their present location, but whereas Fafhrd no doubt based his supposition on his barbarian-bred senses, he based his own on a knowledge of the positions of the stars and constellations, a distinction about which he felt quite smug.

Fafhrd, clutching Graywand in his hands, exposed a portion of the blade then slammed it back into the sheath, a gesture that was both an insult and a curse to his northern people. "This is the Great Salt Marsh," he said, his lips curled back in puzzlement and anger as he turned to face the west. "We're back in Lankhmar where we swore we would never come again."

The Mouser pursed his lips thoughtfully. The night wind brushed through the dark locks of his hair as softly as a woman's fingers, and he remembered a girl named Ivrian, a delicate, pretty little wisp with flowing blond hair and laughing eyes, who had been his first true love. He remembered also returning home one evening to find rats gnawing her murdered corpse and that of another woman, Vlana, who was Fafhrd's first love.

The quest to avenge Ivrian and Vlana had cemented the Mouser's friendship with the big Northerner, and grief had driven them from that despised city when their vengeance was complete. Like Fafhrd, he had no desire to return.

He touched his companion's arm. "Turn away, Fafhrd," he said. "A road still runs two ways, and nothing prevents us from giving our backs to Lankhmar twice."

But when the Mouser turned, something did block their way. Limned by the dim glow of the campfire, an old thatched hut stood on tall, stilted legs. The brittle straw that made its roof jutted up like hair on a wild man's head, and the black, blanket-covered door seemed to yawn like a toothless mouth.

The Mouser rubbed his eyes. Had he been so busy with his stargazing, or had the night been so dark that he had missed this sight before? The hairs prickling on the back of his neck, he slipped his sword, Scalpel, from its mouseskin sheath. The slender blade gleamed redly in the light of the coals.

"Either I have lost both booty and senses in the same evening," the Mouser said softly, "or that hut was not there a moment ago."

From within the hut came a muffled coughing and hacking. A barely perceived hand, more blackened bone than flesh, or so it seemed in the gloom, drew back the curtain draping the entrance. Like a slow-moving shadow, a cowled and black-robed figure emerged. It climbed down a rickety ladder, pausing after each labored step, to the ground. Reaching the bottom, it surrendered to a brief coughing fit. Then, the stooped figure shambled toward them.

From across the campfire's coals, it looked up. There was nothing to see inside that cowl, but a rasping, almost serpentine voice issued forth as the creature introduced itself.

"I am Sheelba."

The Mouser lifted the point of his sword. "This is Scalpel," he said, adding as his other hand touched the hilt of his dagger, "and this is Catsclaw. Come closer if you would make their more intimate acquaintance."

Fafhrd held his own huge blade level with the Mouser's. "I can smell a woman or a wizard a mile away," he said, scowling, "and your perfume is no dainty orchid juice."

From out of nowhere came a wind that blew through the coals of the campfire, snatching hot sparks and glowing ash into the air. A spinning vortex swiftly formed about the Mouser and Fafhrd. Like angry, swarming insects the burning bits and pieces flew around and around.

Then, just as suddenly, the wind ceased, and the coals settled harmlessly back to their original place, and the campfire was just a campfire once more.

A fit of coughing wracked the creature that called itself Sheelba. "Now that we have each displayed our manhoods," he said quietly, "let us speak of dreams and the reason you find yourselves once more in Lankhmar."

Sensing no further immediate threat, the Mouser lowered his weapon. The creature plainly desired to talk, rather than fight, and there was something almost pathetic in its uncontrollable coughing and its bent, weakened posture. "I gather," he said at last, "you are the source and cause of both."

Sheelba nodded. "I sent the dream to occupy and divert your minds while I transported your sleeping forms across the great vastness of space. The story it tells is a true one, but there is more, much more, for you to learn.

"Malygris killed Sadaster," Fafhrd said. The Northerner squatted down on his haunches and leaned on his sword as he stared across the coals at Sheelba. His eyes gleamed, and his face shone weirdly in the dim, ruddy light.

Sheelba's robed form seemed to shake and tremble, but whether from anger, fear, or ill health, the Mouser could not tell.

"Ah, he fell to a subtle and masterful spell," Sheelba said with grudging admiration. "It should have been beyond Malygris's meager talents, but jealousy and hatred drove him to surpass himself. Sadaster was near death before he even realized the cause of his affliction."

"I saw Sadaster die," Fafhrd said, grimly remembering his part of the dream. "Some hideous illness seemed to rot him from the inside out. At the end, he was no more than a living skeleton, and finally not even a living one."

A bitter note sounded in Sheelba's voice when he spoke. "That is the beauty and horror of Malygris's work," he said. "It begins as a little cough—just a little thing. Sadaster could not defend himself, because he didn't know he was under attack until the spell had already touched him." Sheelba's voice caught, and the wizard hesitated before finding strength to continue. "Would that it had ended there," he said. "Revenge is, after all, a thing understandable."

The Mouser eyed the creature before him with suspicion. "Malygris's black art has touched you, too," he said warily.

Hearing, Fafhrd rose slowly to his full seven-foot height. "It's no sickness that saps your vitality, stranger?" he said. "But evil Lankhmaran magic?"

Sheelba raised a withered fist and shook it at the sky. "Malygris was brilliant," he hissed, "but utterly inept. He had no true conception of what he had created. The spell possesses a mindless life of its own. It hangs in the ether like an arcane predator, waiting as it waited for Sadaster."

"Waiting for what?" Fafhrd asked nervously.

A swallowing sound issued from within the creature's black, faceless hood. "This spell was created to slay a wizard," Sheelba continued at last. "But Malygris, blast his soul, wove no controls into his creation. Now it strikes with purpose at every wizard, every magician, attracted by the simplest acts of legerdemain. Grand sorcerers, herb witches, young girls with their love potions, wearers of charms and talismans—they are all at risk. Indeed, many who walk the streets of Lankhmar are cursed already and know it not."

A wind sprang up again, and the Mouser's gaze shot toward the coals of the dwindling campfire, but this was seemingly a natural wind, no whim of Sheelba's, and the coals and ash performed no tricks, but stayed in their bed.

"Is there no counter-spell?" the Gray One asked. "No way to undo what has been done?"

Sheelba bent down over the campfire. A long-fingered hand snatched up one of the coals and popped it inside the hood as if it were a snack, a delicacy to be savored. Sheelba gulped, then belched.

"After much work and diligent study," he said with grim satisfaction, "I have found the counter-charm. However . . ." He paused, and the hood lifted ever so slightly until the Mouser felt the power of unseen eyes directly upon him, peering from the blackness contained in those folds of cloth. "There is one ingredient which I must have, and which you must steal for me."

Fafhrd bristled. "Steal?" he said. "Steal? You mistake us, sir!" He glanced at his gray-clad companion with a hurt expression. "We do not steal! We liberate. We pilfer. We purloin and even filch. But we do not steal!"

The Mouser ignored Fafhrd's comments. He peered closely at the strange figure on the other side of the coals. "You wear desperation like a pair of new boots," he said. "Uncomfortably. I, too, feel a sudden pinching on my soles."

Sheelba's voice was a serpentine hiss. "Even here in the Great Marsh, far beyond the city's walls, his wretched curse reaches." That black, empty cowl turned upward toward the skies, and a long sigh issued forth. "I will die from this evil unless you two bring me what I need."

Fafhrd puffed out his chest as his gaze narrowed contemptuously. "Us?" he said, his voice gruff. "Do you take us for errand boys?"

"I take you for the best thieves and adventurers ever to pass through Lankhmar's gates," the wizard answered. He raised a withered finger to stem their surprise. "Oh yes. Though I live in the swamps and marshes, nothing transpires in the City of the Black Toga that I don't know about. I am called Sheelba of the Eyeless Face. Yet I have eyes, and they are everywhere, and my ears, too. I know your reputations, as I know your deeds and your skills."

Fafhrd's contemptuous expression yielded to a prideful grin. "Indeed?" he said more pleasantly.

The Gray Mouser frowned. His companion was such an easy target for flattery, but his own suspicions were running in dangerous directions. His right hand tightened imperceptibly around Scalpel's hilt, though he wondered what good his blade could do to a being with power enough to transport two grown men halfway around Nehwon. "What is this errand you would have us run?" he asked, "and tell us if we have a choice in the matter?"

Sheelba stretched out his hand above the coals, which began to crackle and spark new flame. Then with a whooshing roar, the flame shot up into a writhing column nearly as tall as Fafhrd.

The Mouser jumped back, whipping out his sword with one hand, shielding his face from the heat with the other.

The fiery shaft quivered wildly, lighting up the landscape, coloring the sky with a blood-red hue. Two smaller prominences exploded from either side of the column, and each in turn sprouted fingers of flame. Those arms and hands began to move up and down, shaping fire as if it were potter's clay. Wherever the hands touched the flames turned silver and took seemingly solid substance.

From his dream, the Mouser recognized the form and features of the wizard called Malygris as they emerged from the fire. In only moments, a gleaming silver statue stood where the campfire had been. A penumbra of flame danced around its edges, then flickered out.

"It's alive!" Fafhrd cried in alarm, raising his sword defensively as the statue's head turned to take them in with a gaze.

"Because Malygris is alive from moment to moment in my thoughts," Sheelba explained. "Have no fear, Northerner. This is only a construct. The real Malygris is hiding somewhere in Lankhmar."

"Hiding?" the Mouser said.

Sheelba's empty cowl nodded, and his words dripped with disdain as he spoke. "Too late, the bumbling fool realizes what he has done, but he hasn't the knowledge or skill to unmake what he has made. Frankly, it's taken me a year to research a counter-measure, and I am many times his match in wizardry." He paused abruptly, seeming to choke on the last word before a bout of coughing seized him. His cloaked frame shook with the strain, and he wheezed for breath.

Despite his reservations, the Mouser started forward to help in whatever manner he could, but Sheelba held up a hand, refusing any offer of support.

"You must roust Malygris from whatever hole he has crawled into," Sheelba said, his voice noticeably weaker, when he could speak again. "My life is not the only one at stake. Many others will die if you deny me. Anyone who uses magic or is touched by it—even the simplest charms—is at risk." He pointed to the gleaming image of Malygris with a shaky finger. "No one is immune, not man, woman, or child. I have the spell that can stop this madness, and I have all the ingredients for it save one."

"Return to Lankhmar City," Fafhrd murmured. His mouth set itself in a firm, tight line as he clenched his jaw. Clearly, he found the idea as distasteful as the Mouser. "But if we do this thing for you, creature, we are hirelings, not errand boys. What rate of pay do you offer?"

"Ever the businessman," the Mouser muttered. "Ever an eye to profit."

Sheelba ignored Fafhrd, turning to the Mouser. "You understand, don't you, Gray One?" he whispered, leveling one frail finger near the Mouser's nose. "You see the choices."

With lightning quickness, the Mouser reached out and caught that finger, expecting to snap it like the twig it resembled. Instead, it bent bonelessly backward toward the wizard's wrist, and if it caused Sheelba any pain at all, he gave no sign of it. "Bah!" he cried, releasing the useless grip and stepping back.

The image of Malygris quietly watched everything with its silver eyes.

"What is it, Mouser?" Fafhrd said, moving closer to his friend, his gaze sweeping back and forth distrustfully from the silver statue to the brown-cloaked wizard. "You have better instincts for sorcery than I, and the look upon your face . . . !"

"He speaks of choices," the Mouser shouted angrily, "but this Sheelba's left us no choice at all!"

"Of course you have choices," Sheelba answered with icy calm. "You can walk away right now. In a couple of months you might even make it back to the Mountains of the Elders where I called you from. You might even find your treasure where you left it."

The statue of Malygris glanced toward Fafhrd, grinned, then did its best to wipe the grin away.

Sheelba's voice took on a nastier edge. "You might even live a long and happy life."

"Might, might, might," the Mouser shot back, "More likely, we'll cough our guts up like you're doing now and rot to death!" He slammed Scalpel back into its mouseskin sheath. "Put your sword away, Fafhrd," he said. "We don't dare gut him, much as I'd love to!"

"Couldn't we nick him a little, here and there?" the Northerner suggested, his sword still in his hand. Plainly, though, he didn't understand the situation.

The Mouser explained it to him. "Transporting us from the Elder Mountains all the way to Lankhmar took a mighty spell," he said. "Our very bodies passed through the magical ether from that point to this. There is every chance that Malygris's damnable spell has touched us."

Fafhrd stared at the Mouser, his lips pursed thoughtfully as he weighed the implications of his comrade's speech. "So," he said at last, swallowing as he turned to Sheelba of the Eyeless Face. "What is this last ingredient we're all so desperate for?"

The wizard's twisted finger resumed its natural shape, and he folded his hands together as if giving thanks for reasonable minds. As he did so, the Mouser's slender blade floated up from its sheath without any help from its owner, then through the air to prick the heart of the silver statue.

As it withdrew, a tiny bit of flame flickered on the end of the sword, then died, leaving not so much as a scorch mark on the metal.

"The final and most necessary ingredient," Sheelba whispered. "Bring me a single drop of Malygris's heart-blood."

"Why can't it ever be just a cup of sugar or a pound of salt?" Fafhrd grumbled, frowning again.

"So we are not errand boys at all, Fafhrd," the Mouser spat as he snatched his sword out of the air and returned it to its sheath. He kept his hand on it this time so it could not fly free again. "We are assassins."

The Northerner turned his gaze in the direction of Lankhmar City, and the Mouser's followed. It was still too far away and much too dark to see its soaring walls, but memories of that hated place were enough to draw them both like beacons. "I must admit, Mouser," Fafhrd said slowly, "if what this Sheelba says is true, no one ever more deserved killing."

"Then let us do it quickly, my friend," the Mouser agreed. "Find Malygris and steal his heart's blood, then put this vile city behind us once more."

"Steal?" Fafhrd began. "Steal?"

The Mouser was in no mood for his companion's bluster. He turned back to Sheelba, but the faceless creature was no longer there, nor was the silver statue of Malygris. Far out on the marshy expanse, barely visible against the starlight, Sheelba's elevated hut walked away on its stilted legs toward the deeper swamps.

TWO

SUNLIGHT AND SHADOWS

Muttering curses under his breath, the Mouser watched Sheelba's hut walk away. Those strange, stilted legs made wide, graceful strides, yet it moved soundlessly until it disappeared in the darkness.

"Giddiyup, house," Fafhrd said in quiet wonder as he sheathed his great sword. "I guess this means we go on to Lankhmar after all."

The Mouser growled, curling his lips and causing the sound to rattle deep in his throat. Wordlessly, he bent and scooped handfuls of damp earth over the coals of the campfire. Then he snatched up his blanket only to throw it down in disgust, finding it sodden with the ground's moisture.

Fafhrd only looked at his bedroll, scratched his short red beard, and shrugged.

As if by unspoken agreement, they turned and walked in the opposite direction from the way Sheelba had gone, the moon and the brighter stars lighting their way. There were few trees and few bushes. The Great Salt Marsh was little more than a sea of grass. In some places, the grass grew tall as their shoulders while in others it barely broke through the spongy earth, alternately creating sharp-bladed forests and vast open stretches.

Emerging from one such forest, Fafhrd stopped and threw an arm across the Mouser's chest. The Mouser, who had been looking downward at his feet, gave a grunt as if he'd walked into a tree. On the verge of an acid comment, he held his tongue as he stared across the expanse that confronted them.

Farther out across that wet plain, thousands of tiny golden-yellow lights swam in the air, blinking rhythmically as they bobbed and darted and danced, always orbiting, never venturing far from a squat, dome-shaped hive constructed from marsh mud.

"Glow wasps," Fafhrd whispered uneasily.

The Mouser nodded as he listened to the low, droning hum the creatures' wings made. The tall grass had muffled the sound before, and it was only upon reaching the clearing's edge that the terrible music had caught his attention.

Left alone, the insects were no threat, but the venom of a single wasp was potentially lethal. Few men ever had to worry about a single buggie, however. Once enraged, glow wasps attacked in swarms—and being temperamental by nature, it didn't take much to enrage them.

The two friends slipped silently back into the tall grass, deciding to take a wide course around the open plain and its glow wasp population, and keeping a sharp eye peeled for single hive-scouts.

The ground became damper. Water began to trickle up around their footsteps. Soon, little pools and thin streams, half hidden by the darkness and thick grass, revealed themselves. The Mouser cursed as, unexpectedly, he sank past his ankle in a muddy patch.

"Were this not midsummer," Fafhrd said, trying to hide a snicker as his comrade shook mud from his foot, "we'd be wading in muck up to our necks."

Daybreak began to slowly color the eastern sky while the moon yet lingered low in the west. For a time dawn painted the marsh with a glimmering chiaroscuro. Waves of grass quivered in a rising breeze, and silvery patches of water rippled. Here and there, gleaming spiderwebs stretched among tall cattail reeds vibrated as the wind murmured through the sticky strands. Birds wheeled gracefully overhead, and unseen creatures, barely perceived by their splashing, scampered or swam away from the immense, elongated shadows that preceded the two advancing human figures.

When the ground began to rise subtly, the Mouser gave a sigh of relief. Moments later, he stood atop a kind of winding, natural causeway that seemed to divide the marsh. On either side lay moist, grassy expanses, but the earth beneath his feet was fairly packed by centuries of horses' hooves and wagon wheels and the tread of traveling feet.

"Causey Road," the Mouser said. He pointed westward. The highest tips of the highest towers and pinnacles of Lankhmar could barely be seen by his straining eyes. "We stand upon an artery to the heart of Nehwon."

Fafhrd had found a stick—a dried reed stalk, actually—and sat down on the roadside to scrape black mud from his boots with it. A sour expression clouded his features. "Lankhmar is the heart of Nehwon?"

The Mouser nodded. "In all the world there is no city greater."

"Certainly none I hold in greater scorn," Fafhrd shot back. "The anus is as important to a body as the heart, so if we must speak in metaphors, let Lankhmar be Nehwon's arsehole."

"You're in a foul mood, to speak of arseholes," the Mouser said.

Fafhrd was sullen. "Arseholes are foul, and Lankhmar is fouler."

The Mouser grinned secretly. "Some call the city fair."

"They are unfair in their judgment," the Northerner answered curtly as he rose and cast aside the stick.

Walking westward on Causey Road, the two spoke little and kept their thoughts to themselves. The Mouser felt a weighty oppression of spirit as he approached the city, and he could tell from the slump of Fafhrd's mighty shoulders and by the sullen expression on his friend's face that the Northerner felt the same.

The marshlands were soon left behind, and the stark gray walls of Lankhmar City rose before them. Well on its way toward zenith, the morning sun beat uncomfortably on the left side of the Mouser's face. He tugged up the hood of his light gray cloak to block the burning rays, though honesty might have moved him to admit it was more to hide his own unhappy expression from Fafhrd.

Causey Road led straight into the city's Marsh Gate. There were no merchants with pitched tents clustered outside the gate as travelers would find at the city's three southern gates, nor was there any traffic. Causey Road ran eastward eventually through the Mountains of Hunger, past the Great Dike, and into the Sinking Lands. In spring and autumn a few caravans and the more adventure-minded traders set forth that way, but most businessmen found the trade far more lucrative further northward along the shores of the Inner Sea.

Two pairs of guards stood wearily in the shadows of the massive gates, sweltering in their armor and red cloaks, pikes leaned against the walls and helmets set by in the roadside dust, boredom and discomfort plain on their sweat-stained faces. As Fafhrd and the Mouser approached the gate, the four exchanged glances as if mentally choosing straws. Finally, one picked up his pike, set his helmet on his head and trudged forward.

"In the name of that peach-sucking, sheep-loving, decadent little pervert who, to Lankhmar's everlasting shame, calls himself our Overlord—halt!"

Fafhrd caught the Mouser's arm with one hand and clutched his other hand over his heart in feigned shock. "That's the prettiest speech I've heard all day, Captain," he said, grinning.

The guard, no captain at all, but a mere corporal of middle age who probably had not advanced in rank in years, looked up at the seven-foot-tall Northerner. If he was impressed he hid it well. "And the truest, I'll wager," he answered. "You look like a pair of rogues to me. Come to steal our treasury and rape our women, have you?"

The Mouser answered drily. "Be assured. Your treasury is safe from us."

The corporal smiled appreciatively, then glanced back over his shoulder at his three comrades to make sure they were safely beyond earshot. "You haven't seen our women." He grimaced as he faked a shudder. "Trust me, our gold is warmer."

Fafhrd laughed aloud. "Our captain speaks like a married man," he said.

The Mouser put on a grave face. "Is it true, good captain?" he said. "Are you so afflicted?"

The corporal hung his head as he nodded, and his shoulders slumped. "It is exactly as you have deduced," he admitted sadly. "A shrewish woman she is, who spends every coin I make and heaps debt upon my poor head." He cast another glance back at his comrades. "Why at this very moment I haven't a penny in my pocket for even a cool pint."

The Mouser eyed the guard with greater understanding. "That is a sad state in which to find oneself," he agreed. "I can fully and completely sympathize." Easing back the folds of his light gray cloak, he turned his own empty pockets inside out.

The corporal's brow furrowed in disappointment. He turned expectantly toward Fafhrd, but the red-headed giant shrugged apologetically as he turned his palms upward. "Money and these hands rarely share long acquaintance," he said.

The guard's frown only deepened.

"On the other hand, these hands," the Mouser said in reassuring tones, "have a handsome skill at finding it." He licked his lips slightly as he brushed his fingertips together. "Do you know an inn called the Silver Eel?"

"The Silver Eel?" the corporal repeated. "On Dim Lane halfway between Cheap Street and Carter. An infamous dive. I see you are not strangers to Lankhmar."

"We shall be at that infamous dive tonight before the witching hour," the Mouser informed. "If you should come around, my friend and I would be happy to buy you and your fellow threesome guards a pint. Or should you come alone you can have their share."

The corporal smiled as he rubbed a hand over his mouth and chin. "A merry and generous offer, indeed," he answered, glancing around again. "If all travelers were such understanding gentlemen as yourselves my job would be a far happier one."

"Not to mention more lucrative," Fafhrd added, rolling his gaze toward the blue sky.

The guard pretended not to hear. "Come then," he said. "It's too hot to stand in the sun like this." He made a grandiose gesture with his right arm. "Prepare yourselves to enter this stinking, rat-infested hell-hole . . ." he paused to wipe the leer from his face. Then he winked. "I mean, 'Welcome to our beloved city.'"

He led them past the other three guards, who eyed the odd-looking adventurers suspiciously as they passed through the open wooden gates and under the great arch where empty watchtowers perched on either side. The Street of the Gods stretched before them, a broad lane paved with white marble. To the left and right ran Wall Street, another wide lane cluttered with shops and merchants' kiosks.

"The Silver Eel, near witching hour," the corporal repeated quietly as he turned to resume his post.

"Refreshing," Fafhrd commented as he watched the man go, "to deal honestly with an honest guard."

"There are so few men of integrity left," the Mouser agreed.

The pair strolled south on Wall Street. The shadows of Lankhmar's towers and minarets drew dark hatchings across the dusty road. The massively stout wall on their left rose in stark contrast to the rickety wooden apartment buildings and old warehouses that stood jammed in too-close proximity on their right.

An ox-drawn cart loaded with rough barrels trundled by; the driver, a bone-thin old man, barely seemed to notice them. A raspy noise issued from his throat, and he coughed into his hand as he passed. The white parts of his eyes were as yellow as old parchment. From a leather cord around his neck depended a small monkey's paw, considered a good-luck charm by the residents of the southern city of Tisilinit, and a bestower of virility by the men of Ilthmar.

The Mouser reflected glumly that the talisman had brought this poor workman neither luck, nor virility.

At Fafhrd's suggestion, they turned and headed west on Craft Street. The sounds of industry were a welcome change from the quietude of Wall Street. Blacksmiths and metalsmiths worked their trades, hammers ringing on anvils, hot steel hissing in tempering waters. Potters' wheels whirred merrily. The mingled smells of leather and fabric dyes wafted richly in the air. Basket weavers at their shops and kiosks sat cross-legged on carpets or short stools among piles of their products, working straws in their callused fingers, glancing up in hopeful expectation as the pair passed by, then giving their interest to their work again, sure that swordsmen had no use for their wares.

At Cheap Street the pedestrian traffic increased sharply. Silk-draped palanquins, borne on the shoulders of servants, ferried nobles up and down the wide avenue. Merchants stood before their shops and stalls, barking enticements to the throngs of shoppers. Old women bent over displays of fruits and vegetables, wrinkling their noses, complaining of quality, trying to haggle the venders down. Chickens, ducks and geese in wooden pens made a squawking cacophony as prospective buyers eyed and prodded them. Small plump dogs, hobbled and bound with leashes, sprawled in the dust beneath one particular tent, whining and hopelessly teary-eyed. Like the penned fowl, they were destined for someone's dinner table.

A pair of youthful, shirtless jugglers worked the corner at Cheap and Craft Streets while a young female assistant, her shiny black hair tied back with a bright bow, moved among the onlookers shaking a plain wooden bowl as she trawled for coins. Daggers flashed between the young men, who were plainly masters of their art. The hot sun glinted on their sweaty skin and on the flying steel, but the jugglers laughed and taunted each other and called distractions, each daring the other to miss.

Only a few coins fell into the young girl's bowl. The Mouser frowned and wished that he had even a single copper penny with which to reward such showmanship. "The audience is stingy," he commented. "They take pleasure from the entertainment and give nothing back."

They proceeded south, pushing their way through the crowded street, the sun hot on their heads and necks. Fafhrd licked his lips and craned his head left and right; the Mouser suspected his comrade was thinking of a tavern and a cool draught.

Suddenly, the huge Northerner bolted through an opening in the traffic, and an unsuspecting Mouser found himself dragged along by the front of his gray tunic. At the same time, an immense roll of carpet, precariously balanced on the shoulders of a lone bearer making his way down the road, aimed straight at his head and a half-starved hounddog, scavenging for scraps, tangled in his feet.

Fafhrd gave another yank, pulling his smaller partner out of the bearer's path, and setting him on his feet again. With a frightened bark, the hounddog bolted the other direction, straight into the feet of the unseeing carpet-bearer. The bearer screamed, the dog yelped, and half a score of pedestrians shouted curses and obscenities. For a brief instant the air was filled with a blaze of woven color. Carpet and bearer went flying, then sprawled in the dust, in turn causing other passersby to trip over them in the confusion. In full panic now, the dog leaped across the backs of the fallen, crashing into still other shoppers, sending bags and packages sailing.

Putting on an innocent expression, Fafhrd gave out with a musical whistle and turned away from the chaos. The Mouser glared at the Northerner's broad back, following him, even as he kept one eye over his shoulder. The insanity in the street seemed to feed itself. A gang of street urchins took advantage of the confusion to snatch tomatoes from an unwary vendor. Noticing the theft too late to prevent it, the vender launched a handful of tomatoes after them, striking some innocent citizens, who turned irate and decided to approach the vendor.

A pair of old women wrestled over a dusty head of cabbage one of them had dropped. The Mouser swore to himself he'd never heard such language from ladies of such mature years. He watched as both women suddenly got hands on the unfortunate vegetable. Leafy greenery flew in all directions. The pair looked stunned with surprise for a moment, then went for each other's throats.

In little time at all a full brawl was underway. A merchant's kiosk collapsed under the weight of a trio of men bent on pummeling each other. A goose pen smashed; fowl ran squawking in goose-hysterics.

The Mouser quick-stepped to catch up with Fafhrd, who had advanced a little before him as they left the tumult behind. It was only then as he reached Fafhrd's side that he noticed the small rosewood lute his companion was clutching to his chest.

"Pardon me," the Mouser said politely, "but a lute seems to have attached itself to your hands."

"Has it, indeed?" Fafhrd answered curiously. "Why, I believe you're right, Mouser. You have a keen eye."

The Mouser grunted. "When last my keen eye spied such an instrument, it was hanging on a peg on a tent-post by the counter of a lettuce merchant."

Fafhrd said nothing, but his fingers brushed lightly over the lute-strings, not strumming, but picking out a small flurry of individually harmonic notes.

"You have nimble fingers, my friend," the Mouser said, knowing the double-entendre would not be lost on Fafhrd.

The Northerner grinned. "We'll need food and lodgings," he said, "not to mention coins to pay a certain gate guard his bribe at the Silver Eel tonight. I've decided to sing for our supper."

Rubbing his chin, the Mouser cast another look over his shoulder. "That's well enough," he answered. "But first let's move a little farther from the lettuce merchant and all that annoying, noisy calamity."

Three blocks farther along, by a public fountain at the intersection of Cheap Street and Vintner's Lane, Fafhrd struck a pose, lifted the lute and prepared to give out with a tune. The Mouser elbowed him in the ribs before he could loose a note.

"A bowl, you great idiot," he whispered, watching the crowd around them. "A begging bowl, or a cup. What do you expect them to put their coins in?"

Fafhrd lowered the lute and scratched his short red beard with a puzzled expression. Then without further hesitation he removed his right boot and perched it before him. Lifting the lute again, he struck an introductory chord and began to sing.

"Oh, the northern women
are sour as lemons,
and make for miserable wives.
They're bitchly witches,

and with spells and switches
They rule their menfolk's lives."

During his youth in the icy land called the Cold Wastes,
Fafhrd had received training as a bard. His voice was as fine as
any the Mouser had ever heard, and as the Mouser listened, he
watched Fafhrd's hands, as well, marveling that they could wield
sword and dagger with such deadly skill, yet dance with a gentle,
almost bewitching surety over the strings of a lute.

Pedestrians, hearing Fafhrd's song and fine playing, drifted
closer and stopped to listen. Ever the ham performer, Fafhrd
stepped up onto the low wall that surrounded the fountain so
that he could be better seen, mindless of his somewhat ridicu-
lous, one-boot appearance.

"Oh, it's ice for dinner
to keep them thinner—
They like a look that's lean,
But I'll tell you, pal,
till you've had my gal
you don't know what frigid means!"

An appreciative chuckling went up from the audience.
Fafhrd's size and red-gold hair gave away his origin and heritage,
and his listeners seemed to enjoy the song more for his poking
fun at his own people. A number of hands made passes over the
top of the empty boot; a few even dropped coins. One man
dropped a rosy apple.

The Mouser screwed up his face in muted horror. No man in
his right mind would sink his teeth into an apple that had rested at
the bottom of Fafhrd's boot. Indeed it was luck that a stout,
cleansing wind was blowing through the streets or Fafhrd, with one
foot bare and fuming, would never have held his audience, but sent
them running holding their noses and crying out for mercy.

"On a fateful night
When the world was white
I crawled into our bed—
took her in my arms
to taste her charms
and discovered she was dead.

Now I'm a filthy sod,
and you'll cry, 'My God!'
But I'll confess it true and well—
It wasn't nice,
but I had her twice,
and no difference could I tell!"

The audience, having grown to a considerable size, roared with laughter, men and women alike. The Mouser drifted among them, studying their faces with sidelong glances as they gave Fafhrd their rapt attention. With one hand he fingered the hilt of his dagger, Catsclaw. With the other he supported the cumulative weight of the purses he had deposited down the front of his tunic.

"Then, damn my eyes!
I had her thrice!
I know I'm bound for hell—
Four times, then five!
When she was alive,
She never fucked so well!"

Fafhrd threw himself into his performance, and the crowd cheered him on. The Mouser couldn't manage with a subtle nod or gesture to catch his eye and let him know it was time to move on. Finally, he gave up and slipped away from the fountain, trying not to jingle noticeably as he walked, taking up residence

in the shadow of an alley a little distance away. Putting his back
to the outside of a shop wall, he sank down on his haunches and
prepared to wait.

Fifty-seven verses later, Fafhrd's song ended. The Mouser
roused himself and peered out into the street to see the big
Northerner climb down off the fountain wall, pick up his boot,
and glance around. With the show over, Lankhmar's citizens
went quickly about their business.

When Fafhrd glanced his way, the Mouser waved a hand,
summoning him out of the sunny street and into the cooler
shade of the alley. "I was beginning to think you were audi-
tioning for court minstrel out there," the Mouser scolded as
Fafhrd limped over. "I thought the day would end before your
dainty little ditty did."

The Northerner leaned the lute against the wall and shook
his boot, a disappointed look growing upon his face. Up-
ending his odoriferous footwear, he spilled into his palm six
copper tiks, a single silver smerduk, and a no-longer-quite-so-
rosy apple. "These Lankhmarans truly are cheapskates and
penny-pinchers," he grumbled. "In any other city this would
buy us a bed and a decent bowl of stew with buttered bread,
but in high-priced Lankhmar we'll be lucky to find a stall and
a bag of oats!"

Disgusted, Fafhrd shook his head and absently took a bite of
the apple.

The Mouser made a loud, retching sound.

"I still have the lute, and I still have the boot," Fafhrd announced in more optimistic tones as he lofted the core toward
the alley's rear. "There's better profit waiting on a different
corner perhaps."

"Spare your warbling throat," the Gray Mouser said, lifting
his tunic to reveal one fat purse. He had poured all the others
into it and hidden the empty purses back near where the apple
core now lay.

Fafhrd's eyes lit up at the obvious weight of the purse. "Why, Mouser," he said with quiet admiration, "you are a cutpurse and a thief. The best in the business, from the looks of that."

"Thief? Cutpurse? Nonsense!" The little man in gray raised one eyebrow. "These coins are tribute to your incredible vocal talents. I've only aided your audience to suitably express the appreciation that a somewhat misplaced modesty prevented them from expressing on their own."

The Northerner grinned and proceeded to tug on his boot. "I trust your *contributions* came only from the well-heeled, who could afford it?"

The Mouser grunted. "The bulk of it came from a pair of heels, period," he answered. "A couple of Thieves' Guild amateurs were working the crowd, too. I saw no reason for them to benefit from your performance."

At mention of the Thieves' Guild, Fafhrd's face clouded over with a mixture of anger and sadness. "We settled our score with them, didn't we, Mouser?" he said grimly. "Remind me that we indeed settled it, lest I give thought to settling it again."

"We settled our score with them, Fafhrd," the Mouser answered as old memories came surging back upon him. "But they may not have settled theirs with us."

"That is good," Fafhrd said, rising to his full seven-foot height and clenching his fist as he stared out from the alley's shadowy gloom into the bright street. "It will make me very happy if they learn we are here and try to settle them."

THREE

THE SILVER EEL

The Mouser stared out through the open shutters of the only window in their small room above the Silver Eel. The black towers and minarets of Lankhmar stabbed at the star-speckled sky. Midsummer's Moon, waxing toward fullness, hung like a solemn, disapproving frown above the tallest spire.

A tendril of pale mist wafted across the sky, diffusing the moon's light. In the street below, a thicker, white fog rolled slowly through the city, southward and eastward from the Inner Sea and the River Hlal.

A lone figure, barely visible in the darkness, waded quietly through the fog down the narrow road called Bones Alley and entered the rear door of the Silver Eel. Laughter from the inn below suddenly penetrated up through the floorboards. The Mouser cast a glance toward the only bed, but the sound failed to disturb Fafhrd, who lay sprawled on his belly, like a great starfish taking up the entire mattress.

The Mouser had slept but little, himself, clinging to the very edge of the bed lest he be smothered or crushed in Fafhrd's unconscious embrace. Adding to his restlessness was the sullen afternoon heat that had lasted into the early evening. They had been lucky to get this room for only five coppers, but it had been a mistake for the Mouser to try to catch up on lost sleep.

Still, he felt rested enough. It was not yet near midnight, he reckoned, but he could abide the room no longer. His mind churned with thoughts of Malygris, Sadaster, and the strange creature called Sheelba. Folding his arms across his bare chest, he gazed out the window again and drew a deep breath.

The rising mist half-obscured the moonlight now, and the silvery fog glimmered in the weakening light. Somewhere out there, the Mouser thought glumly, a terrible enchantment crept through the city as silently and surely as the night-mist, stealing under closed doors, pressing against shuttered windows.

Involuntarily, he edged back into the room's shadows, his gaze never quite leaving the soft, white tendrils and wisps that eddied just beyond the sill. Then, with crisp, abrupt movements, he stepped forward, leaned out the window, seized and drew the shutters, and latched them tight.

For a long moment, he stood in the darkness, aware of nothing but the frantic beat of his heart and the dryness in his mouth. "I need a drink," he muttered, disgusted with himself for the undeniable fear he felt.

Groping his way around the room, he snatched his garments from a narrow rope line strung up high near the ceiling. Cherig One-hand, the owner of the Silver Eel, had provided them with a basin and water enough to wash their clothes and themselves at no extra charge for the service. Though still slightly damp, his things were dry enough to pull on. Quietly, he eased into his boots by the door, fastened his weapons belt around his waist, and slipped out into the hallway.

A lantern mounted on a sconce at the end of the narrow hall provided the only light. The Mouser paused long enough to reach into the purse on his belt and draw out a small strip of leather, which he used to tie back his lengthy black hair. Then, determined to forget about spells and wizards for a while, he squared his shoulders and went downstairs to the tavern.

The Silver Eel was arguably one of the most notorious dives in Lankhmar. Here, on almost any night between the right hours, a man could expect to fence a pretty bauble or contract out a murder. Yet, such was Cherig One-hand's reputation for keeping the peace in his establishment that one could find the city's most ruthless denizens rubbing elbows with some of the more adventurous-minded nobles whose tastes ran to "slumming."

A small crowd was gathered tonight. Some of the customers paused in their conversations to see whose soft tread creaked on the seventh stair. While most resumed their talk after a casual glance, a few watched, suspicious and steely-eyed, until the Mouser settled on a stool behind a rough table in the tavern's farthest corner.

The Silver Eel's owner strode to the Mouser's table, an earthen mug dangling from the hook where his right hand used to be, and a pitcher of dark beer clutched in his good left hand. With practiced ease, he set the mug upright before his customer and filled it to the brim. "First one's on the house for renters," he grumbled good-naturedly. "How do you like my fine suite, Gray One?"

The Mouser grinned. "Most excellently," he said, raising the mug to his lips. "The rats bowed with exquisite grace to welcome us, and the fleas waited a full hour before biting us in our bed, which, by the way, is too small."

Cherig One-hand laughed. "It's not the bed that's too small, but your companion, Fafhrd, who is too large."

The Mouser swallowed a cool draught and smacked his lips. Cherig's home-made brew was legendary in Lankhmar, another reason for the Silver Eel's popularity. "Hmmm," he murmured with a roll of his eyes, "a complaint he often attributes to his wenches."

Cherig topped off the Mouser's mug as he set it down. "Well, now you and me are men of the world, are we not? And we've taken the measure of such boasts before."

A short cough sounded somewhere in the tavern. The Mouser momentarily forgot Cherig, and his gaze roamed around until he spied a trio casting dice at another table. A mustachioed bravo, dice clutched in a frozen fist, seemed in some distress. He gave a second, sharper cough as he lifted his mug with his free hand and took a quick, deep drink. Then, his discomfort apparently eased, he returned to his gaming.

Cherig resumed his serving duties, and the Mouser, his spirit sinking even lower, tilted his stool on its rear legs to lean his back against the wall. Raising his vessel to his lips, he drained half its contents.

The tavern door opened. Fingers of white mist curled around the edges, preceding a small girl-child with tangled yellow-gold hair and a haggard, dirty face. On her hip, she carried a shallow basket. Shyly, she approached the table nearest the door. "Would you like to buy one of my poppets for your sweetheart?" she asked in a weary, high voice as she reached into the basket and held up a doll made of braided and woven straw in a handmade scrap of a dress.

Deep in his cups, the lone figure who sat at the table growled and waved her away without looking up. Wisely, the child backed off and turned to make her pitch at another table.

Again, the door opened. Though the hour was well before midnight, the Mouser recognized the corporal from the Marsh Gate. The fog rose like smoke off the shoulders of the man's red cloak as he closed the door and looked around the tavern.

Raising his mug, the Mouser cried, "Ho, Captain! Can this be the hour of our appointment, already?"

The corporal strode through the crowd, unlacing his cloak as he came. Tossing the garment carelessly across one end of the Mouser's table, he then removed his helmet and set that down, too. "I was afraid if I waited until midnight," he said, seating himself unceremoniously across from his host, "that you'd have spent my bribe on ale and women by eleven."

The Mouser, suddenly glad for company, grinned. "I, sir?" he said, feigning offense. "Have I not dealt with you honestly?"

"Aye, sir," the corporal answered smartly. "And though you obviously have coin now when you had none before, I shall not ask with whom you have dealt dishonestly."

Laughing, the Mouser slapped the table. "I like you well, Captain. Tell me your name, and I shall buy you a drink." He beckoned to Cherig on the other side of the tavern.

"Nuulpha is my name," the corporal said. Then he paused as Cherig set a mug of beer before him. Lifting the beverage, he drained it to the last drop and ran his tongue around the rim before he placed it back on the table. "Nuulpha, the long-suffering," he continued. "But, gods willing, a few more of these, and I'll be suffering a little less."

"Your head may suffer the more," the Mouser responded as he motioned for Cherig to refill both their mugs. "Our host brews a devilish strong potion."

Cherig shrugged as he poured. "Consider the devils who make up my clientele," he grumbled in a voice dripping with good-humored sarcasm. "I get few such honest gentlemen as yourselves."

Nuulpha raised an eyebrow, smirking as the Silver Eel's owner departed. Then, he lifted his mug in salute. "If I may?" he asked, and when the Mouser politely nodded, he continued with gracious formality. "To my host. Though diminutive in stature, his generosity is larger than his guest's fat and spendthrift wife— and that is no small compliment."

With a low chuckle, the Mouser raised his own mug and added, "Let's hope it's as large as your capacity for this fine beer."

Putting his elbows on the table, the corporal leaned forward and rubbed one hand over his grizzled chin. A weary look passed over his face, then faded. "Speaking of things large, where is your red-bearded companion?"

An exaggerated sigh slipped from the Mouser's lips as he lowered his beverage. "Sleeping like a babe, but with nothing more than a pillow on which to suckle." He leaned forward as well, laying his hands on either side of his beer, and lowered his voice to a conspiratorial whisper. "I would ask you a question, Captain."

A grin turned up the corners of Nuulpha's mouth. "So the brew has a price, after all," he said, lifting his drink. He swallowed noisily and smacked his lips with satisfaction as he set the mug down again.

"Not so," the Mouser assured. "Your company averts a dark mood that earlier besieged me, and no matter your answer, I'll pay for the privilege of drinking you under the table."

Nuulpha casually glanced around the tavern before speaking again. "You must have robbed a rich man, indeed," he said.

Preparing to drink, the Mouser spoke nonchalantly over the rim of his mug. "Three members of the Thieves' Guild," he answered.

His guest's eyebrows shot up. "I salute you once again," he said, lifting his drink. Swallowing, he wiped his mouth with the back of a hand. "They're a dangerous lot to trifle with, however. I'd be remiss not to advise you to watch your step where they are concerned." He drank again, and shrugged. "But I forget you are not new to Lankhmar. Ask your question, good host."

The Mouser called for Cherig to refill their mugs yet again, and waited quietly while the owner poured. Cherig eyed them closely, then as if sensing some business was underway, he departed without comment.

The Mouser leaned forward again. "Do you know of a wizard named Malygris?"

Nuulpha sputtered and spewed half a mouthful of beer across the table before he slammed his mug down and clapped a hand over his face to stop the spray. "Abject apologies!" he muttered hastily when he could draw a breath. Red-faced, he pushed his stool back slightly from the table as if he expected trouble.

The tavern grew silent as all eyes turned their way. Cherig, pitcher and tray balanced on one hand, turned, stern-faced. The little girl with the basket of dolls scurried down between a pair of tables for safety.

With icy calm, the Gray Mouser dabbed a finger at his dripping eyebrows. "Think nothing of it, Captain," he said, and if there was a bit more emphasis on the last word, it was purely unintentional. "I shall take care not to startle you again."

When trouble failed to start, the tavern patrons resumed their conversations. The little girl crawled out to continue her enterprise, and Cherig disappeared momentarily to return with a clean, soft towel, which he deposited wordlessly at the Mouser's elbow.

Embarrassment still coloring his cheeks, Nuulpha leaned forward again and spoke in a nervous whisper. "That's not a name one speaks aloud these days in Lankhmar."

"Perhaps that was the reason I spoke it in such an exceedingly low voice," the Mouser suggested pointedly as he wiped the towel over his face and set it aside.

Before either could say more, once again fingers of pale mist pushed open the tavern door, admitting a pair of roguish-looking Ilthmarts whose tattered cloaks could not hide the long swords they wore. The pair swaggered toward the last empty table, sat down, and swept the Silver Eel with sullen glares.

Nuulpha turned his attention back to his host. Leaning close over his beer, he whispered, "If I may ask, what is your interest in . . . this person you named?"

The Mouser wondered just how much to explain, but his thoughts were interrupted when the little girl ventured shyly up to his elbow. "Please, sir," she said. "Would you like to buy one of my poppets for your sweetheart?" She held up a tiny straw doll. "Guaranteed to bring good luck to her kitchen or . . ." she hesitated, then blinked her eyes, ". . . or your bedchamber, should she place it there."

A sudden cough caused the Mouser to look past the child toward the table where the dice game was still in progress. The same mustachioed bravo coughed violently into his fist, his face reddening. With a visible effort, he controlled himself and tossed down the remains of his beverage, but the coughing seized him again. When he moved his hand away from his mouth, a green phlegm smeared his chin. With barely muttered apologies to his two companions, he cast down the dice, rose and fled the Silver Eel.

The Mouser stared hard at the little blond-haired huckster by his table. When he pulled out a gold coin, the child's eyes grew large, and she stood still, trembling like a small bird.

The coin seemed to move of its own accord from between the Mouser's thumb and forefinger, pausing between the next set of fingers, then the next before it made the journey back to thumb and forefinger. Nuulpha, as well as the child, watched in amazement.

The Mouser passed his other hand over the coin, then held up both his hands, turning his empty palms outward. The gold was gone, seemingly vanished into air.

Nuulpha snorted. "My wife does that trick, only she makes money disappear even faster."

Winking, the Mouser reached toward the child's ear and retrieved his coin, eliciting a girlish giggle as he held it close to her large eyes. "Count nothing on luck, my young merchant," he told her. "Do not even speak of luck or magic. This is an ill time for such things. Now, I will buy not just one, but all these dollies you call your poppets, and you will take this single gold coin, which is wealth enough to feed you and your family for a month."

"All my dollies?" the child exclaimed, her gaze locked greedily on the coin.

"All," the Mouser affirmed. "In return, you must promise me to make no more of these so-called lucky trinkets."

The child clearly didn't understand his request, but her desire for the coin was plain. "Oh, master," she said, "supposing I promise to make no more poppets for as long as the value of this pretty metal feeds my tummy?"

Nuulpha thumped the table, hooting with mirth. "The little beggar would haggle with you!"

The coin disappeared once again, seeming to melt inside the Mouser's closed fist. The child looked crestfallen, but the Mouser, opening his empty hand, blew on his palm, and closed his fist once more. When he opened his hand again, the coin was back. "One cannot ask a pretty little girl to starve," he said, "but so long as you can make this last, fashion no more poppets."

The child nodded. Slowly, she set her basket on the edge of the table. With surprising speed, she shot out one hand and snatched the gleaming bit of gold, lest it should disappear again. "Now, master," she said, breathless with excitement, "you have the market to yourself, for I'm out of the business for a month or so at least—a lady of leisure!"

With that, she spun about and ran for the door, flung it open, and vanished into the foggy night of Lankhmar.

Cherig stomped across the tavern, scowling and waving his hand to disperse the fog that poured through the door the child had neglected to close. A kick from his booted foot sent it slamming shut.

When the Silver Eel's owner turned, the Mouser beckoned him over.

"Do you have a stove or hearthfire in your kitchen?" he asked, waiting for Cherig to nod before he put the basket of dolls into that one hand. "Burn these," he instructed. "They're probably harmless, but burn them, anyway. Every one." He tapped the rim of his mug with a fingertip. "Then we'll have another cup of your fine, delicious piss."

"At the rate you're consuming it," Cherig answered as he walked away, "I'll just bring the chamber pot, and you can serve yourselves."

When they were alone again, Nuulpha leaned once more across the table and whispered, "I'm impressed, not just with the generosity of my host, but with his wizardry. Why buy the dolls if you meant to destroy them?"

The Mouser looked askance, once more taking note of the Silver Eel's clientele. The volume of the conversations had risen to match the intake of liquor, and the clatter of dice elicited curses and growls with increasing frequency. In the too-easy laughter that issued from several knots of customers, there was a strained quality. The Mouser, a cautious man, observed it all and turned back to his guest.

"No wizardry," he answered quietly. "Just some simple sleight-of-hand." He raised his mug, adding with a brief smile before he drank, "it's a useful skill for impressing children and officers of the Overlord's Guard." Lowering his nearly empty mug again, he continued. "Your question brings our conversation back to the person whose name we shall not mention for fear of once again engaging your gag reflex."

Cherig reappeared long enough to place a full pitcher of beer between them.

"I can tell you only this," Nuulpha said in a voice turned serious. "Few men have ever seen Malygris, but his very name is considered a curse in some quarters of the city. In the darkest dives and gutters, grown men shiver and turn away at mention of it."

"He could be Death's personal valet," the Mouser said, unfazed, as he refilled his guest's mug, then his own, from the pitcher. "I still must find him."

"God's balls, man!" Nuulpha hesitated, then gulped from his beer. A quite audible thump sounded when he set it down again, and his gaze locked with his host's for a long moment, as if he were trying to probe the workings of the Mouser's mind.

The volume of the crowd seemed to rise around them, and yet, huddled over their table, isolated in the farthest shadow-filled corner, they might have been an island in a sea of noise.

With scant subtlety, wrapping his hands nervously around his mug, Nuulpha glanced over both his shoulders. "Most of the populace is too stupid or too complacent to notice the things that happen in this town," he said, his voice a mixture of fear and bitterness, "but the common, lowly guards who work the streets have eyes and ears, nor are we fools." He took a short drink. "Three of Lankhmar's most powerful wizards have died of sickness this past year, and this even our great bloat of an Overlord knows. But along with the rest of this city's pampered nobility, he disdains to observe that others have died—fortune-tellers, charm peddlers, priests. Also common merchants, shop-keepers, housewives and whores . . ."

He paused and looked sharply around again before continuing. "In the barracks, a few have dared to whisper the word, *plague.*" The corporal frowned. "Their superiors had them whipped. I, myself, believe it is no plague." Touching the tip of a finger to his temple, he added, "I've been around, my friend, and I know a candle from a quarter moon. Some sorcery haunts the streets of Lankhmar, and something evil stalks our foot-steps."

Nuulpha picked up his mug again, drained it, and looked uncomfortably away. "My host knows this, too," he said as he wiped his mouth with his sleeve. "I saw it in his eyes and heard it in his voice when he warned that child to have no traffic with luck or magic."

The Mouser narrowed one eye, impressed with his guest's perceptive powers, as he reached for the pitcher again. The handle appeared fuzzier than it should have, and it took two tries for him to close his fingers around it. When he refilled their mugs, some of the amber contents splashed onto the table.

"I'll tell you honestly, good Captain," the Mouser said. "I know precious little, save that I must find this Maly . . . Malygris, and I haven't a clue where to begin." With a heavy sigh, he raised his mug in another salute to his guest. "Come, the subject has made us a pair of humorless gargoyles. See how you sit hunched over your beer?" He slapped his palm against the table. "No more of this tonight. Cherig's cellar is not yet dry, I'll wager, and that should be challenge enough for a pair of good men."

Nuulpha's expression remained gloomy. Both hands clasping his mug, he stared down into its contents. "I like you well, gray friend," he whispered, "but if some geas compels you to pursue this madness, then pay heed." He lifted his gaze to meet the Mouser's black-eyed stare. "There is a rumor—no more than that. In one of the forbidden temples of the Ancient Gods that stand near the riverfront, some hint that Malygris has taken residence, although in which of those accursed and abandoned structures . . ."—he shrugged—"no one says. Treat this as you will, but remember: if you are caught trying to enter or disturb those ruins, it's Lankhmar's law that your lives are forfeit."

Grinning, the Mouser touched his mug to his guest's. "Well, if I'm arrested and hauled off to your famous city dungeon, I'll trust in you to effect for me an escape of such breathtaking derring-do that the bards will sing of it throughout this and the entire next season."

Picking up his mug, Nuulpha returned the salute. "Indeed," he answered, "however, that will cost you a considerably larger and more ornate bribe than this milk of Cherig's."

Once again, the Silver Eel's door opened. Raucous laughter preceded a pair of slender young men, whose richly embroidered black cloaks marked them as noblemen or sons of noblemen. The fog swirled around their feet and clung to their garments like thick smoke as they entered, and to the Mouser's inebriated eye it seemed that a wispy tendril shifted and coiled with noose-like menace around the throat of one of them, but the door closed and the clinging mist swiftly diffused in the growing heat of the tavern.

With the young men came their paramours, two elegantly clad beauties, whose gowns of splendid silks shimmered in the Silver Eel's shadowy lamplight, whose arms and fingers sparkled with jeweled rings and bracelets. Both women wore their hair piled high on their heads and held in place with glittering pins and combs. One stood tall and dark as a raven's wing, but it was the smaller blonde who held the Mouser's eye. A child, really, no more than fourteen, she appeared thin as a willow wand, yet possessed of a grace an older woman would have envied. Her gaze swept around the tavern, and for a brief instant, her eyes met the Mouser's.

With his mug halfway to his lips, the Mouser's heart froze. "Ivrian," he muttered, for it was the face of his one true love staring back at him across the smoky room.

Then, she turned away again and threw her arms around the neck of her lover, laughing at some comment from him, as the four of them moved into a corner to call for drinks.

Slowly, the Mouser sipped from his mug and set it down. The beer tasted bitter in his mouth. With an effort, he swallowed, his eyes still on the blond woman, who never looked his way again.

"Stirs your blood, does she?" Nuulpha said, turning his head to regard the foursome.

"She . . ." the Mouser hesitated, his voice dropping to a soft whisper, ". . . reminds me of someone."

Nuulpha grinned as he reached for the pitcher to refill his mug. "You can buy an evening with her for half again what you gave the child."

The Mouser's eyes widened. "She's a prostitute?"

"I'm a man of the streets," Nuulpha said proudly. "I know them all. Her name is Liara, called by some the Dark Butterfly, and she belongs to the House of Night Cries on Face-of-the-Moon Street."

The Mouser fell silent as he regarded Liara. All the tables in the tavern were occupied, so she and her friends leaned against the wall, their celebratory spirits undampened. No common beer for them; Cherig stood at their elbows with four rare and delicate crystal goblets balanced on his tray as he poured wine of Tovilyis from a slender brown bottle. The lamplight gleamed on the blood-red wine, and the glasses shone like huge fiery rubies as hands reached out to seize them.

Liara clinked the rim of her goblet with her companion's, then rose on tiptoe to lightly kiss his lips. Her dark eyes, subtly shadowed with traces of kohl, locked with his as she tasted the expensive liquor, while with one hand he stroked her breast.

The Mouser rose suddenly, accidentally knocking over his stool. Grabbing his mug, he drained the contents and slammed it down again. "Got to pee," he told Nuulpha, slurring his words as he pushed away from the table.

He weaved carefully through the crowd. Beneath the stairs that led to the sleeping rooms on the upstairs level stood a narrow door. The knob tried to dodge his grasp, but on the third attempt his fingers caught and turned it. Beyond was a narrow hallway, then another door that opened outward into Bones Alley.

The white fog hung like a pall in the air, eerily still and cool upon his face. When the Mouser paused to stare up and down the alley, neither end was visible. So thick was the mist that it even obscured the rooftops of the buildings opposite the tavern.

The Mouser pushed the outer door closed, muffling the laughter of the Silver Eel's customers. In the silence, he walked several paces down the alley and loosened the front of his trousers.

The door opened again. A silhouetted figure turned quickly to the wall, muttering to himself as he raised a mug to drink, while fumbling one-handed with his clothing. The soft sound of his urination joined the Mouser's. "Leaks out fast as I put it in," the man grumbled drunkenly.

The Mouser grunted noncommittally as he watched the dark stain he was making on the inn's wall grow. His thoughts were on the prostitute, Liara, who so resembled his dead love. A dull ache grew in his heart, and he began to spell Ivrian's name wetly above the stain as a pair of sentimental tears welled in the corners of his eyes.

Through the alcohol that dulled his senses, the Mouser heard soft footsteps coming up the alley. Yet another figure approached, emerging ghostlike out of the fog. Dark eyes locked on the Mouser, and from under the edge of a cloak, rose the long, broad blade of a sword.

"I'll ha' yer purse, shorty," the newcomer ordered, leveling his point near the Mouser's nose. "An any other bauble or bit o' value ye might be holdin'."

The Mouser shifted his lower, hidden hand. "The most valuable thing I've got for you," he said, turning his body away from the wall just enough to whip his own slender blade from its sheath in a high head parry that knocked his foe's point away from his face and sent the larger sword flying, "is this piece of advice . . ." His riposte put his own point beneath the taller man's chin. Suddenly empty-handed, the fellow's eyes snapped wide with surprise and fear.

"Never interrupt a man in mid-stream." The Mouser finished his business on the man's boots.

Behind him, almost forgotten, the other man, who had relieved himself by the door, chuckled. "An' never ferget that thieves are like the boots yer pissin' on."

At last, recognizing their Ilthmart accents, the Mouser reacted too late. An earthen beer mug came crashing down on his head. Red stars exploded behind his eyes. He staggered, then sagged against the wall where he'd written Ivrian's name.

"We usually come in pairs, little man."

FOUR

SHADOWS IN
THE MIST

Fafhrd yawned, stretching his arms above his head as he sat up on the side of the bed. The muffled sounds of laughter and general carousing rose up through the floorboards from the tavern below. It was not the noise that had awakened him, however, but a nightmare from which he had struggled to awake.

Frowning, he rubbed his nose. Born and raised in the open spaces of the Cold Wastes, the smells of city living constantly offended his senses. At the moment, though, such odors were a welcome distraction, for they forced his mind farther from the specters that even now reached for him and called to him from the receding dream.

Only a feeble light from the lamps in the hallway seeped beneath the door. Otherwise, the room was black as pitch. Throwing back the sheet, Fafhrd rose naked and groped for the chamber pot at the foot of the bed. In the darkness, however, he kicked it, and sent it clattering into some other corner of the room.

Muttering curses, the huge Northerner hopped up and down on his right foot as he clutched his left. His big toe throbbed.

Yet he thanked his god, Kos, for small favors, for his nose told
him that the Mouser had not used the pot before him. Squinting,
he tried to locate the overturned vessel in the blackness. Then,
with a shrug, he gave up and limped to the window.

Somebody had closed the shutters, Fafhrd noted sleepily, but
he flung them open and leaned against the sill. Damn the
chamber pot. He would only have emptied it into the alley
below anyway. Yawning again, he released his urine and watched
it fall steaming into the cool, foggy night while he listened to
the voices coming up through the floor.

Outraged screams and curses rose up through the floor!
Fafhrd grinned as he continued with the task at hand. Cherig's
guests were a rowdy lot tonight. No doubt his companion, the
Mouser, was downstairs in the thick of it.

Then, another sound jarred against his ears, and suddenly
Fafhrd realized the curses were rising, not through the floor, but
from the alley below his window. Steel rang on steel, a note
played only by one sword blade upon another.

As he continued to pee, Fafhrd leaned his head out the
window, curious to see what transpired below. Through the
dense fog, he barely spied one small shape fending off two larger
attackers. At the same time, he heard his own name shouted.

"Fafhrd, you ill-mannered oaf, you're drenching me in your
damnable rain!"

His personal business nearly complete, Fafhrd shouted back
in surprise. "Mouser?" he called, the sleep-fog lifting from his
brain. "Is that you?"

The small shadow below called back as he dodged and
feinted, and steel rang out again. "None other, and covered in
your foul stink!"

While one tall shadow engaged the Mouser another stepped
away from the conflict and shook his sword at Fafhrd's window.
"As am I, you faceless, bottomless bladder! After we dispatch
this puny runt and relieve him of his purse, my comrade and I

will be pleased to knock upon your door and deal you similar treatment!"

Fafhrd considered for a moment while all three shadows resumed the fight. "Mouser," he called over the clash of blades. "Do I take it this bout is not just the friendly play of good-natured tavern-mates engaged in peacock displays of skill and manhood?"

A heavy wisp of fog shifted through the alley, momentarily obscuring the combatants from Fafhrd's view, but the Mouser's voice came to him clearly, if a bit breathlessly. "This pair of Ilthmart thieves?" There was a pause, followed by a loud hawk and sound of spitting. "Skill and manhood are both small things to these cowards. I am giving them a fencing lesson!"

Despite the Mouser's bravado, Fafhrd thought he detected a certain slur to his friend's words, and when the fog parted slightly, it seemed to him that the Ilthmart thieves, blades weaving in tandem, were pressing the Mouser to the wall.

His own sword, Graywand, stood sheathed near his pillow. Swiftly crossing the room, Fafhrd stubbed another toe on the bed's leg. With a roar of pain, he drew the blade. A stream of curses flowing from his lips, he returned to the window, leaped over the sill, and plunged through the fog to the street below.

One of the Ilthmarts turned to face Fafhrd. Raising his sword to strike, the thief and would-be murderer hesitated, his eyes widening as he looked up at his seven-foot opponent. No small man, himself, his jaw gaped.

"Now then," Fafhrd said as he took a two-handed grip on his huge weapon and leveled the point near the man's throat, "which of you called my friend a *puny runt?*"

The thief wet his lips. Without taking his eyes from Fafhrd, he inclined his head toward his partner, who was furiously fending off the Mouser's attacks. "Uh, not me," he answered with an innocent-seeming shrug. "It was my friend. He's always had a big mouth. I'm a quiet one, myself."

"I see," Fafhrd said, drawing a circle before the man's eyes with his sword's point, "No reason to run you through, then." He brought his foot up into the Ilthmart's groin. The man's eyes snapped wider as he dropped his sword, clutched himself between his legs, and sank to his knees; his mouth made a pained oval, and he elicited a pitiful, low moan. "Next time," he gasped as he slumped forward, "just run me through."

Planting the point of Graywand in the dirt, Fafhrd leaned on the pommel and peered through the ever-thickening fog. The clang of blades made a sweet music for a pair of dim shapes dancing a few paces away. "How fares the puny runt?" he called to the pair.

Barely visible in the hazy mist, the remaining Ilthmart scowled contemptuously, though his breathing was ragged. "His sword is a small threat."

Fafhrd smirked. "Play with him a while, and it'll grow."

"I have taught him the parry from the third, fourth, and fifth positions," the Mouser called merrily, his words wine-slurred, "as well as the direct and indirect ripostes." Blades clanged again, mingling with the sounds of boots scraping desperately in the road, ending with a scowled curse and the harsh intake of breath. "Ah, there!" the Mouser cried. "Now he knows the fleche!"

Patting his lips with the palm of one hand, Fafhrd faked a yawn. "Haven't you dispatched him, yet? A spectator might think you were in some trouble."

Again, a ring of steel as blades slid against one another. "A mouser likes to play with its catch before he eats it," the smaller figure laughed. "Ah hah! There! An arm-cut!"

The larger shadow growled. "No more than a scratch, you little braggart! And there's one lesson I learned long before this." Stooping, he grabbed a handful of dirt and flung it at the Mouser's face. "That's when to run away!"

Recoiling, the Mouser shielded his eyes with one hand as the Ilthmart thief disappeared down the fog-enshrouded alley. "I think I should mention he's got our purse," he said, sputtering dirt from his lips as he spoke to Fafhrd. "And I've run up quite a tab with Cherig. There'll be no beer for you tonight if he gets away."

Spurred to action by such a prospect, Fafhrd snatched his sword out of the ground and raced after the Ilthmart, guided only by the sound of fleeing footfalls. Down the length of Bones Alley he ran, emerging into Plague Court. There, he paused to listen and to determine the direction the thief had taken.

The Mouser crashed into him from behind. With a groan, he bounced off Fafhrd's huge form and fell backward on his rump. "Mog's blood!" he cried angrily, invoking his tutelary god. "What do you mean, stopping in the middle of a chase like that, particularly in this pea-soup fog!"

Fafhrd offered a hand to help his friend up. "Maybe I should have called a warning," he whispered derisively. Then, pitching his voice toward an imitation of a woman's soprano, he continued, "*Oh, Mouser, I'm stopping now. Don't run into me like some stupid, drunken sot!*"

The Mouser grumbled unappreciatively, waving his narrow blade before he wisely sheathed it. "I should have put Scalpel's point up your backside!"

A crash and a now-familiar snarl sounded out of the fog off to Fafhrd's right. Wasting no more time on witticisms, he ran in that direction with the Mouser close behind. At a corner of the next intersection a rain barrel lay overturned and smashed. The muddy ground betrayed how the thief had fallen and scrambled up again, and wet footprints indicated his direction.

Fafhrd stepped carefully around the broken pieces of the barrel, cool mud squishing between his bare toes. It was an abrupt reminder that, in his enthusiasm, he had jumped naked from his window to rescue the Mouser. Standing bare-assed in an unnamed alley with muddy feet and nothing but the night's fog to cover him—and a chilly fog at that—the stolen purse suddenly seemed less important than his dignity.

Unfortunately, at the same moment that he came to this realization, a door opened further down the narrow road, and a dim light spilled briefly out. For a moment, muffled laughter echoed up the way before the door closed again.

"The rat's ducked into some dive of a tavern," the Mouser whispered, unsheathing his sword again as he advanced purposefully past Fafhrd. "Lucky for me—I've quite a thirst this evening."

"Mouser!" Fafhrd hissed, hoping to stop his friend. "Mouser!" But the Mouser continued on, determined to retrieve his purse from the Ilthmart thief. With an aggrieved sigh, Fafhrd followed, covering his groin with one hand while his other hand tightened around his sword's grip.

The fog nearly swallowed the weak light of a lone lantern that hung on a jut above the tavern's door. The establishment's name, painted over the same door in long-faded letters, was impossible to read.

"I can't go in there!" Fafhrd insisted. "I'm naked as a babe!"

One hand on the door, the Mouser paused to give Fafhrd an exaggerated wink. "Wait here, then," he said. "I'll find him and chase him out to you."

Before Fafhrd could protest, the Mouser pushed open the door and disappeared over the threshold. Within, the laughter immediately ceased. A moment later, the Mouser reappeared.

"It's too crowded," he said gravely, "and too poorly lit to see faces."

Keeping to the shadows, Fafhrd leaned one shoulder to the wall and looked patiently down at his smaller partner. "Let us go home then," he suggested. "It's not so bad to tuck your tail between your legs when there's nothing else to keep you warm."

The Mouser rubbed his chin thoughtfully. "I have a plan," he announced. "Stay here, and keep hidden." With that, he turned, pushed open the door once more, and stepped inside. His voice, however, could plainly be heard.

"Your mothers sleep with Mingol stableboys," the Mouser shouted. "So do your fathers. And you've all got faces like the rumps of buggered sheep."

A general cry of outrage followed, and the crash of furniture being thrown about. Fafhrd felt a shock through the wall where he leaned, as if a weighty object had struck the other side. An instant later, the tavern's door flung back, and the Mouser dashed out.

"The one that stays behind will be our man!" he cried as he ran past Fafhrd's place of concealment.

"Good plan," Fafhrd complimented sarcastically, stepping out of the way as a score of insulted customers, brandishing swords and knives, in varying stages of inebriation, charged through the door and after the Mouser. Even the cook gave chase, waving a large wooden spoon, his apron flapping around his knees as he vanished in the fog.

Fafhrd listened to the fading sounds of their cries, then cautiously opened the door and stepped inside.

The Ilthmart thief sat at a table, pouring himself a mug of ale as he clutched the wrist of a serving wench and tried to drag her closer. What the woman lacked in looks, she made up for with ample bosoms. "Now that we're alone, my purty birdie . . ." the thief was saying when Fafhrd walked in.

"You're covered with mud and stink like a pisspot!" the woman protested as she tried to pull away.

Hinges creaked as Fafhrd pushed the door closed, and a board groaned under his foot.

The Ilthmart looked up. "Bleedin' hell!" he raged, releasing the woman's arm so suddenly that she pitched backwards and fell. The Ilthmart paid her no more attention. Pushing back his chair, he drew his sword.

Legs straddled and skirts splayed about her, the wench sat up and rubbed her backside, which was as impressively abundant as her breasts. Pushing back a thick strand of hair that fell over her face, she stared wide-eyed at Fafhrd. "I dunno, dearie," she said. "That looks like heaven to me!"

Moving slowly across the floor, Fafhrd raised Graywand. "I'll match you steel for steel and inch for inch, my friend," he said, touching the tip of his longer sword to the Ilthmart's blade.

The wench scrambled out of the way, her gaze still on Fafhrd's nude form. "I'll wager he's got you on either count, luv," she said to the thief.

The Ilthmart backed up nervously. On the sleeve of his sword arm a rip and a slight red stain showed where the Mouser's blade had earlier nicked him. His gaze darted about the gloom-filled room, seeking a way out. "Perhaps we can come to some accommodation?" he said, lifting the Mouser's purse by its strings from under his belt.

"No doubt we can," Fafhrd replied in calm manner. "Return my partner's purse, and we'll consider it a short-term loan. And that ring you're wearing, we'll consider that interest on the loan. Your sword, too." Then he smiled. "Your cloak, that's a bribe to the middleman who arranged your loan—me. In fact, just leave all your clothes."

The Ilthmart blustered. "Why, my things won't begin to fit you!"

Fafhrd smiled. "I know, but I'll feel much better knowing I'm not the only one running buck-naked in the middle of the night through the streets of Lankhmar. And since you're responsible for my current state of undress, it seems fitting that you share my discomfiture." He rested the tip of Graywand on the Ilthmart's chest. "Do I need to emphasize my point?"

The Ilthmart cast his sword down at Fafhrd's feet and scrambled swiftly out of his boots and clothes. In moments, he stood as naked as Fafhrd, but far less at ease.

"Out you go, now," Fafhrd said, inclining his head toward the door.

Nervous eyes regarded Fafhrd, then flickered toward the wench, who still sat straddle-legged on the floor, then toward the door, and back to Fafhrd. "That's it?" he said warily. "You're letting me go?"

"What worse can I do to you?" the Northerner answered. "Your humiliation's between your legs."

"Ain't it the truth!" said the wench, making a wry face as she measured a small piece of air with thumb and forefinger.

Face reddening with anger and embarrassment, the Ilthmart clenched his fists. Without another word, he bolted past Fafhrd for the door. Fafhrd, laughing hugely, swung his blade, the flat side of which made a loud, sharp crack on bare buttocks. With a yowl, the Ilthmart flung open the door and raced into the night.

The thick fog crept surreptitiously over the threshold, seeming to pause as it touched the warmer interior air. At a slower, more cautious pace, it flowed along the floor.

Fafhrd picked up the Ilthmart's discarded trousers, frowned, and cast them aside.

"Why not try me on for size, dearie?" the wench suggested with a lewd wink.

Fafhrd considered it for a moment as he extended a hand to help her to her feet. But there was still the Mouser's safety to ascertain, and this nameless tavern's customers might return at any moment. Wrapping one arm around her waist, he drew her close for a quick kiss before stepping away. "Except for this cloak," he said, snatching up the garment and lacing it at his throat, "these clothes and sword are yours. Hide them before someone returns and sell them for what you can."

The wench's eyes widened at such generosity. "I'm not used to no gentlemen," she said, swiftly collecting the Ilthmart's belongings. Straightening, she clutched them to her breasts. "But you come back this way any night, and I'll treat you right well, and charge you nothing for it."

Fafhrd smiled at her earnestness. Prying one hand from her new possessions, he planted another kiss on the tips of her fingers, and bowed. Then, gathering the folds of his acquired cloak to conceal his nakedness, he went out into the street.

The fog seemed thicker than ever. It flowed over the ground like a white, feathery river and filled the air with an obscuring, chilly mist. Fafhrd paused long enough to tie the Mouser's purse strings around his left wrist, struck with a curious awe and foreboding by the eerie atmosphere. He drew the cloak closer about his shoulders, unable to see the garment's hem or the lower portions of his legs as he waded through the night.

Hidden in fog, an overturned rain barrel waited for Fafhrd, and the unsuspecting Northerner howled as he smashed the already-abused big toe of his right foot against it. Cursing, he hopped away, slipping in the mud created by the barrel's spillage. With another yelp and a loud curse, his left foot slipped out from under him, and he fell in a sloppy splash.

"Hounds of filthy hell!" Fafhrd grumbled, shaking mud from his hands as he got to his knees and clambered up. Groping in the fog, he seized a piece of the barrel and flung it away. In midflight it disappeared in the fog, but the noisy racket it made as it struck some wall gave a small satisfaction.

"Hello?"

The voice drifted out of the fog, distant and muffled. Fafhrd listened as he wiped Graywand's blade on a piece of his sodden cloak, wondering if he should answer.

From another direction, a different voice responded. "Who's there? Hello?"

"Can't see a thing," the first voice called. "Who made that noise?"

Fafhrd repressed a shiver. The overturned barrel was a landmark that told him he stood at the point where the alley joined Plague Court, but he could not see the other side of the street, nor anything up or down it. The callers were virtually invisible, disembodied voices crying in the fog. He thought of answering, then reconsidering, kept silent. These might be the men chasing the Mouser.

Moving slowly into Plague Court, he turned to his left, sure that in that direction lay the Silver Eel, where the Mouser, if he knew what was good for him, would be waiting with a reserved table and a pitcher of beer.

Far down the street, he spied the faintest amber light floating in the misty limbo that Lankhmar had become. The hairs prickled on his neck, and he froze again, until he convinced himself it was only the obscured gleam of someone's torch or lantern. He saw no figure, though, only the light bobbing in the mist. When it disappeared a moment later, he told himself it was because its bearer had turned a corner or entered a building.

The voices continued to call. There seemed to be more of them now. Barely perceived, a shape passed with outstretched arms and faltering steps near to Fafhrd. "Gamron?" the shape murmured nervously. "Is that you?"

Heeding the counsel of his own natural caution, Fafhrd kept silent and moved on, holding his sword low and before him as if it were a blind man's cane.

Never had he seen such a fog. In the Cold Wastes, that distant land of his birth, he had seen the ice witches of his village call great mists, but always they came with a numbing, marrow-freezing chill that set the air to glimmering with ice crystals and coated everything with a white rime.

His mother, Mor, had been such a witch, and with such a spell—damn her jealous eyes—had she killed his father, Nalgron, as he climbed the frigid peak of White Fang Mountain, from which could be seen the very top of the world and all the gods of Nehwon.

He forced the bitter memory away. Fafhrd had not thought of his mother or father, nor of the Snow Clan he had left behind, for a long time. Pausing again to frown and scratch his head, he wondered if he had passed the Silver Eel. Could he have run so far in pursuit of the Ilthmart thief?

Squinting, he tried to penetrate the gray veil with his gaze, spying nothing to left, nor right, before, nor behind. At last, deciding that the middle of the street was the wrong place to be, he took a perpendicular course, expecting eventually, within a few steps, to encounter a wall, along which he could then grope his way.

He encountered no wall. Instead, he found himself in another alley or street. Still the voices, heavily muffled, drifted out of the gray night, and an increasingly worried Fafhrd tried to cheer himself with the wry thought that half the city seemed to be wandering lost and unable to make contact with anyone else.

A superstitious dread suddenly seized him. Reaching out to the right with his sword, he raked the point lightly along a stone construct, reassuring himself that he was not lost in some unnatural wasteland. With a quiet, half-embarrassed sigh, he put his hand on the side of an unknown building and began to feel his way along.

"Fafhrd."

He stopped. Was that his name he'd heard, or did his imagination play tricks on him? Listening, he waited, uncertain if he should continue. He raised the point of his sword. "Mouser?" he whispered.

No response came, nor any sound at all. Feeling foolish, Fafhrd lowered his blade. Only his imagination after all, he told himself. Starting forward again, he stopped just in time when a random eddy in the fog revealed another rain barrel directly in his path. He gave a hearty laugh that was more relief than genuine mirth, thinking that at least this once he had spared his poor toe.

Stepping around the barrel, he advanced through the fog, considering that it might be better simply to wrap himself in his muddy cloak and curl up under some stairway or in some alley until morning and sunlight evaporated the veil enough to let him find his way home. But he licked his lips, and the thought of a cool mug impelled him to continue. If not the Silver Eel, surely he could find another tavern to take pity on a naked and filthy man. Thankfully, he had the Mouser's purse.

"Fafhrd."

The voice drifted to him again, and once more he stopped, certain that he had heard his name this time. Should he answer? He bit his lip, chewing a corner of his beard as he did so. How many people knew his name in this city?

A sudden suspicion filled him.

"Mouser," he grumbled, staring ahead into the fog to where the voice seemed to emanate. "If you're playing some trick to get even with me for peeing on you, I'll pound on your head until you're six inches shorter than you presently are!"

Fafhrd grinned with inward satisfaction. If it was, indeed, the Mouser playing games, such a taunt should draw him out. His partner was quite sensitive about his height and refused to abide comments under any circumstances.

Slowly, however, the grin turned to a frown. He might have shouted at the moon, had the moon been visible, for all the response he got.

Suddenly a breeze whispered through the lane, stirring the fog, parting and lifting it. A few paces away, a figure stood aswath in the vapor, quietly regarding him. A beauty she was, clad in a dress of black velvet with strands of raven hair riding the wind about her strong, Lankhmaran features. Around her waist, gleaming with an impossible light, hung a belt of silver links, and from that depended an empty silver sheath where a dagger might once have been.

The breeze swirled the mist once more, briefly revealing her face.

Fafhrd's heart seemed to stop in his chest. "Vlana?" Trembling lips seemed scarcely able to form her name. Extending one hand, he took a lurching step and stopped, unwilling to believe his eyes. Still, he cried, "Truest love!"

The wind ceased, and the mist enshrouded once more the figure before him, the only woman who had ever claimed his heart. With a wild outcry, Fafhrd thrust the point of his sword in the earth and ran forward, flinging his arms around the space where she should have been, encountering nothing. Nearly maddened, he flailed at the fog, spinning around and around like a drunken dancer, calling for his Vlana, until at last, he fell exhausted to his knees.

She was gone, if she had ever been there at all.

Once again, like a teasing serpent, the breeze slithered down the narrow way, and the heavy, gray fog parted before it. Lifting his head, Fafhrd stared across the road at the charred ruin of a once-familiar apartment dwelling and realized with a horrible, heart-wrenching certainty where he was.

In the uppermost floor of that building, his true love and the Mouser's had been set upon and devoured by hordes of rats under the control of a wizard in service to the Thieves' Guild. The women had fought and died while their men were off buying wine from the Silver Eel for a party.

The horror of the sight that greeted his eyes upon returning to those bloody rooms still haunted Fafhrd. It was the substance of all his nightmares, that Vlana called out, cursing his name and begging for aid as the vermin ripped out her throat and drank her eyes from their sweet sockets.

Such was the dream he had dreamed even this night and from which he had struggled to awake.

For the first time in this stranger than strange evening, he felt truly lost.

Alone and unseen, veiled by the darkness and the fog, even a barbarian could weep without shame. On his knees in the street, the big Northerner's head sagged forward onto his chest, and his arms fell limply to his sides as sobs of grief and aching loss filled the night.

The fog hid the building from sight once again, and misty tendrils, offering cool comfort, enwrapped Fafhrd in his pain.

FIVE

CITY OF A THOUSAND TEMPLES

The front door of the Silver Eel opened quietly, and the pale gray light of an early misty morning seeped across the threshold. The heavy fog of night had retreated, but the sun had not yet warmed the streets, nor chased the chill from the air. Hugging his cloak about his shoulders, Fafhrd eased the door closed.

The tavern was silent and empty but for a single figure. Slumped over a table in the farthest corner, the Mouser raised his head sleepily and peeled open one eye. Fafhrd said nothing to his companion as he passed by, but he set a soft leather purse near the Mouser's hand before he proceeded up the stairs and sought the room they shared.

The lamp in the hallway had long since burned out, and within their rented room, darkness still held sway. The morning light, weak as it was, had not yet penetrated into the narrow alley beyond the open window. Putting aside his sword, Fafhrd pulled the shutters closed and latched them. Turning, he gazed around the room and wondered what he should do next. At last, he sank down to the floor, leaned his back against the wall beneath the window sill, hugged his cloak closer still, and put his head wearily upon his knees.

With the mildest of creaks, the door opened and shut. It was Fafhrd's turn to look up. An orange glow surrounded the Mouser as he held high one of the tavern's lanterns. In his other hand, he bore a pitcher. Placing the lantern beside the wash basin on the room's only table, he handed the pitcher to Fafhrd, then crossed the room to sit on the edge of the bed.

"Rough night?" the Mouser asked. "Looks like you spent it in a pig sty."

Fafhrd took a long pull from the pitcher. The beer tasted warm and bitter, but it drove the chill from his body, and lifted his spirits a little. "Nice of you to wait up," he said.

With the strings looped around his first finger, the Mouser twirled the purse around and around until the speed of its motion made a small humming sound and the purse, itself, blurred. "I gather you encountered the Ilthmart of questionable character?"

Fafhrd only nodded as he rose and went to the table. Setting aside the pitcher of beer, he cast off his cloak and began to wash himself with an old cloth using the water that already half-filled the crude earthenware basin. The sound of gentle splashing filled the room.

The Mouser put aside the purse. "Did you kill him?" he inquired carefully. "Is that why your mood seems bleaker than this crippled daylight?"

Fafhrd cleaned mud from his feet and shins. "He preferred to be reasonable," he answered. "As for my mood—" he paused in his ablutions and glanced toward the shutters before rinsing the cloth with a violent effort. Water splashed from the basin, spilling onto the table and floor. Fafhrd ignored it. "Blame it on this fog-haunted city. I wish we were away from here."

A strangely grim expression shadowed the Mouser's face. Fafhrd looked away from his friend as he gnawed his lower lip.

He wondered if he should speak of Vlana's ghost. Yet, could he be sure he had, indeed, seen the spirit of his one true love? Perhaps it was only his imagination or the fog playing tricks with his head. Perhaps it was only his grief catching up with him.

The Mouser patted the mattress. "Let us take a few hours' sleep," he suggested, "then, we'll rise and begin this evil quest. The sooner begun, the sooner done."

Fafhrd scowled as he threw the cloth back into the basin, splashing more water. "Sleep," he said, turning down the lantern's wick. Crossing to his side of the bed in the near-darkness, he crawled under a corner of the only blanket. "Then rise and head to work like good common little hirelings."

The Mouser's boots clunked onto the floor as he cast them off. His tunic followed, and he claimed his own piece of the blanket. "You should never go to bed angry," he said in a lighter tone.

"You are not my wife," Fafhrd grumbled as he turned onto his side, a movement that dragged the entire blanket to his half of the bed. "Shut up."

The Mouser snatched it back again, beginning a silent war that would continue until well past noon.

A drizzling rain fell from slate-gray skies, turning the backstreets and alleyways to ribbons of mud, slicking the cobblestones and paving tiles of the better thoroughfares. Along the Street of the Gods, the gutters roiled with dirty, refuse-strewn water. Huddled under hooded cloaks or brightly dyed parasols, pedestrians hurried in and out of the many elaborate temples that gave the way its name.

Impatiently watching the traffic, Fafhrd waited outside the columned gates of the Temple of Mog, the spider god. The droning intonations of Mog's priests reached his ears, muffled only slightly by the rain's steady pitter-patter. The temple was actually a huge amphitheater with a cone-shaped administration building at its center. Come rain or shine, from dawn until sundown, priests and acolytes and worshippers ranged about the grounds singing the praises of their deity.

Huddled under a single blue and yellow parasol, a pair of old women passed by Fafhrd and through the columned entrance. Immediately they began to sing, weaving their voices in a squeaky, tuneless harmony. Drawing the folds of his hood closer about his face, the Northerner turned his back to the gate and shook his head. How, he wondered, could any god abide such prayer?

He resumed watching the traffic until the Mouser emerged from the temple gate and tapped his shoulder. Fafhrd look down at his comrade. "I didn't hear your dulcet tones soaring among the voices of Mog's heavenly choir," he said with unveiled sarcasm.

The Mouser, looking miserable in his sodden gray cloak, took Fafhrd's elbow and steered him through the street in the direction of the riverfront. "You know I sing like a frog with a fly stuck in its throat," he answered. "Instead I convinced the priests of my piety by making an offering of the Ilthmart's ring."

Fafhrd grunted. To his mind, the ring was now wasted wealth. If Mog ever saw the pretty bauble, it would be adorning the finger of one of his priests. But above all the other gods of Nehwon, the Mouser worshipped the spider god, and when asked for permission to donate the ring, Fafhrd could not deny his partner.

"With such business as we are upon," the Mouser said, almost apologetically, "currying a little favor with the gods cannot hurt."

"Can't it?" Fafhrd said, giving a sidelong glance toward a line of saffron-robed priests of Issek as they marched down the middle of the rainy street, shaking chipolis and bells in accompaniment to some chant. "What is prayer, but a poor man's magic-making? What if it also attracts Malygris's deadly curse?"

The Mouser stopped in his tracks and pushed back the edge of his hood to regard his companion. His face seemed paler than usual. He looked up and down the Street of the Gods at all the citizens entering and exiting the various temples. "All these people . . ." he said. Wiping rain from his eyes, he pulled up his hood again and resumed the course. He muttered to Fafhrd, "You have a talent for making a gloomy day gloomier."

Where Silver Street intersected the Street of the Gods, a team of four brawny slaves bearing a gaily draped palanquin momentarily blocked the way. The white wood frame, carved in relief with small figures of animals, resembled expensive ivory. Even in the rain, its cloth-of-gold and red silk curtains shimmered, and tiny golden bells on the bearing poles jingled in rhythm with the bearers' steps.

As the palanquin passed them by, delicate fingers with long, painted nails parted the curtains ever so slightly. A wisp of blond hair flashed, and kohl-blackened eyes focused briefly on them. Then the curtain closed again.

"Liara," the Mouser whispered, staring after the vehicle as it hurried on.

Never had Fafhrd seen such a strange expression on his partner's face. The Mouser's jaw hung, and his eyes seemed glazed, nor did he show any inclination to move. "Who?" he said. "You know that pretty dish?"

The Mouser seemed to shake himself, but still he stared after the palanquin, finally tearing his gaze away. "The Dark Butterfly," he said gruffly, abruptly leading the way across the busy intersection. With a note of scorn, he added, "Some whore, who happened into the Silver Eel last night. On her way to some assignation, no doubt."

The rain abruptly stopped. Fafhrd glanced up at the sky and observed the thick clouds that rolled and rumbled above the city. The sun, barely visible through the pall, floated like a pale, blinking eye, watchful and vaguely ominous.

A pair of shepherds drove a bleating flock of sheep through the intersection. Small hooves rang on the cobbled pavement, and a dog barked and nipped at the ankles of woolly stragglers. A wagon, pulled by two oxen and laden with heavy barrels, trundled noisily on huge wheels of solid wood after the shepherds, the driver scowling and cursing the slowness of the procession.

"Watch your step," Fafhrd said to the Mouser when the way was clear and they started forward again. He wrinkled his nose. "That's not mud, where you're about to plant your boot."

The Mouser did a dainty dance around a series of small sheep pies. "Brag now about the sharpness of your barbarian senses," he said in a nasal voice, his mood lightening again, as he pinched his nostril shut with a finger and thumb.

They made it across Silver Street at last. Continuing down the Street of the Gods, they passed the five-storied Temple of Aarth, the largest and most lavish of all the Lankhmaran temples. A semi-circle of white-washed columns formed its gate, and white-robed neophytes with shaven heads greeted the lines of worshippers that filed through.

In all his travels, never had Fafhrd seen a city with so many gods and temples. The Street of the Gods ran from one side of the city to the other, from the Marsh Gate to the River Hlal, with nothing but temples on either side of it, or shops selling incense, herbs, or other offering materials to hurried worshippers. Every god or goddess in Lankhmar had a temple on this street, as did many gods from other nations.

Only Godsland itself, in the far north where the gods lived, could have more temples, Fafhrd figured.

Aarth's temple marked the end of the Street of the Gods, but it was not the last of the temples in Lankhmar. Turning south, they started down Nun Street, and Fafhrd spied the first of the seventeen black towers of Lankhmar's forgotten gods.

No one knew the names of the gods those black structures had been erected to honor, nor when they had been built. Already ancient and abandoned when the first Lankhmaran settlers came to this land, they were places of crumbling mystery, foreboding and forbidden. Some stood slender and tall, like thin claws thrust up from the earth to rake the sky, while others sat squat and low, like dark-skinned frogs watching the river.

Despite the oppressive shadows those temples cast, a bustling commerce flourished all along the riverfront. Lankhmar sat near the mouth of the River Hlal, which opened into the Inner Sea. Trading ships from Ilthmar, the Land of the Eight Cities, and even the far-off Cold Wastes from where Fafhrd hailed regularly docked at Lankhmar's busy wharves, and Lankhmar's own merchant navy stood second to none.

Shops and industries lined the streets of the riverfront. In addition, many of the city's nobles had built their homes and established fine estates in the district.

Another palanquin passed them, jangling with scores of tiny golden bells, born by four powerful men in red liveries who wore long dirks sheathed on their belts. Crimson and silver draperies fluttering somewhat in the breeze allowed no clue as to the occupant. A trio of servants, dressed in the same red garments, followed hurriedly after it, bearing packages and covered baskets.

Fafhrd scratched his short red beard. "She had a familiar face," he said thoughtfully.

"Who?" the Mouser asked, glancing from Fafhrd to the palanquin and back again.

"Your whore," he answered.

A dark look clouded the Mouser's face. Wordlessly, he strode off toward the first of the forbidden towers, stepping off Nun Street and taking Fishbloat Lane, which ran straight to the wharves. With long-legged strides, a puzzled Fafhrd easily caught up with his smaller companion.

"I want a look at each of the towers," the Mouser said quickly, as if preventing Fafhrd from reviving the previous subject. "If necessary, all seventeen."

Fafhrd nodded agreement. "Will Malygris be waving a hanky prettily out a window, or are we just reacquainting ourselves with the city's sights?"

"I don't know," the Mouser snapped with uncharacteristic rudeness. "Nuulpha's rumor may be just a rumor. But it's also a place to start. Do you have a better suggestion?"

Stung by his partner's tone, Fafhrd hesitated. "No," he finally admitted.

Forcing a path through a crowd of shoppers at an outdoor fish market, the Mouser spoke over his shoulder. "Then do me two favors," he said. Pulling back a corner of his hood, he forced a grin. "First, forgive me for my harsh speech." He held up one finger, then another as he abruptly stopped. "Second, look over the heads of this rabble and tell me where in Mog's name is the tower?"

Fafhrd laughed, his hurt forgotten. A narrow street, the shops and warehouses that lined Fishbloat Lane formed virtual walls on either side of the way, and so thick were the crowds, now that the rain had ended, that his short friend was nearly engulfed in a sea of humanity. Even with the advantage of his height, Fafhrd could barely see the tip of the forbidden tower that marked their goal.

"Through here," he said suddenly, catching the Mouser's gray-clad arm and jerking him into an alley. The passage was barely worthy to be called such. The rough wooden walls on either side, so close that they forced the two friends to walk sideways, scraped their backs and chests as they inched along. Mud squished under their boots, and the smell of rancid fish seemed trapped in the air.

Fafhrd dared to look down. The thin ribbon of ground glimmered with fish scales, old and new. It was not mud alone they walked on, but mud and fish guts. Rolling his eyes, he uttered a short prayer to Kos that no merchant dumped more garbage until he and the Mouser reached the other end.

"Come here often?" the Mouser muttered sarcastically as he shook a fish-head off his toe.

Fafhrd didn't answer. The alley joined another street where the shoppers were fewer. Fafhrd stepped out and let go the breath he'd been holding. Instantly, he jumped back as an ox pulling a cart nearly ran him down. His sudden lunge for safety caused him to collide with the Mouser, who was not yet clear of the alley. The Mouser gave an awkward cry and clutched frantically at Fafhrd's borrowed cloak with one hand, at the wall with the other.

The big Northerner caught his friend's arm and apologetically set him on his feet again.

"Pissing on me last night, that I can forgive," the Mouser warned. "Knocking me into this slime, however, would have demanded retribution."

Fafhrd peered carefully around the edge of the alley before stepping out again. The way was clear. At the end of the new street where they found themselves the tall masts of a sailing ship rocked gently to and fro. On the wharf, half-naked men busily loaded barrels and sacks of grain onto the vessel.

Halfway down the street, the line of warehouses parted, yielding to the cracked marble tiles of an old courtyard. Surrounded by an iron fence that offered no gate, a slender, black-stoned tower rose three stories high. Only the third and highest story offered any windows or apparent openings. Birds flew in and out, having made their nests in its shadowed recesses. The courtyard, even the side of the tower, was stained with centuries of droppings.

The Mouser approached the fence, walked back and forth before it, ran his fingers along the spear-pointed iron bars. Fafhrd stood back. His gaze climbed the stones, noting the crumbling mortar, the gaping rent in the structure near its parapet, the way the birds cooed in their nests while their mates circled.

"He's not here," he said in a low voice to the Mouser. When his partner turned toward him, he explained. "The birds are too carefree. The nests would be empty if the tower were inhabited."

Nodding agreement, the Mouser backed away from the fence.

Returning to Nun Street they worked their way south through the growing throngs that choked the busy thoroughfare. Exerting itself, the sun made slight headway through the clouds, and though the sky remained gray, the air warmed.

A pair of temples stood side by side on Sailors' Row. The taller one stood two stories and loomed over the second temple, which was a low, square building. The tower, badly crumbled on one side, leaned at an unlikely angle. *Slumped over,* Fafhrd thought to himself, *as if the god it was built for had died.* The box-like temple appeared ageless, seamless in construction. Neither structure showed doors or windows. They shared a common courtyard, and in the center of that lay the shattered ruins of an ancient fountain. A common iron fence separated the grounds from the rest of the city.

The feeble sun slipped toward the horizon, and twilight stole quietly through Lankhmar. The sounds of industry lessened in the riverfront district, and the streets slowly emptied of shoppers and workers.

Frustration gnawed at Fafhrd as he wandered with the Mouser to the southern end of the wharves and stared across the glimmering water of the wide Hlal. A rising wind played an eerie tune in the riggings of ships moored in their berths. He listened, noting also the creaking of the boards beneath his feet as the river lapped at the pilings. It all made a strange, lonely music.

"I think I have never felt so thin as now," Fafhrd murmured to himself.

Overhearing, the Mouser raised an eyebrow. "Thin?"

Far across the river, a black-cloaked old man poled a flat skiff patiently across the dappled water. Fafhrd watched with an odd foreboding, that he attributed to fatigue. "The wind blows," he said cryptically to the Mouser, "but it blows through me. The music, too, seems to pass through me."

"Music?" the Mouser repeated. "What music?"

Fafhrd continued to watch the skiff. Though the boatman worked his pole with practiced skill, he progressed but slowly over the darkening waves. "I can't explain it, my friend," he said without looking at the Mouser. "I feel . . ." he hesitated and hugged himself against a chill before finishing his thought. "Insubstantial."

A small sharp pain flashed suddenly through Fafhrd's rump. Giving a yelp, the Northerner jumped a foot in the air and clutched his backside.

The Mouser smiled wickedly as he held up thumb and forefinger and made a pinching motion. "So much for insubstantiality," he said. "Now come on."

The Mouser turned his back to the river and started away. Fafhrd followed, but before they rounded the corner of yet another warehouse, he glanced around abruptly and stopped.

The air became dead still without a breath of wind. The guy wires and riggings of the moored ships hummed no more, but fell suddenly silent, as if struck dumb. Even the constant creaking of the wharves seemed to cease.

Fafhrd studied the river. Nowhere upon that gently swirling surface was there a sign of a skiff or boatman.

"Blood of Kos," Fafhrd muttered, taking long strides to catch up with the Mouser. "This city is getting to me."

Where Nun Street joined Cash Street, yet another temple stood. The four-storied black structure cast its shadow over a neighborhood composed mostly of small shops and the estates of wealthy merchants and ship-owners. Taller and more slender than most of the forbidden towers, and leaning at a riverward angle, it looked to Fafhrd like some stygian sword thrust by a giant hand into the earth. Narrow balconies beneath windows on either side even gave the impression of tines.

A fair number of citizens still ventured abroad in this part of town even as night drew close. Many still carried their shopping baskets as they drifted from door to door. Others, dressed in finery and accompanied by servants or personal guards, on foot or in palanquins, headed east on Cash Street toward Carter Street, bound for the Festival District or the Plaza of Dark Delights.

Fafhrd started toward the iron fence that surrounded the ancient tower, but the Mouser's hand closed firmly around his arm and steered him in a new direction.

"Pull up your hood," the Mouser whispered sharply, his dark eyes darting suspiciously from side to side.

Without seeming haste, Fafhrd covered his head and continued down the street past the temple. A fountain and public drinking well gurgled prettily at the center of the intersection of Nun and Cash Streets. Fafhrd allowed the Mouser to guide him there, and the two men dipped their hands in the water to drink.

"So, gray friend," Fafhrd said as he brought his cupped hands toward his mouth, "what spurred this sudden fondness for my elbow?"

"Glance toward the lace-maker's shop across the way," the Mouser said as he pretended to drink. "What do you see leaning in the doorway?"

Smacking his damp lips, Fafhrd wiped his hands on his trousers. "Why, nothing but two fellows in idle conversation," he answered, scrutinizing the pair. Under the cloaks they wore, however, he thought he detected the outlines of swords.

"Now, over by the white wall of that estate," the Mouser continued, dipping his hands for another drink. "Just down the road to your left."

Splashing a little water on his face, Fafhrd wiped at his eyes with one sleeve. As he did so, he gazed where his partner directed. "Another pair of fellows," he noted. "Also in idle conversation."

"Also cloaked and armed," the Mouser said. "Also shaven of face and trimmed of hair, like the pair by the shop. Four sturdy men without an ounce of merchants' fat around their bellies or on their bare cheeks. Their eyes sweep everywhere."

"Private security?" Fafhrd suggested. "Perhaps they are positioned to keep the neighborhood safe from crime."

The Mouser snorted. "Let's continue casually around the tower," he suggested. "For the moment, observe it without approaching it."

By the time they finished their reconnaissance, night had fully settled. "How many did you count?" Fafhrd asked as they drank once more from the fountain at the intersection of Nun and Cash.

"Twenty-two," the Mouser answered quietly, "lounging in various doorways and gateways, under trees, on rooftops."

From the doorway of the lace shop, a pair of stout men paused in their conversation and glanced their way. They were a different pair, but acting out the same conversation, striking the same nonchalant poses. Their eyes, though, gave them away, for they watched everything.

"The guard has changed," Fafhrd murmured.

"The question is," his companion said, "what are they guarding? My money is on the tower."

Together, they left the fountain and started eastward on Cash Street away from the forbidden temple. "Why this particular temple and not the others?" Fafhrd wondered aloud. Then, the obvious idea occurred to him. "Could they be seeking Malygris as well?"

The Mouser gave a low chuckle. "So many curious questions," he said. "And if your archery skills are sufficient to put an arrow and a climbing line through one of those upper windows, perhaps after midnight we can find some answers."

SIX

DEATH KNELLS

og once again moved through the streets of Lankhmar. Tendrils of mist crept up every lane, poured into every plaza, seeped through the smallest alleys. The heavy gray blanket extinguished the moon and stars, dimmed the watch-fires that burned atop the city walls, threatened to swallow even the tiny flames in the lanterns of the few citizens who dared to venture forth.

Once more crouched in a shadowed doorway near the inter-section of Cash and Nun streets, the Mouser growled a low curse. The midnight hour was far off; the deepening fog had forced them to hasten their plans.

In the shadows beside him, Fafhrd stood ready with a newly purchased line and iron grapnel. "Getting over the fence would be easy," the Northerner whispered. "But in this pea soup, I can't even see the tower, let alone pitch a hook through a third-story window."

Fafhrd exaggerated their predicament only slightly. Only the lower portion of the tower remained visible, and that was little more than a silhouette. The fog thoroughly concealed the upper half.

The Mouser cursed again, marveling at how swiftly the damned stuff had moved up from the river and into the city. Even as he watched, it seemed to swirl languidly around the forbidden tower, engulfing it. The lower portion, too, vanished from sight.

"There's no adventure for us there this night," Fafhrd muttered, shifting nervously in the doorway.

A sharp cough from the far side of the street caught the Mouser's attention. He tugged the hood of his cloak over his head as he rose from his crouched position. "Not so," he answered. "If we can't get into the temple, let's see if we can discover the identities of its guardians."

With Fafhrd close on his heels, he darted to the far side of Cash Street and pressed himself against a wall. An upward glance told his companion what he planned. In cupped hands, Fafhrd accepted the Mouser's foot and boosted him to the low roof. Once secure in his perch, the Mouser reached down and took the grapnel his partner extended to him. Then, with a powerful jump, Fafhrd caught the edge of the gutter. For an instant, he hung there, then, silently he muscled his huge body upward.

A moment later, the two squatted side by side. "A fine pair of gargoyles we make," Fafhrd murmured as he took the grapnel and line back from the Mouser.

"I'm too good-looking for a gargoyle," the Mouser whispered in reply. "You're just about right, though." Rising with a big grin on his face, he quickly tip-toed away over the rooftop before Fafhrd could form a rejoinder.

The shops in this part of the city stood close together, many sharing adjoining walls. Moving carefully over the mist-slick tiles, the pair of adventurers crouched down again and peered over the edge of a certain lacework establishment facing Nun Street. Needlessly, the Mouser glanced at Fafhrd and, holding a finger to his lips, cautioned silence.

Soft, muttering voices rose up from the doorway just below their rooftop perch. Stretching out on his belly, pushing back his hood, the Mouser crawled forward as far as he dared and peeked downward. Two cloaked men sat on the small stoop, casually swapping stories of fishing in the Hlal. One balanced a sheathed sword across his knees.

The Mouser crawled away from the edge and sat up again. Farther up on the roof, a patient Fafhrd sat cross-legged, lovingly stroking a thin gray cat that was curled up in his lap. Luminous eyes blinked as the beast settled its head upon a brawny thigh and purred.

"Where did that come from?" the Mouser dared to whisper.

Fafhrd drew his fingers gently between the cat's ears, down its neck, along its furry spine. "I seem to attract gray mousers," he answered. Then he put a finger to his lips exactly as the Mouser had done earlier, but whether to warn against disturbing the cat or the men below, the Mouser wasn't sure.

Leaving Fafhrd with his newfound friend, the Mouser crawled back to the roof's edge and stretched out on his belly again. Perhaps if he listened long enough he might learn something from the conversation on the stoop. The voices droned boringly on about the weather, the fog, the river, the coming midsummer celebration.

Without warning, a weight suddenly landed in the middle of the Mouser's back. Every hair on his neck stood on end, and he barely stifled an outcry. On his belly, he could reach neither sword, nor dagger.

The sound of purring touched the Mouser's ears. His attacker was none other than Fafhrd's cat. The impudent little animal walked in a circle on the Mouser's spine before curling up comfortably in the small of his back.

This is carrying kinship too far, the Mouser thought. About to shoo the creature away, he froze abruptly to listen as the conversation below took a more interesting turn.

"Damn this fog," one of the voices said. "There's beer and warmth back at the barracks."

The stoop creaked as someone shifted. "Quench your thirst at the fountain," said the second voice in a weary tone.

The Mouser pursed his lips in a thoughtful frown. Any number of Lankhmar's nobles quartered their own private guards, but surely such a casual reference to *barracks* indicated the involvement of the city's guards. His frown deepened.

Shifting position, Fafhrd sat down near the edge and proceeded to stroke the cat again. Fickle as only a cat can be, it rose, flexed one claw in the Mouser's right buttock, then transferred itself to the Northerner's lap once more.

The pale gleam of lanterns penetrated the thick fog. Six tall men in nondescript cloaks emerged from the mist, walking south on Nun Street. Without a word to the others, two separated from the party and approached the laceworks shop.

"Report," said one of the newcomers.

A now-familiar voice answered wearily. "All's quiet from this station."

"Take the lantern then," said the newcomer, "and remember you're celebrants, albeit quiet ones. Return by a roundabout course to the Rainbow Palace."

With the lantern's light to guide them through the fog, the men on the stoop walked around the corner to Cash Street while the newcomers made themselves comfortable in the doorway below.

Putting the cat aside, Fafhrd rose and beckoned the Mouser away from the roof's edge. But he didn't stop when they were safely out of hearing. Indeed, not until they had reached Cash Street, themselves, and dropped to the ground did Fafhrd speak.

There was no sign of a lantern's glow in the fog, which continued to grow ever thicker. "These are the Overlord's men," he stated, adjusting the grapnel, which was now slung by its coiled line over his shoulder.

"Your ears are sharp as ever," the Mouser answered.

A gray streak leaped from the roof, rebounded from the rim of a rain barrel, and landed between their feet. The Mouser jumped back, his narrow blade flashing out of its sheath.

Unimpressed, the cat blinked and gave a quiet meow before it rubbed against Fafhrd's ankle.

Grinning at his partner's startled reaction, Fafhrd shrugged. "Think of him as a mascot," he suggested.

The Mouser slammed his sword back into its sheath. "Think of him as victuals," he responded. He wagged a finger at the cat. "One more time . . ."

Fafhrd drew the Mouser against the wall. A dull amber glimmer, coming from the direction of Nun Street, warned of someone's approach. Drawing up his hood, the Mouser crouched down by the rain barrel. When he glanced back for his friend, Fafhrd was simply gone.

The lantern and still another pair of men passed right by the Mouser's hiding place. He might have put out one foot and tripped them, they came so close. Unaware, they wandered on until the night swallowed them.

The cat rubbed its head against the Mouser's rump.

Fafhrd swung lithely down from the rooftop, where he had taken refuge. "Why would the Overlord keep a round-the-clock watch on a forbidden temple?" he asked.

"Why are the guards out of uniform?" the Mouser replied.

Fafhrd rubbed his bearded chin. "To trap and apprehend Malygris?" Fafhrd suggested uncertainly.

An ugly scowl settled over the Mouser's face as suspicion filled him. He picked up the cat and hugged it close. His dark eyes, narrowing to slits, burned almost as luminously as the feline's. "Or to protect him?" he said sharply. Pushing the cat into Fafhrd's arms, he started down Cash Street again. "Come on, there's nothing more we can do here tonight."

The black shapes of buildings loomed as Fafhrd and the Mouser made their way through the thickening fog back toward the Silver Eel. Here and there, the silhouette of a minaret or an obelisk jutted up half-seen. In the murk, a statue affixed to a fountain at the intersection of Cash and Gold Streets took on a menacing appearance. To the north, the ten-story Spire of Rhan, the tallest structure in Lankhmar, rose barely visible over the shadowy rooftops to stand like a spear upon which the misty night had impaled itself. Over it all hung the palest silvery moon, its weakening light causing the air to glisten and sparkle.

Voices, then the high-pitched sound of a woman's laughter came out of the fog near the corner of Cheap Street. Fafhrd and the Mouser paused to watch in silence as four men and two ladies, all in cloaked finery, passed by with lanterns to light their way to the Festival District. Their gay spirits were a distinct contrast to the depressing weather.

An unexpected beam of frosty light suddenly lit the street, causing the Mouser and Fafhrd to glance skyward. A brief rent widened in the mist and clouds, and the moon, like some brightly burning pupil in an arcane eye, stared down upon the city. The clouds moved in again, and the rent sealed from the top to the bottom as if that godlike eye had slowly closed.

The cat in the Mouser's arms gave a soft meow, and he gently scratched the soft fur beneath its chin. The greedy creature encouraged his strokes by lifting its head to give him freer access to the tender parts of its throat as it began to audibly purr.

Fafhrd glanced up toward the sky again, then his gaze seemed to comb the shadowy mists as if he were watching for something. The Mouser thought he had never seen his friend quite so tense.

"That woman's laughter," Fafhrd explained slowly. "Coming out of the fog like that. It . . ." he paused, and when he spoke again there was an odd note in his voice. ". . . reminded me of someone."

"Lord Hristo's whorish wife?" the Mouser guessed.

Fafhrd offered no response, just started forward again. With a puzzled shrug, the Mouser followed, but before they took ten paces another sound caused them to stop in their tracks and stare northward.

The deep tone of a huge bell sent a chill creeping up the Mouser's spine. Once, twice, three times it rang, and still it did not stop. Precisely spaced and measured, those dreadful tones echoed across the city. Not even the thick fog could muffle the lonely sound, and the air seemed to shiver with every mournful stroke.

"... nine ... ten ... eleven ..." Fafhrd counted, murmuring each number.

Even the cat in the Mouser's arms pricked up its ears. No longer purring, it arched its back, as if aware of the bell's significance. "The Voice of Aarth," the Mouser said reverently, speaking the name of the great bell, which resided in the highest minaret of Lankhmar's most important temple. "A priest has died."

The doleful chime continued, but Fafhrd stopped counting and shook his head. "Not even those egotistical shave-heads would disturb the city in the dead of night for a mere priest."

"The Patriarch?" the Mouser wondered aloud.

The grim look on Fafhrd's face was agreement enough, and the Mouser admitted his companion was probably correct. The bell continued for twelve more strokes while they stood listening, unwilling to move, as if frozen by the sound.

Then Aarth's Voice went silent. For a long moment, the night seemed to hold its breath. Nothing moved, not even the fog; the dense vapors ceased to swirl and eddy, and lay leaden in the streets.

From far across the city, a new sound came, shrill and sharp as a blade, to tear the stillness. A lone voice cried out a trilling zaghareet. Before the eerie cry died, another voice joined it, then another, and another as the priests and followers of Aarth took to the streets to fill the night with the almost inhuman sound of their mourning.

Fafhrd drew his cloak closer about his shoulders. "If there are any ghosts in this fog tonight," he muttered half to himself, "that noise will surely drive them away."

The Mouser frowned. "The death knells have not yet faded from my ears," he scolded, "and you talk of ghosts. You'll bring bad luck with your careless words."

"Superstition, Mouser?" Fafhrd mocked. "From a son of the civilized south?"

The Mouser squared his shoulders and drew a hand along the gray-furred spine of his new-found pet. The cat resumed its purring. "You northern barbarians are not the only ones that pick up pins and study the way the crow flies at dawn," he said defensively. "You have no corner on irrational beliefs."

The light-hearted exchange brought a certain sense of relief. Both friends breathed sighs and clapped each other's arms. "Back to the Silver Eel?" Fafhrd suggested, shouldering the weight of the grapnel and its line under his cloak.

The Mouser nodded. "That finely seasoned lamb Cherig served for dinner was exquisite," he said, trying to relieve the tension with small-talk. "I could barely taste the near-rot. Perhaps he has some left."

"I leave the lamb to you," Fafhrd answered. "Nothing but a keg, or even two, of our host's strongest beer will settle me this night."

The mournful zaghareets of Aarth's faithful, spreading southward from the Street of the Gods, served to hasten the footsteps of Fafhrd and the Mouser as they hurried toward Cheap Street. Like the muffled cries of wind demons, the weird sound bounced among buildings, echoed from rooftops and towers. Distorted by distance and the fog, it chilled the blood and fueled the imagination until every shadow became a crazed and menacing shape poised to attack.

A gray, misty sea hid the plaza where Cash and Cheap Streets intersected. The shops and apartments on the far side of the square could not be seen at all. Hesitating, the Mouser looked down and bit his lower lip. The mist curled with intimate familiarity about his thighs. He could not see his own knees.

"Give me your hand, that we might not get separated," Fafhrd said, his voice little more than a whisper.

"Am I some maiden?" the Mouser answered curtly. "As if I could lose a mountain like you, even in this soup. Lead on, Mountain."

They moved up Cheap Street, nearly missing the entrance to Dim Lane, down which lay the Silver Eel. Wishing for a lantern, the Mouser tugged at Fafhrd's sleeve. "This way," he insisted, turning into the narrow lane.

A muted percussion reached their ears. Dumbek drums rumbled under furious hands, brass zills clashed, and tambourines rattled. Up ahead, a weak lantern lit the sign above the Silver Eel's entrance.

"Sounds like a celebration," the Mouser commented, his step quickening now that their destination was in sight.

But Fafhrd caught a piece of the Mouser's cloak and jerked him backward. With a sweep of his other arm, the huge Northerner intercepted a spreading rope net that dropped from a rooftop. Catching its edge, he flung the net aside and reached for his sword.

Four men stepped out of the shadows before them. Crouching for action, they brandished clubs or short swords—darkness and fog made it impossible to tell which. "Four more behind us," Fafhrd whispered. His huge sword made a whisking sound as he whipped it from its sheath. The Mouser glanced upward. On the rooftop, two more men stood in plain sight, silhouetted against the gray-black sky.

"These walls are too close for that great skewer," the Mouser murmured to his companion as he calmly stroked the cat and watched the eight men on the ground advance menacingly. He turned ever so slightly so that he could keep a better eye on the men at their back while Fafhrd watched the four at their front. The pair on the roof offered no immediate threat unless they decided to jump.

Down the lane, behind the thin door of the Silver Eel, the dumbeks and zills and tambourines strained toward a feverish tempo.

With his own weapon still sheathed, the Mouser murmured again, "Be ready, my friend. They are almost upon us."

Taking a two-handed grip on Graywand's hilt, Fafhrd responded with sarcasm. "Some might think it impolite of you to greet such gentlemen with empty hands."

"Tut, tut, my dear Fafhrd," the smaller man said. "My hands are full of weapons."

With that, he spun suddenly about and flung the cat, which let out a horrible screeching as it found itself flying through the air. Claws dug deeply into the face of the nearest man, who let out a shriek to match the cat's. "Demons!" he screamed in terror. Wrestling with the beast that ripped his flesh, he leaped back into two of his comrades, sending them toppling.

The Mouser hit the fourth man with his shoulder, smashing him into the wall before he could recover from his surprise. The Gray One ran toward Dim Lane's entrance into Cheap Street.

One of the figures on the roof leaped into Fafhrd's path. Before his feet even quite touched the ground, a heavy pommel broke his jaw. A huge hand caught the shoulder of a rough tunic and hurled the slack-faced man into the paths of the other team of four as they rushed forward.

"Amateurs!" Fafhrd called, taunting them as they scrambled to get up. A knife whished by his ear suddenly, and his grin vanished. Spinning about, he ran back up the lane, pausing long enough to put a boot in the face of the man the Mouser had downed, and to sweep up the cat.

The Mouser waited for him at the mouth of the lane, his narrow sword drawn now, his breathing quick, his eyes bright with excitement.

"I think this belongs to you," Fafhrd said, delivering the cat into his arms. But the beast gave a growl, leaped away, and disappeared into the fog.

Footsteps raced toward them. Their attackers were not yet discouraged.

"The puss is on his own," the Mouser declared, forgetting about the cat as the first foe charged out of the fog. A blade cut toward the Mouser's head. Ducking the swing, he put a boot between the wielder's legs. "The better part of valor?" he suggested, inclining his head in the direction of the plaza.

"But of course!" Fafhrd called over his shoulder, his heels already ringing on the paving stones as he ran.

The plaza was a virtual fog-bound limbo, an ocean of gray mist. Neither intersecting Cash Street, nor the other end of Cheap Street could be seen. "Where?" Fafhrd cursed, his head whipping from side to side as he searched for the best course.

The Mouser whirled to meet their onrushing attackers, who surged into the plaza right behind them. The ten formed a circle around them. The weapons they carried were plainly swords now, not clubs, and the looks in their eyes were murderous.

The broken-jawed man stepped slightly forward and pointed his sword toward Fafhrd. "Ah wan' ma cloak, 'ou filthy barbaran! An' ma ring! Then ah wan' yer miserble lives for the embarrassmen' you've caused me!"

"It's our Ilthmart friend," the Mouser said in a tone of mockery as he turned back-to-back with Fafhrd.

"Aye," Fafhrd answered, "and nine of his dumbest, ugliest sisters."

"Ugly I may well be, you ignorant lummox," one of the nine said harshly. "But I take offense at 'dumb.'" With serpentine quickness, a length of rope flashed from his hands, uncoiling, whiplike, to snap around Fafhrd's sword. The blade went flying.

The Ilthmarts charged. The Mouser's blade rang against another. A knife flashed at his ribs. Twisting, he avoided the thrust and slammed his elbow into a face. Pain flashed across his left bicep, and the warm rush of blood poured down his sleeve. A fist toppled him to the street, and for a moment he was submerged in a foggy sea under a pile of bodies. A knee pinned his sword-hand to the ground, and a knife waved before his eyes. A vaguely familiar face appeared suddenly close to his, and the Mouser recognized the other Ilthmart who'd tried to rob him in the alley behind the Silver Eel.

"That's twice ye or yer pal have put a boot in me family treasures, shorty," the Ilthmart said angrily. "Now I'm gonna slice yers off an' wear 'em fer earrings!"

But before the Ilthmart could carry out his threat, his eyes widened with fear, and he leaped away. All the Mouser's attackers fell back as a whirring sound filled the air, growing louder, deeper. Rising first on an elbow, then to a nervous crouch, the Mouser gripped his wound and stared.

Standing protectively over him, Fafhrd swung the heavy grapnel on its length of rope around and around. Letting out more line with each rotation, he drove the Ilthmarts back. A blow from that weight meant crushed bones or death. Just beyond the lethal arc, the Ilthmarts cringed, but kept their weapons ready, looking for some opening to renew their attack.

The grapnel whooshed; Fafhrd's breath came out in great exhalations as he whirled the make-shift weapon, letting it out to the full length of its line. On the ground, the Mouser groped for his sword, finding Graywand as well as Scalpel.

Just out of the grapnel's range, the Ilthmart's broken-jawed leader raged. "Ge' in there!" he encouraged his men. "Cu' their damn throa's! Avenge the honor of Ilthmar'!"

In his enthusiasm, he caught the arm of the nearest man and propelled him forward—straight into the path of the grapnel. The weighty prongs missed the startled unfortunate, but the line arced around his throat and upper body, snapping his neck before the grapnel finally tangled itself.

Giving a tug on the line, Fafhrd found it would not come free. "Oops," he said with a shrug to the Mouser. He extended a hand for Graywand.

The Ilthmarts stared in disgust at their leader. Nevertheless, they now had something more than mere honor to avenge. Gripping their weapons, they stalked forward with fiercely determined expressions.

Then, up from the foggy sea, dense tendrils of mist snaked languidly upward, surrounding the Ilthmarts. Like the tentacles of some horrid sea squid, those tendrils coiled about the terrified men with such power that some were lifted from the very ground. The Ilthmarts screamed, those whose throats were not gripped. Spines and ribs, arms and necks cracked with brittle snapping.

Back to back with Fafhrd, even the Mouser cried out in fear and horror. Cold sweat ran down his neck; wide-eyed, dry-mouthed, he watched the killing, his ears ringing with screams, his hammering heart near to bursting. He shrank from the arcane tendrils, cowering against his trembling partner, his sword useless in a fear-numbed hand.

The last scream ended with a strangulated gurgle and a gasp. Not a single Ilthmart remained alive. Their deadly work completed, the tendrils lost their seeming solidity, dissolved, and melted away into the murky night.

The Mouser turned slowly to stare at Fafhrd. The Northerner, pale of face, shivering like a child in the cold, stared briefly back. As if with one thought, they ran from the plaza, ran up Cheap Street, ran as fast as their legs would carry them down Dim Lane for the warmth and light of the Silver Eel. Bursting through the door, the Mouser tripped over the threshold and spilled full upon the floor. Fafhrd slammed the door shut. Ignoring his small partner's plight, he braced his muscled frame against the wood as if to hold it against a pursuing foe.

The Mouser raised his head, suddenly aware of a powerful quiet. Every pair of eyes in the hotly crowded tavern locked on them. Around the room, men half-risen from their chairs put hands to swords or daggers. A dancer, raven hair plastered to her bare, sweating shoulders, stood frozen in the middle of a movement. Behind her, a band of drummers hesitated in mid-beat over now-silent dumbeks. Another trio of scantily clad women ceased to shake tambourines.

On the far side of the inn, Cherig waved his hook in the smoky air. "It's only my favorite tenants," he called merrily to his customers. "Play on! Play on!"

Like a tableau come back to life, the drummers struck their hides, and the dancer resumed without seeming to miss a step. Gruff men pushed their weapons back into sheaths, sat down again, and turned their gazes once more to shimmying hips and breasts, some clapping appreciatively to the throbbing beat of the dumbeks, others sipping beer or thin wine. Near the door, a comely woman leaned on the arm of a pot-bellied noble, but the wink she gave Fafhrd held no subtlety.

Red-faced with embarrassment, the Mouser banged his forehead on the floor three times before he drew a deep breath, got to his feet, and sheathed his slender blade. "I pray," he said to Fafhrd, summoning an air of bravado as he straightened his cloak and tunic and patted his stomach with one hand, "let Cherig have some of that seasoned lamb . . ."

He didn't finish the thought. Across the tavern in the gloomy corner near the rear door, standing between a pair of handsome young men, he spied the Dark Butterfly.

SEVEN

THE DARK
BUTTERFLY

In the gloomiest corner of the inn, the Mouser leaned his back against the wall and ate cold lamb and gravy on a trencher of bread. He chewed slowly without appreciating the taste at all, dripping sauce on the front of his gray tunic without noticing.

The percussion continued, but the music turned softer with the addition of Fafhrd's lute-playing. The dark-haired dancer worked the center of the floor, her movements slow and sensuous to match the more romantic mood created by the lute's strings. Her audience watched, entranced, but her flashing eyes glowed only for the red-bearded Northerner.

Between her two paramours, Liara paid little attention. She sipped her violet wine, sometimes lifting a small, ivory-skinned hand to hide a smile or quiet a laugh as one of the men whispered some secret in her ear. The deep purple of her silken gown and cloak shimmered in the inn's lantern light, and with her every slight movement, golden threads woven throughout the fabric seemed to spark with fire. A huge amethyst, depending from a golden chain, blazed at the opening of the valley between her breasts.

The Mouser watched her, frowning at the intimate way the two men touched her, whispered to her, pressed themselves against her in their dark corner as if they were about to take her, standing, right there. Liara laughed, drew down the face of one of them, kissed his nose, then his lips, before she pushed him away again. The other moved in then, bending close, expecting similar treatment, and she gave it.

Casting the remains of his meal on the floor, the Mouser wiped his hands on his trousers and tried to look away. She drew him, though, as if she were a flame and he a helpless moth. With his gaze turned from her, he still felt her there. Her presence called to him, demanded all his attention. Try as he might, he could not resist for long.

Just looking at her filled him with a fire, a heat he had not known since his beloved Ivrian held him last. Mog's blood! How could one woman look so much like another?

She laughed again, a sharp little sound, and stroked her own breast while her companions grinned hungrily down upon her.

The Mouser could stand her teasing no more. Leaving his place by the wall, he chose a spot where he could better watch his partner's playing. The blond noblewoman who had earlier winked at Fafhrd had sidled closer to him while the dancer bent backward before him, letting her hair brush over his feet as her breasts spilled nearly out of their cups. With soft percussion for accompaniment, Fafhrd played sweetly, enjoying the attention it won him.

Cherig One-hand appeared suddenly by the Mouser's side and pushed a mug of beer into his hands. "Perhaps the barbarian isn't such a barbarian, after all," he said with a hint of drunkenness. The Silver Eel's owner snatched another mug from a startled customer's hand and swallowed from it. "I think he's good for business, and I'd like to have a drink with his manager." Without thanks or apology, he handed the vessel back to the same customer.

The lantern light reflected in the amber contents as the Mouser swirled the liquid thoughtfully without drinking. "No," he murmured, more to the beer than to Cherig. Without even looking, he could sense Liara in the corner as he passed the beer back. "I'd like a small glass of Tovilyis wine."

Cherig raised an eyebrow. "Your boy's popular for one night, and already you're making demands!" He lifted the Mouser's mug to his lips and drained it, spilling some of the contents down his bare chest and into his apron. "I'll get it then to make you happy," he said, wiping his mouth with the back of his arm. "Festival comes, and all my friends must be happy!"

The music ended, and the percussionists took over. A wild, frenzied beat filled the inn. A different woman leaped up onto a table and began to gyrate, uncaring when someone snatched at her clothing. Indeed, she began to cast it off, herself, throwing blouse and then skirts into the air to fall where they would while the rest of the customers clapped and called encouragement.

She was indifferent-looking, however, and the Mouser's gaze strayed toward the tavern's rear door. Did he imagine it, or was Liara watching him, too? She raised her glass and sipped the wine. Her eyes, catching the liquor's color, shot violet fire.

Then Cherig blocked his view. The tiny crystal goblet he held for the Mouser was not much bigger than a thimble, yet the rare wine's bouquet blossomed like the finest perfume. Accepting the drink, the Mouser closed his eyes and inhaled delicately, letting old memories wash gently over him.

Ivrian had loved this wine of Tovilyis. On the first night of their love-making in Lankhmar she had poured a bottle over him and, laughing, licked it off. "To my noble father, who tried and failed to keep us apart," she had toasted as she filled his armpit and drank from it. "To my father's soldiers, who couldn't find their own arses, let alone the two of us in this huge city," she had said with her head between his legs.

"To you, Ivrian," he whispered as he raised his small glass to the memory of his one true love and opened his eyes. To an observer, however, it might have appeared that it was Liara he toasted, for Cherig no longer stood between them.

Putting the crystal to his lips, he poured the thick, flowery nectar down his throat. Surely the gods vinted no more wondrous beverage, he thought as he savored the burst of flavor.

When he lowered the glass, over the rim he spied the Dark Butterfly slipping out the rear door with her pair of suitors.

Fafhrd, in a generous effort to lower class barriers, had one arm wrapped around the dark-haired dancer and the other on the waist of the blond noblewoman. As the Mouser watched, the noblewoman held a mug to the Northerner's lips, and he drank deeply while the dancer kneaded the corded muscles in his neck.

Cherig passed by again to claim the precious glass. Without a word to his partner, the Mouser slipped through the crowd and exited through the rear door.

The fog swirled through Bones Alley. The moist air felt cool on his face, and he drew up his hood as he gazed up and down the narrow passage, hoping for a sight of the Dark Butterfly. The mist, of course, thwarted that desire, but a short, familiar laugh established his direction.

The haunting zaghareets of Aarth's followers still floated in the night, but the close walls of the alley muffled the weird cries. He felt his way along carefully until he reached Carter Street.

Rounding the corner, he caught just a flash of a silk cloak before the fog concealed Liara from his view again. Fortunately, her companions, made ebullient by liquor, gave forth with an endless stream of brags and jokes, as men too often did in the presence of beautiful women. Their voices made them easy to follow.

At the corner of Damp Street, a gaunt-faced man in a ragged cloak raised a smoking pitch torch as he called out to the trio.

"Light your way!" he cried, his dirty face shining under the bright flare. "Light your way! Five tik-pennies is what you pay! Light your way!"

The Dark Butterfly laughed as she stopped before the enterprising fellow. "What a clever way to earn your bread, and a worthwhile service it is," she said. "Have you turned much business tonight?"

The torch-bearer bowed elegantly. "This damned fog, if your ladyship will pardon a poor man's language, keeps many folks inside. But Midsummer Festival approaches, and there's always them that likes to get an early start on their celebrating. I just walked a couple to the Plaza of Dark Delights." He winked salaciously.

A chorus of shrill zaghareets and a barely human scream ripped through the night. The torch-bearer shrank in fear, nearly dropping his money-maker. One of the paramours drew Liara protectively into his arms while the other whirled with a drawn dagger.

Unseen, the Mouser flattened against a wall, his sword whisking from its sheath. For a moment, all the horrors of the Cheap Street Plaza, forgotten in his desire for the woman he followed, surged through his mind.

A small mob of Aarth's priests and followers charged down the road, saffron robes flapping and torn, the light of tiny lanterns swinging in the mist as they ran. Again, they screamed zaghareets, and again one of their number, unable perhaps to make the intricate sound, answered with a blood-curdling scream. In only a moment they were passed and lost once more in the dense fog.

Liara's guardians gave a visible sigh of relief and sheathed their daggers, though Liara seemed quite calm, almost amused. "I have no fear of the night," she said to the torch-bearer, "but to soothe the nerves of these big strong men,"—she indicated her companions—"I will hire your services." She held up a finger. "One tik."

The torch-bearer scoffed, feigning offense. "Five tiks," he insisted. "But for such a beautiful lady, I will lower myself to accept four."

Liara held up another finger. "Two," she offered.

The torch-bearer rubbed his chin, looking stern. "Shall we say three and call it a bargain?"

"Two," Liara said firmly. Then she smiled. "And a kiss at the end of your hire."

The torch-bearer's eyes grew as bright as his flame.

"On the cheek," she added, folding her arms beneath her silken cloak.

"Left or right?" the torch-bearer grinned, unwilling to end the haggle.

Liara shrugged, reached out with a fingertip, and touched the left side of a broken-toothed mouth. "Here."

The little man smiled, then jumped up and clicked his heels. "Lead the way!" he sang. "Lead the way! Two tiks and a kiss is what you pay!"

Now four, Liara's party continued down Carter Street surrounded by a wavering circle of amber radiance. Concealed by the fog, the Mouser followed a few paces behind, his sword once more in its sheath. The smoke of the pitch torch tickled his nose, and he pressed a finger against his nostrils to stifle a sneeze.

She even walked like Ivrian. Her laughter, speech, her smallest movement reminded him of his dead love. The color of her hair, her eyes, her face was Ivrian's. Only in her boldness, her disdain for the dangers of the night, did she differ, and in her open, flagrant flirtation.

Drawn almost against his will, the Mouser crept along just past the edge of the light, a shadow of her shadow, haunted and mesmerized.

Suddenly, as they passed the mouth of a narrow alley, another pair of shadows sprang out. The torch-bearer whirled, shoving fire into the face of Liara's largest suitor. In the fire-gleam, daggers flashed. The remaining suitor, his dagger free, slashed at the torch-bearer, and the torch went spinning into the street. The burned man's screams turned into a bloody, choking gurgle. Then the second suitor went down, too.

Liara struck with her own dagger at one of the shadows, but the figure caught her wrist and twisted it. The blade flew out of her fist, but with her other hand she clawed at his eyes and hurled herself upon him like a hellion.

The second attacker slit the burned suitor's throat to silence him, then tangled a hand in Liara's hair, jerked her head back and slapped her hard enough to knock her sprawling into the street.

"Strip 'em of any valuables," the second man said gruffly to his partner, who wiped blood from several oozing scratches. "Then we'll strip this whore, an' have some fun."

Liara rose up on one elbow, rubbing her smarting cheek. As a rough hand reached to rip her gown, a slender dagger suddenly sprouted from the man's neck. His eyes snapped wide, and with a choked cry, he fell upon her.

The second thief had no more opportunity. Gray-gloved hands caught either side of his head and twisted sharply. A loud *crack* resulted, and the thief fell like a puppet whose strings had been cut.

The Mouser moved swiftly into the concealing fog again, certain that Liara had not seen him. With a string of curses that would have made Fafhrd grin, she pushed the first thief's body off, and got to her feet. With another curse, she put a delicate slipper forcefully into the dead torch-bearer's face.

"Pick up the torch," the Mouser whispered, pressed out of sight near a wall. "I will see you safely to your home."

"You'll see me?" Liara shot back nervously with nothing to address but a voice in the fog. "I can't see you."

"Pick up the torch," he repeated. "I'll protect you. A beautiful woman should not walk these streets undefended."

Liara snorted as she recovered the sputtering torch and lifted it. "Well, that at least tells me you're no god or spirit. Only a man would concern himself with my looks." Using the light, she glanced down at her murdered companions and picked up one of the thieves' daggers, a larger and more dangerous-looking blade than her own tiny sticker. "I thank you for this, mysterious defender. For all their vanity, these were good servants, undeserving of treachery and slaughter."

"Servants?" the Mouser said with surprise. "I thought they were your paramours."

She drew herself stiffly erect, her eyes blazing with pride. For a moment, the Mouser thought she might be able to see him where he hid. "I treat my servants as well as my paramours," she answered. "They give much better service for it."

Turning, she started down Carter Street again, her blond hair mussed, her cloak ripped, but her bearing regal. There was no fear in her voice, only a hint of mockery and amusement when she whispered, "Are you still there, defender?"

"Lead the way, lead the way," the Mouser answered softly, imitating the torch-bearer's song as he withdrew Catsclaw from the thief's throat and wiped it clean.

Liara gave a small, scoffing laugh. "And how much will I pay?" she asked, finishing the rhyme.

The Mouser swallowed, his thoughts full of Ivrian, his eyes full of the Dark Butterfly. His heart pounded in his chest. Why did he hide in the fog when he might walk close beside her? He couldn't tell. The confusion that filled him swirled thicker than any mist in the street. Still, he dared a brazen response. "You may keep your tik-pennies," he said. "I will take the kiss."

Liara laughed again, nodding to herself. "Yes," she murmured. "Though you conceal yourself, you are certainly a man."

They walked in silence after that, the Mouser alert for any threat, Liara seemingly unconcerned. At Barter Street a throng of pedestrians crossed their path, swinging lanterns, singing as they headed toward the Festival District. Another pack of Aarth's maddened followers ran screaming after the celebrants, overtaking them, passing them, and disappearing in the fog.

A gilt palanquin born on the shoulders of four slaves approached, surrounded by four more servants bearing torches. At a quietly spoken command from the palanquin's occupant, the bearers came to a crisp halt. Slender, well-manicured fingers parted the vehicle's gauzy curtains, and a face peered out. The torchlight reflected on an oiled beard and sharp features.

"Liara," a voice said smoothly.

The bearers lowered the palanquin until it rested on ornately carved legs, then stood at silent attention. One of the torchbearers hurried forward, unrolled a small carpet on the ground and set a step stool upon it. The speaker parted the curtains a bit more, but did not get out. "By what strange whim of the gods do I find you alone and unescorted on this dreadful night?" Without waiting for an answer, he offered, "Come, give me your company, and let's see if we can't make it pass more pleasantly."

The expensive, silver-trimmed black toga that enwrapped the man's shoulders revealed him as one of Lankhmar's highest ranking nobles. Only the Ten Families, the descendants of Lankhmar's ancient founders, were allowed the honor of the garment.

Liara seemed unimpressed. "I am not alone, Belit," she answered in a familiar manner, disdaining even to call him *lord.* Such impudence from any other citizen would have brought a public whipping in Punishment Square. "I am protected by my shadow."

Belit gave her a strange look, then leaned out of his vehicle to search the fog with his gaze. Shrugging, he straightened. "Another time, then," he said without further questioning. "But be careful. Attavaq has died this night, and his damned priests are running like hysterical demons through the city."

Hidden in the fog, the Mouser listened and rubbed his chin. So it was Aarth's Patriarch, after all, for whom the great bell had rung.

Belit waved a hand casually through closing curtains, and his bearers once more lifted his palanquin onto broad shoulders. A torch-bearer quickly rolled up the carpet, snatched up the stool, and fell into step with the others as they proceeded into the mist.

"You have powerful friends," the Mouser whispered as they resumed their journey.

"I have no friends," Liara said coldly. "But I have the goods on powerful people." She laughed again, harshly. "Lankhmar is a marvelous place. A clever whore can excel here."

The Mouser's voice dropped a note lower as he gazed upon her from the shadows. "I will never call you such a name."

The Dark Butterfly laughed again and drew her purple silk cloak closer about her throat. "You have already proven yourself a fool," she said. "By following me thus."

Leaving Carter Street, she turned up the narrow way that led to the entrance of the Plaza of Dark Delights. White gravel shifted softly under her slippered footsteps. Cautious as ever, the Mouser followed far to the side of the path, making no noise, hiding in the fog just beyond the flickering border of her torch-light.

Tall, immaculate hedges and fantastically shaped topiaries dominated the plaza, which was actually a park on the edge of the Festival District. Secluded niches with marble benches offered privacy and solitude for lovers and philosophers alike, and in truth, at night the plaza was known more for debate and discourse than as a place for illicit assignations. The carefully maintained greenery blocked any view of the towers and rooftops of the city, nor did the hubbub of the city penetrate into the park. Indeed, a citizen could stop for a while to meditate and utterly forget that the greatest city on Nehwon swirled around them.

By tradition, no one carried more than the dimmest of lanterns into the park. Liara's torch would have drawn scowls and curses had there been anyone in the plaza to complain, but only the mist occupied the niches tonight.

"One should not pass this way," the Mouser whispered, "without speaking or hearing some sage word."

Liara seemed not to hear, or chose not to answer. Or perhaps, the Mouser considered, her silence was an answer, and if so, there was wisdom of a sort in it. He peered around at the giant topiaries that stood along the pebbled path. The fog and mist lent them a menace that made his skin crawl. They reminded him of tendrils rising up from the mist of another plaza; they reminded with a sudden shivering fear that the fog concealed something more than just himself.

He stopped with an abrupt realization. Those tendrils had reached out only for the Ilthmarts. The fog had spared Fafhrd and himself—or saved them.

"Why do you stop, my defender?" Liara said, turning. The torchlight lit up her features. Her eyes shone with reflected fire, and the amethyst at her throat gleamed as her cloak gaped open.

Surprise prevented the Mouser from responding at once.

She laughed that small, tinkling laugh. "Did you think I couldn't hear you? Oh, you're an excellent sneak, little defender, but I have sharp ears." She laughed again. "As every official in Lankhmar knows."

The Mouser frowned. "Why do you say *little?*"

"I hear the length and quickness of your stride," she answered. "Take it as no insult."

"The wound," the Mouser admitted, "is to my pride, for I thought no man could hear my tread when I crept with earnest intent."

"No *man* did," she said with dignified emphasis. Turning again, she continued through the park, from which they shortly emerged.

Face-of-the-Moon Street made a paved crescent around the southeastern corner of the park. Elegant manses on one side of the street faced the great circling hedge that defined the park's circumference. These were not the dwellings of nobles or wealthy merchants, however, but houses of pain-pleasure where men could experience darker enjoyments than those commonalities found on Whore Street.

Such a place was the House of Night Cries. In keeping with the park across the way, a hedge separated the manse's grounds from the street. Among its leafy greenery bloomed black-petaled and white-tipped mooncrisps, called by some Roses of the Shadowland. Droplets of mist shimmered on the petals under Liara's torchlight.

At the entrance, she paused.

"Step into my light," she commanded.

The Mouser hesitated, licking his lower lip uncertainly, suddenly nervous. Finally, he obeyed. She stood a few inches taller than he, and he gazed up into the brightness of her eyes, his heart hammering, his loins full of desire.

Perfunctorily, she leaned forward and kissed his right cheek. "I have paid your hire," she said, straightening, turning to leave him.

He caught her hand.

Liara jerked away, anger contorting her beautiful features as she raised the torch like a weapon and backed a step. "You are paid!" she shouted, clutching the hand he had grabbed to her breast as if he had injured her.

"I only touched . . ."

She lowered the torch, but her anger did not subside. "No man touches me for free!" she cried. "No man!"

Hurt, surrendering to his own rising anger, the Mouser shoved a hand into his purse, found a coin and tossed it at her feet.

The torchlight gleamed on a silver smerduk, and she laughed again with a harsh sound. "That would not get you in my door."

Then, Liara seemed to relent somewhat. Snatching a black mooncrisp from the hedge, she flung it into the Mouser's hands. "I cannot be courted with coins, my gray defender," she said with softer gentility. "If you wish, bring me a gift, and I will not turn you away. But when you choose your gift, be mindful that I have entertained the wealthiest men in Lankhmar. Then, come to me again. Come to me, and I will show you the finest perfections of love."

The Mouser opened his hands and let the mooncrisp fall into the street. "The Dark Butterfly," he said with bitter sadness. "You are only a harlot with a fancy nick-name."

Her eyes narrowed again. "You said you would never call me a whore."

Turning away, he spoke over his shoulder as he started back toward the park. "And I kept my word," he said specifically.

EIGHT

A SHIP ON THE
SEA OF MISTS

Fafhrd kissed Ayla and patted the belly-dancer's backside playfully as he opened his room's door and let her out into the dimly lit hallway. Flashing a smile, she wrapped herself in her veils and hurried downstairs.

In the darkness near the bed, Sharmayne fastened a blue silken cloak around her shoulders and pulled up the hood to conceal her face. Approaching the big Northerner, the noblewoman rose on tiptoe and lightly pressed her lips against his. "That was what I call a midsummer celebration," she whispered before she, too, hurried away.

Grinning, smugly pleased with himself, Fafhrd closed the door. Alone, with only a tiny lamplight for illumination, he drew a deep breath and sighed. Idly, he wondered where the Gray Mouser had gone and if his partner's evening had proved as pleasant.

Throwing the covers over the rumpled bed, he discovered a small quantity of wine remaining in one of the three bottles on the floor. With a single pull, he drained the last drop. Then gathering the empty bottles, he carried them to the window, pushed back the shutters, and cast them into the narrow alley below.

He lingered at the window, taking mischievous pleasure in the shattering crashes as the bottles exploded. The feather-soft touch of a random breeze played over his bare chest. Drawing a deep, refreshing breath, he sighed.

The fog still blanketed the city. As he watched, a thick finger of mist stole across the sill, dissipating even as it seemed to spill down the wall and flow over the floor. Abruptly, he stepped back, heart hammering, his brows knitting with suspicion and dread.

The wisp of fog in his room, no more than a tenuous vapor now, rose ghost-like into the air, like a spirit uncurling itself to stand erect. A shiver ran up Fafhrd's spine. Then some unlikely draft swirled through the room, caught the vapor, and bore it back outside.

With a carefully maintained calm, Fafhrd closed the shutters and locked them. The fight at the Cheap Street Plaza was still a fresh memory in his mind. He remembered the arcane tendrils of mist that had risen to crush and strangle the Ilthmarts. The screaming still echoed in his ears.

Not even the charms of two beautiful women, he discovered somewhat guiltily, had driven that terror from his heart. He had used Ayla and Sharmayne as distractions to hide from his fear. In their arms he had tried to forget what he had seen, what he had heard. But Ayla and Sharmayne were gone, and now his fear returned.

He couldn't quite explain it. He had seen men die horribly before, and he himself had faced vile deaths. Yet all the superstitious dread he thought he had left behind in the Cold Wastes seemed once again to press in upon him, and he could not shake a peculiar premonition.

Something lurked in the fog beyond his window, waiting. It waited for him.

Quietly, he walked to the lamp and turned the wick higher. Although the taller flame brightened the room a little, the shadows also seemed to darken and grow in number. Each time the light wavered or the wick sputtered, the shadows stirred, shifted, striking macabre poses on the walls, the ceiling, the floor.

Attempting to shake his black mood, Fafhrd picked up his lute and settled down on the bed with his back against the wall. His fingers brushed softly over the strings as stubbornly he tried to ignore the shadows. Instead, he thought of the noble-blooded Sharmayne and Ayla the dancer, the fine wine they had shared, the laughter that had so softly blessed his ears. The sweet smell of Sharmayne's perfume yet lingered in the bedclothes, mingled with the odor of passion-sweat. Barely audible, Fafhrd sang in a low voice.

"Nothing finer for me and you
Than the belly-jig danced by two,
Unless, of course, it be
The belly-jig danced by three—
Me and thee and thee!"

Abruptly, he stopped and listened. Not a sound drifted up through the floor from the tavern below; apparently the customers had all gone home. Even the infernal cries of Aarth's followers seemed to have ceased. The unexpected silence hung about his shoulders like an oppressive weight.

He set his fingers to the strings again and prepared to pluck a note.

Fafhrd. . . .

A draft teased the lamp's flame; the shadows whirled around the room and settled down again. Was it Fafhrd's imagination, or did they strike new and improbable postures? He was drunk, he decided, disgusted with himself. Setting the lute against the wall near the head of the bed, he crossed to the table and turned the wick down again.

"Take that, you tormenters or poor, inebriated sots," he said
to the shadows. The deepening darkness seemed to drain them
of life. Before he could truly gloat, a disharmonic chord, powerful of volume, rang through the small room with eerie effect.
The Northerner jumped, nearly bashing his head on the low
ceiling. When he spun about, he spied his lute, which had
slipped from the place where he had leaned it and now lay upon
the floor, its strings still vibrating faintly.

Fafhrd. . . .

His heart skipped a beat, and his mouth went dry. The darkness quivered and rippled, as if the shadows it had swallowed
were struggling to get out. The room seemed suddenly too close,
too small. The weak and tiny light retreated even farther into
the lamp. The walls themselves began to pulse, and a labored,
breathing sound whispered from the boards.

"Blood of Kos!" Fafhrd cried.

At Fafhrd's outburst, the room stilled. Then it all began
again—darkness writhing like something alive, the breathing
louder than ever. The pulsing became a painful thunder that
filled his head and set his senses to swirling.

With a shout of terror, Fafhrd snatched up his sword from
where it lay buried beneath the pile of his clothes. He whipped
the blade from its sheath. For a moment, he hesitated, half in a
panic. The walls of the room, like the chambers of some monstrous heart, throbbed. With another cry, he lunged, driving his
point deep into the woodwork.

The pulsing ceased instantly. The room seemed to give a final
long sigh, then a gasp that faded away.

Fafhrd pulled his sword free. For a long moment, he stood in
the center of the room, breathing hard, his gaze darting nervously to every gloomy corner. Rubbing thumb and forefinger
over his eyes, he shook his head as if to clear it. Perhaps he was
drunk, after all.

Sheathing his sword, he sat down on the edge of the bed. With his hands wrapped around the guard-tangs, he leaned his head wearily on the weapon's pommel and closed his eyes. It had to be near dawn, he figured. A little sleep would help to clear his head and let him see things more rationally.

Hugging the sword to his chest, he tipped sideways and curled up on the blanket. The bed creaked under his shifting weight, but the soft feather mattresses embraced him with comfortable warmth. The pillow beneath his head smelled pleasantly of Sharmayne's expensive perfume, and a strand of Ayla's dark hair tickled his nose until he brushed it away. He turned over twice, finally settling on his back, and threw one arm over his eyes. At last, he lay still.

The lamplight flickered. The wick sputtered and hissed.

Slowly, Fafhrd uncovered his eyes and stared up at the ceiling. Had he slept? He wasn't sure. But something had disturbed him, not a sound or a movement, something else. He sniffed, and inhaled the odor of a sweet perfume that was not Sharmayne's.

He knew that fragrance, though—Vlana's perfume.

The lamplight flickered once more. With careful deliberation, Fafhrd turned his head toward the window. The shutters, which he had closed and locked, hung open. Beyond the sill, the fog stirred and eddied.

Fafhrd . . . .

It was not wind, nor the lute-strings, nor the effect of too much wine, nor his imagination. Vlana whispered his name. From somewhere in the dark and misty night, his one true love called him to rise from his bed and join her. How such a thing could be when she was dead, he did not understand, but he reached for his trousers and his boots. Wordless, he pulled them on.

Strapping Graywand around his waist, he went to the window and leaned out, seeing nothing but the fog. He would go down to her then, find her wherever she might be, make whatever amends he could for his part in her cruel and untimely death.

Leaving the room, he made his way down the stairs. Empty wine bottles, beer mugs, overturned stools and chairs lay scattered about the Silver Eel's floor. There was no sign of Cherig One-hand. With all his customers gone, no doubt he had retired to his own bed, leaving the clean-up until morning. Only an old brown dog glanced up at Fafhrd before it resumed eating the scraps that littered the floor.

Fafhrd slipped through the passage beneath the steps and opened the back door to emerge into Bones Alley. His open window and Vlana's whispering voice had suggested she might be waiting here, but he saw no one.

He thought he better understood the strange occurrence in his room now that he knew who was behind it. The fear he had earlier felt was gone, replaced almost by a sense of relief. He thought he understood now the strange occurrences in the Cheap Street Plaza and in his room. Something indeed waited in the fog. Or rather, someone. And she waited for him.

He did not yet see Vlana, nor did she speak his name again. As he gazed up and down the mist-filled alley, a lingering grief compelled him to speak.

"Why do you haunt me, love?" he whispered to the fog. "What do you want from me?"

A little way down the alley, the mist parted like a slowly opening curtain to reveal his beloved. A wind he couldn't feel teased the folds of diaphanous white silk that clothed her form, and black tresses whipped about her face. With mesmeric grace, her arms rose and fell in a serpentine undulation, while her hips floated in a tantalizing circle. One pale hand waved in the air, a gesture that seemed to invite him closer even as it warned him away.

"Vlana . . ." he said, taking a single step before halting again.

She spun in a triplet pirouette and stopped, flinging out her arms, her eyes flashing like ice in sunlight. Pressing her palms firmly together beneath her chin, she began a new, far less sensuous dance. Her bare feet moved in a series of intricate patterns, while she held her upper body with rigid, courtly formality.

"I love you," he whispered, his voice pleading.

Again she stopped. Her cold gaze fixed him accusingly across the distance. With a dramatic toss of her head, she bent at the waist, and swung all her hair forward to conceal her face. Then straightening, she parted it with her hands. Vlana's face was gone, replaced by a glaring red-eyed skull whose teeth chattered an angry rhythm.

Fafhrd gave a cry of despair, but before the sound had escaped his lips, Vlana spun again. When she stopped, she wore her own beautiful face again. Reaching up with one hand, she drew down a piece of the mist and drew it teasingly across her face like a dancer's veil. With a flourish, she tossed it away. Her fingers began to move with dazzling speed. Unable to tear his gaze away, Fafhrd watched, feeling stirrings, a strange excitement. Like frantic birds, her hands worked in the air, fluttering, fingers darting between fingers, nails tapping on palms, tips snapping together.

Only once before during their too-short time together had he seen Vlana perform the subtle and beautiful finger-dances of Tisilinit. A culture dancer of immeasurable talent and reputation, she held in her repertoire dances and dance-tales from scores of Nehwon's many lands and nations. She danced alone now and made no effort to approach him, but played upon the palms and fingers of a lover, the movements were said to bring on an erotic passion unmatched by any herb or aphrodisiac.

He remembered the night when he first saw her dancing on a crude stage with poor lighting for the benefit of even cruder men who could not possibly appreciate her art. With a caravan of traders she had come, just one of a small troupe of actors and entertainers, to the village of the Snow Clan in the Cold Wastes. Only the adult men had been invited to the performance, but he had climbed a high tree, shinnied out on a limb, and from such a precarious perch, he fell in love.

How different his life would have been without her, he realized. It was Vlana who had lured him away from his mother, his clan, from the plain village girl to whom he had been betrothed, from a life devoid of hope, empty of dreams, Vlana who had severed the chains of expectation and lifted the yoke of duty from around his neck. It was she who had brought him to the southlands and the warmer climes, ultimately to the exotic city of Lankhmar and taught him the ways of civilization.

In return, he had sworn always to love and protect her. Succeeding in the first, he had failed horribly in the second.

"Even with death's chilly rime on your lips," he murmured, "grant me forgiveness with a kiss."

Resolutely, he walked toward her. Vlana ceased her dance. The fire went out in her eyes, and a look of horror flashed over her face. Holding out a hand to warn him away, she took an involuntary step backward. At the same time, the fog seemed to thicken and rush in from all sides, snatching her away.

Fafhrd ran forward until he stood on the spot where she had danced. The fog swirled about him, filling his eyes with a cold, numbing vapor, blinding him, choking his lungs. Stumbling, he fell to his knees.

From out of the night came a harsh, mocking laughter.

Coughing, rubbing his fists against his half-frozen eyes, Fafhrd looked up. The high walls of Bones Alley no longer loomed over him. Indeed, he could not say exactly where he was, in Lankhmar, or even on Nehwon. A shallow sea of cold mist flowed around him, gently tossing with low, smoky waves. From horizon to horizon, as far as he could gaze, it rolled beneath a featureless, fog-filled sky.

Struggling to his feet, Fafhrd closed one fist around the hilt of his sword. Again the night reverberated with derisive laughter. Knee-deep in streaming white fog, he turned toward the sound.

Far off in the darkness, a lamp burned dimly. Yet even as Fafhrd watched, it drew nearer and nearer. In its sickly amber glow, he spied the prow of a boat or a barge, a black shape sailing upon the fog. Barely visible in the lamp's glow, a pale figure stood in the prow.

Closer and closer the ship drew. The unmoving figure stood stiff as a mast in a white silk gown that billowed, sail-like. As the vessel continued to approach, the brightening lamplight reflected on heavy steel chains and manacles locked about the figure's wrists and neck, and on raven hair that streamed about proud and shapely shoulders.

Sad eyes turned Fafhrd's way.

"Vlana!" he cried, his heart brimming with anger and despair.

Another, taller figure worked in the vessel's stern. Until now, the brilliance of the lantern had prevented Fafhrd from seeing him. The black robes he wore snapped in the wind like the wings of a huge vulture, and a voluminous hood concealed his features. From his sleeves jutted a skeleton's bony hands and forearms. Leaning upon a long pole, he propelled the unusual boat forward.

The vessel's low, black rails gleamed with intricately worked gold and silver inlay. Amidship, a slender mast spired upward. Without sail or rigging, it was covered with the same swirling inlay work as the rails, indeed, the rest of the ship. Immensely old and beautiful, it also gave off a sense of alienness.

Without word or warning, the pilot lifted his pole from the misty sea and swung it. Vlana's face contorted with pain as the end struck her in the side, yet she made no sound at all as the impact sent her sprawling upon the boat's deck.

Fafhrd drew his sword. "Villain!" he shouted. As rapidly as he could manage against the currents and eddies that worked

unseen beneath the surface of the strange sea, he waded toward
the boat. On its present course, he feared that it would sail right
past before he could reach it. "Damned villain!"

From within the black folds of the pilot's hood came a now
familiar mocking laugh. Setting aside his pole, the creature bent
down and effortlessly lifted a huge iron anchor, which he threw
over the side. It disappeared without a splash or crash, and the
anchor chain drew tight. The boat jerked to a stop. Once more,
the creature took up his pole.

"Let her go!" Fafhrd demanded as he struggled toward the eerie
craft. Over the low, wooden rail he could see the limp form of his
one true love, and he fought all the harder to reach the ship.

A raspy voice spoke from within the hood. "Will you fight
me for her, barbarian?" the creature said. "Is your blade as strong
as your heart?"

Fafhrd did not answer with words. At last he stood within
sword-reach of the vessel. Gripping Graywand's hilt in both
hands, he swung the blade high and brought it smashing
down on the rail. The boat rocked under the impact; wood
splinters and bits of gold and silver flew into the air. Impossibly, they sparked with brilliant, white-hot fire and flared
out.

Reflexively, Fafhrd flung up an arm to protect his eyes from
the unexpected light and heat.

The creature laughed. The pole whirled in his skeletal hands,
becoming a blur. Then one end lashed downward at Fafhrd's
head. At the last instant, Fafhrd recovered his senses and brought
his great sword up in a defensive block. Pole and steel clashed.
Again, searing sparks leaped at the contact.

"You can't win back the lovely Vlana," the figure taunted
him. "You'll fail her again, just as you did before."

"No!" Fafhrd screamed. Desperately, he swung Graywand
again, striking at the creature's legs. At the same time, he caught
the side of the boat with his free hand and tried to pull himself

aboard. Deftly evading Fafhrd's cut, the creature smashed downward at Fafhrd's fingers.

Barely in time, Fafhrd let go of the rail and jerked his hand away. The other end of the pole came spinning toward his unprotected head. Voicing a deep grunt, he brought his sword up in a mighty swing. With powerful force, wood and steel met again. Shimmering sparks seemed to set fire to the mist before fading, and the ship's inlay flashed.

They fought in earnest now, the creature striking from his higher vantage with both ends of his weapon, Fafhrd swinging his sword with consummate skill, thwarting every attack. The boat rocked precariously, and the lantern, depending from a peg on the mast, cast a pendulum of light over the gray sea.

Yet, strive as he might, Fafhrd could gain no advantage from his lower position. Finally, he risked a dangerous gambit. Chopping at his foe's knees, he drove the creature back a step. Then, springing up with all the power in his muscular legs, he threw himself across the boat's rail. Under his sudden weight, the vessel tipped violently. Still clinging to his pole, the creature catapulted over the side, wildly aflutter in his robes, and sank out of sight beneath the sea of mist.

Sword ready, Fafhrd whirled, his gaze locked on the spot where his foe had disappeared under the gray waves. Not for a moment did he believe he could vanquish such an opponent so easily. He ventured only the swiftest glance toward Vlana, who cowered with her arms wrapped around the base of the slender mast, her eyes wide with terror.

With lightning quickness, one end of the pole arced upward out of the mist, and whistled toward his skull. Fafhrd hurled himself backward. Still, a stinging blow glanced off his brow. Dazed, he caught himself on the side of the boat.

The robed and hooded being rose laughing out of the river of mist. Fafhrd had yet to win even a glimpse of the face within those funereal garments.

"What are you, monster?" Fafhrd shouted, stalling for time while his vision cleared. He gripped Graywand's hilt in both hands and swayed lightly back and forth on the balls of his booted feet.

The creature's laughter ceased. The voice that issued from within the black hood turned grim. "I am the Inevitable," it said pompously, "that all men must face."

"Spare me your riddles," Fafhrd said. He lunged, describing an elusive circle with the point of his broad blade, hoping to slip past the creature's defense and drive home through its heart, if it had one.

"No one will be spared," the creature said. "Not even the most innocent, the newest born." Undeceived by Fafhrd's tactic, it slammed the pole downward, intercepting the fatal thrust, diverting it.

But Fafhrd only pressed his attack. With renewed fury, he rained deadly blows upon his foe, driving him backward away from the ship. Again and again, pole and blade met, and the darkness glowed with the heat and lightning they created.

"Vlana must be spared," Fafhrd cried.

"Fool," the creature said coldly. "She is already dead."

With an anguished shout, Fafhrd swung Graywand with all his might. One more time, sword and pole met. Fire and heat erupted, and a thunderblast shook the night. Steel cleaved through wood; a fragment of the pole exploded into flame and spun across the sky like an arcane comet.

For an instant, the creature stared in amazement at the shattered weapon. Fafhrd didn't hesitate. Putting the entire weight of his giant body into a back-handed effort, he sliced through his foe's chest.

But the blade met little resistance. Black robes buckled inward, like a sack containing nothing. The creature, whatever it was, fell forward into the sea with the remains of its pole, and the mist swallowed it.

With a triumphant bellow, Fafhrd turned toward the boat, intent on a successful rescue of his one true love. His heart swelling, he thought of breaking her chains and gathering her in his arms, of tasting the ruby wine of her lips once more.

The boat, however, was already far away, its anchor and chain neatly curled on deck. Vlana stood amidships, watching him from the mast, while a cadaverous pilot in black robes propelled the vessel with a long pole.

"I beat you!" Fafhrd shouted, bitter with frustration and renewed grief. "Let her go! I fought for her, and I won!"

The much-hated sound of the creature's laughter rolled back across the mist, followed by a rasping voice. "You lost, son of Nalgron." The sea itself seemed to carry the words to him. "Before this little amusement began, you had already lost."

The boat sailed onward, growing smaller and smaller, until only its lamp could be seen, and even that passed out of sight.

"Vlana!" The desperate shout ripped from Fafhrd's throat as the lamp's light vanished.

Alone in a gray limbo, he tried to think what he should do. Slowly he turned, attempting to spy some landmark in this desolate, featureless place by which he could navigate. Nothing caught his eye, no sound touched his ears, no odor wafted through the air. Even the pale, thin grayness that pervaded this world—wherever it might be—was fading, leaving him in darkness, deep and impenetrable.

Blind, guided by nothing except hope and determination, he started in the direction he thought the boat and Vlana had gone. How far he walked, he could not guess, nor for how long before the chill fog began to freeze his legs, and the cold crept into his lungs and all through his extremities.

With Vlana's name on his rime-caked lips, his weary limbs gave out, and he stumbled. Falling, sinking, the shallow sea seemed suddenly to have no bottom at all.

The mist enfolded him in a feathery soft embrace as unseen currents caught and carried him—somewhere. *Yet again I fail you, Vlana,* he thought bitterly as consciousness left him. *Yet again I fail.*

NINE

SHADOW ON THE SUN

The first sunlight of dawn burned across the fog, coloring the sky with watery pastels. Swaths of pink and palest blue washed over a canvas of grays and silvers, creating a chiaroscuro edged with the black of retreating night.

Wearily, the Gray Mouser pushed open the Silver Eel's door and made his way up the stairs. On tiptoes, with no desire to wake either Cherig One-hand or the inn's other tenants, he crept down the hall to the room he shared with Fafhrd, turned the knob, and entered.

Fafhrd's big, booted feet stuck out from under the only blanket and hung over the end of the bed. Still in his clothes, the Northerner lay face down on the pillow, his red hair splayed about on the case, snoring with somnolent abandon. His left arm hung off the side of the bed, and the knuckles of that hand brushed the floor.

The Mouser frowned. There was no room on the bed for him to lie down. Unfastening his weapons belt, he set sword and dagger aside, placing them beside the only chair. Stripping off his gray tunic, he moved quietly across the room to a table and poured cool water from a pitcher into a ceramic basin. Enough light slipped through the unshuttered window to make the small oil lamp unnecessary, and he gently blew out the tiny flame. Unbinding his hair, he let the black mass spill forward as he bent over the basin and laved his face. He felt dirty, in need of a bath.

The bed frame creaked. Wiping his face with his tunic, the Mouser glanced sideways as Fafhrd sat slowly up and looked around the room with the curious, wide-eyed expression of one not quite awake. His gaze finally fastened on the Mouser.

"How did you get that plum over your eye?" the Mouser asked, returning to his ablutions.

As if in a daze, Fafhrd reached up and gingerly explored the red bruise that showed just below his hairline. Then, throwing back the blanket, he ran a hand over his trousers. "It wasn't a dream," he murmured distantly. But his face screwed up with an expression of confusion as he patted the bed. "Or was it?" Staring toward the window, he became pensively silent.

Wadding up his tunic, the Mouser dipped it in the basin and used it to wash under his arms, over his chest and neck and back. He scrubbed until his dusky skin turned red, and still he scrubbed. Liara's soft face seemed to stare up at him from the water in the basin, and her words echoed in his mind.

. . . *I will show you the finest perfection of love*, she said.

He scrubbed some more, forgetting about Fafhrd, gritting his teeth until he threw the wet tunic forcefully into the basin, shattering the image he imagined there, splashing water across the table and floor. Struck by a wet sleeve, the lamp pitched over the table's edge. Lunging, the Mouser caught it and set it safely upright again.

A little oil had leaked over his fingers. For a brief moment, he noted how the faint morning light played in the oil on his skin, how it shone like the cold light in Liara's eyes.

He pushed his hands into the basin and washed them thoroughly.

"Fog or no fog," he said suddenly, his jaw firmly set, "we search that tower tonight and find Malygris. This corrupt city will taint our very souls if we linger here. We're made for open skies, you and I, and for carefree adventure."

Fafhrd spoke with uncharacteristic softness and regret. "I can't leave, my friend," he said from the bed. He wore a haunted look, and his gaze seemed fixed on something beyond the open window, something the Mouser couldn't see. "I have a new mystery, and I'm compelled to solve it." Pausing, he swallowed hard. "Twice, I've seen Vlana—or her ghost. Truly, I know not which. But she, or her spirit, walks in the fog."

"In the fog?" the Mouser said doubtfully.

"I believe it was she that saved us from the Ilthmarts."

The Mouser scoffed. Turning back to the basin, he took up his shirt and wrung it, his arms bulging, knuckles turning white with the effort he exerted. "Ghosts don't wield witchly powers," he said. Unwinding the garment, he shook it violently, snapping out the wrinkles, flicking droplets everywhere.

"I know what I have seen," Fafhrd answered stubbornly.

"You know what you've dreamed," came the Mouser's harsh reply. "Or what the bottom of some wine bottle has shown you." He spread the tunic over the back of the only chair and moved it next to the window so the sun would dry the cloth quickly.

Fafhrd shook his head. "I can't get her out of my mind, Mouser. I swear to you. Vlana, or her spirit, walks the streets of Lankhmar."

Agitated, the Mouser began to pace about the room. Abruptly, he stopped. Liara's face seemed to float in the air before him, though he knew he only imagined it. . . . *The finest perfection of love*, she seemed to say to him, her voice drowning Fafhrd's earnest insistences.

"All night I wandered in the Plaza of Dark Delights," he said suddenly, his voice a bare, choking whisper, "through that mist-filled maze of hedges and topiaries. Over white-pebbled walkways, down grassy paths slick as ice with dew. For hours I sat, then reclined, on a marble bench and stared into the gray limbo overhead where stars used to burn so brilliantly." He paused, and for a moment, he stood unmoving as a statue before he continued. "Not another soul ventured through the plaza all night. I was utterly alone. I felt so empty—"

"Perhaps our souls are already tainted, my friend," Fafhrd said, "though not by the city, but by our own memories."

The two men looked at each other for a painful moment. Then Fafhrd grinned and smacked his palm on the bed so hard the blanket leaped up around him. "Come and lie down on something softer than a marble bench," he invited. "When we wake up again, these black moods will have melted with the fog."

The Mouser drew a deep breath and shrugged. Bending down, he pulled off a boot and cast it aside. "Later, I'll sneak into the kitchen and forage for breakfast."

"You distract Cherig," Fafhrd said, holding back a corner of the blanket for the Mouser to slip under. "I've got a bigger appetite and deeper pockets in which to stuff his delicious victuals."

The Mouser chuckled. "Just don't hog the bed," he warned as he stretched out.

Huddled under the single blanket, the two turned their backs to each other and grew quiet. After a while, Fafhrd's snore broke the silence, rising in volume until it rocked the bed. Snatching the only pillow, the Mouser covered his head and stoppered his ears with his hands.

Gradually, he relaxed. As sleep crept over him, he thought of Liara, and when he dreamed, he dreamed of the finer perfections of love.

A knock at the door awakened them. Without waiting for a response, Cherig One-hand walked into the room and strode to the foot of the bed. In his arms, he carried a large bundle wrapped in black cloth.

"Move your smelly feet, my favorite of guests," he said to Fafhrd with a subtle grin as he dropped the bundle on the mattress. "The Lady Sharmayne has sent you a token of her, shall we say, appreciation."

Throwing back his part of the blanket, Fafhrd sat up. "She seemed sufficiently appreciative last night," he said, reaching for the large bundle. Rolled inside an expensive black cloak, he found a complete set of new clothes.

Pinned to the cloak, he found a note. "For Fafhrd's large shoulders," he read aloud. A sleeveless tunic of black silk and a black jerkin trimmed with the soft white fur of the snow bear bore another note. "For Fafhrd's broad, powerful chest and back," the note said. Among a pair of studded arm bracers, he found still another note. "For Fafhrd's strong arms."

The Gray Mouser reached toward the bundle and curiously lifted a studded leather groin guard. Swinging it from one finger, he started to read the note attached. "For Fafhrd's great . . ."

Fafhrd snatched the guard from his partner, and flipped a corner of the blanket over the smaller man's head. "Unhand my trousseau, you cad." He picked up a wide, studded belt that matched the bracers and the groin guard and raised it admiringly. "I think I'm in love!"

"Mostly with yourself, I suspect," Cherig said with a chuckle as he prepared to take his leave. Pausing at the door, he winked at the Mouser. "For a giant, he is too pretty by half."

The Gray Mouser rose out of bed as the door closed behind Cherig. Going to the chair by the window, he picked up his tunic, sniffed it, and satisfied that it was clean enough, pulled it over his head. "You must have made quite an impression on the Lady Sharmayne," he grinned.

Fafhrd continued to admire his new finery. "Her teeth made quite an impression on me," he said, rubbing a shoulder. "And Ayla . . ."

Hesitating as he reached for his boots, the Mouser raised an eyebrow. "Ayla?" he asked.

Fafhrd regarded him innocently. "The dark-haired dancer," he explained.

The Mouser's other eyebrow went up. "Both?"

The Northerner gave a sheepish, half-embarrassed shrug.

"You filthy sod! Say no more!" The Mouser, stamping quickly into his boots, continued, muttering, "Lest I throw myself from the window in a fit of envy." Seizing up his gray cloak and weapons belt, he crossed to the door. "I'll be downstairs scaring up some breakfast."

"Good, I'm hungry!" Fafhrd called as he fitted one of the bracers around a tanned, brawny forearm.

"Your hungers have been sated," the Mouser called back with a smirk as he tossed his light cloak around his shoulders. "It's my own belly I'm working for now."

The Mouser passed quietly down the narrow hallway and descended the stairs to the tavern below. Cherig One-hand paused from mopping the floor, wiped sweat from his brow, and glanced toward him. "Bread, sausage, and fruit on the table in the kitchen," he said gruffly. Returning to his task, he dipped the mop in a wooden bucket and pushed a veritable tide of water across the old boards, scrubbing them until they gleamed.

The Mouser pushed open the kitchen door. Cherig's dog, curled up by the hearth, opened one disinterested eye and closed it again. The Mouser stepped over him and piled an earthen plate with food, which he carried back into the tavern.

As the Mouser straddled a stool and sat down at a table, Fafhrd descended the stairs. In his new clothes, his black cloak flowing and braided red hair shining, he looked almost regal. In his left hand, he carried his lute.

Cherig paused from his mopping again and smirked. "Sharmayne always pays well for her nights of pleasure," he said.

Fafhrd took a stool opposite the Mouser, rested his instrument against the table's edge, and helped himself to half the loaf of bread and one of the two apples on the Mouser's plate. "Cherig's been very generous," he whispered as he twisted the apple and broke it neatly into two pieces. "Our funds are starting to run low, however, so I'm going to spend this afternoon playing the minstrel over by the wharves and in the River District. I can pick up a few coins and keep an ear out for any clue to Malygris's whereabouts."

"Keep an eye on that tower," the Mouser said. "I'll prowl around some of the shops and merchants. See if I can pick up any useful information. I may need some lubrication."

Fafhrd grinned around a mouthful of breakfast. "Lubrication," he repeated. "A pretty word for bribe money."

The Mouser shrugged. "Grease a few palms, loosen a few tongues." He didn't need to explain to his partner how he would obtain his lubrication.

A chorus of screams interrupted as he lifted a bite of sausage to his lips. The tidbit fell untasted on the table; he reached for his sword, half-rising from his stool.

The Silver Eel's door stood open and the window shutters were flung back to air the place after the night's festivities. Outside, a score of Aarth's followers ran shrieking through the streets, their saffron robes in dirty tatters, sunlight gleaming on their shaven heads and sweat-streaked faces. Past the tavern they ran, their shrills fading after them.

Easing his sword back into its sheath, the Mouser sat down with a scowl. "Fanatics," he muttered, reaching for the sausage again.

Cherig pushed his wet mop around the floor, speaking without looking at his guests. "That's twice today they've serenaded me with that damn song," he said. "You must've slept through their first pass. Sharmayne's servant, when he brought your new clothes, claimed that things were pretty tense up in the Temple District. Half of Aarth's priests are runnin' around

the city like bloody shriekin' idiots, and the other half are
schemin' to take Attavaq's place and become the next Patriarch."

Grabbing the neck of his lute, Fafhrd rose. With his mouth
still wrapped around a chunk of bread, he grinned and nonchalantly tossed his apple into the air, catching it again. "Be careful
where you put your sticky fingers, Mouser," he said, sputtering
crumbs as he headed for the door. "I don't want to have to break
you out of the Overlord's prison."

"And you be careful where you stick your . . ." The Mouser
paused, then waved his friend away. "Never mind. You just
earned a new set of clothes with it."

Fafhrd's grin widened. With a flourish of his expensive black
cloak, he left the Silver Eel.

Alone, the Mouser stared at the empty breakfast plate and let
go a soft sigh. The swishing sound of Cherig's busy mop and the
drone of a fly somewhere in the room were the only sounds. The
tavern dog padded noiselessly over, curled up at his feet, and
closed its huge, moist eyes.

The Mouser shut his own eyes and rested his head on his
hands. Unbidden, a vision of Liara floated through his mind.
Her cruel eyes sparkled with the cold fire of diamonds, and he
imagined he heard her taunting laughter. She held out a hand to
him, and blood dripped from her slender fingers.

Snapping his eyes open, he expelled the vision. The dog
whined and lifted its head, as if sensing the Mouser's change of
mood. "Lie down, pooch," the Mouser murmured, scratching
the homely mutt between the ears until it relaxed again.

A frown creased the Mouser's lips. If his fingers were sticky, as
Fafhrd had said, it was with blood. He thought bitterly of the
men he killed last night to protect the Dark Butterfly. He did
not like killing. A smart thief, or any man with wit or cleverness,
could usually achieve his ends without stooping to murder.

But when those rowdies threatened Liara, a deep crack in his heart suddenly opened wide, and rage spilled out. He had seen, endangered in that street, not Liara, but Ivrian, whom he had failed to save before, and who, in his dreams, time and time again he had failed to save, and suddenly his sword was in his hand.

He had neglected to tell Fafhrd of the killings, and he realized he had no intention to do so. They shared much, he and Fafhrd, but he would not share this shame. He wanted only to forget the incident as he planned to forget Liara. For all her outward beauty, he perceived now the petty blackness that filled her soul, and he resolved never to see or think of her again.

Rising, he nodded to Cherig and went through the doorway into Dim Lane. Drawing up the light hood of his cloak, he set a brisk pace and hurried northward while he kept an eye out for a fat merchant or a plump nobleman with a foolishly exposed purse.

The main thoroughfares of the city teemed with people. Creaking carts inched their way through the masses. Beggars and entertainers worked the street corners. With loud voices, merchants hawked their wares from open doorways or kiosks, from hastily spread blankets scattered with trinkets or basketry. Wide-eyed farmers and peasants from the outlying villages and towns, arriving for the Midsummer Festival, rubbed elbows with Lankhmar's elegantly clad nobility.

A trio of dirty-faced children raced suddenly through the crowd, laughing merrily. A little blond girl, whose hair was a tangled mess and whose face was streaked, collided with a shopper. Though uninjured, the huge man took offense. Scowling angrily, he caught the girl's hair with a meaty hand and flung her into the street.

Sent sprawling in the dust, the child squealed with pain and fear.

The Mouser's eyes narrowed as the shopper's light cloak parted to expose an elaborate toga of black silk and silver embroidery. A nobleman, then. He studied the man's face with its neatly trimmed and oiled beard, pinched eyes and bulbous nose.

Two servants hovered near, well-armed, but heavily burdened with their master's packages.

As if blind to the tableau, the crowd parted subtly and moved on. On the ground, the frightened child cried. Cursing her and all children, the shopper beckoned to his servants and turned away, only to collide again with a short, gray-hooded man.

"Pardon me," the Mouser said gently.

"Idiot!" the shopper shouted. For an instant his face clouded with rage, and he raised his fist, but then his gaze fell on the hilt of a slender sword, which just peeked from under the fold of a gray cloak, and he thought better of it. Lifting his misshapen nose skyward, he moved on.

The Mouser watched him disappear in the human tide. Then his right hand emerged from under his cloak and lightly tossed a plump, blue velvet purse. The purse's contents jingled and clinked. "Pardon you," the Mouser muttered.

Extracting a smerduk from the purse, he bent and offered it to the child. "No more crying, little one," he said, putting on a smile for her benefit.

She stared at him with doubtful eyes, though her tears ceased and her fear abated somewhat.

The Mouser pressed the silver coin into her pudgy hand. "Find your friends and buy them all honey cones. It's too nice a day for weeping."

The Mouser helped her to her feet and brushed the dust from her thread-bare dress. She opened her hand, as if disbelieving she really held the coin. Then, making a tight fist around the silver piece, she made a short curtsy. "Thank you, sir," she murmured in a barely audible voice before she took off running up the busy street.

With a sigh, the Mouser added the coins in the velvet purse to his own and tucked his new wealth under his belt. Resuming his course toward the Temple District, he whistled pleasantly to himself.

Fewer people congested the Street of the Gods. In deference to the passing of Attavaq, many of the shops were closed. The pedestrians who walked there kept their voices and their heads lowered. In contrast to the celebratory mood that filled the rest of the city, a muted and funereal atmosphere dominated.

Wandering slowly up the street, the Mouser entered the first shop he found open. Rings and necklaces and bejeweled ornaments glimmered upon counters covered with black velvet. The proprietor, a thin, elderly man in plain, but well-made garments, emerged through a curtain at the rear of the shop to greet his customer, and the Mouser made a show of taking out his heavy purse and bouncing it on his palm.

The proprietor smiled with subtle greed as he noted the purse. "The sweetest music ever played by man," he said as the Mouser shook the purse again and set the coins to jingling. "And you, sir, are obviously a maestro."

The Mouser bent over one of the counters, frowning as he pretended to study the workmanship of a diamond pendant. "What is obvious," he said to the proprietor in a petulant tone, "is that this stone is glass, and the setting is of poor quality." He jingled his purse. "Have you nothing better?"

The proprietor scrutinized him, then eyed the purse again. "I can see you know quality, sir," he said. He waved a hand around the shop. "I display these trinkets for the casual shopper. You are a connoisseur." He crooked a finger, beckoning. "Come into my back room."

The Mouser followed him through the curtain into a room lit with several oil lamps. Jewelers' tools, bits and flakes of stone, pieces of chain, shards of metal lay scattered chaotically about a long worktable. The proprietor turned the wicks of the lamps higher, and the room brightened with golden firelight. Going to a chest in one corner, he took a key from a ring on his belt, bent over a massive trunk, and put it into the lock. A soft click. Standing aside, gesturing grandly, he raised the lid.

The Mouser's eyes snapped wide. Wildly colored fire flashed as the lamplight touched the contents. The proprietor lifted a flat tray upon which was displayed half a dozen elaborately jeweled necklaces. Beneath that tray lay another covered with bracelets and rings, all held in appropriate place by loops of thin wire.

With gaping jaw, the Mouser bent over the first tray as the proprietor placed it on the worktable and moved a lamp closer. The gems dazzled under the shifting light. He caught his breath and leaned nearer.

"I salute you, sir," he said at last to the proprietor. "Never have I beheld such remarkable fakes. How do you make them?"

The proprietor's face colored, and the muscles in his neck corded. For an instant, he swelled up like a man who'd taken a severe insult. Then he relaxed. "No sir," he said. "It is I who salute you. I see you are, indeed, a connoisseur who knows his stones, and I cannot fool you." He shrugged as he tugged a ring loose from its velvet backing and held it up. When he spoke again, it was with the voice of a man who took pride in his work. "I cut every piece, myself," he said, "and inject the smallest amount of dye into the glass. Rare is the man who can tell them from real stones. But tell me, how did you gain such a keen eye?"

The Mouser rubbed his chin as he continued to examine the trays. "I am a sometime-procurer of gems for a great northern prince," he said. Inwardly, he smiled, thinking of how Fafhrd would laugh at that. "I'm afraid I'm looking for something a bit more, shall we say, unusual. Perhaps even talismanic."

The proprietor shook his head and began to replace his trays within the trunk. Closing the lid and locking it, he turned once again to the Mouser. "As hungry as your fat purse makes me, I

can offer you nothing. If it is precious objects of a religious nature you seek, may I recommend Demptha Negatarth. He runs a
shop one block north on Temple Street, and some say he dabbles
in minor sorcery, as well."

The Mouser led the way back through the curtain to the
shop's outer room with its display cases of cheap baubles. At the
door, he paused. "Since most men cannot discern the true nature of your wealth," he said, "how is it that you have no guards
to defend it?"

The proprietor smiled. "You have a keen eye for stones, sir,"
he said, pointing a finger toward the ceiling, "but only the gods
are all-seeing."

Among the shop's high rafters four stout, dark-faced dwarves
sat swinging their legs with ankles crossed. They grinned wickedly down at the Mouser, showing the huge, glittering knives
they held on their laps. Despite their size, they had the look of
dangerous men.

With the briefest of bows to the proprietor, he left the shop
and stepped out into the street again. Pushing back his hood, he
paused and frowned.

The quality of the sunlight seemed muted, and the bright
blueness of the sky had leeched away.

Shading his eyes with a hand, he glanced squinting up toward
the sun. Did he imagine it, or did the tiniest piece seem to be
missing? Jerking his head away, he wiped at stinging tears and
blinked hard.

From the east, saffron-robed priests of Aarth ran shrieking
down the Street of the Gods, their bare feet slapping furiously
on the cobbled paving. Then, without warning, the gates of
Mog's temple flung open. Black-robed priests of the Spider-god
poured out with upraised swords to intercept Aarth's fanatical
followers.

Now the shrieking took on a new note—of terror. Swords
rose and fell mercilessly, flinging blood. Mog's priests swarmed

over Aarth's followers, hacking and chopping until none stood. Still, in a grisly fury, they swung their swords, beheading and dismembering the corpses.

Shoppers and pedestrians ran screaming from the streets. The Mouser pressed himself into the narrow alley between a pair of shops and dragged a rain barrel across the opening. Over the rim, he watched with his own sword in hand.

Covered with blood, Mog's priests ran down the Street of the Gods. Scores of them fell upon the lines of faithful gathered before the pillared entrance to view the body of Attavaq the Patriarch before its burial. A new chorus of screams rose up.

Then, from around both corners rushed squads of Aarth's followers. Brandishing swords and clubs, they surged through the gates, entering their own temple behind Mog's invading priests.

The clash and clangs of weapons rose over the temple walls. Bloody acolytes stumbled into the streets. Worshippers ran out in terror. The battle followed them, filling the street outside the temple.

Yet another cry drew the Mouser's attention. From farther down the street, the gates of the Rat God's temple opened. Red-robed priests, waving spears and blades, charged forth to attack the followers of Mog.

Above it all, the sun slowly vanished. The sky turned the color of gray slate, and still it darkened. An unnaturally cool wind blew through the narrow passage where the Mouser nervously crouched.

Madness swept through the street, growing, feeding upon itself. Armored soldiers from the North Barracks raced down Nun Street and Silver Street to meet the fray. At first, they attempted to break up the fighting, but soon, they battled for their lives in a chaotic sea.

Up from Nun Street and from the wharves, yet more squads of soldiers ran. Common citizens, supporting one god or another, or striving to protect shops and homes, or merely trying to get out of the way, drew steel and fought.

Suddenly, the Mouser leaped up. He slapped his thigh and slammed his sword back into its sheath as he shot another look toward the sun. His heart pounded in his chest. Overhead, nightbirds began to caw and circle, confused by the fading light. Here, in the midst of insanity, lay an opportunity!

Hurriedly, he slipped back through the passage, emerging in another narrow alley, and then another, until he found himself on Pimp Street. In the road or on their rooftops, citizens screamed or prayed at the tops of their voices, faces filled with terror as they pointed at the black shadow that crawled across the sun.

The Mouser paused, swallowing hard. The hand of fear squeezed his heart as he stared at the horrifying sight. Stinging tears clouded his eyes, forcing him to look away. Then, gathering his courage, he ran.

Cherig's dog stood howling in the open doorway of the Silver Eel, its muzzle thrust toward the darkening sky. The Mouser leaped over the beast and ran inside, finding no sign of Cherig or anyone else. Rushing up the stairs, he pushed open the door to the room he shared with Fafhrd, snatched up the coil of rope with the grapnel attached, and dashed out again.

Two at a time, he descended the stairs, and collided with a breathlessly ascending Fafhrd.

"The tower!" the northern giant shouted excitedly as he clutched the rail to keep from falling backward.

Of course, Fafhrd had had the same idea, seen the same opportunity. They thought alike, Fafhrd and he. Sometimes they seemed even to share the same mind.

The Mouser picked himself up and rubbed his bruised rump. "There's a good chance the guards are busy elsewhere," he said, moving past his partner. Outside, he paused again to stare upward. Now the great shadow obscured fully three-quarters of the sun. In the west, a pair of premature stars twinkled.

"Come on!" Fafhrd urged, grabbing the coil of rope from his partner and throwing it over his own broad shoulder. "What's the matter? You've never seen an eclipse before?"

The Mouser struggled to feign a sophisticated calm. "Eclipse?" he said. "Of course it's an eclipse." He ran on before Fafhrd could see the look of relief on his face. He'd heard of such things. He wasn't uneducated, and he knew more than just a little astronomy. He'd just never seen one.

"An eclipse," he muttered under his breath, disgusted that Fafhrd had known something he hadn't.

TEN

THE TOWER OF KOH-VOMBI

Over Lankhmar, a fiery crescent burned in the darkening sky. Unexpected night swallowed the city while fear and madness spread through the streets.

A terrible lamentation rose as panicked citizens fled into the roads, pleading for mercy, begging their gods to spare them from the destruction of the world. In the southern part of the city, many hurried northward to seek their temples, unaware of the slaughter going on as priests made war on each other.

In the deepening shadows of Nun Street, Fafhrd and the Mouser crouched down and stared toward a lonely black-stoned tower.

"Can you hit that window?" the Mouser whispered.

Fafhrd eyed the narrow, dark opening halfway up the tower's facing wall. "Not if we lose the light entirely," he answered grimly. His gaze swept around. Rising, he adjusted the weight of the grapnel and line concealed under his cloak. "I don't see any soldiers or guards."

"Called to the Temple District," the Mouser said. "I expected it." He nodded ahead. "Let's go."

They charged the iron fence that surrounded the tower. Reaching the ten-foot barrier first, Fafhrd bent low and braced his hands on the rusted metal bars. Running hard, the Mouser leaped, one foot barely brushing Fafhrd's shoulder. Fafhrd sprang erect, catapulting his smaller companion into the air. Waving his arms for balance, his gray cloak flapping, the Mouser landed lithely in the tall weeds that filled the space between the fence and the tower.

Briefly, Fafhrd studied the top of the fence, which was only three feet above his head. Backing a few paces, he took a quick running step. One foot pushed off an iron bar as his hands caught the top cross-bar, and he vaulted over.

"It should be a crime to be so tall," the Mouser muttered as his partner landed beside him.

"It's a crime to be on this side of the fence," Fafhrd reminded. Looking quickly around, he noted people on the rooftops along Nun Street. The eclipse held them in thrall, and he doubted anyone had witnessed the tower's invasion. Still, he bent low, using the weeds for concealment as he ran toward the mysterious edifice.

After twenty paces, the soft ground and weeds gave way to a broken paving of large flat stones and a terrace of steps that ringed the tower. No entrance or opening revealed itself at ground level.

"How in Mog's name does Malygris get in?" the Mouser wondered, frowning.

His gaze fastened on the window high above his head, Fafhrd freed the hidden line and grapnel. Stepping back, he let out a few feet of line and lofted the clawed weight upward. Metal scraped on stone. Grapnel and line plummeted downward.

Covering his head, the Mouser cursed and jumped backward as the grapnel crashed on the spot where he'd stood.

With a sheepish look and a shrug, Fafhrd rapidly coiled the line again and made a second toss. This time, the grapnel sailed expertly through the dark opening. Fafhrd tugged on the line until it snapped tight.

Without a word, the Mouser drew Catsclaw from its sheath and put the dagger between his teeth. Taking the line, he climbed rapidly, hand over hand, his soft-booted feet making no noise on the tower wall. Like a small, gray spider on a web, he rose.

Fafhrd glanced skyward. Icy stars flickered in the black heavens. Only the barest trace of the sun remained.

In the far northern land of his birth, he had seen eclipses and partial eclipses and stranger things. He recalled the cold, shimmering auroras of colored light that danced sometimes above the frigid mountains. Magic, some of his people claimed. Not so, said the sailors and seamen among them.

To him, they were awesome mysteries to be appreciated, not feared. Nevertheless, he understood the dread such phenomena instilled in many human hearts.

The line jerked in his hand—the Mouser's signal. Fafhrd returned his attention to the task at hand and began to climb. In moments, he squeezed through the narrow window.

"It's dark," he commented as the Mouser touched his arm to help him through.

"Inside and out," the Mouser commented drily. "We should have brought a lamp."

Quickly, Fafhrd drew up the line, coiled it, and hung the grapnel over his shoulder again, while the Mouser probed the darkness of the corridor in which they found themselves. Creeping noiselessly after, Fafhrd caught up with his partner and touched his shoulder. "Look," he whispered, pointing back toward the window.

Beyond the slender opening, the sky of Nehwon blazed with stars.

"It's just an eclipse," the Mouser muttered with casual disinterest, but in one tight fist he held his dagger, Catsclaw, and he set his jaw more firmly than usual, and his lips drew into a thinly nervous line.

Loosening sword and dagger in their sheaths, Fafhrd slipped past the Mouser, and led the way into the deeper blackness that filled the tower. With one hand on a cool stone wall, he felt his way along, and with each careful footstep he probed the old boards that made the floor before transferring his weight forward.

The air smelled of bird droppings and rat dung, damp and musty and stale. Each breath filled his nostrils with a repulsive perfume that left a dry and bitter taste in the back of his throat. He covered the lower part of his face with one hand as he groped in the darkness with the other.

Mortar crumbled suddenly under his fingertips, and he paused, listening to the soft patter of the fragments in the thick pounce that covered the floor. A softer skittering of tiny feet sounded ahead as rats retreated further into the darkness.

Gritting his teeth, Fafhrd shuddered. Memories of Vlana and Ivrian swam unwelcome in his head, and he recalled the rat-chewed corpse of his first true love.

The corridor curved subtly to the left. Behind, the window with its starry panorama could no longer be seen. Though virtually invisible, the Mouser's steady, low breathing reassured Fafhrd that his partner still followed. Licking dry lips, Fafhrd held up his hand and brought it slowly toward his face, unable to see palm or fingers.

Frantic wings beat suddenly in the dark. A bird, disturbed by their intrusion, sprang from an unseen nest cradled in the corridor's rafters. Feathers brushed sharply at Fafhrd's eyes. Cowering back against the wall, he covered his face with a protective arm, biting his lip to prevent an outcry. The bird surged past, seeking the window and the safety of the sky.

"Piss and defecation!" the Mouser hissed. "Watch your next step, Fafhrd—my heart's thumping somewhere on the floor."

Fafhrd squeezed his comrade's shoulder and replied in the lowest of whispers. "Then if I slip, we'll know the cause."

Continuing forward, they reached the end of the corridor. A stone staircase curved downward into the tower's stygian depths. Reaching out, Fafhrd discovered no guarding rail or baluster on the inner sweep, so he pressed his back to the wall and descended one cautious step at a time.

Abruptly the stair widened, and Fafhrd's hand brushed a round metal knob. Blindly, he explored the outline of a smoothly polished wooden door. Placing his ear against it, he listened, detecting no sound from the other side. His fingers curled cautiously about the knob; it refused to turn.

The Mouser tapped his shoulder. Creeping to the precipitous edge of the staircase, they peered downward together.

A faint ruby glow burned near the far-off bottom of the stairs, no brighter than a slowly dying coal. The light wavered in a subtle manner, dimming and ebbing with heartbeat precision.

Fafhrd knew the ways and whims of fire. No flame caused the glow he gazed upon. With soundless tread, braving the unguarded edge, he eased down the stairs again, always with one eye upon that weird redness.

The staircase spiraled lower and lower. Here and there, steps flattened into wide landings. Black, stale-smelling corridors and locked doors temptingly presented themselves, but Fafhrd and the Mouser ignored them. By unspoken consent, the glow became their destination.

Finally, they reached the bottom of the staircase. Ten paces away, a pair of huge, arched doors stood partially open. No longer only a small glow, scarlet light poured from a chamber beyond the doors and lit up the Mouser's face as he paused on the last stair, clutching his dagger in a ready fist. His grim, wide-eyed expression betrayed excitement, fear, and wonder all at once as he gazed toward that light.

Fafhrd pulled up his hood, concealing hair and face. In his black cloak, he looked like any other shadow. Still, he hesitated before moving toward those inviting doors. The light that shone on his partner's face also revealed black markings upon the wall at his back. As far as he could see up the soaring walls, those markings went. On the steps, too, and barely visible under the thick carpet of dust, on the floor.

Stooping down, he brushed his fingers over one of the markings. They were too regular for burns, forming a definite pattern that covered the walls and floors, the steps, perhaps even the ceiling high above. He glanced upward, noting the beams and rafters barely visible in the red glow. Paint, then? Some kind of artwork?

The Mouser slipped past him. On the balls of his booted feet, leaving prints that showed visibly in the thick dust, the small gray man stole toward the waiting doors. Catsclaw's polished blade gleamed like a scarlet flame in his gloved hand as he crouched low and peered through the opening. Cautiously, he straightened and, putting one hand on the nearest door, eased it wider.

Putting aside the mystery of the markings, Fafhrd overtook his comrade, but rather than showing himself in the opening, he concealed himself behind the nearest door. Putting one eye to the narrow gap between the door and the wall, he peered over the top of a hinge into the chamber beyond.

A ring of elaborately carved chairs greeted his vision. Some lay crumbled in pieces with legs and arms rotted away, while others still stood, as if immune to the centuries, with high, polished backs proudly gleaming in the red glow.

The smell of fresh oil touched Fafhrd's nostrils. Taking his eye from the slender space, he touched the hinge, and his fingertip came away with a faint, wet smear. With a start, he gazed back at the floor. The dust betrayed not only the Mouser's footprints and his own, but someone else's.

Before he could warn the Mouser, his comrade threw the doors wide, stepped over the chamber's threshold, and boldly strode inside. "Behold a wonder!" he murmured.

Frowning at his partner's lack of caution, Fafhrd followed the Mouser inside, his gaze sweeping around, his fist closed tight around the hilt of his sword, Graywand. Even so, he caught his breath.

The small range of vision through the crack between door and wall had allowed no sense of the chamber's ancient grandeur. A domed ceiling soared overhead. Against the north wall, on a white marble dais, a huge Y-shaped altar of black obsidian stood, its once-sharp edges worn smooth. Brownish stains on the stone hinted of blood sacrifices.

Elaborately worked candelabras of purest gold stood on either side of the altar. Standing at least six feet high, the bases resembled the intertwined forms of serpents, and eight fanged serpentine mouths opened to hold the candles. Only melted stubs and wax drippings filled those gaping jaws now.

These discoveries paled, however, in comparison to the source of the slowly pulsing glow. Ten feet above the obsidian altar hung a jewel the size of Fafhrd's fist. Four rods, two of gold and two of silver, jutting from the walls at the four cardinal points, joined to form a circlet where the ruby—if such it was—perched.

"In all of Nehwon," the Mouser said, forgetting to whisper, "there can be no other stone so marvelous as this!"

Fafhrd nodded agreement. But as the Mouser walked toward the altar and climbed upon it, Fafhrd's gaze swept about the chamber again. The same black markings covered the floors and walls and ceiling of this inner chamber. Like twisted teardrops, he thought, wondering at their significance.

"Malygris doesn't seem to be home," the Mouser said, standing on the altar, staring up at the jewel. "But our effort won't be totally wasted." Replacing his dagger in its sheath, he drew his rapier and jabbed the point at the ruby to dislodge it. It lifted slightly in its resting place, then settled back again.

The wizard's name seemed to echo in the domed chamber. The sound sent a chill up Fafhrd's spine. He turned slowly, hand tightening upon his sword. "Leave it," he whispered, eyes narrowing suspiciously as he drew his long blade. Some sixth sense jangled nervously. Did he detect a new glow in the outer hall? "I don't think we're alone."

The Gray Mouser seemed not to hear. "Why don't you give me a hand, you great giant?" he said without looking at Fafhrd. Jumping straight up, he thrust his rapier at the ruby again. The point scraped on the gleaming facets, and the jewel popped out of its golden circlet. For a moment, it teetered on the metal edge, threatening to fall back into its resting place. Instead, after a moment's hesitation, it tumbled into the Mouser's waiting hands.

The Mouser cried out triumphantly, his face eerily lit by the arcane gem he held.

In the same instant, the chamber's arched doors flew wide. Five armored soldiers, dressed in the livery of Lankhmar's Overlord, surged across the threshold with torches and drawn swords. A huge knight rushed Fafhrd, and gleaming steel flashed toward his head.

As Fafhrd parried the first blow, the Gray Mouser screamed, and the red light shifted wildly as his prize struck the edge of the altar and rolled across the floor. Slamming an elbow into his attacker's face and leaping back to give himself room to wield Graywand, Fafhrd risked a glance toward his comrade.

The four rods that had held the jewel whipped about like living tendrils. In an instant, they ensnared the Mouser's arms and legs, jerked him off his feet, and forced him down upon the obsidian altar.

A second soldier ran at Fafhrd, and two more tried to flank him. A fourth thrust a torch at his face; he knocked it aside, and put a boot in the man's stomach, knocking him back between the doors.

A sword rose, but before it fell the soldier that held it hesitated, his gaze going toward the ceiling. Fafhrd might have run the man through, but for a sudden vertigo that weakened his knees and sent him stumbling backward.

The chamber seemed to swirl. The black teardrops on walls and ceiling and floor began to move. A strange humming rose, soft at first, but turning angry. The arched doors slammed shut, and a short, sharp scream followed as they crushed the head of the soldier Fafhrd had sent sprawling between them.

A weird chorus of unearthly whispers swelled over the humming and the Mouser's cursing and struggling. *Koh-Vombi,* those ancient, rasping voices called, *Koh-Vombi!*

Fafhrd struggled to regain his balance. The soldiers reeled before him, their faces filled with terror. "Mouser!" Fafhrd called as he groped toward the altar where the whipping rods held his partner spread-eagled.

A ripple passed through the candelabras. Tiny red eyes snapped unnaturally open on eight serpentine faces, and gold-scaled forms untwined and collapsed to the floor. Of one will, however, the creatures undulated to the altar, and the rods forced the straining Mouser's wrists and ankles down toward wetly glittering fangs.

Koh-Vombi, called the ancient voices, *Koh-Vombi!*

With a mighty effort, Fafhrd lurched to the altar. Gripping Graywand's hilt in both hands, he swung the blade in a powerful arc and brought it smashing down on a golden rod. Metal rang on metal, and the force of his blow shivered up his arms. A second time, he struck the rod, and the Mouser screamed, feeling the impact in his wrist, but the rod snapped, and his left arm was free!

A flat, scaled head leered up over the side of the altar. With a shriek of near panic, the Gray Mouser snatched his rapier from his still-prisoned right hand and swung it. The creature's head flew across the chamber, spraying green ichor.

Three more swift blows freed the Mouser. The rods lashed wildly, like injured things, spraying the same horrible, warm fluid. Gathering his feet under him, the Mouser sprang from the altar, clearing the serpents by a goodly distance, and fell flat on his face among the struggling soldiers.

Fafhrd backed more slowly, carefully placing each foot, making sure of his balance. The serpents turned away from the altar to follow him. If he fell, their fangs would find him. But the chamber's swirling filled him with a senses-stealing sickness that threatened to topple him.

He dared to glance away from the serpents at the walls.

Koh-Vombi! Koh-Vombi!

The black teardrops moved like creatures in a hive. No longer flat, two-dimensional markings or bits of paint, they gleamed with a wet slime, and from the rapid beating of thin, membranous wings issued that angry humming.

One of the Overlord's soldiers managed to rise unsteadily to his feet. Turning toward the door, intent on escape, he reeled unexpectedly to the left and fell on one of the chairs, which shattered under his weight.

A serpent came within reach of Graywand, and a second severed head splatted against the wall.

The rasping voices of unseen summoners rose in volume, chanting, *Koh-Vombi!*

Black teardrops leaped from the walls, filling the air with furious flight.

Something smacked wetly on Fafhrd's neck. He grabbed for it and scraped it free, even as another struck his right cheek. Opening his fist, he found a pulpy shape and a smear of blood. "Leeches!" he shouted, horrified.

Flying leeches. They attacked the soldiers, the Gray Mouser, and Fafhrd.

Ripping away the beast on his face, Fafhrd lunged for a torch that lay on the floor and waved it desperately through the air. Touched by the flames, some of the leeches exploded, but more attacked Fafhrd's hands.

Two soldiers writhed screaming on the floor. One clutched his eyes, which were crawling black masses. The other clawed frantically at his ears. Another, working with the Mouser, tried to drag the corpse of the crushed soldier from between the doors while the Mouser threw his shoulder against them. They refused to open.

The remaining soldier, though covered hand and face with leeches, sought to fulfill his orders. Sword upraised, he lumbered toward the Mouser's unprotected back.

Screaming a warning, Fafhrd hurled Graywand. The long blade flashed across the chamber to slam forcefully between the soldier's shoulder blades even as the Mouser, alerted, spun and plunged Scalpel through the man's heart.

With one hand free, Fafhrd grasped the edges of his hood and drew it closer about his face. He felt the creatures striking him, attaching themselves to his clothes. More than a few had wormed their way under his garments.

He smashed the torch down on the head of another serpent, then snatched up a soldier's fallen sword to cleave its body in half. That still left five crawling about the room.

The Mouser was having no luck at the doors. Only the crushed body of the first soldier prevented them from closing and, no doubt, sealing them in.

Koh-Vombi! chanted the voices, *Koh-Vombi!*

"Koh-Vombi up your nose!" Fafhrd shouted at his invisible tormentors. He shot another look around the room. The last remaining soldier whirled blindly about, smashing chairs, tripping over a fallen comrade, screaming as he ripped leeches from his unprotected face. Coiled on the altar, a golden serpent hissed and showed its fangs.

Gripping the torch tightly, Fafhrd called to his comrade. "Look out, Mouser, I'm coming through!"

Running across the chamber, he leaped, hurling himself at the doors. Wood shattered and hinge-metal shrieked. Fafhrd struck the floor amid shards and splinters, and the Mouser flew over him to bound across the hall and up the staircase.

The voices followed them from the inner chamber. The hallway began to swirl with leeches.

Springing up, Fafhrd hit the staircase at a run, torch in hand, his new cloak thick and weighty with slimy bloodsuckers. Three at a time he took the stairs, climbing as fast as his legs would go.

"Want to go back for your sword?" the Mouser suggested sarcastically as Fafhrd overtook him.

"Want to go back for that damned jewel, you greedy-guts?" Fafhrd called over his shoulder as he passed his partner.

Leeches darted and dived at them. Bloated shapes covered the backs of Fafhrd's hands. Blood trickled down his neck. A wet warmth settled suddenly in his right eyebrow. With a gasp, he tore the bloodsucker away, and pushed himself to even greater speed.

"This way, Mouser!" he called desperately to his comrade, uncertain if the Mouser was still behind him. "This way!"

And ancient voices answered, *Koh-Vombi! Koh-Vombi!* The tower echoed with that sound. The very stones seemed to shiver with it.

At last, he found the window through which they had come. The Mouser slammed into him, nearly knocking him through it, as he struggled to free the line and grapnel from about his shoulders with one hand, while with the other he used the torch to fight off the leeches.

"Hurry!" the Mouser shouted, clutching his hood tightly about his face so that he saw only through the narrowest space of cloth. Still, fear and panic shone brightly in his dark eyes.

Setting the grapnel firmly on the sill, Fafhrd cast the line out. "Go!" he ordered, grasping the Mouser's shoulder, half-flinging him out the window.

While the Mouser scrambled over the edge and down the line, Fafhrd braced himself before the portal and swung the torch with both hands, igniting scores of leeches as they flew at him. Tiny burning bodies fell like stars at his feet, smoking and stinking with a hideously foul odor.

As many as he killed, though, far more struck his face, his hands, burrowed beneath his clothes. With fearful desperation, he touched the torch to one of the rafters overhead. The old wood took fire immediately. With a small curtain of flame burning before him, he threw down the torch and squeezed his great bulk through the window's slender space.

A leech slapped his nose and stuck.

Fafhrd's hands closed about the line. Without any control, he slid halfway down, burning his ungloved palms. The leech crawled toward his eye. In utter panic, he let go of the line with one hand and clawed at the creature. With only one tortured hand on the line, his weight and momentum proved too great.

The Mouser cried his name as he fell.

ELEVEN

THE RAINBOW'S BLACK HEART

Screaming his partner's name, the Gray Mouser watched horrified as Fafhrd lost his grip on the line and, tangled in the folds of a fluttering black cloak, plummeted earthward. His horror doubled when a darkly violet hole opened in the star-flecked heavens beneath Fafhrd. The Northerner fell through it, vanishing in midair, and the hole blinked out of existence.

For an instant, the Mouser stared, open-mouthed. Then his own survival instinct asserted itself. Fafhrd was gone, beyond help for the moment, and the Mouser had to think of himself. Ripping away his garments, he scraped desperately at the black leeches that fed on his flesh.

To his amazement, they crumbled at his touch, flaking into pieces, then into a black ashen powder. Trickles of blood and painful red blotches on his skin proved the creatures' menace. They had settled in his hair, wormed under his clothes, into his armpits, his crotch, even down inside his boots. But outside of the tower, beyond the range of whatever magic spawned them, they were dying a quick and strange death.

Naked, he gave a whoop of triumph and brushed the remains of the last leech from between his toes.

"Halt, criminal, in the name of the Overlord!"

At the sound of that authoritative command, the Mouser dived and rolled, reaching his weapons belt, drawing his rapier, Catsclaw, in one smooth motion as he came to his feet again. Swiftly, he saw his predicament and the futility of resistance.

A ring of soldiers stood knee-deep in the weeds inside the iron fence that surrounded the tower. A dozen grim-faced men-at-arms stood ready with pikes or drawn swords. Another dozen bowmen, bowstrings quivering with tension, sighted carefully down drawn shafts.

The Mouser glanced hopelessly to his left and right. Even if he could reach the fence, those archers would make a pin cushion of him before he could climb it. He looked back at the tower. Thick smoke poured from the window above his head, and tongues of red flame licked the sky.

"Damn you, Fafhrd," he muttered disgustedly. "Once again, you've left me in the lurch."

Scowling, he threw down his sword. Covering his groin with his hands, mindful of the arrows trained on him, he stood meekly until the Overlord's men seized him. A pair of guards roughly twisted his arms behind his back and applied ropes to his wrists. A soldier in a corporal's livery knotted another rope loosely about his neck and gave it a jerk. The Mouser's head snapped up. Forgetting himself, the Mouser cursed the corporal's unfaithful mother.

They beat him for that, slapping and punching him until he fell on the ground. They kicked him and jabbed him with the butts of pikes. Covering his vitals as best he could, he rolled on the harsh, broken paving stones and waited for it to end, biting his already bloody lip to keep from giving further offense.

Finally, the guards wearied of such easy sport. Using the rope around his neck, they hauled him cruelly to his feet, mocking him with great mirth. The guard whose mother he had insulted seized the leash and reeled the Mouser close until they stood nose to nose. He let fly a slimy wad straight into the Mouser's left eye, then turned away, laughing.

The Mouser burned with embarrassment and rage. His mouth quivered, and he bit his lower lip until his own teeth drew new streams of blood. *Puss and piss!* he thought bitterly, staring at the broad back of his abuser. *My sentence is already death for violating a forbidden tower.*

He snapped his right foot up sharply, smashing his heel into the guard's lower spine. A wet crack! The man's scream achieved a satisfyingly high note, and he fell, arms and legs thrashing convulsively.

"No one spits on me," he warned in a cold, deadly voice. Ready to fight, no matter his bonds, he met their startled gazes steadfastly. "No one."

For a moment, they stared back, as if impressed. Then, of course, they beat him again, and quite thoroughly. But this time, no one laughed, and no one dared to spit on him.

When they were through, they dragged him to his feet again. Though he could barely stand on his own, the Mouser did his best to remain erect. Naked, bruised, and bleeding, he managed yet to look defiant.

Nearby, the corporal lay whimpering on the ground, his legs absolutely still, his arms twitching, eyes filled with pain and fear. A small circle of his fellows clustered around him, shaking their heads. A few knelt beside him, murmuring words of comfort.

The Mouser felt a twinge of guilt as he gazed at the fallen man and watched another guard quietly, secretively slide a knife from a belt sheath. Still murmuring assurances, he laid one hand across the corporal's eyes, then cleanly slid the blade deep into his comrade's windpipe and sliced sideways.

A moment of convulsion, a gurgling gasp, and the corporal's suffering ended. The rest of the soldiers turned accusing glares upon the Mouser. He knew by those looks that his suffering had just begun.

The soldier with the knife wiped his blade and sheathed it. The others looked to him for orders now, though he wore no officer's insignia. Someone gathered the Mouser's belongings. Someone else picked up the end of the rope around his neck. At a word from the new leader, they marched the Mouser to the north side of the tower and toward the iron fence.

A pair of ladders straddled the iron structure. A pike at his back urged him up. Awkwardly he climbed the narrow rungs, unable to steady himself with his bound hands. At the top, he nearly fell. With the point of another pike to encourage him, he caught his balance and descended.

"We'd hang you on this fence if it was up to me," the new leader said grimly. "Hissif wasn't too bright, but he was a good man, and deserved a better death."

With a mouth full of coppery-tasting blood, the Mouser studied the thin scar that ran from the man's chin to his right ear. "It's my experience," he muttered, "that people usually die exactly as they deserve."

The guard's voice remained impassive, but his eyes betrayed anger. "Shortly, we'll broaden your experience."

Naked and leashed, the Mouser simmered inside as the soldiers marched him through the streets of Lankhmar, up the wharves past the sailing ships and fishing boats. The wind sang in the ships' rigging; the wharves creaked and groaned. Otherwise, an eerie quiet haunted the streets.

One by one, the stars faded away. Darkness retreated, giving way to a creepy shade of twilight. A burning red crescent marked the slow return of Nehwon's sun. On the rooftops, in windows, from the doorways of homes and shops, Lankhmar's citizens watched the brightening sky with nervous, pale-faced relief.

As they crossed the plaza where the Street of the Gods met the wharves, the Mouser tried to slow the pace. Turning his head to catch a glimpse down the broad avenue, he witnessed carnage. Bodies lay sprawled in the road. Cobblestones gleamed darkly with blood. Soldiers, many bleeding themselves, worked to pile the corpses and tend the wounded.

A sharp jerk on the leash rope caused the Mouser to look forward again, and a rough push from a guard propelled him onward.

Every muscle and bone aching, the Mouser's thoughts turned to Fafhrd. What was that violet light that had swallowed his partner? Was Fafhrd dead? Captured by Malygris? If the guards had noticed Fafhrd at all, they seemed strangely disinterested. Perhaps they thought the Mouser had violated the tower alone.

He glanced at his shoulders, still mottled from the kisses of the leeches, and in his mind he heard again Fafhrd's final falling shriek. What had compelled Fafhrd to lose his grip on the rope?

"Damn the misbegotten creature that brought us back to this city," he muttered to himself. "Damn Sheelba. Damn his stinking swamp, his unlikely hut, and his eyeless face." He lifted his head and swept his gaze around. Directly ahead, the wall of the North Barracks rose, and off to the right of it, on a graceful hill, stood the Overlord's Rainbow Palace.

"Damn all of you," the Mouser swore under his breath, yielding to increasing bitterness. "You've cost me the truest friend in all the world."

The North Barracks gates stood open. Straight into the sprawling compound his guards marched him. In the yard, arranged in three neat rows, lay a score of corpses, soldiers killed in the melee before the temples. Now, his captors added one more to the nearest row as they placed their corporal's body on the grass.

Shortly after that, they flung the Mouser into a windowless cell and slammed the door. A heavy metal bolt slid home on the other side, and the little bit of torchlight that slipped under the jamb vanished as his guards left him. In utter blackness, he lay on his side on a bare stone floor. For a long while, he remained there, without hope, awash in his pain and grieving for Fafhrd.

Then slowly, he sat up, wincing at the effort. Licking caked blood from his lips, he wriggled his bound hands beneath his hips, under his legs, and over his feet. Bringing the rope to his teeth, he chewed and pulled until the knots loosened enough to let him slip free. He cast the coils disgustedly at the door.

Thoughts of Fafhrd stole into his mind again, and he grew morose. Dead, or in the clutches of Malygris—or worse, Fafhrd caught by whatever remnant god once resided in that evil tower whose defenses the Mouser, himself, had so foolishly triggered. Curse him for a fool for ever laying eyes on that huge, ruby jewel. Fafhrd had paid the price for the Mouser's greed.

Cross-legged, he sat on the floor, hands in his lap, head hung, blaming and shaming himself until a new possibility entered his mind. "Sheelba," he muttered to himself, grasping at a small hope. Could Sheelba have saved Fafhrd from his fall? That mysterious wizard had transported them across the world with his arcane art. Could he not have transported Fafhrd to safety?

Clearly, some magical hand had reached out to snatch the Northerner from midair.

The Mouser's shoulders slumped again. Surely that was a false hope. Sheelba dwelled in the marshes beyond the city's walls and was sick near to death, in need of errand boys to go where his magicks could not. What would he think of his errand boys now, the Mouser wondered bitterly.

Reaching behind, he fingered the leather thong that bound his black hair away from his face. At least he still had one weapon. Crawling on hands and knees, he searched the floor until he found the coil of rope that had bound his wrists. Undoing the knots, he tested its strength, nodding grimly. It would make an adequate garrotte, and now his weapons were two.

Sitting again, listening alertly for any sound beyond the door, he conserved his energy and shut from his mind all awareness of pain from the beatings the guards had given him. He might yet, with luck and daring, break out of this prison. Then nothing would keep him from learning Fafhrd's fate.

Before much time had passed, he heard a sound in the corridor, and a key grated in the lock of his cell door. Moving swiftly, he rose and concealed himself in the gloom next to the door, gripping the two ends of the rope. The door swung outward, and lamplight spilled across the threshold, but no guard stepped inside.

"Prisoner, show yourself," a deep voice called from the corridor.

Some guard's natural caution had undone him. Silently cursing, the Mouser dropped the rope and, blinking, stepped into the light. Four soldiers stood in the narrow passage with short swords drawn. The tallest guard gestured to two of the others. "Take him," he said.

The guards seized him roughly by his arms. For an insane moment, the Mouser considered fighting them. In the close confines of the corridor, though, their swords would cut him down easily. At least, when he made no effort to resist, they relaxed their grips.

Down the corridor they led him, up a stone staircase, and into a room. Sunlight streamed through a pair of barred windows. On a table in the center of the room he spied his clothes. No sign of his weapons or his purse. Another soldier leaned over the table, frowning distastefully as he stirred the Mouser's belongings with a finger.

When the soldier looked up, the Mouser recognized him by the scar on the right side of his face. On the shoulder of his scarlet cloak, he wore a corporal's pin. Apparently, he had succeeded his superior.

"Get dressed," he instructed as he pushed the gray bundle across the table.

Reaching for his garments, the Mouser asked in a sarcastic tone, "Is it a formal occasion?"

Corporal Scarface regarded him coldly. "As formal as it gets."

The Mouser pulled on his clothes, taking his time, studying the room, the corporal, his guards, looking for any opening that might suggest an opportunity to escape. Nothing presented itself yet. He slipped on his boots and tied the lacings.

"Leash him," Corporal Scarface ordered when the Mouser was dressed.

One of the guards sheathed his sword and produced a short rope. With practiced speed he bound the Mouser's hands securely together. When the knots were tied, the guard slipped another rope around the Mouser's neck. Grinning, he gave a tug on the line.

"I can tell you're a man who loves his work," the Mouser said drily, trying to hide a grimace. The ropes bit deeply into his flesh. Already, numbness crept into his fingers.

Behind, another guard rapped him sharply on the head. "Silence!" he ordered.

Scarface, no man for long speeches, headed for the door. "Bring him."

The guard holding the other end of the Mouser's leash gave it a jerk, spinning his prisoner about. Two guards fell in behind the Mouser and two before. Scarface led the way from the room into the corridor, through a large hall, and out into the grounds of the North Barracks.

A large tarpaulin had been cast over the stack of corpses. A number of soldiers wandered aimlessly about or sat in the shade of other buildings, sporting bandages and wounds. Most of the barracks, the Mouser reasoned, would be out in the streets attempting to restore order and reassure the citizenry.

Scarface set a brisk pace. Out through the barracks' main gate they went. To the Mouser's left, the ancient Citadel of the Overlord squatted on a low hill, bleak and gray as old steel behind high walls. The northernmost point in the city, it overlooked the vast Inner Sea and the Royal Docks. In past centuries, during an attack, the Overlord and his generals conducted battles from that stronghold, but it was seldom used now. No nation on Nehwon dared make war against Lankhmar.

The Mouser appreciated what a rare tour he was about to receive. Commoners were not allowed in the Noble District without permission or an escort. He might have wished for friendlier companions, he admitted, and better circumstances.

For a short time they walked toward the Citadel past several well-kept estates, past walls lined with roses and greenery, down a road paved with wide, flat stones and well-shaded with stately trees. Orchards and floral gardens filled the air with a sweet perfume. Expensively sculpted fountains offered cool water to pedestrians.

Then, one long and unbroken wall of gleaming white sandstone began to border the right side of the road. No trees grew near this wall, no roses, no greenery. Slender, mushroom-shaped watchtowers, artfully constructed, stood atop the wall at every fifty paces. Archers in ornamented, highly polished armor and bright scarlet cloaks, scrutinized every movement in the street below while pairs of foot soldiers walked patrol.

Another pair of soldiers stood duty before a small, arched gateway. With a gesture, Scarface signaled his men and his prisoner to halt while he approached the sentries. Reaching inside his jerkin, he brought out a folded parchment and displayed it for the guards, who studied it closely.

The Mouser couldn't hear the exchange of words, but the gate guards looked up from the writ and eyed him with the kind of disgusted, disbelieving look usually reserved for the idiot who drinks too much and pukes on himself. Shaking heads, the two opened the gate and stepped aside to allow Scarface, his prisoner, and his men to pass through.

Beyond that gate lay a place of beauty, a dreamland—Lankhmar's Rainbow Palace. Four stories high, made of the same sandstone as the wall that surrounded it, the palace shimmered

in the late afternoon sun. White colonnades supported gracefully curving porticos and terraces. Spires and minarets floated
splendidly skyward above the fourth level.

Majestic obelisks and sculptures stood scattered about the
perfectly manicured lawns. Beds of blossoming flowers, carefully tended, spread bright color about the grounds. Isolated
fruit trees, placed strategically for artistic and olfactory effect,
sang with wind chimes that hung from their branches.

A sharp jerk on his rope and a push from one of the guards at
his back reminded the Mouser of his predicament.

Flat stones made a narrow walkway from the gate leading toward the Rainbow Palace. His guards fell into a cadenced military
step now, and carried themselves with stiff bearing. The Mouser
pushed out his chest and lifted his head higher. A prisoner he
might be; and though he had been beaten, beaten he was not.

Even the least significant entrance to the palace was double-
guarded. At a tiny yet ornately gold-embossed garden door,
Corporal Scarface flashed his parchment for the soldiers on
duty. Wordlessly, they stepped aside.

The bright beauty of the Rainbow Palace ended at the
threshold. Beyond the door only a single smoky cresset relieved
the cavern-like gloom that filled a low-ceilinged passage. In the
next corridor, another lone cresset burned, and in the next. In
the chamber beyond that, a trio of suspended lamps illuminated
huge earthen jars taller than any of the guards. Covered and
sealed with cloth and wax, they smelled of mysterious oils.

Past that chamber, they climbed a staircase. On the second
level, lamps and cressets lit the hallways with noonday brightness. Servants drifted by, casting curious glances at the Mouser
and his guards, saying nothing.

Reaching a set of grandly carven doors, Scarface once more
showed his writ. The sentries posted there examined it carefully,
then eased open one of the doors. The Mouser's guards drew
their swords and closed in around him.

"Little man, you stand in a place of honor," Scarface warned. "Conduct yourself accordingly."

The Mouser glared at him. Then he sent his gaze past the corporal to take in the lavish richness of the vast hall, its wooden columns, its tapestries and carpets, the dais and the high-backed, ivory throne at the far side.

"Why am I here?" he whispered in a tone unbecoming his status as a prisoner.

Scarface matched his glare and raised his sword slowly until the point rested on the Mouser's nose. "Abase yourself at his feet when you approach," he instructed, ignoring the Mouser's question. "If you hesitate, I will sever the tendons behind your knees."

The Mouser raised one eyebrow and gave Scarface a sardonic, challenging look. Defiance would ill-serve him now, however. Instead, he turned smartly, moving so quickly that he pulled the leash from a lax guard's hand, and led the way toward the Overlord's throne, trailing the rope tied about his neck, leaving his guards to hurry after.

At the foot of the dais he paused. The royal seat was empty. The Mouser looked around. Off to the side, between a pair of gracefully fluted pillars, a trio of men stood in muted conversation. The light of a single brazier gleamed on their oiled beards and hair, and on the elaborate silver embroidery that adorned their black tunics and cloaks.

The Mouser needed no urging from his guards to stand silently and wait to be noticed. The Mouser used the time to test his bonds. Straining subtly against the ropes, he tried to flex some feeling into his fingers.

One of the three, a well-built and muscular man with the look of a wrestler, suddenly turned around. The brazier's light shimmered on a thinly delicate coronet of gold that adorned a stern brow. Dark eyes focused on the Mouser, and the observer pursed his lips in study. Abruptly, he waved off his two companions.

Executing curt bows, the nobles obediently departed through a shadowed doorway. The wearer of the coronet strode slowly toward the throne.

Scarface raised his sword in salute, and his voice boomed. "Hail, Rokkarsh, Overlord of Lankhmar, Lord of . . ."

A gesture of irritation from Rokkarsh cut him off, and Scarface fell silent. His lowering blade, however, came to rest on the Mouser's right shoulder.

Scowling and grumbling inside, the Mouser bent his knees. With his hands tied behind his back, he dropped awkwardly to the floor, nearly cracking his chin on the expensive marble tiles.

"In Aarth's name," the Overlord said, grimacing as he fanned the air with one hand and with the other selected a plump peach from a bowl on a small table beside the throne. "I told you to bathe him. His stink fouls the palace."

The Mouser raised his head, eyes narrowing to slits as he regarded the man before him. Slowly, he drew his knees under himself. Let Scarface put a sword in his back; he would grovel and crawl no more, particularly not before an oiled, pomaded effete with the audacity and bad taste to tattoo a rose around an exposed left nipple.

"If the palace stinks," the Mouser said through clenched teeth, his temper barely in check, "the cause must be that whore's perfume in which you've drenched yourself."

Scarface bellowed. "Let me strike off his head, my lord!"

The Overlord held up his peach as if to display the proud bite his royal teeth had taken from it. "No, not his head," he said with calm bemusement. "However, you may take from him the finger of your choice."

The Mouser's dusky face took on a serpentine quality, and he fixed Rokkarsh with his gaze. "If one of your dogs dares to touch me again," he boldly threatened, "I'll lay a curse to rot off a more important appendage than your finger."

The Overlord waved Scarface back and took a bite from his peach as he studied the Mouser. With a curious grin he asked, "Do you have such power, little man?"

The Mouser scowled at the reference to his height. "Lankhmar's walls will echo with the lamentations from your harem," he promised.

Rokkarsh licked a droplet of juice from his lips. "Well, we couldn't very well have that, could we?" he said. "I take it that you're some kind of wizard?"

"The great Overlord of Lankhmar may take whatever he likes," the Mouser sneered. "You can take my life if that pleases you, and you can take your fiddle and go up to the roof of the Rainbow Palace and play for the gulls while the city burns around you."

Rokkarsh set aside his peach and leaned forward as he licked his fingers. "The only thing burning in Lankhmar, little wizard, is the tower you set afire." The Overlord leaned forward, and his voice took on a new tone of menace. "Why did you enter a forbidden temple, and where is the partner witnesses saw with you?"

The Mouser feigned a look of surprise. "Partner?" he said, glancing over his shoulders and down between his legs before he shrugged. "Your witnesses must be drunkards."

The Overlord assumed an expression of boredom as he reached again for his peach. "I think I shall risk your curse and let the corporal strike off your finger after all. Then perhaps you'll answer honestly the next time I ask."

Scarface stepped close and, grasping one of the Mouser's bound hands, began to pry at a finger. The Mouser's heart thundered in his chest as he resisted by making fists, but he had little control over his rope-numbed hands. Desperately, he fixed his gaze on the Overlord.

"I'm looking for Malygris!" he shouted.

Rokkarsh held up a hand and Scarface became still, though he maintained a grip on one of the Mouser's fingers.

"The wizard?" Rokkarsh asked with interest. "Why?"

The Mouser glared back at the Overlord. "To end the thrice-damned plague he's conjured on Lankhmar and surrounds."

Rokkarsh turned pale. Trembling, he rose from his throne and, drawing back his arm, an enraged scream bubbling on his lips, he let fly the half-eaten peach.

TWELVE

TUNNELS OF
HOPE AND
HEARTBREAK

The half-eaten peach flew past the Mouser's head and struck Corporal Scarface with such force that it knocked his helmet askew.

"Great shot," the Mouser complimented.

"Get out!" Rokkarsh, purple-faced, screamed at his guards. "Leave us!"

Scarface sputtered as he struggled with his chin strap and tried to set his helmet aright. "But, my lord!" he exclaimed as juice dribbled down his cheek and chin, "the prisoner!"

Rokkarsh reached as if for another peach, but his hand slipped down between the throne and the table that held the bowl and came up again with a short, gleaming sword. Brandishing it, he gestured with the point toward the great doors.

"Insignificant fart," he said, his voice low with menace as he glared at the corporal, "your new rank goes to your head. Should the Overlord of Lankhmar fear a lone, bound man? Get out! And if one of you repeats a word of what he heard here, I'll hang the lot of you from the city walls."

Scarface shot a look of purest hatred at the Mouser, and the Mouser responded with a crooked grin and a mocking lift of his eyebrows. Retreating from their Overlord's fury, the other soldiers hurried to the doors. Slamming his sword back into its sheath, Scarface stalked after them.

"Now, little man." As the great doors closed behind the last of the soldiers, Rokkarsh descended halfway down the steps of the dais and stopped. His eyes narrowing to slits, he waved the point of his blade hypnotically before the Mouser's face. The red light of the braziers seemed to turn the silver metal to flame, and the Overlord himself appeared to grow subtly in power and stature as he struck a pose.

"You are not native to Lankhmar," Rokkarsh observed, studying the Mouser closely. "Your dusky skin suggests Tovilyis. I think you've come, an agent of some foreign power, to sow seeds of discontent, fear, and false rumor among my people."

"I know nothing of my parentage or my specific origins," the Mouser acknowledged, lifting his head high in stubborn pride, "but my guardian, Glavas Rho, raised me in the southlands of Lankhmar, steeped me in her traditions and customs, weaned me on her tales and legends. Lankhmar's gods are my gods, her ways my ways, and her people are my people as much as yours."

Rokkarsh sneered. "A pretty speech, but your arrogance puts the lie in your mouth. A true son of Lankhmar wouldn't dare to speak so to his Overlord. You're a spy and a rumor-monger."

With numbed fingers the Mouser surreptitiously explored the knots of his bonds, working clumsily to loosen them, gaining nothing. He fought to conceal his disappointment, considering his options. Perhaps he could reason with Rokkarsh, reach him with words.

"Forgive my urgency, which you mistake for arrogance, most noble lord," the Mouser said. "Don't you see that our people are dying in their homes from an evil plague, and that damned wizard, Malygris, is to blame?"

Rage flashed across Rokkarsh's face, and he raised his sword as if to strike off the Mouser's head. "Hold your tongue, rogue, lest I cut it from your mouth! There's no plague in Lankhmar, and the loyal citizen, Malygris, has done me the dearest of favors with his magic."

The Mouser felt the blood in his veins turn cold, and for a moment he ceased to work against his bonds. "Favor?" he said suspiciously. "What favor?"

A faint smile danced over the too-handsome face of Lankhmar's Overlord. Abruptly, he lowered the sword he held, turned, and climbed the few steps to his throne. Languidly, he sank upon it, throwing one arm over its high, velvet-cushioned back.

"Malygris undertook to rid me of important rivals and ene-mies," he said with a bemused grin. "The Patriarch of Aarth, for one, that meddling old fool." He gazed down upon the Mouser to measure the effect of his words as he touched the golden cir-clet he wore with a fingertip. "This rests a little easier on my brow with certain priests and powerful wizards out of my way. And if a few insignificant fortune-tellers and herb-witches have been incidentally brushed aside by Malygris's spell . . ."—he hesitated, looked thoughtful, then waved a hand—"well, their sacrifices are for the betterment of the state."

As he glared at the monster on the throne above him, the Mouser trembled with poorly hidden anger. "You fool!" he hissed. His life was forfeit; he knew that now beyond all hoping. Rokkarsh would not have confessed so much, otherwise. "Your ass disgraces the honored throne upon which it sits!"

Rokkarsh selected a new peach from the bowl close at hand and took a deep bite. Juice squirted upon his chin and dribbled downward. Contemptuously, he spat the pit at his prisoner's feet.

The Mouser cursed his inept, swollen fingers because they couldn't manage the knots. How he wished he could squeeze

Rokkarsh's neck and choke the breath from his body. "You stationed soldiers around the tower to protect Malygris," the Mouser accused. "Your villainy is even blacker than his!"

Rokkarsh inclined his head indifferently. "As the only wizard who can safely practice his art, he has some value to me." Setting aside the sword that dangled from one hand, he clapped his palms together sharply. "You, however, have no value at all. While you pose no real threat to a mage of Malygris's caliber, I can hardly let you run around the streets screaming 'plague!' and upsetting the citizenry."

On either side of the Mouser the nearest of the tall, fluted columns suddenly popped open. Unseen in the smooth stone, narrow doors flung back. From each, a giant emerged, men as tall as Fafhrd, clad only in loincloths and gleaming with sweat. Each carried an axe of impressive size.

The Mouser shot a worried look over his shoulder, wondering how many more of the scores of columns supporting the massive roof also housed a defender. Shouldering their axes, the pair of giants seized him roughly by his arms, lifting him up to the very tips of his toes. "Take a bath, pigs," the Mouser said, clenching his teeth against the pain that shot up into his joints. He wrinkled his nose in disgust. "You've been in your larders too long."

Rokkarsh chuckled softly. "They can't answer you," he said. "They surrendered their tongues to better serve their Overlord."

"Good at keeping secrets, huh?" the Mouser said, wincing as the pair lifted his bound hands high, forcing him to bend forward.

"Very," Lankhmar's Overlord agreed. "I trust them to repeat nothing said within these walls." Throwing back his head, he laughed.

The Mouser's head slumped forward, and droplets of sweat rolled from his brow onto the floor as despair and anger filled his heart. Then slowly, even as his arms were twisted higher still, he lifted his head and glowered at Rokkarsh. "One way or another," he promised, "I'll see you in hell."

The Overlord ceased his laughter and rose slowly from his throne, and when he stood erect, in the brazier's flickering red glow, he seemed to keep on rising, growing until he filled all the Mouser's tortured vision. "Indeed you will," he whispered in low, dangerous tones that echoed through all the hall. "Indeed."

He gestured to the pair of giants. "Take him to the dungeons below," he instructed. "Strike off his head and cast his corpse into the worm pits." Sinking down on his throne again, he seemed to resume his normal size once more. He reached for a fresh peach, took a bite, and threw one leg over the carved arm of his royal seat, half-reclining. "Ah," he sighed, paying the Mouser no more attention. "I am in need of a nap."

The axemen jerked the Mouser off his feet and dragged him away, his heels scrabbling and kicking futilely on the marble tiles. Out of the great hall and through a darkened archway they went and into a shadowy passage illumined only by regularly placed, low-burning cressets. The axemen paused long enough to put the Mouser on his feet, then still gripping his arms, they escorted him at a brisk pace through windowless corridors, down flights of stone steps, deep into the bowels of the Rainbow Palace.

A damp, foul-smelling seepage coated the rough floor of the lowest sub-basement. From lightless, locked cells soft murmurings and groans issued as the Mouser's muttered cursings and the footsteps of his guards disturbed prisoners who had not seen the sunlight in countless days.

The sound chilled the Mouser's soul. He grew quiet as he eyed those cold, iron-barred doors, imagining the half-starved and tormented humans shut behind them. Suddenly he felt the pain in his bruised ribs again, the cuts and lacerations on his face, all the places where Rokkarsh's soldiers had punched and kicked and beaten him.

His guards dragged him into another chamber. More locked cells, barely perceived shuffling behind the bolted doors— someone pacing mindlessly. Rats, licking at the slime on the floor, scuttled out of the way, squeaking in protest. Here stood instruments of torture. Chains, racks, strappados, thumbscrews and ankle-vices, other devices unidentifiable even to the Mouser.

The next chamber contained only one device, a wooden platform with manacles for arms and legs. The Mouser's eyes widened in fear. He lunged against one of his guards, knocking him sideways, and turned to make a desperate escape. A huge hand caught his long hair, halting him painfully, and a meaty fist slammed against the side of his face. The Mouser hit the floor hard, his vision full of a red haze and bright pinpoints of light like a bloody sky burning with stars.

He felt himself lifted, placed on the platform. Manacles snapped around his ankles, then a knife swiftly cut his ropes. Forced down upon his back, cold iron bracelets clamped around his wrists. One of the giants laughed now, a harsh and ugly sound. From above the other guard fitted a leather strap under the Mouser's chin and jerked it tight, forcing the Mouser's head back until it nearly cut off his breath, and the muscles of his throat stood out with the tension.

The Mouser stared upward, terror gripping his heart. What a devilish device, to force the victim to witness the descent of the blade that meant his own execution. The largest of the giants stepped close, chuckling low as he regarded his helpless captive, an ugly sound from a tongueless mouth. He raised the axe in his two hands, chest swelling, muscles tensing, and swung it down.

Despite himself, the Mouser screamed.

A scant inch from the Mouser's throat, the axeman checked his swing. Looking to his partner, he chuckled again. The second guard ripped a piece of string from the hem of his loincloth and measured the distance from the Mouser's Adam's apple to the edge of the axe. Marking the string with his thumb, he handed it to the first guard and, taking up his own axe, moved into killing position.

Though he bit his lip, swearing not to give them the pleasure of a second scream, the Mouser nevertheless cried out as gleaming death hurtled down upon his offered throat.

Again the axeman checked his swing, and his partner measured an even shorter distance with the piece of string. Swallowing, the Mouser could just feel the sharp metal edge brushing his skin. Grumbling, the first guard took up his axe again.

A movement near the chamber entrance caught the Mouser's attention. A black-cloaked figure swept into the room, its features concealed beneath a hood. A long-bladed sword arced high and whistled down upon the first guard's unprotected neck. A spray of hot blood fountained into the air.

"Fafhrd!" the Mouser croaked, straining at his manacles, twisting his head as far as the strap beneath his chin allowed.

The figure made no answer. Knocking the corpse of the first guard aside before it could fall, his rescuer leaped upon the platform, nearly putting a boot in the Mouser's stomach as he swung his sword again. The second guard ducked and tried to swing his axe. Before he could lift it, a bolt sprouted from his left eye.

Surprised, the Mouser strained to twist his head again. Another cloaked figure stood in the doorway, a crossbow still braced against one shoulder. "You're not Fafhrd!" he said, rolling his eyes toward his nearer savior.

A gloved hand pushed back a concealing hood. Nuulpha grinned, his face flush with excitement. "Want me to leave?" he said.

The Mouser did his best to shrug. "As long as you're here . . ."

Nuulpha's partner found a ring of keys on a peg near the entrance and tossed them. "Hurry!" the second figure insisted, shooting a nervous glance back over one shoulder.

Nuulpha fumbled with the keys, trying one after another in the manacles until he found one that fit the locks. Freed, the Mouser sat up, and with Nuulpha's help, stood.

"Aarth!" Nuulpha muttered. "Your face . . . !"

The Mouser touched his right cheek and winced. His right eye was nearly swollen shut, too. His whole face felt like over-ripe fruit. "You're not so pretty, yourself," he said, forcing a grin. Then he shook his head. "No, forget that. Right now, you're the prettiest thing I've ever seen."

"Kiss him later," hissed the figure guarding the doorway as it loaded a new bolt on the string. "Let's get out of here."

"Can you walk?" Nuulpha asked worriedly.

The Mouser nodded, relaxing his steadying grip on Nuulpha's arm. "If you don't particularly mind, I'd rather run. This damp environment is bad for my complexion."

"Walk, run. Just be prepared to fight," said the second figure, in a harsh whisper. Sweeping back one side of a cloak, a slender arm tossed a bundle toward the Mouser.

"Scalpel!" the Mouser exclaimed, as he unrolled his gray cloak and found his weapons. "Catsclaw!"

Nuulpha took the Mouser's arm again and steered him into the next chamber with an urgency. "When I heard someone had tried to break into the forbidden tower on Nun Street," Nuulpha whispered as they hurried through the dungeon, "I knew it was you. At the North Barracks I found your weapons and learned that Rokkarsh, himself, had demanded to see you."

A body sprawled in the corridor, blood oozing slowly from one ear to pool on the slimy floor. From the leather apron and the keyring at its side, the Mouser guessed Nuulpha had jumped the jailor.

Glancing at that keyring the Mouser asked, "Is there time to open some of these cells?"

"No!" said Nuulpha's partner, who prowled the corridor ahead as an advance scout. "Now shut up—before we're all caught!" Reaching the bottom of the staircase, the partner ignored the steps and instead ducked into the shadows below the stone cascade.

The sound of well-oiled gears turning shivered faintly through the air, followed by a barely audible scraping. A gleam of light drew a line near the floor, illuminating the partner's boots, then calves, knees, and thighs as it widened. A door, hidden beneath the stairs, rose. Just beyond its threshold, a lantern, suspended on a peg, limned Nuulpha's partner with a golden radiance.

With concealment no longer an advantage, the partner pushed back the concealing hood and shook free a curly mass of black hair before seizing the lantern and beckoning them onward.

The Mouser gaped, taking a full instant to realize through the surrounding light, that the face before him belonged to a young woman. Before he could say anything, she turned away and hurried down a narrow, stone-lined tunnel whose ceiling hung so low it nearly brushed her head.

Stepping into the tunnel, Nuulpha leaned on an iron lever embedded in the dusty floor. A narrow panel, seemingly made of thinly sliced granite, dropped into place with a clinking of chains. But for the lantern's light, which was moving ever farther up the tunnel, darkness ruled.

Crouching to avoid banging his head in the low passage, Nuulpha touched the Mouser's arm and urged him after the light. The Mouser, quickly as his aching muscles and injuries allowed, chased after that singular glow with his friend and rescuer close on his heels. As he went, he strapped on his weapons and tossed his light cloak over his shoulders, feeling a little better in familiar accoutrements.

"What is the lady's name?" the Mouser whispered over his shoulder as they strove to overtake Nuulpha's swiftly moving partner.

"Jesane is a lot of things," Nuulpha answered, "but she's no lady."

"Even better," the Mouser said with a grin. "Women with crossbows excite me. I've got a quarrel I'd like to fit to her string."

"You'll have more than a quarrel if she overhears you," Nuulpha warned, nudging him along. "Limp faster."

A narrow, stone-lined archway marked another passage that abruptly forked off to the right. Slowing his step, the Mouser stared into impenetrable darkness and repressed a shiver. Though he could not say how, he felt sure that something unseen not so far down that tunnel stared back at him, a malevolence so cold and ancient that he perceived it on a level deeper and more primitive than any of his five senses.

Humor deserted him. He hurried on until he stood at last in the umbra of Jesane's lantern, and when he spoke again, he kept his voice to the barest of whispers for fear of disturbing things best left undisturbed. "No rats," he muttered, eyeing the tunnel floor. In a place like this there should be hundreds of rats, thousands of rats. A queer urgency crept into his words. "Where are the rats?"

Neither Nuulpha, nor Jesane, answered, but in the lantern's yellow glow the Mouser caught the look on the soldier's face. He noted the grip Nuulpha kept on his sword and the manner in which Jesane held her cocked crossbow ready.

Swallowing nervously, he put a hand on his own slender sword and loosened it in its sheath. The walls seemed closer than ever, and he felt the weight of earth and rock above him as surely as if it rested on his shoulders.

Another archway and another darkness-filled passage branched off to the left. Only a few paces beyond that, yet another passage offered itself. Jesane led them under its low arch, and they soft-footed in a new direction. The lantern seemed a tiny shield against the overpowering blackness, and the Mouser found himself praying someone had remembered to fill its reservoir. The thought of getting lost down here. . . .

They turned into yet another tunnel, and the floor turned slick with slime, then muddy.

Without warning, the darkness burst with a glittering and glimmering. Neat pinpoints and jagged shimmering streaks of brilliance flared to sudden life. Jesane lifted the lantern higher as the Mouser caught his breath.

They walked no longer in a man-made tunnel, but in a natural cavern whose roof dripped spectacularly with stalactites. Bits of quartz and mica embedded in the formations, in the walls and roof, caught and scattered the lantern's glow, creating an eerie and awesome display.

"The underworld of Lankhmar," Nuulpha whispered. "A honeycomb of man-made tunnels, natural caves, and deep caverns. A secret closely guarded by the Overlord and the Great Noble Families with the cooperation of the high priests of certain powerful religions."

Instinctively the Mouser softened his step, and his gaze searched the shadows and gloom-filled crannies, the upper reaches, and the unyielding darkness beyond the reach of Jesane's small light. Such horrible, mysterious grandeur! Putting out a hand, he dragged his fingertips over the rough limestone surface and the jagged point of a stalagmite that rose as high as his waist. An overwhelming sense of age shivered through him.

Letting go of the stalagmite, he gazed upward again and imagined himself in a stygian mouth, between powerful jaws, monstrous teeth about to crush out his life.

Jesane moved ahead quickly, and Nuulpha, glancing back the way they had come, again put a hand on the Mouser's shoulder and urged him onward. Once more the Mouser caught the narrow, worried look in his friend's eyes; he perceived the way Nuulpha listened as if to the very darkness and the tension revealed by the grip that never eased on the hilt of his soldier's sword.

Quickening his pace, the Mouser turned his eyes from the beauty the cavern offered. Beauty sometimes made tender bait for deadly traps, and every attitude of Jesane and Nuulpha suggested danger lurked near. He resolved, not just to follow Jesane's light, but to stay within its wavering, yellow circle.

Their journey through the cavern ended abruptly when the lantern's light fell upon another man-made archway cut into the limestone wall. Upon one rough-hewn stone block a queer symbol stood out in a faded, ancient black paint—a crude, leering face with a crescent moon above its brow, a dagger beside its right cheek, a bone beside its left, and a pentagram below.

Without knowing its meaning, the Mouser recognized it for a darkly evil sign. "Where do all these tunnels lead?" he asked, following Jesane into the new passage. The thin smoke from her lantern rose and spread upon the low ceiling.

"To nearly every important edifice, public or private, in the city," she answered quietly without slackening her pace. "The Overlords built them originally as storeplaces during times of war and invasion, and as a means of moving unseen between the Rainbow Palace, the Citadel, the garrisons and the Royal Docks."

"Over the centuries the Great Families expanded the network, taking advantage of the natural caverns, until they had secret access to every public building, temple, even to the private estates of their enemies."

"The temples?" the Mouser said thoughtfully. "Even the Forbidden Towers?"

"No doubt," Nuulpha said.

"Of course," Jesane affirmed.

Nuulpha nodded. "She knows the network better than anyone."

The Mouser pursed his lips and thought of Fafhrd, a black anger filling his heart, mingling with fear and grief. "That explains how Rokkarsh's soldiers caught us off-guard. There was no other visible entrance save the window we used."

Jesane paused and turned suddenly, holding up a hand for silence as she peered into the darkness behind them. For a tense moment, all three listened, hands on their weapons. She lifted the lantern a bit higher, throwing its light back down the passage. Finally, her finger eased off the crossbow's trigger.

Letting out a slow breath, the Mouser uncurled his fingers from around Scalpel's hilt. The look of fear on Jesane's face still lingered in his mind. Even as they resumed walking, he cast a sheepish glance back over his shoulder, noting with some relief that Nuulpha did the same.

What dangers lurked in these tunnels, he wondered, to cause his comrades to start at the smallest sounds? No rats, he remembered nervously, casting his gaze upon the floor. Some ravenous creature, then, prowling the black maze? Or creatures? Though the question gnawed at him, it suddenly seemed wisest to preserve the silence.

Jesane led them through yet another archway and into another tunnel. The way twisted through a natural cave, then entered another man-made passage. Abruptly, a staircase carved crudely out of the rock presented itself. At the top stood a door painted with the same ominous sign the Mouser had seen in another tunnel.

"What is that?" the Mouser dared to whisper as Jesane stepped aside. Drawing his sword, Nuulpha moved to the fore and slammed the pommel against the stout wood.

Jesane stared at the symbol. In the wavering lantern-light, the leering face seemed to regard them with subtle hatred. "No one remembers," she answered simply, tearing her gaze away.

Nuulpha moved down a step as a heavy bolt slid back on the other side, and the door opened into the tunnel. A dim light oozed outward, mingling with Jesane's lantern to brighten the gloom. An emaciated, thinly bearded face, large eyes bulging from shrunken sockets, cheekbones stretching the sallow skin, peered around the door at them.

The Mouser caught his breath at sight of the corpse-like being, and his hand shot downward once again to grasp his sword.

Those large eyes fixed on the Mouser. A lipless gash of a mouth moved. "You got him."

Nuulpha nodded as he caught the edge of the door and opened it wider. "Yes, Mish, now let us in."

The man named Mish—for the Mouser saw that, indeed, it was only a man and not some litch or revenant—moved back beyond the door and took down a torch from a sconce on the wall. A small stool beneath the sconce suggested Mish had been waiting for them.

When they were all across the threshold, Nuulpha tugged the door closed and threw the iron bolt that sealed it shut. Jesane, visibly relaxing, set her lantern upon the stool and brushed a hand through her hair. The slightest of smiles turned up the corners of her mouth as she removed the quarrel from her crossbow, returned it to a small quiver on her hip, and uncocked the bowstring.

The Mouser watched her with new interest. That faint smile offered the first hint of her true beauty. Her hair shone like liquid gold as she bent to retrieve the lantern again.

Mish, with his torch, led the way up the corridor. Stone tiles formed the floor, and the walls, though ancient, glimmered smoothly under the flow of the light. Making a sharp right turn, then a left, they approached a solid wall—a seeming dead end. Undaunted, Mish put one foot against the lower left corner of the barrier and depressed a barely visible stone. A narrow section of the wall slid back.

Soft light, cook smells, and the sounds of voices spilled out. With widening eyes the Mouser stepped beyond the barrier into a vast chamber filled with slender white columns, each lit with a torch or lantern, and scores of people.

Unlacing her cloak with one hand, Jesane smiled as she greeted a gnarly old man whose only garment was a dirty loin-cloth. Bowing, obviously pleased to see her, he took her crossbow and held out his other hand for the black garment.

A small throng quickly gathered around them, but farther into the chamber more hung back, watching uncertainly. Men and women of varying ages, small children—most bore the marks and trappings of poverty and deprivation. Their faces were gaunt, and rags made their clothing. Some reclining on pallets strained weakly to raise up to see who had come from the tunnels. Others continued disinterestedly at small tasks.

Standing near the Mouser, Mish covered his mouth with a hand and suddenly coughed. Somewhere in the chamber, someone echoed him. A low moan followed that. In the farthest corner a child wept softly while a woman's weary voice cooed a quiet lullaby.

The Mouser caught Nuulpha's arm and gripped it, struck by the horror he saw before him. "Are they all sick?"

With stiffened jaw and clenched teeth, Nuulpha nodded. "This is Malygris's legacy."

The throng parted to reveal the new speaker, an old man with dark, glittering eyes under white, bushy brows, with a snowy, unkempt beard that covered his chin. Torchlight gleamed on his pale, shirtless torso, on blue-veined skin thin as parchment. He extended a hand; the fingers, gnarled and brittle as dead twigs, trembled.

Before him, the Mouser realized, stood the leader of this troubled band. Gently, he shook the offered hand as he stared into those dark eyes to see the power and wisdom they contained. "I think I have you to thank for my rescue," he said with a short bow.

The old man laughed. "Oh no!" he said. "You owe the corporal for that."

"Over drinks," Nuulpha reminded, grinning. "You promised me a great ballad if I ever hauled your fat out of Rokkarsh's dungeon. So when word spread through the garrison that a little man dressed all in gray had broken into and burned one of the Forbidden Towers, I saw my chance to be immortalized in song."

The Mouser grew suddenly glum. Fafhrd, not he, was the singer and composer of songs. Fafhrd would write a ballad worthy of Nuulpha. Of course, he'd make Jesane the centerpiece of it—that was Fafhrd. But it would be a song to make an audience laugh and applaud. The Mouser, himself, had no bardic skill, certainly none to match that of his northern companion.

"Where is your companion?" the old man asked suddenly, his gaze fixed steadfastly on the Mouser's face.

The Mouser glared sharply at the old man. Those dark, glittering eyes locked with his; a vague sense of vertigo washed over him, and for a moment he felt as if he might fall. They were wells, those eyes, deep yawning wells. The Mouser blinked and backed half a step.

"Who are you?" he murmured suspiciously.

The old man did not bow, but lowered his eyes politely. "I am called Demptha Negatarth," he answered.

"The jeweler on Temple Street?" the Mouser rubbed his chin. "I have heard of you, that you also dabble in sorcery."

Demptha Negatarth forced a tight smile as he held up his brittle, nearly fleshless fingers. "And so, like most others here, I have fallen victim to Malygris's legacy." Lowering one hand, he beckoned with the other for the Mouser to follow. "But you regard me suspiciously, wondering how I know of your friend. I could confess that Nuulpha told me, but in truth I think we have been expecting both of you for some time."

Jesane took his arm, and with feeble steps he led the way to the far side of the chamber, weaving carefully among the pallets, greeting the sick with small, reassuring nods. The Mouser stared at them, feeling a growing weakness in his stomach. Some were covered with sores and strange black patches. Many appeared wasted, starved. A man too weak to hold up his own head coughed bits of sputum and mucus while a tearful woman tried to soothe him.

Blackened samovars perched over pots of hot coals poured pungent, herb-flavored steam into the air.

"Parents," Demptha Negatarth whispered to the Mouser as he nodded toward an elderly couple who knelt laving water over a sweating younger man. He nodded to a man who smeared salve over a young woman's sores. "Relatives," he said. He paused to lay a sympathetic hand on the shoulder of woman who merely sat holding another woman's hand. "Friends," he whispered.

But the Mouser barely heard. A numbing cold shivered through him. Wrapped in a tiny blanket, a beautiful little girl-child slept fitfully, her skin pale in the lamplight, her brow beaded with droplets. A strand of blond hair clung wetly to one cheek. Tucked neatly in the crook of one arm, she held a familiar straw dolly.

"She has no one," Demptha Negatarth said, coming to his side. "We found her an hour ago unconscious in an alley. Perhaps we'll locate relatives in time."

"Or perhaps not?" the Mouser said grimly.

Again, Demptha turned that potent gaze upon the Mouser. "You know her?"

The Mouser shook his head, fighting the emotion that tried to choke him. "No," he answered. "She came into the Silver Eel a few nights ago selling dollies."

Nuulpha bent down beside the child for a closer look. "I remember," he said as he brushed the strand from her cheek and wiped her face with a corner of the blanket. "You bought them all—her poppets, she called them."

The Mouser's hands clenched into tight fists. "How can Rokkarsh turn his back on this? How can he turn a blind eye?"

Jesane spoke with surprising bitterness. "Since when did an Overlord, or any of the Great Families, give a damn for the common people and the poor?" She turned to the rest of the room, waving her arms as she shouted. "Be quiet, everyone! Be quiet! Listen!"

But for a muffled cough, the entire chamber grew silent.

As if from far away a softly merry music came. The play of pipes and the beat of a dumbek swelled, but distantly, then faded only to be replaced by lutes and tambourines and bells. Those, too, faded against the swell of laughter and voices and more music.

A hacking cough in the chamber set off a chorus of coughing. Someone began to cry, and someone else cooed gentle words of consolation.

Jesane turned back to the Mouser, her eyes burning with fury. "That is the Midsummer Festival above our heads. From hundreds of miles around, people are pouring into Lankhmar, bringing goods to trade, spending money, pouring untold wealth into city tills and coffers. But should word spread that a plague held sway in Lankhmar—festival or no festival, do you think they would come then?"

Nuulpha rose, his face appearing suddenly weary, his demeanor haggard. "Rokkarsh has turned no blind eye, my friend," he said. "People have been quietly disappearing in Lankhmar for some time. A few, we have brought down here to care for in hidden safety. More lie in the Overlord's secret lime pits far outside the city, and any who dare to hint or speak of a plague are swiftly seized. They, too, disappear."

Trembling with anger, Jesane raised a hand to her mouth, turned her head away, and coughed.

With a worried look, Demptha Negatarth took her hand in his and patted it. "Come, daughter. Rest awhile and have some broth. You've done enough this day."

"There's more to do," she said stubbornly, freeing her hand and brushing back her hair. Still, she allowed a tight smile. "But I'll take the broth."

The Mouser watched as she left them. A few paces away, she paused beside a column to speak to someone.

A shadow of a memory flitted through his mind—something in the juxtaposition of her silhouette beside that column. He tried to grasp it again, but ghost-like, it slipped away.

"Your daughter?" the Mouser said, turning back to Demptha Negatarth.

A deep grief settled over the old man's features. "Tainted by my magicks," he said in a voice thick with regret. "This illness has changed her, made her harder and stronger than most men. Yet, I am more proud of her than I have ever been."

The Mouser nodded, turning for one more glimpse of her. "Grief is nothing if not a sword," he said.

Demptha Negatarth tugged at the Mouser's sleeve. "Grief we have in plenty," he said, leading the Mouser again toward a long table at the farthest end of the chamber. "It is you, I think, who will provide the sword."

On the table lay a deck of Lankhmaran tarot cards. Two cards, separated from the rest, lay exposed faces up. As Demptha Negatarth gestured, the Mouser bent for a closer look.

"I believe they represent you and your comrade," Demptha Negatarth pronounced.

But the Mouser wasn't looking at the cards. He ran a hand along the table, and again memory flashed through his mind. He stared up at the low ceiling, listened with straining ears to the music from the street far above. Turning, the torches and lamps seemed to dim as he gazed around. He remembered the columns, remembered the music, the chamber. The table—he remembered alembics and decanters and phials, a red smoke.

Malygris.

"The Temple of Hates," he whispered.

Demptha Negatarth and Nuulpha regarded him queerly. "What?" the old man said.

"The Temple of Hates," the Mouser repeated, recalling all the details of his dream. "This is where it all began." He leaned on the table, eyes squeezed tightly shut as the dream washed over him again, and the others backed a step away, leaving him alone, as if afraid to interrupt something they didn't understand.

When it was over, when the dream passed, he opened his eyes again, but he saw nothing, nothing but the pair of cards in the center of that table where foul instruments once had set, where evil, midwifed by a madman, had sprung to writhing life.

Reaching out, he touched the cards. His own shadow threw a cloak of darkness over them, and he turned them toward the light until he could see them clearly.

Cards of vengeance—

Cards of retribution—

The Knight and Knave of Swords.

THIRTEEN

SHROUDCLOTH

From the depths of sleep's black ocean, Fafhrd floated slowly toward wakefulness. Pain throbbed in the back of his head, a distant awareness at first, a mere discomfort. It grew sharp and constant as it spread down the right side of his face. Even his teeth ached. He fought waking, tried to sink back into blissful unconsciousness. Pain buoyed him upward.

Opening one eye, he winced at the sunlight that streamed through an open window. With a low groan, wondering where the hell he was, he opened the other eye. Too quickly, he sat up.

A lightning bolt of pain shot through his skull, and a wave of disorientation seized him. For a moment, the room whirled. He clutched at the side of the bed in which he found himself. Fearful, confused, he squeezed his eyes shut and waited for the wave to pass. The pain subsided somewhat, and when he dared to open his eyes again, the room remained still.

He ran a palm over the colorful, finely pieced quilts that covered him as he took note of the thick feather mattress that made his bed. Seldom had so sumptuous an accommodation supported his head. Gilt-threaded embroidery decorated the pillow cases, and the sheets were of exquisite red silk.

The bed and all the room's furnishings betokened wealth. Plush carpets dyed a deep, royal blue covered the floor. Two matched intricately carved chairs fashioned from rare seahawk wood stood in opposite corners. A wardrobe and a desk, each of Quarmallian thorn-wood, stood against one wall.

Yet, a closer look revealed a fine patina of dust on the furnishings and carpets, and despite the open window, a vaguely stale odor lingered.

Fafhrd pushed back the blankets and carefully swung his legs over the bedside. The room began to spin ever so slightly, and he hesitated. Then, naked, he stood. Pain hammered the inside of his skull again. Raising a hand, he probed delicately at a goose-egg knot on the back of his head, wincing at the blood-crusted cut he found there.

He remembered the forbidden tower, the leeches and fire, falling. . . . Nothing beyond that. He scratched his chin, then his crotch, pompously pleased with himself that he had survived a plummet guaranteed to crack a lesser man open like an egg.

But where was he? Where, for that matter, was the Mouser?

With measured steps, he walked to the window, gaining confidence as the vertigo subsided. Leaning on the narrow sill, he peered out.

Below lay the ruins of a formal garden. Now weeds strangled the flower beds. Oranges, lemons, and persimmons hung brown and unpicked from untended fruit trees, or rotted on the ground. Flies and gnats swarmed. Marble fountains that once flowed with sweet water stood dry and stained, covered with bird shit and filth. Old leaves from the previous winter half-concealed the pebbled walkways while dead, broken limbs thrust up from the earth like old black bones.

From the trees hung rusted wind chimes and broken bells. When the breeze touched them, they played a plaintive, sad music—whisperings and murmurings of music, really—ghostly memories of once-happy melodies. The wind rose, yet they played quietly, as if ashamed that anyone might hear.

Fafhrd turned away, disturbed by the sight. Something stirred in his mind, a memory, some image. No, some dream. He turned back to the window. Peering out, a chill passed through him. He knew with a certainty where he was.

Once more, he turned, noting the bed, the red sheets, the carpets, the arrangement of the room.

Sadaster's bed. Sadaster's sheets.

Fafhrd swallowed hard, his throat suddenly dry. On that bed, Sadaster had slept, his wife in his arms. Through this window—Fafhrd jerked his hand away from the sill—had come Malygris's evil spell.

Fafhrd had seen it all in his dream. A renewed rage at Malygris's treachery filled him. Fear filled him, also, and set his heart to racing. How had he come here? What hand had brought him? Surely not the Mouser's.

Nudity caused him no shame, but an overwhelming sense of vulnerability propelled him toward the wardrobe in search of garments. Ignoring his headache, he flung open the thorn-wood doors and found his clothes neatly cleaned and hung on pegs fashioned in the shape of little hands.

"My lord!" a woman's high voice called behind him. "You should not be out of bed!"

Fafhrd whirled, and the room whirled with him. Unexpectedly, his vision blurred. He struggled to regain focus as he clutched one of the wardrobe's doors to keep his balance.

A young girl moved swiftly from the entrance and set a tray containing steaming bowls upon the thorn-wood desk. "My lord!" she cried again, alarm in her voice as she took his arm to steady him. "You are not yet well. Come, lie down."

The vertigo passed again, but Fafhrd let the girl slip her arm around his waist, and he put his arm around her shoulder. He dared not lean on her, though. Her head barely rose to his chest, and she was slender as a willow branch.

She looked up at him with a worried expression as she tried to steer him toward the bed. Her eyes were green as a cat's, her face round and white as the full moon. He ran a hand boldly through the black sweep of her hair.

She hesitated, as if sensing that he didn't need her help. Her gaze ran down his torso. A blush colored her cheeks. Averting her eyes, she stepped away. "My lord, you should get back in bed. Your poor head . . ."

Out of consideration for the girl, Fafhrd drew his black cloak out of the wardrobe and wrapped it around himself. "I'm not a superstitious man," Fafhrd interrupted. He reached for the rest of his clothes and, turning his back to the girl, began pulling them on under the cloak. "But I'm damned if I'll crawl willingly into a dead man's bed."

He glanced back at her suddenly, acutely aware of how silly he looked wiggling and struggling into his garments with only the cloak to screen him from her eyes. "It would be easier if you turned around," he suggested. "Who are you, anyway? How did I get here?"

The blush deepened on her cheeks as she turned quickly around. "I am Sameel," she answered. "My mistress will answer all your questions. If you feel well enough, I'll take you to her."

Fafhrd put his cloak back onto a peg long enough to draw on his tunic and lace his jerkin over it. "Is that hot gahveh I smell?" he said, casting his gaze toward the tray with its steamy bowls.

Sameel went to the thorn-wood desk and picked up a small bowl. "Most of these contain aromatic herbs to ease your slumber and speed healing," she answered. With a quick, nervous glance to assure herself that Fafhrd was decent, she carried the bowl to him. "But I brought gahvey to drink while I sat by your bedside. Please take it." She made a small curtsey as she offered it to him.

Draping the cloak over his right arm, Fafhrd took the cup with his left hand and drained half its contents. Satisfaction lit up his face, and he exhaled a dramatic sigh. "The nectar of the gods," he proclaimed. "Or it would be if the gods had any taste."

Sameel's face lit up. "I grow the beans myself, lord."

Taking a smaller sip, he smiled. "Now lead me to your mistress, Sameel," he said with a gracious bow, careful not to spill his precious beverage. For an instant, the room spun a little. Fafhrd righted himself and touched the tender place on the back of his head. A vaguely crooked grin flickered over his lips, and he added in a self-mocking tone, "But perhaps at not too swift a pace."

She led him from Sadaster's bedroom through a hallway made airy by numerous narrow windows that overlooked the once-beautiful garden. At the opposite end of that corridor stood a pair of tall double-doors ornately carved with figures of trees and flowers, birds and deer, and such.

Catching hold of gold knobs, Sameel pushed open the doors.

Fafhrd caught his breath, struck by two wonders at once.

Never had he seen so many books, nor even dreamed of so many! From floor to ceiling, books lined three walls. On a stand in one corner, a thick tome lay open. On a table in another corner stood more books neatly stacked. In all the rest of Lankhmar, an awestruck Fafhrd thought, there could not be so many books.

However, in the very center of the room, waited another, more mysterious wonder. Fafhrd moved a step closer, treading carefully upon the room's rich carpet with its lushly embroidered vines, flowers, and garden motifs to marvel at a silver sarcophagus, nine feet tall and fashioned in strange form.

Upon its polished front, the gleaming shape of a nude woman, eyes closed as if in slumber, emerged in carefully sculpted relief. Three pairs of graceful silver arms reached as if from behind the amazing box to modestly embrace her. The fingers of those hands clasped tightly over her breasts, her navel, her most private region.

No lid or seam showed to mar the perfect finish.

Fafhrd walked slowly around the device, admiring it. How it shimmered in the beam of sunlight that speared in through the only window!

Sameel knelt down before the carven figure. Her black hair spilled forward over one shoulder as she bent lower still to press her head upon the elaborately woven carpet. "Mistress?" she whispered.

A moment of silence passed as Fafhrd watched. Without warning, a metallic creak sounded. A single finger on the top-most pair of hands twitched. One by one the interlocked digits stirred to impossible life. The second pair of hands, then the lowest pair, also came alive, trembling and shifting eerily, as if unlimbering. Three sets of fingers wiggled eerily, creaking and groaning in a cacophony of straining metal.

Suddenly the hands let go of each other. Once more silence dominated. Then with a soft hiss of escaping air, a seam appeared down the front of the sarcophagus, and a feathery vapor leaked out.

"Aarth's blood," Fafhrd muttered, retreating a step as that pale fog glided upon the carpet and crept around his ankles. The hackles rose on the back of his neck.

"Do not fear," Sameel said, rising from her knees and stepping aside. Her gaze fixed expectantly on the silver construct.

Fafhrd gulped the last of his gahvey. Another loud metallic groan filled the room, and a narrow beam of white light lanced forth from the widening seam. Startled, Fafhrd let the empty cup fall from his hand. It shattered on the carpet. Embarrassed, he shot a glance toward Sameel, but the gleaming box held her rapt attention. Surreptitiously, he bent and picked up a jagged shard.

With that poor weapon, he prepared to greet the unexpected.

The sarcophagus yawned open, splitting in half. White fog spilled out in a rush, revealing the still form of a dark haired woman swathed from neck to foot in folds of white linen. A strip of the same material covered her eyes, and a chilly rime paled her red lips.

A vision of strange loveliness, Fafhrd thought, noting how regally the woman sat upon her narrow, cushioned chair. He stared, an odd sadness filling him. Death sat gently upon that perfect face, diminishing none of its beauty.

Off to one side, Sameel bowed again.

From within the sarcophagus, the woman spoke. "Welcome, son of Mor and Nalgron." An amused smile turned up the corners of her lips. "Be careful not to cut yourself with that piece of crockery."

Fafhrd's heart lurched as the corpse spoke. Then he realized the woman was not dead, as he had thought. Casting a brief glance at the shard he held, he wondered how she could have seen it through her blindfold. With an embarrassed shrug, he dropped it, brushed his hands with an exaggerated motion, and clutched them before him. "You have the advantage of me, Lady."

"I have not saved your life twice to take advantage of you, Northerner," she answered calmly. "I am Laurian . . ."

Surprise compelled Fafhrd to interrupt. "Sadaster's wife?" He took a step closer, peering at her face. Even through the mask of her blindfold he recognized her from his dream. "You say you've saved me twice?"

A delicate ivory hand rose from one of the chair's armrests. A slender finger slowly extended upward. Every motion Laurian made seemed unnaturally slow through the thin veil of mist that lingered about her. "Once," she said, "when thugs attacked you and your companion in the Carter Street Plaza."

Fafhrd stiffened, remembering tendrils of mist that had risen out of the night-fog to crush and strangle the Ilthmarts, who sought to kill both him and the Mouser. He noted with sudden nervousness the pale vapor that wafted about his feet, like a cat rubbing him as it wandered between and around his legs.

Laurian lifted a second finger. "Twice when you fell from the window of Malygris's tower." Her hand sank slowly back to the armrest. "Unfortunately, I acted too slowly and snatched you from midair. You struck my floor awkwardly with all your accumulated momentum. I apologize."

Fafhrd touched the goose-egg on the back of his head. "Not to sound ungrateful," he said, wincing, "but why save me at all? Of what interest to you can I be?"

"We shall be allies," Laurian answered. "I saw you in a dream, Fafhrd, and your friend the Mouser, too. I have watched for you, and watched out for you."

"Sheelba," Fafhrd muttered under his breath.

"Sheelba?" Laurian echoed. She looked thoughtful, as if searching her memory. Her gaze strayed past Fafhrd toward the bookshelves. "Yes, Sheelba of the Eyeless Face—one of the Transfigured, who are so steeped in magic that their bodies, their very souls have twisted into arcane shapes. Their ways are as unfathomable as the gods. Why do you speak of him?"

"Sheelba, sender of dreams," he answered with cryptic bitterness. "Sheelba the manipulator." He glared suddenly at the woman who claimed to be Sadaster's wife. Had she really saved his life? How could he trust her?

Her eyes. He must see her eyes. Then he would know the truth. "Take off your blindfold," he said. "Let me see through those windows into *your* soul."

A blue-veined hand lifted from the armrest. Fingers curled and clutched at silk, and the blindfold came away. Gripping the strip of cloth, the hand settled into a black silk lap. Laurian turned her face toward him.

Fafhrd froze inside as he stared at those sightless orbs. Only a hint of color remained in the irises, but pools of thin red blood floated in the large whites. "You really are blind," he said in a voice suddenly regretful.

"Malygris's spell," she said stonily. "It killed my husband. It is killing me."

"You were not a sorceress in my dream," Fafhrd said.

Laurian laughed bitterly. "Indeed. I was but a pampered wife deeply in love with a man who gave me everything I wanted. And all I wanted were flowers and fruit trees, chimes to sing in the wind, fountains and pebbled walkways—a perfect garden in which to sit in the sunshine with Sadaster's head in my lap while I read poetry to him and stroked his brow."

Laurian's hands clutched the armrests of her chair. Slowly, with great effort showing on her face, she pushed herself up and stood. The veils of mist inside the sarcophagus swirled lightly about her as she pressed her hands together, the blindfold trailing from her fingers.

"Malygris made a grave mistake when he killed Sadaster," she said. With one frail hand, she gestured around. "He left me alive with my husband's magnificent library and a heart full of hatred."

Fafhrd felt a chill pass over his heart. "You studied magic, knowing the consequences," he said.

She laughed again. "I immersed myself in it," she answered with defiant anger. "Sadaster meant everything to me. I watched him rot day after day while he struggled uselessly to find a counter-measure to Malygris's evil curse . . ." She pressed a palm to her head and stopped suddenly, trembling, as if unable to continue.

"I would walk through hell," she said at last in a quieter, more controlled voice, "challenge Death, himself, in the Shadowland to strike Malygris down for his crime." With a weary sigh, she sank into her chair, positioned her arms on the rests, and leaned her head back. "I am too weak. Knowledge I have, and power, but too little. And only my shroudcloth keeps me warm now."

Laurian's voice trailed away, and her head turned a little as if she had fallen asleep. Fafhrd watched her, uncertain of what he should do. Wait? Leave? He still had unanswered questions. He studied her face, so beautiful but for her ravaged eyes and the faintest lines of grief etched across her brow.

He found himself admiring Laurian. Love and vengeance, and the desperations to which they drove a person, were things he understood well. He thought of his own Vlana. Had he not stormed Thieves' House with all its traps and horrors to slay the thrice-cursed sorcerer, Hristomilo, who had killed Fafhrd's one true love?

He looked with a potent sympathy upon Laurian, who dared to claim Sadaster's magic for herself, caring not if Malygris's spell claimed her life so long as she found the power to take that hated wizard in the bargain. Fafhrd nodded approvingly.

Aye, he understood Sadaster's widow.

Sameel nudged his arm and offered him another cup of steaming gahvey. He accepted with surprise, unaware that the girl had slipped from the library and returned. Her moist gaze settled upon Laurian as she passed the cup into his hands.

"My mistress is dying," she whispered sadly. "Only the box sustains her life force, and in it she lingers, seeing beyond sight, hearing beyond hearing, pursuing her vengeance. I fear her time is short."

As if waking, Laurian's head snapped forward. "I am not dead yet, child," she said.

Fafhrd held his cup without drinking. "How is it that you see?" he asked.

Lifeless eyes turned his way. "The mist and the fog tell me things," she answered, waving a hand with slow grace, setting the mist that yet lingered in the sarcophagus to swirling. "We are great friends, the fog and I. The fog touched you in the street, and the one you call the Mouser. It overheard you and whispered to me that you also seek Malygris." A hard smile turned up the corners of her mouth. "And by my dream I knew that I could trust you. The enemy of my enemy. . . . I'm sure you've heard."

Fafhrd sipped his beverage. "Has the fog told you where to find Malygris?"

"I've found several of his hiding places," Laurian answered, her hands curling into small fists, "but never Malygris, himself."

"I can sense your disappointment," Fafhrd said, attempting a bit of levity while he considered. "I thought that Malygris loved you. In my dream, he slew Sadaster out of jealousy."

Laurian's face reddened. "I met the fool but one time, Northerner—at the celebration of my engagement to Sadaster. He and my husband once were friends. In his warped mind, he fancies that he's loved me ever since, and that only some black spell of Sadaster's kept me from returning that love."

Fafhrd shrugged as he took another sip of the hot, strong-tasting beverage. Beneath his calm demeanor, his thoughts churned with schemes and possibilities. "Still," he said slowly as he fingered the rim of his cup, "sometimes the simplest plans are best. Have you invited him over for gahvey?"

Laurian started. "What?"

"He's a man, isn't he?" Fafhrd said, raising his cup in a mock-toast. "Open your window, wave a hanky, and call yoo-hoo." Fafhrd quickly swallowed the rest of his gahvey and handed the cup back to Sameel. "Trust me," he added. "If he's in love, he'll come."

Laurian touched a fingertip softly to her lips as she considered. "I could set traps, magical snares . . ."

Fafhrd interrupted. "Just stick a knife in him."

Laurian froze, her mouth half-open, facing Fafhrd as if she actually saw him. "Have I been such a fool?" she whispered disbelievingly. "Could it be so easy?"

"It's never easy to knife a man," Fafhrd answered gravely, "no matter how much you hate him. That's why I'll be hiding behind a curtain with a sword." He clapped a hand to his side

where Graywand should have been, abruptly remembering—
he'd lost it in the Tower of Koh-Vombi. He looked up sheepishly. "I seem to have misplaced my weapon."

". . . right into my very bedchamber," Laurian ruminated,
murmuring to herself. She paused again, then she gestured toward her handmaiden. "Sameel, fetch Sadaster's sword."

Obediently, the girl hurried from the room.

"You will have my husband's sword, Northerner," she said,
her voice firm with determination. "But do not doubt. If
Malygris proves fool enough to walk into my home, it will be
my dagger that drinks his heart's blood."

Fafhrd paced to the open window and stared outward. In the
distance, Rhan's spire rose above all the rooftops of Lankhmar.
Behind it, the sun sank slowly toward the horizon. Soon darkness would fall.

Where, he wondered, was the Mouser?

"Dagger or sword," Fafhrd said quietly, vaguely troubled by
the impending night. "It matters not, so long as I have a drop of
that blood."

"A gruesome request," Laurian said. Then she spoke a name
as if it were a question. "Sheelba?"

Fafhrd nodded, his back to her. His gaze still upon the horizon, he covered his mouth with a fist and allowed the small
cough he had been resisting. A chill and a shiver of dread rattled
through him. Squeezing his eyes shut briefly, he mastered himself. Now was not a time for fear.

Realizing Laurian had not seen his nod, he explained. "With
that last ingredient Sheelba can cast the counter-spell to end this
nightmare Malygris has dreamed for us."

Laurian's voice softened again as she leaned back within her
silver sarcophagus. "A counter-spell?" She sighed as she tied the
white linen blindfold once more over her ravaged eyes. "Then
more than vengeance will guide my blade. Lankhmar is my city,
and I know the suffering of its people."

With a second sigh, she folded her fragile hands upon the shroudcloth that draped her lap, and her head sagged forward upon her bosom.

Fafhrd moved around the room again to face her. Once more, she seemed to sleep. No matter how he tried to deny it, a troublesome fear grew within him. He whispered a question. "Why didn't you bring the Mouser, too?"

Laurian did not stir. Even the thin mist that surrounded her seemed to hold perfectly still.

Fafhrd repeated, strangely unable to raise his voice. Did he want her to hear? Did he want an answer?

"She dared not snatch your friend," Sameel said, standing nervously behind him. In her hands she carried a magnificent great-sword in an elegantly crafted leather scabbard. "She had only strength enough for one of you. And your friend has not yet been touched by Malygris's curse."

Fafhrd's mouth went dry. He stared at Sameel's moistening eyes, reading the fear and uncertainty he suddenly saw in those limpid green pools. Groping beyond his own uncertainty, his heart went out to her. "You, too?"

Wordless, she nodded.

A cold anger filled Fafhrd, and his hand went to the sword. He curled his fingers around its hilt. It fit his grip as if it had been made for him. Grimly, he drew the blade. Streaming through the window, the last sunlight touched the keen edge with a glittering fire.

Red fire, Fafhrd thought, turning the sword in the light— deep and rich as the color of blood.

FOURTEEN

PIECES OF DREAMS, NIGHTMARE SHARDS

F afhrd slipped naked between the sheets of Sameel's bed and eased his head carefully down upon the pillow. The vertigo troubled him less than before, and the constant hammering inside his skull had eased somewhat. Still, he saw the wisdom of resting a while. Later, he would rise, go out and search for the Mouser.

Turning on his side, his gaze fell upon his new sword, which leaned against a chair where his clothes were hung. Sameel's room had no windows, and the lambent flame from an oil lamp lent the polished black pommel stone a starlight glow.

Sameel entered the room quietly, bearing another tray of fresh herbs and steaming bowls. Noting the direction of his gaze, she said, "My master called the sword, *Payday.*"

"I'll name it Graywand," Fafhrd said, "as I name all my swords."

"Why is that?" Sameel asked. Setting down the tray, she crumbled herbs and scattered them in varying portions over the bowls. Immediately a sweet aroma perfumed the air.

He closed his eyes for a brief moment, and the face of his father floated in his mind—dark eyes, sweeping hair as red as Fafhrd's own, a handsome visage clouded by a melancholy and regret that Fafhrd had never understood.

"To honor Nalgron," he said, opening his eyes again, speaking as if to the sword itself. "After his fatal fall on White Fang Mountain, I inherited his sword, which he called Graywand. An uncle presented it to me when I was only a small boy." He paused and crooked one arm under his head. "But my mother, Mor, despised my father. Fearing I would grow to be just like him, she took the sword, broke the blade, and ordered the pieces melted."

Old memories washed over him, and he imagined at that moment that his face looked not unlike the clouded, brooding face of his father. "When I grew old enough to claim my own blade," he continued, "I gave it the name of my father's sword to remember him—but also to spite my mother. And every sword I've owned since that day I've named Graywand."

With a long piece of straw she took flame from the lamp and lit a small candle beneath a slender copper samovar. "I never knew my parents," she said softly. "Laurian found me living in the streets when I was very small and took me in." She hesitated, holding the straw's flame close so that it uplit her face. Then she blew it out. "Sometimes in my dreams, I see the shadow of a face that might have been my mother." She shook her head. "But I don't know."

Fafhrd watched her as she bent over the tray again and crumbled some herbs into a delicate white kerchief. Lamplight and gloom played about the soft lines and curves of her body, lending her an aura of mystery and beauty Fafhrd had not noticed before. He rose up on one elbow, the better to observe her.

Folding the kerchief carefully, she turned from the tray and approached the bed. "Breathe these fragrances," she said, sitting down on the edge of the bed's wooden frame. "They will ease your pain."

Sameel lifted the pomander to his nose, but Fafhrd caught her wrist. Though she stiffened, she did not pull away. Their eyes met. For a long moment neither moved, and the only sound came from the soft sputtering of the lamp and the candle. Without taking his eyes from hers, Fafhrd drew her hand and the pomander closer. As he breathed in the woodsy aroma, he lightly kissed her fingertips, and when she did not protest, he drew her gently down beside him.

He shifted position, drawing her closer as he unfastened the brooches that held her simple dress upon her shoulders. She trembled against him. "I've never . . ." She bit her lip, her eyes brimming with tears. She squeezed them shut. "My lord, I don't want to die without tasting love."

Fafhrd shushed her, putting a finger upon her lips as he gazed down upon her frightened beauty. "Death has no business here tonight," he whispered, stroking her cheek, "nor any thought of Malygris, or curses."

Easing aside her dress, he drew the sheet over their bodies. Again he hesitated, studying Sameel's face, noting the play of the light in the tears that hung upon her lashes. She was not Vlana, not his one true love, but he saw within her something rare and special, something courageous in the face of a terrible fear—and for that moment, at least, he loved her.

In her sarcophagus, Laurian saw with a sight beyond vision. Nothing transpired in her home of which she was not aware. She felt in her mind and heart, like a tide on her skin, the waves of emotion emanating from her guest and her handmaiden. Simultaneously she experienced joy for Sameel and intense sorrow for the loss of her own beloved.

The ornate box cracked open, and the strange fog, her constant companion, seeped about the darkened library. It radiated a faint, yellowish light. In that glow, Laurian rose weakly. For an instant, she hesitated, summoning her courage and strength. Then she stepped from the sarcophagus. A moment of uncertainty and dread shivered through her. Immediately a cold determination replaced it.

The fog seemed to cushion her footfalls. Soundlessly, she glided across the floor and pushed open the library doors. Her blind gaze turned down the hall that led to Sadaster's room. An ache filled her heart, and beneath the blindfold, her eyes misted. Steeling herself, she blinked back the threatening tears and moved, instead, in the opposite direction toward her own suites.

The fog that accompanied Laurian swirled ahead, played over the knobs, and opened the doors for her. In its unnatural light, she entered her room with its clutter of treasures, whose value could be weighed only in memories—small figurines, delicate pillows embroidered with bright-dyed thread, trinkets, pieces of jewelry, and vases of colored glass, precious gifts all, tokens of Sadaster's love and their years together.

A fine layer of dust covered everything. Waving a hand carefully over a table near the door, she found the remains of a single dead rose, drew it from its vase, and hugged it to her heart. It crumbled to pieces. The brittle petals fell from her fingers to the carpet. Another wave of sadness washed over her. Drawing a deep breath, she groped toward a thorn-wood chest at the foot of her bed. The hinges of the heavy lid creaked as she opened it.

Folded neatly within lay her wedding trousseau. Despite her resolve, tears came freely now, saturating her blindfold, leaking down from the edges of the cloth. With loving care, she lifted the items and spread them upon the bed. Then, she removed her blindfold, unwrapped the swaths of pale linen from about her body, and dropped them upon the floor.

One by one, she pulled on her wedding garments. The underskirts rustled crisply, and the white dress glittered with diamond chips sewn into the weave. She ran her hands over it, smoothing the folds and creases, pleased to find it fit her as perfectly as on that distant day when Sadaster took her for his wife. Setting the sheer veil over her head and face, she fixed it in place with a silver circlet that blazed with sapphires.

Slowly, she closed the trunk and approached a nearby table. Among the many trinkets sat a small chest. Opening it, she groped among strands of pearls, rings, and silver chains, pins and brooches, and lifted a slender dagger in a jewel-encrusted sheath. Carefully she inserted it beneath a tight-fitting sleeve.

Tears ceased; her mouth drew into a tight, determined line.

Returning to the library, she sat down once more upon her velvet-cushioned chair. A soft sigh escaped her lips as she put a hand beneath the veil. Touching her face, she explored fine new wrinkles, and old ones that had deepened, and skin that had lost its softness—the price she paid for leaving her elaborate sarcophagus.

Closing her blind eyes, she gathered her strength and planned magic. The night exhaled a soft breath, sending a wind that blew through the open window and fluttered the pages of a book on a table. When the wind ceased, silence and stillness dominated the room.

Laurian rested, letting her head roll back against the chair. Patience, she had learned, was sorcery's paramount virtue. The mist that perpetually filled her sarcophagus caressed her like a soothing friend, coolly kissed her, reassured her with its presence. When she lifted her head again, it spread itself before her feet.

Once more, Laurian turned her inner sight upon her handmaiden and her guest. Their tender coupling touched her heart as the fervency of their passion suffused her home and filled it with a radiance only she could see. With tender care, not wishing to disturb them, she distilled the essence of their desire and collected it as a fine moisture in her cupped hands. Then, leaning forward, she shook the glimmering droplets into the mist, which rose up and seemed to lick her fingers.

"Go," she whispered.

Over the carpet the mist flowed, turning gray and thick as it oozed out the window and poured down the side of her house, thicker still as it crawled across the lawn and climbed the wall to reach the street.

Not far away, the fog that hovered upon the waters of the River Hlal turned toward the shore. Thickening, it engulfed the ships moored at the docks, swallowed the wharves, poured eastward into the city. In the north, more fog moved in from the Inner Sea, extinguishing the street lamps that lit the roads in the Nobles' District, obscuring the lights of the Rainbow Palace as it drifted inexorably southward.

Fafhrd cradled Sameel's head on his arm and stroked her throat lightly. Lying on her back, gazing toward the ceiling, she caught his hand and entwined her fingers with his. Her expression, so recently filled with rapture, reflected a thoughtful worry, and when she spoke her words seemed tiny and distant.

"Do you fear the decay in our bodies?"

Fafhrd sat up and swung his legs out of bed, turning his back to her. "No," he said in a quiet voice.

Sitting up, Sameel hugged her knees. "I guess I'm not as brave as you."

The lamp flame glimmered steadily, and the samovar sighed as it poured out a soft, fragrant steam. He stared into the shadowy corners of the room where the small light did not reach, as if the darkness might somehow show him his future.

"Malygris's curse won't have the chance to rot me," he said grimly. "His heart's blood contains the cure, and I'll kill him to obtain it. Or he'll kill me. Either way . . ."

Sameel put a hand on his back. "I try to be brave," she said as if she hadn't heard him. "But I remember my master, how thin and weak he grew, and I see myself in a corpse's skin, struggling against the grave."

"It's all right to be afraid," Fafhrd said softly, turning to take her in his arms. "There's no courage without fear, girl." He drew her closer still, his heart hammering as he warmed himself in the fire of her body. Suddenly he buried his face in her hair. "I lied. I am afraid."

She laid her head upon his shoulder. "But you're also brave, my lord."

Her words calmed him. Sitting up, he composed himself and kissed the top of her head. He was a man of the north, and a warrior, he reminded himself, and it was Sameel who needed protection and reassurance.

His right hand cupped a bronze-colored nipple, and a grin turned up the corners of his mouth. "This doesn't feel like the skin of a corpse," he said.

She laughed lightly and slipped a small hand down his belly. "I think something is rising from its grave."

They fell back onto the bed and into each other's arms once more.

Fog rolled through the streets of Lankhmar, veiling the city in white. Down silent roads it poured, into alleyways, into the parks and city squares, swallowing whole blocks, entire districts.

In Pinchback Alley, a rat-catcher in pursuit of a fine black rodent felt the feathery touch of cool mist on his neck. Fog swirled around him. Squeaking, the rat scampered to freedom. The rat-catcher shrugged and turned toward home, his thoughts suddenly full of his wife, who waited for him.

The fog enwrapped the Spire of Rhan, concealing it from view. The five-storied Temple of Aarth sank beneath the tide of a gray sea. The great silos in the River District bowed away behind a misty curtain.

A carriage moved northward on Gold Street, its way lit by lanterns swinging on either side of the driver's seat. Within, a merchant's wife sat trembling, biting her lip as she peered out the carriage window, horrified by a strange and unnatural desire for her young son, who sat on the seat beside her.

Silently, the fog moved into the Garden of Dark Delights, enfolding the elaborate topiaries, obscuring the pebbled pathways. In a secluded place, two late-night philosophers shared a marble bench. The conversation turned gradually, seemingly naturally, from Kleshite theories of celestial mechanics to the finer points of Tovilyan erotic poetry.

The fog continued southward and eastward.

While quiet dominated much of the city, the sounds of music and drunkenness rose throughout the Festival District. Night brought no cessation to the weeklong midsummer celebration. Arm in arm, couples staggered from one crowded tavern to another. Some purchased bottles from temporary shops that wine merchants had erected in the streets. Dancers and jugglers, mimes and acting troupes entertained on every corner. Musicians strolled the lanes, serenading at the tops of their lungs to be heard over the din.

Countless lanterns lined the streets, hung from posts by the city planners. More lanterns burned above the entrances to businesses that remained open. Tall torches provided flaming light for the scores of performing stages.

One by one, the fog devoured them all.

Undaunted, the celebrants continued. But now, the plays went ignored. Musicians cast aside their instruments, and jugglers abandoned their props. Couples stumbled into alleys to grope each other's bodies. Some crawled beneath the stages and beer wagons. Some fell upon each other in the streets, trusting to the fog to conceal their lusts.

Men and women, men and men, women and women. In-hibitions melted. A pair rose suddenly upon a stage to dem-onstrate their prowess. A female pick-pocket of exceptional skill pilfered one man's purse as she slaked another man's de-sires.

Throughout the district, tavern doors stood wide open. The silent fog slipped inside. Wherever a window gaped, or a shutter hung open, wherever a crack in a wall allowed, or an unpatched hole in a roof, the fog slipped in.

High atop the Tower of Koh-Vombi, in the shadows of the par-apet, Malygris studied the heavens, noting the descent of the evening star, Astarion, on the western horizon, and the ascent of bright Shadah in the east. Overhead, Akul burned like an em-erald. In the north, the Targe constellation, with its seven vivid points of light, slowly turned.

Vaguely troubled, he raised one spidery hand to rub his chin and waited for Midsummer's Moon to rise. Its shape and posi-tion in relation to Shadah would determine his next move. He set his hand upon the parapet and quickly jerked it back, frowning in disgust at the crusted bird shit that covered the an-cient stone. It covered the rooftop, too, and within, the very rafters dripped with it.

If the moon rose precisely where he calculated, and if he could draw a straight line from it, through Shadah, to Akul, then he would gather his power and leave this crumbling place. He had long ago grown tired of its filth, its mysteries, and the incessant monotonous whispering of its damnable ghosts driving him to annoyance.

For months the tower had provided him shelter and safe hiding, as the stars had promised it would. He had walked care-fully in a dangerous place, drawing no attention to himself, avoiding rooms and objects best left undisturbed, respecting whatever ancient god once had dwelled here.

Now, however, invaders had breached his security through the only window and from below through a tunnel previously unknown to him, and damn near roasted him alive! Fortunately, finding little to feed on, the flames had extinguished themselves without seriously damaging the tower. Or perhaps the gods and ghosts of this place had stopped the fire.

But the invaders, what was he to make of them? Most, by their liveries, he knew for soldiers and men of the Overlord. The other two, the warrior-thieves, he knew not. He remembered a snatch of conversation he had overheard from the shadows.

"Malygris doesn't seem to be home," the short gray one had said.

They had come seeking him, those two. To what end? In whose service?

And what part did the ruler of Lankhmar play?

Too many questions and no answers.

He dared not set magical protections on the tower. Such might anger the spirits of this place. Certainly it would betray him to the wizards and sorcerers he knew were seeking him— might as well send a beacon of light up into the darkness.

No, it was best to change his hiding place. He waited only for the moon and the stars to verify his judgment.

But glancing up, he frowned. A thin veil of mist dimmed the stars. He shot a look toward the river, and his heart quailed. A thick white fog crawled over the banks, swallowing ships, wharves. The fishing district faded from sight, and still it came on, unstoppable.

One by one, the stars vanished. The fog advanced, approaching his tower, swallowing everything in its path. Malygris cried aloud in despair and thrust out his hands as if to hold back the massive tide. It swept around him, soft and warm as breath.

Cursing, he flung up the roof's trap door and descended into a large, round room, the tower's uppermost. A dozen candles illuminated the chamber. A crude pallet marked the place where he slept.

A small stack of books and parchments lay scattered around it. Tiny pieces of down drifted in the air, and scattered about the floor lay small bones and the plucked corpses of raw, half-eaten birds.

Malygris waved a hand under his nose, silently cursing the thick smell of smoke that pervaded the air. He paced nervously back and forth. An overwhelming sense of danger buzzed like a wasp in the back of his head. Chewing his lip, he began to gather his books, which, like everything else, smelled of smoke. From hiding place to hiding place he had carried them, his few treasures, and now they were nearly ruined with the horrible reek. Dumping them disgustedly on his blanket, he tied the corners and shouldered the bundle.

Then, slowly he set it down again.

A strange feeling of calm settled over him. He turned back to the steps that led through the trap door to the roof, climbed them. The door, so old and rarely used, hung warped and swollen upon its horizontal jamb. He had neglected to close it carefully. Wisps of vapor floated at its edges where one corner gapped. It mattered nothing to him. Pushing the door back, he ascended and stepped out into the white night.

The fog reduced Lankhmar's skyline to a few ghostly silhouettes. In the thick mist that drifted through the air, the distorted shapes of towers and minarets seemed to waver. The nearest rooftops appeared and disappeared as the thinnest of breezes stirred the currents.

Staring northward from the parapet, Malygris felt a rush of joy. He whispered a name. "Laurian."

The fog quivered as if in response, white as Laurian's skin, soft as the body of the woman Malygris loved. He closed his eyes as he thought of her. Was it her perfume he smelled riding on the vapor? Her cool touch that brushed, delicate as a feather, over his face and throat?

His eyes snapped open, and he chided himself. Why was he hiding? Sadaster was dead, and—however inadvertently—most

of Lankhmar's mages with him. What mattered if his greatest
working had somehow gone awry? He was still Malygris, and
the city feared him.

"Laurian," he whispered again as he gazed longingly in the
direction of her house. He licked his lips. Her name in his
mouth tasted sweet as honey. His heartbeat quickened with a
building desire.

He had allowed her time—a proper period to mourn and to
forget her husband. A year this very night since the Great
Casting of his spell, and six months since Sadaster's funeral. The
time for mourning was over.

He clutched his fists, shivering inside even as his skin seemed
to burn, and his mind churned with thoughts of love. Out of
courtesy, he had denied himself long enough. No longer would
he wait to claim his heart's desire.

Forgetting all else, he climbed the parapet and plunged
head-first over the side. But he did not fall. Spider-like, he
crawled down the side of the ancient tower, defying nature.
Even the mist seemed to recoil in revulsion from the scuttling
shape he made on the crumbling black stone. Once he paused,
and his head jerked back and forth as he surveyed the empty,
fog-bound streets. When he reached the ground, he laughed
softly.

The fence that surrounded the tower offered no greater challenge. Climbing it, he strode up Nun Street and into the heart
of the River District. Even in the fog, he knew the way to her
estate. In his mind, in his heart, in his dreams he had made this
trip a thousand times, a groom going to claim his bride.

On the street-side of a white wall, he stopped. Again, his gaze
swept cautiously up and down the misty avenue. No sign of life,
not even a sound. The fog smothered everything. He might
have been walking through a dead city.

A leer that resembled a snarl curled his lips. Considering the
power and effect of his Great Casting, the analogy was apt.

Employing his peculiar talent, he climbed the wall and scuttled down the other side to stand within Sadaster's estate.

Through one window only, a light shone. That lonely amber beam spilled down through the limbs of dead lemon and orange trees, through the twisted and brittle branches of lifeless rose bushes, to weave upon the ground a shadowy webwork that spread throughout the ruined garden.

Malygris drew himself erect. Boldly, he strode forward, crushing old mint and juniper under his tread, scattering old leaves, brushing aside the limbs. A sense of triumph filled him. Reaching the house, he looked up again at that window, whose shutters were thrown wide in invitation. In a matter of moments he crouched upon the sill.

His heart soared! In the center of the room in which he found himself, stood all his dreams and hopes fulfilled. Breath caught in his throat, and his heart hammered.

The lamplight played with dazzling effect upon the diamonds in the folds of white that draped his bride. Veiled, Laurian turned toward him and lifted her arms.

"I've been waiting for you," she said, silken-voiced. "Come, and receive my Wedding Vow."

Malygris sprang forward, passion burning in his blood, desire expelling all reason. Laurian's arms went around him, and he caught the edge of her veil, seeking the taste of her lips.

"Receive now, my Wedding Vow," she said as he drew the concealing cloth from her face.

Malygris gasped as she turned her eyes upward. Horror surged through him—he saw his own handiwork in those blind, blood-specked orbs. He tried to recoil, but her arms tightened about him. A sharp pain lanced into his back. Screaming, he pushed her away. "What . . . ?"

"My dagger," Laurian hissed, brandishing the bloodied blade. Droplets of red splattered upon her shimmering dress. "I named it for the occasion." She threw herself at him, catching his garments with a determined grip. With all her force she drove the blade upward. "Now receive it again!"

In Sameel's bed, Fafhrd rose suddenly up on his elbows, pleasure forgotten, as a shrill scream reverberated in the corridors. Before he could react, a second and higher-pitched shriek followed.

Sameel's eyes widened with fear. "Mistress!" she cried.

Instantly, Fafhrd threw back the sheets and sprang to the floor. Grabbing his sword with one hand and his breeches in the other, he flung open the door and raced for the library on the upper story.

Launching himself up the marble stairs, taking them two and three at a time, he tripped on the topmost step, fell heavily, and rolled to his feet again, leaving his garment behind. Down the hall he ran with Laurian's scream still echoing in his ears, straight for the library.

Fafhrd smashed through the ornate doors and whipped Sadaster's sword from its sheath.

A ragged, shriveled figure bent over Laurian's half-prone form, fingers locked and squeezing her throat as he cursed her with incoherent snarls. Blood spattered Laurian's white dress. Even as she gurgled for desperate breath, she beat one fist at her attacker's face and groped with the other hand for a dagger just inches beyond her reach.

Thin tendrils of fog, reaching in through the window, curled about the invader's waist, one arm, an ankle. Another snaked about his neck. Quivering and weak, they tried to drag the man off Laurian, but he resisted with a hideous strength, tightening his deadly grip.

Fafhrd screamed his challenge as he leaped to Laurian's rescue. "Malygris!"

The wizard's head snapped up. An animal-like growl issued from a thin mouth. Dark eyes gleamed with a horrible power.

Shrugging off the gray tendrils that sought to hold him, he rose to meet Fafhrd. "Another man in your house already?" he raged at Laurian. "Unfaithful whore!"

As Fafhrd charged across the carpet, his senses unexpectedly whirled. The embroidery beneath his feet moved strangely, and the pattern shifted. Impossibly, the stylized vines and creepers woven into the rug assumed three-dimensions and rose up to thwart his attack.

Like some monstrously camouflaged man-eating plant, the carpet came to life. With a startled cry, Fafhrd swung the huge sword, slashing left and right. For every vine he cut, two more lashed at him. Serpent-like, they struck at his face, at his eyes, constricted his chest, tried to crush the breath from him. Coils ensnared his legs and sought to topple him.

Heart pounding with fear and fury, he caught a slender shoot as it looped about his neck. With all his might, he ripped it away. A sticky ichor filled his palm, ran down his arm. It burned his skin!

Malygris laughed harshly, his visage a frightening mask of anger, hatred, and pain. Turning his bloody back to Fafhrd, he bent over Laurian once more. Weakly, she dragged herself the few inches across the floor and reached for the dagger. Malygris pushed it away with a slippered toe. Then he began to throttle her once more, slowly and with relish.

"Leave her alone!" Fafhrd shouted, winning a few steps' progress into the room through the murderous jungle that assailed him. Vines whipped up immediately to encase his thighs, his waist. "Damn you to hell!"

Malygris showed no concern. "I am in hell already," he answered with grim savagery. "Without love, without hope, without Laurian."

The snap of bones filled the room. Laurian's eyes opened wide, then a sigh escaped her parted lips, and her feeble resistance ended.

"No!" Sameel streaked into the library. "I'll kill you! I'll kill you!" she cried hysterically. The vines and creepers that filled the air seemed oblivious to her presence. Before Malygris could react, she tackled the wizard, knocking him to the floor.

In her hands, she held Fafhrd's bunched breeches. Riding Malygris's back, she wrapped the leggings around his head, blinding him, choking him. At the same time, she struggled to reach Laurian's dagger.

Ensorceled vines and branches recoiled back into the carpet. Fafhrd grunted in surprise, suddenly freed, but wasted no time questioning the how or why. Raising his sword, he lunged forward. Now, with a stroke, he would avenge Laurian and Sadaster, and claim the drop of heart's blood that would end this madness.

Sheelba had sent him on an errand of cold-blooded murder, but leaping past Laurian's body, his blood ran very hot, indeed.

Before he could strike, however, Malygris rose. With little more than a shrug, he flung Sameel backward directly into Fafhrd's path. Whirling about, he clawed the breeches from his head.

Dark fire flared in the pits of his eyes. Again, the carpet's pattern came to life.

"Don't look at his eyes!" Sameel cried, throwing herself at the wizard again.

Malygris batted her aside with the back of his hand, sending her crashing into the silver sarcophagus. As she sagged to the floor, he glared at Laurian's body and backed warily toward the open window.

Fafhrd fought the vines again as they sought to entangle him. But Sameel's outcry rang in his ears, and suddenly he understood. "Illusions!" he cursed. "Here's a trick for you, monster!"

He flung the sword with all his strength, straight for Malygris. But the wizard dived headfirst through the window. The blade flashed through the space where only an instant before he had stood. The point bit deep into the woodwork, quivering. For a moment it protruded there, then fell to the carpet.

Malygris's mad spell dissolved again. Fafhrd snatched up his sword and leaned out the window. Halfway down the wall, clinging to the side of the house like an insect, Malygris looked up and snarled.

"Naked fool! I am not done with you!"

Fafhrd hawked and spat. The wad of saliva splashed on Malygris's bald head. Without a word, he catapulted over the sill and landed in a crouch on the ground directly below the wizard.

"Then come down and have done with me!" he called angrily, all fear gone now. Only the desire for vengeance boiled in his heart.

But Malygris refused to descend. With his strange talent, he crawled sideways upon the house, seeking escape around the corner. Fafhrd ran after him, leaping high and swinging his sword. Malygris climbed toward the roof out of range.

Drops of blood splattered the dead grass below him. Fafhrd noted the spoor with a grim nod. Laurian had struck a blow, at least. Fafhrd determined to make his own mark.

Keeping one eye on the wizard's position, he shot a look around the garden. A ring of dirty white stones made a border around a withered rose bush. Driving the point of his sword into the earth, Fafhrd tore up two rocks the size of his fists.

"Hey, spider-face!" he called. Malygris paused at the very roof edge and foolishly looked back.

The first stone impacted the side of the house, cracking the stucco and causing a shower of plaster. The second struck Malygris's elbow.

The wizard howled in pain, an inhuman sound that chilled Fafhrd's blood, yet pleased him bitterly. He bent to snatch up another stone, but when he drew back to throw it, Malygris had achieved the roof. His shadowy form melted into the dark-tiled background.

Grabbing his sword, Fafhrd ran with his rock through the garden to the opposite side of the house, ready to continue the battle. Squinting, breathing furiously, he scrutinized the gutters, the roof summit, the walls, the grounds. Then he ran back to the other side again.

With a curse, he swung his blade in a powerful arc and carved a deep gash in the sod. Tasting failure, he remembered Laurian and Sameel. He would have another chance at Malygris—both he and the wizard had sworn it.

Flinging open the garden doors, he made his way through a darkened foyer and found the stairs to the upper floor. The library doors hung crookedly on their hinges. He rushed inside.

Sameel cradled Laurian in her arms on the carpet. She turned a tear-streaked face toward him. "Malygris?" she asked hopefully.

"Gone," he answered. "Laurian?"

Sameel brushed hair from her mistress's face. "She's with Sadaster now."

Fafhrd picked up the scabbard he had cast aside and sheathed Sadaster's sword. A new anger welled up within him as he clenched his fist around the hilt. "Why?" he raged. "Why did she challenge him alone? We should have planned it together, chosen the time . . ."

Sameel smiled wanly. "You didn't know Laurian."

I know she's dead, Fafhrd nearly snapped. Instead, he bit his tongue and shook his head. "She should have let us help."

Sameel leaned her head forward until it touched Laurian's brow. "I helped," she whispered. "Didn't I, mistress?"

"What?" Crouching down beside her, Fafhrd lifted her chin, forced her to look at him.

She gave a weak laugh that sent a new chill through Fafhrd. "She asked me for a favor," she said, turning her face away. "Something important, something that would insure Malygris's coming."

Fafhrd knelt closer, confused as well as angry, but suddenly frightened again as he peered at Sameel and perceived in her a new, desperate quality. It seemed as if her mind were unhinging. He started to speak again, but she put up a hand to stop his lips.

A moment of lucidity settled upon her face, and in her eyes he saw a sadness so deep it set his soul to aching. "Don't ask," she said, her words feather-soft, her breath herb-sweet. "The answer might hurt too much. And I will never tell."

Her eyes fluttered, and her head sank down upon Laurian's head again.

"Sameel?" he said.

She didn't answer.

A dark stain spread slowly across the carpet beneath Laurian's body. Fafhrd stared, puzzled. Too much blood for Malygris's wounds, and Laurian hadn't been stabbed. He noted how gingerly Sameel supported her mistress's limp form in her left arm. His eyes spied Laurian's dagger so close at hand.

With a despairing cry, he caught the hidden arm and tugged it free. "What have you done?"

Blood swelled freely from the vein she had opened lengthwise and properly. It ran over her palm, through her fingers, dripped into Laurian's dark hair, into Laurian's shut eyes.

Sameel pulled her arm away and hugged it to her bare breast. "All the kindness, all the joy I have known in this world flowed from my mistress and my master," she said. An eerie happiness filled her voice. "They will need me in the Shadowland."

A hollow silence settled through the room. Fafhrd's eyes burned, and his heart threatened to burst. Kneeling, clutching his sword as if it were a holy relic, he banged his head again and again on the pommelstone.

Looking up, Sameel touched his knee. A dull light, swiftly fading, lingered in her eyes as she sought his gaze. "I didn't mean that—not all the joy," she whispered. She spoke his name once, then leaned down to wrap her mistress in a final embrace.

All through their night together, she had called him only, *my lord.*

Fafhrd raised his fists and screamed in rage and pain. For a long time he remained beside them, awash in memories, paralyzed by old and new regrets. Then, carrying both women, he placed Laurian on her velvet chair and arranged Sameel on her mistress's lap.

Closing the two halves of the silver sarcophagus around them, Fafhrd sat down and leaned his head against it.

After a time, he got to his feet, collected his breeches and other garments from Sameel's room, and dressed. While Malygris breathed, he would save his grief, and hoard his anger like a treasure of incalculable worth.

Meanwhile, there was the Mouser to find.

Carefully he closed the gates of the estate and stepped into the street outside. A soft breeze blew through the avenue, sweeping away a misty fog. Hugging himself beneath his cloak, he turned southward.

But before he went far, a harsh mirth echoed down the night, freezing him in mid-step. Even with its bitter edge, he knew that peeling laugh. "Vlana?" he said, casting a searching gaze about.

In the dark mouth of an alley, he thought he glimpsed a pale shape, a hint of flashing eyes, a wisp of hair floating about a familiar face. But when he rushed to the spot, no one was there.

FIFTEEN

A FEAST OF FEAR

The Mouser peered cautiously around the corner of an old warehouse on Hardstone Street into an alley filled with night's gloom. Adjusting the heavy sack he carried over one shoulder, he cast a glance toward the ponderous silhouette of the city's eastern wall in whose shadow he stood.

An aura of moonlight shimmered above the wall, though the moon had not yet risen above it. Wetting his lips, he slipped into the alley's deeper blackness.

Halfway into the alley, invisible from the road, Nuulpha sat on a low wooden crate, bent forward, elbows on his knees, lost in thought. Moving soundlessly on soft-booted feet, the Mouser reached out and tapped the corporal on the top of his helmet.

Startled, Nuulpha gasped and fell sideways into the dirt, one hand groping for his sword's hilt. Only the Mouser's toe, placed carefully upon the edge of the crate, kept that from toppling and making an unwanted racket.

"By the Rat God!" Nuulpha whispered anxiously, finally recognizing his friend. "I didn't hear you." With some embarrassment, he rose and brushed himself off.

"What are you doing here?" the Mouser asked in a low voice.

"Waiting for you," Nuulpha answered. "Demptha said you'd left on some errand." He eyed the Mouser's burden. "What's in the bag?"

"Decent food and plenty of it," the Mouser answered, passing the heavy bag to Nuulpha. "Everyone below, including Demptha, looked half-starved. A nobleman named Belit happened to cause me some irritation a night or two ago, so it amused me to strip his larders bare."

"Lord Belit?" Nuulpha gave a soft whistle. "I wish I'd been with you for that."

The Mouser shook his head. "Except for Fafhrd, there's no other man I'd take a-burgling. I'm not fool enough to risk a fight or capture on someone else's clumsiness."

A look of hurt slipped over Nuulpha's features, but the Mouser slapped his arm. "No offense intended. But theft is a solo job, my friend. If you ever take it up, remember that. Trust no one."

Nuulpha adjusted the bag on his shoulder. "But you and the Northerner . . ."

"That's different," the Mouser said curtly. "I can't explain it, but that big lummox and I know each other in a manner that's not completely natural." He rolled his eyes melodramatically. "Distasteful as I find the idea, sometimes I think we're two halves of some very old soul."

Suddenly he held up a hand for silence and, poised like an animal ready for flight, turned toward the alley's entrance.

The sound of marching feet grew steadily clearer. Then a soft wavering radiance drifted down Hardstone Street. The Mouser loosened his thin sword in its sheath as he pressed himself against the warehouse wall into the deepest shadows.

A squad of six soldiers bearing torches passed by without so much as a glance into the alley. Exhaling a soft breath, the Mouser stole up to the street, peered around the corner of the warehouse, and watched until the squad marched out of sight.

"Let's go inside," the Mouser whispered, returning to Nuulpha. "Don't let the hinges squeak."

"I oiled them," Nuulpha answered, sheathing his own sword and picking up the bag, which he had placed on the ground.

"You're learning," the Mouser said with a nod and a grin. "I'll make a thief of you yet."

Nuulpha led the way a little further down the alley and found the wooden handles of a pair of large doors. Carefully, he opened one just wide enough for them to slip inside. The hinges made no sound at all, but the bottom of the old door, which hung crookedly, scraped softly in the alley dust.

Pulling the door shut, the Mouser reached for the stout four-by-four wooden bar that leaned against the wall nearby. As quietly as possible, he set it in place, sealing the doors. Relaxing a little, he surveyed the warehouse's stark interior. A score of thick square-cut beams supported the low ceiling, standing like anorexic sentinels guarding a vast dusty emptiness.

A few paces away, crouched beside a wooden box, Nuulpha turned up the wick of a lantern. The dim blue flame within brightened, exuding a soft yellow glow that uplit the corporal's sharp-featured face. Seizing the bale, he lifted the lantern in one hand and the bag with the other.

Just at the light's edge lay a huge crib that might once have served as a corn bin. The Mouser tugged open the lid and pulled back the latticed door before pausing. Pursing his lips, he turned slowly.

"Speaking of my partner," he said quietly, "have you learned anything?"

Nuulpha frowned. "No news at all," he said regretfully. "No one's seen him—the city guards aren't even looking for him. You, however, are a different matter. A certain Corporal Muulsh of the North Barracks is storming all over the city looking for you."

The Mouser drew a finger down his right cheek. "Long scar?" he asked.

Nuulpha nodded. "You know him?"

"A peach of a fellow," the Mouser answered, turning away. He bent to the floor of the corn crib, found a metal ring embedded in the old boards, and curled his gloved fingers around it. Lifting a hidden trap door, he peered down into blackness.

Demptha Negatarth had purchased this abandoned warehouse because of its precise location above one branch of Lankhmar's secret tunnels and had excavated this private access. Down this hole, down these narrow wooden steps, he and his followers came and went, bringing the helpless victims of Malygris's evil magic to hide them from Rokkarsh's night-prowling soldiers.

He felt no small honor at being entrusted with such knowledge. Taking the bag from Nuulpha again, he motioned the corporal to go down. The light shone dimly up from the hole as the Mouser closed the crib door and lowered its heavy lid into place. Descending the first few steps, he lowered the trap door above his head.

The ponderous weight of the earth seemed to close about him, and the smell of dirt and dampness filled his nostrils. A sense of unease settled upon him; he was no mole, and rooting around in the ground held no appeal. Fixing his eyes on the lantern's glow, he descended as quickly as the heavy bag and the narrow steps allowed.

Nuulpha waited at the bottom, his upturned face betraying a nervousness he hadn't shown before. His shoulders slumped, and he crouched subtly, though his head cleared the tunnel roof by inches.

The Mouser knew how the corporal felt. The darkness possessed an intimidating solidity that the lantern barely penetrated. The closeness of the walls and the low narrow ceiling suffocated, and the earth still bore a fresh-dug odor. He could practically feel, he imagined, the hungry maggots and worms burrowing nearer.

Perhaps because he felt so intensely the absence of his friend, he recalled the words of one of Fafhrd's songs. Softly he whispered, seeking to buoy his spirits by mocking his own fear as he crept forward into the gloom.

> *"Lay me down in the cold, dark ground;*
> *Make of the earth a soft round mound;*
> *Worms and maggots gather around*
> *To bear me off to Shadowland."*

The stale air seemed to shiver, and the lantern's flame reacted with a barely perceptible waver as if some undetectable wind had danced around it. The Mouser's skin crawled, and the hair stood on the nape of his neck.

> *"There is a road we all must brave—*
> *King and peasant, saint and knave—*
> *No man is born who is not a slave*
> *To the Lord of Shadowland."*

With a shaking hand, Nuulpha turned up the lantern's wick another notch. The flame brightened a little, but failed to push back the darkness. "Have you no other song?" he grumbled.

"A tisket, a tasket, two bodies in a casket," the Mouser persisted, forcing the words through clenched teeth.

But suddenly he stopped. Catching Nuulpha's arm, he jerked his companion around. "You're trembling," he said. "So am I." He squeezed past Nuulpha, daring to venture a few paces beyond the boundary of the light, then stepped back into its amber circle. "Grown men shivering in the dark," he whispered. He licked his lips thoughtfully, admitting his fear, feeling it growing inside him like a pressure.

"Why am I afraid?" he said, as much to himself as to Nuulpha. "I've been under the earth before. Why does this seem different?"

"My heart is hammering," Nuulpha confessed in a hushed voice. "And there's weakness in my knees. It shames me . . ."

"Then there's shame for both of us," the Mouser said, clapping his friend on the shoulder. He set down the bag of stolen victuals and put a hand over his own heart. "I am almost overwhelmed," he said. "As if I were wading deeper and deeper into some black sea . . ."

". . . About to be dragged down by some unseen tentacled monster . . ." Nuulpha added, wiping sweat from his brow.

Rubbing his chin, the Mouser paced to the very edge of the light and stopped with only his toes challenging the horrible border. He squinted into the blackness, half-expecting some red-eyed demon to stare back.

"Eclipses," Nuulpha muttered, picking up the bag and going to the Mouser's side, "a Patriarch's death, all this damnable fog of late—bad omens, all, I tell you."

Forcing down his fear, the Mouser ventured slowly forward. Yet he felt in his bones some pervasive, unseeable change in the tunnels, an unearthly strangeness that tainted the air. Even the very darkness, the shade and texture of the gloom, struck him suddenly as alien.

They emerged finally from the narrow, man-made tunnel into a larger natural cavern. Here, too, the oppressive strangeness dominated. The Mouser stood still and listened. Was it Nuulpha's breathing he heard, or his own? Or was it . . . something else.

He thought of the rats and bats that should have occupied this underworld, the insects and countless crawling creatures. Yet no living thing dwelled here. He remembered wondering if some monster, stalking these grim passages, had eaten the rats. Now he wondered if, following some animal instinct, they simply had fled.

Again, leaving Nuulpha on the tunnel threshold, he stepped beyond the range of the light to turn slowly in the darkness.

Above, the ceiling's stalactites glimmered coldly with hints of phosphorescence, of crystal, and mica. In either direction the cavern walls seemed to vanish, and the black gloom extended into some void, an infinity of fearsome night.

"Glavas Rho," he whispered, invoking the memory of the herb-wizard who, in the absence of father or mother, had raised him through boyhood. "I think you have not prepared me for this."

Nuulpha crept to his side. The lantern's wick was now turned as high as it would go, but the flame and its light seemed smaller than ever. He raised the lantern over his head, surrounding them both in a circle of faint radiance.

The Mouser drew a circle in the air with his left hand, one of the holy signs of his spider-god. "Let no evil thing pass into this glow," he intoned, his black eyes glittering sharply.

"Stop!" Nuulpha cried. The light wavered dramatically as, dropping the foodbag, the corporal clapped a hand around the Mouser's head and over his mouth. Instantly, he released the Mouser again, but spun him around. "You invite Malygris's curse with such careless words!"

Stunned briefly, the Mouser hugged himself against the chill Nuulpha's words caused as he looked up into his comrade's stricken face. "Thank you, Captain," he said, recovering himself. Yet, a thought flashed through his mind—had he just doomed himself with that stupid charm-casting? He turned to stare once more into the void beyond the light, into the darkness that ate at his reason.

"How easy it was to forget myself," he murmured to Nuulpha, "just once. Despite my cautions, despite knowing the danger, I acted according to my nature."

He bit his lip. Did he dare tell Nuulpha more? A double dread shivered through him, fear of Malygris's wasting curse, and of something else—these tunnels and caverns. Something stirred here, something vaster and more inhumanly malevolent than any mere monster of his imagination. He knew it, though he couldn't explain his knowledge.

Whatever it was, it was not Malygris.

"Let's move on," Nuulpha urged, laying a hand gently on the Mouser's shoulder. "Demptha will be glad to receive this food."

Turning, the Mouser forced a grin as he motioned for Nuulpha to lead the way. In truth, he suddenly preferred not to remain in one spot too long down here. "And Jesane?" he asked in a falsely jaunty voice, giving his thoughts to Demptha's daughter. "Will she be glad to receive me?"

Nuulpha snorted, quickening his pace subtly, as if sensing something more than the Mouser at his back. "Despite what your eyes tell you, she's old enough to be your mother."

The Mouser barked a laugh that sounded strained even to his ears. "Liar, and whoreson jealous dog!" he said, slapping Nuulpha's back. "You think you can turn my interest aside so easily? You want her for yourself."

Nuulpha shook his head emphatically. "I have a loving wife," he reminded the Mouser. "She loves to spend my money, loves to order me about, loves to lie around slothfully. . . . But never mind. About Jesane, I speak the truth. She could be your mother. Mine, too, for that matter. And Demptha is a lot older than he looks."

"But Demptha is far less enticing," the Mouser answered. He cast a backward glance as they left the cavern and entered a brick-walled tunnel. He knew it could only be a trick of the light, but the void seemed almost to stalk them.

When I stop, it stops, he thought to himself. *Yet each time I look around it seems just a little bit closer.* He chewed his lip while Nuulpha continued obliviously on. Finding himself abruptly on the edge of the light, he hurried to catch up.

A soul-wrenching scream ripped suddenly through the tunnels. Goosebumps rising on his flesh, heart hammering, the Mouser froze in his tracks and stared wide-eyed past Nuulpha into the forward darkness. The tunnels magnified the sound, and the echoes rattled from the stones. The food bag slipped from the corporal's grip, and the lantern trembled violently in his shaking hand. A man's cry of pain followed, then a cacophony of terrorized shrieking.

Nuulpha spun about, his face a pale, distorted mask of fear. A moaning cry bubbled on his own lips. Knocking the Mouser down, he ran back the way they had come.

The light vanished with Nuulpha's fleeing figure, and darkness closed about the Mouser like a fist. Cowering, he flung himself against the wall, finding little comfort in having something solid at his back. The screams continued, long blood-curdling waves of horror. Blind in the darkness, the Mouser shot desperate looks up and down the tunnel. He whipped out his dagger, gasping, fear sucking breath from his lungs like a cat. "Nuulpha!" he called. "Nuulpha!"

Then he clamped a hand over his own mouth, afraid that something unpleasant might hear and turn his way.

He twisted toward the screams, and an icy wind seemed to brush his soul as suddenly he thought he recognized some cries among others. *That's Mish's voice! That's Jesane!* They issued from the Temple of Hates, he had no doubt. On hands and knees, clutching Catsclaw, he began to crawl forward, groping at the wall, feeling his way.

A high-pitched child's shriek stung his heart. *The little girl!* he thought with an inward despairing cry. He lurched to his feet. With shambling steps he ran. He opened his mouth and screamed his own scream, a challenging and angry cry, feeling his throat tear with the ferocity of it. He hoped this time to draw the demons to himself and away from the temple—for demons there must surely be!

Pain flashed. Stars exploded inside his skull. Rebounding from the wall, a bend in the passage, he fell backward with a groan and sprawled on the cold earth. The screams became fewer, weaker. Shaking off the impact, he struggled to his knees, fumbled about for Catsclaw, which had fallen from his grasp. His fingers brushed the dagger's hilt.

The metal glimmered against his fingers. Light! He shot a look back over his shoulder. Nuulpha!

The corporal crouched down beside him. "Forgive me!" he begged.

The Mouser seized the lantern and ran ahead through the tunnel. The screams were no more than moans and groans now, yet no less terrible. "Which way?" he shouted, confronted with an unexpected intersection.

"This way," Nuulpha said grimly, squeezing past, taking the lead with his naked short-sword in hand. The Mouser raced beside him through the new, wider passage, envisioning the carnage ahead.

Even the moaning ceased. A dreadful silence filled the tunnels.

Another turn, a few more paces, and they reached the Temple of Hates. The Mouser's mouth went dry as he gazed up the ancient stone staircase. The huge door at the top stood ominously closed. On its wooden surface, the cracked and painted face of some unknown demon or deity mocked them with its leer.

Swallowing, the Mouser crept cautiously up the steps and put his hand against the door. At his touch it swung open with a faint creaking. The lantern's light speared the darkness beyond the threshold, revealing only an empty corridor.

"Black as a bat's arsehole," Nuulpha whispered, close behind him.

The Mouser entered the passage with swift, soundless strides, exchanging his dagger for his sword. With the slender blade held on guard before him, he took each bend in the way and came to the seeming wall that separated the corridor from the Temple.

Nuulpha kicked the appropriate stone. The hidden entrance slid back, and the Mouser sprang inside.

Only darkness greeted them. Side by side they moved through the chamber, shining the lantern about. The many columns that supported the low ceiling cast uncounted shadows, and every shadow seemed a threat. Yet no enemy accosted them.

Every pallet lay empty. Blankets were cast aside, pillows scattered. No real signs of a struggle, though. Water jars stood undisturbed; furniture sat upright; no traces of blood or violence.

"Where'd they go?" Nuulpha whispered incredulously. "Where's Demptha?"

The Mouser shook his head. His skin crawled as he looked about. The screaming he had heard were screams of death and slaughter. He had prepared himself for carnage and battle, not for this—this eerie emptiness.

The light fell upon a small straw doll that lay on the floor. Picking it up, he thought of the little blond girl in whose arms he had last seen it. Was she dead? Should he grieve? He dropped the doll on the nearby pallet where she had slept and moved on uncertainly, searching every corner, every shadow.

"Who put out the light?"

Nuulpha had dropped out of sight behind the Mouser. The Mouser turned to find the corporal standing a few paces away near a table pointing to a fat candle, its wax still soft and warm. "All the lanterns, all the candles and torches," the corporal said. "They've all been recently extinguished."

"Is there any other way out of here?" the Mouser asked. "Another tunnel or some secret passage Demptha might have shared with you?"

Nuulpha shrugged as he lit the candle from the Mouser's lantern. He moved forward, turned slowly about, and shook his head. "I know of only the one way," he answered. A look of puzzlement settled over his face. "There's something else," he said, staring toward the ceiling. "It's too quiet."

The Mouser listened. "The Midsummer celebration," he said with dawning awareness.

"We're right under the Festival District," Nuulpha reminded. "We should hear traces of music and laughter."

Grimly, the Mouser continued his search. The temple's acoustics were tricky. The silence might signify nothing more than a lull in the festivities. He put that puzzle aside to concentrate on the present mystery. Moving toward the farthest end of the temple, he shone his light on Demptha's long worktable. "Look," he said, summoning Nuulpha.

Demptha's tarot cards lay scattered over the table and on the floor as if an angry hand had swept the deck aside.

"Demptha would never have left those behind," Nuulpha said with certainty. "He painted them, himself." Bending, the corporal scooped up the fallen cards. Placing them with the others on the table, he assembled them once more into a neat deck. "Maybe he'll come back for them," Nuulpha added doubtfully.

On an impulse, the Mouser turned over the top card. The miniature painting revealed a long banquet table piled high with bones and skulls and body parts. In elaborate high-backed chairs sat a trio of skeletons clutching goblets of blood.

"The Feast of Fear," the Mouser said, dropping the card with a grunt. He went cold inside as a sudden black irony hit him. "I was bringing them a bag of food."

Nuulpha seized a torch from a sconce behind the table and lit it with his candle. "I'll go to Demptha's shop in the morning. Perhaps he'll turn up there."

The Mouser held out no such hope.

They returned with torch and lantern through the tunnels. Neither spoke. The Mouser's thoughts churned. He felt Fafhrd's absence acutely. With the Northerner beside him, he would have known his next move—or they would have figured it out together.

Instead, he felt defeated, stripped of important allies, and no closer to Malygris.

They came to the bag of food where Nuulpha had dropped it. Scowling, the Mouser gave it a savage kick and stormed on. Nuulpha quietly collected it and swung it over his shoulder. Food, after all, was food even in Lankhmar.

At last they climbed the narrow wooden steps and went through the trap door into the warehouse on Hardstone Street. "Back where we began," the Mouser grumbled while Nuulpha closed the hidden entrance.

"What now, my gray friend?" Nuulpha asked.

The Mouser shrugged in frustration. "Go home to your wife, Nuulpha," he said. "I need time to think. Look for me tomorrow at the Silver Eel."

They left the warehouse together and strode up the alley to Hardstone Street. There they paused once more, gazing up and down the empty avenue. A thick white fog had descended upon the city while they were underground. "More of this damnable stuff," Nuulpha said with an irritated frown. He poked his torch at the mist. "At least I've a light to find my way home."

The Mouser watched Nuulpha walk northward, his light growing fuzzier and fainter, finally vanishing. Sheathing his sword, he started southward toward the Festival District, lantern swinging at his side.

The fog swirled about him, feather-soft, cool on his face. Its damp touch seemed to dampen his mood as well. Morose, suddenly lonely, he drew up his hood. Nuulpha had a home, a wife and a warm bed waiting. What had the Gray Mouser?

Once in this very city such good fortune had been his. Ivrian, his one true love, had waited for him each evening in the small apartment they had shared above Bones Alley. Laughter and joy had been theirs, and love such as he had never known before or since. How delicate and beautiful had been his Ivrian, child-like in her innocence and easy delight. She had showered him with her affection, and he missed her with a pain that threatened to break his heart.

How lucky Nuulpha was, and how seemingly oblivious to the blessings that were his.

A sound disturbed his glum meditations. Curiously, he shone his light upon a hay wagon parked in the shadows near an old smithy shop. A handful of hay flew into the air, and a small cascade fell off the end. The wagon's boards commenced a merry creaking.

Extinguishing his light, creeping closer, the Mouser listened to the soft gasping and sharp breaths that rose from the unseen couple in the wagon. With darkness and fog concealing his actions, he approached them. He thought of peering over the side, but instead, he crouched down by a wheel, listened for a moment to their love-making, then quietly slunk away, feeling lonelier than ever.

He thought of Ivrian, his one true love, and remembered her warmth, her sweet beauty. How he missed her! But when his lips formed her name, the sound that came out said, "Liara."

He stopped in the middle of the street, shocked at his mistake, feeling that he had just betrayed Ivrian's memory. But not far behind him, he could still hear the sounds of the couple in the hay wagon. And from that alley just ahead—did he hear another couple?

The fog swirled through the lane like a white river, sweeping him into the Festival District. He walked in a dream-like state, senses alternately muffled and sharp. A woman danced out of the fog, turning elaborate pirouettes, laughing hysterically. Spying the Mouser, she flung herself at him and tried to press her lips against his face. He tolerated her touch briefly, then pushed her away.

"You're not Liara," he said, his voice sounding distant in his own ears.

Torches and lanterns began to glimmer weakly through the fog. In that crippled light he spied couples rutting on the doorsteps of shops, in the alleyways. Through the open doors of a tavern he paused to witness the orgy underway on its tables and floor.

He moved inside. Unnoticed, he collected coin purses and necklaces, rings and bracelets, cash from the till, a fine crimson cloak with large pockets to carry it all. At the next tavern, he did the same, robbing the place and its customers of every last copper and earring.

In the street, he found many of the kiosks and vending booths untended. If he found a cash box he emptied it into the cloak's pockets. Finding a particularly large and handsome leather purse, he traded the cloak for it and transferred his booty. With the weighty purse over one shoulder, he continued on.

On a stage, an athletic couple wrestled with impressive enthusiasm. From the edge of the proscenium, the Mouser paused to offer appropriate and well-deserved accolades while he rifled the clothes they had cast aside. He also claimed the jeweled necklace with the broken catch that had slipped from the woman's throat during their exercise.

At last, he found himself on the district's southern edge, having pilfered his way from one end of it to the other. No street lamps lit this part of town, and he regretted leaving his lantern somewhere. Adjusting his bag of loot on his shoulder, he walked on.

Liara occupied all his thoughts. The memory of her brief kiss burned in his mind. Her voice whispered musically in his ears, and the soft night wind hinted at her perfume as it stirred the fog. His heart cried out for her, and nothing and no one but Liara could ease its aching.

Abruptly he stopped. With sudden clarity, he found himself on Face-of-the-Moon Street. Appalled, he touched the bag, pushed his hand inside, and lifted out a handful of the treasure within. Coins and jewelry sifted through his fingers, and he burned with shame.

Then the fog eddied around him again. On the verge of retreating, filled with trepidation, he nevertheless continued down the dark lane until he stood before the House of Night Cries.

White gravel crunched under his footsteps. The sculptures on the lawn seemed to turn menacingly as he passed, barring escape—a fancy of his mind, he knew. Strange dread filled him, and stranger anticipation. An unexplainable fever heated his blood, wrung sweat from his brow. One by one he climbed the marble steps to the door. Trembling, nervous fingers seized the brass knocker.

The flat sound of the ring striking the plate reminded him of bones snapping.

For long minutes he waited, shifting uneasily from one foot to the other. Just as he reached for the knocker again, the door slowly opened. A heavy-set bald man with eyes like cold gray stones and a boulder for a face glared down. Bare arms and chest bulged with impressive muscle; a huge leather belt constrained an immense belly.

The Mouser stared at the unlikely doorman. "The Dark Butterfly," he muttered, hugging his bag of booty beneath his gray cloak. "Tell her—" he hesitated. Licking his lips uncertainly, he exposed the bag. "Say that her defender has brought a gift."

The doorman's face betrayed no emotion. "Wait here," he said, closing the door firmly in the Mouser's face.

Turning, the Mouser stared across the fog-enwrapped lawn toward the street and the park barely visible beyond. He warred with himself, wishing to run, not daring to depart. Liara's promise held him like a chain. The finer perfections of love— she said she would show him.

The door opened again, and the doorman beckoned.

Soft lanterns, their wicks turned very low, lit an opulently furnished hallway. The Mouser paid little attention. The fever gripped him completely now. His guide paused and rapped gently on a door, then opened it. He closed it again as the Mouser stepped across the threshold.

She stood in the center of the room, elegantly posed, legs slightly apart, back arched, her head at a haughty, mocking angle. A thin robe of black silk, barely covering her shoulders and the fine curves of her breasts, gaped open. Blond hair spilled loosely down her spine.

Her eyes laughed at him.

The Mouser pushed back his hood. His gaze flickered away from Liara to the veiled bed. Without speaking, he turned the bag upside down and emptied the contents—enough wealth to keep a noble household in style for a year—on the plush carpet.

"Is it enough?" he asked. His voice revealed both a desperation and a bitter edge that reflected the war still raging in his mind.

She sneered, yet her voice was a cat's purr. "For the finer perfections of love?" Coming closer, she stirred the glittering pile with one painted big toe. Her eyes fastened on her guest. "Barely." She turned toward the bed. "Undress."

Swiftly, the Mouser stripped off his garments. Standing at the foot of the bed, Liara watched him, a look of seeming impatience on her face. Her robe gaped open wider as she planted one hand on her hip. In the dim light, her eyes flashed.

The Mouser moved to her side. He drew his fingertips down the ivory flesh of her arms, eliciting no reaction until he tried to embrace her. She put a hand on his chest. "You are not on the Street of Red Lanterns," she said harshly.

A chill passed through him, then a wave of heat as she held back the veils that surrounded the bed. The Mouser gazed up at the tall framework over the bed, eyeing the manacles suspended from above.

Her calculating look dared him. He stared back at her. In that icily beautiful face he saw his one true love, sweet Ivrian, and this other woman, Liara the whore. In his mind, their identities merged and blurred.

His senses reeled. Like a drunken man, he climbed up onto the bed. Struggling to keep his balance on the pile of expensive down mattresses and slick silken sheets, he placed his own wrists in the manacles and waited, his mind awhirl with confusing memories and thoughts, his body on fire with unfettered dark lusts.

Ivrian or Liara climbed up on the bed behind him. He could feel the cool fabric of her robe on his buttocks and calves, but he felt the stab of her bare nipples against his back as she reached up and snapped the manacles' locks.

"Welcome to the House of Night Cries," she breathed into his ear.

She laughed a cruelly taunting laugh as she backed away from him.

"Ivrian," the Mouser whispered. The sound he heard was not laughter, but the voice of the woman he had failed to protect. It came to him like a condemning wind across the years. His knuckles cracked as he gripped his chains. "Forgive me, Ivrian."

He cast a glance back over his shoulder. And he knew with a drunken man's clarity that the woman behind him was Ivrian, or some part of her.

Closing his eyes, he arched his back and prepared himself.

Liara laughed again, then hissed like a cat.

A velvet whip lashed across the Mouser's flesh. For nine strokes, he bore it silently. Still her arm rose and fell with amazing strength. Five more strokes. In his mind he tried to hold an image of Ivrian, but it kept changing into Liara, and with every stroke it mocked him. He bit his lip. A thin string of drool oozed from the corner of his mouth and over his chin.

The whip came down again, shattering the image and his silence. At last he knew why they called it the House of Night Cries.

SIXTEEN

CITY OF THE DAMNED

As dawn broke over Lankhmar, a dispirited Gray Mouser pushed open the door to the Silver Eel. Pausing on the threshold, he stared at the overturned tables and broken stools, the spilled mugs and empty bottles that littered the place. A couple of drunks, slumped shoulder to shoulder on the floor, snored noisily in one corner.

A shirtless Cherig One-hand lay sprawled upon the bar, snoring as loudly as his two unconscious patrons. Someone had folded the tavern-owner's arms upon his chest in funereal manner and stuck a wilted flower between his fingers. A copper tik-coin rested upon each of his closed eyes. His boots had been removed, and his toenails as well as his fingernails had been painted bright scarlet as a woman would do. Likewise, his cheeks had been rouged and his lips berry-brightened.

The Mouser's mood lightened immediately, and he felt a little less the fool than when he entered. Thus decorated, Cherig made quite the comical sight. Obviously the madness that had passed through the Festival District had come this way, too.

The Mouser tiptoed by the sleeping tavern owner, careful not to wake him, and climbed the stairs to the sleeping rooms above.

Reaching the door to his own room, he put a hand to the knob, then paused.

A cough sounded from within.

The Mouser pushed the door inward. "Fafhrd?" he called, glancing eagerly toward the bed.

The Northerner sat upon the mattresses with his back against the wall. He looked thoroughly miserable, not to mention drunk. His clothes were rumpled, and his face wore a long expression. Between his knees he held a half-empty bottle of wine. Another empty bottle rested on the table nearby.

Sitting forward, Fafhrd pushed at the sheets with his bootheels, grinning stupidly as he waved the bottle at the Mouser. "Hey, welcome home!" he cried excitedly. Then his face turned grave. "Guess what? Vlana's haunting me, did you know that?" He waved the bottle in the air again, then took a deep swig. "Chased her half the night, I did, through every damn street and alley in the district."

The Mouser froze. Then softly he closed the door and turned away so Fafhrd couldn't see his face. Vlana's name reminded him of Ivrian and of what he'd surrendered himself to at the House of Night Cries. He felt the lashes and welts underneath his soft silk shirt, and his face burned with shame. Had Liara wielded a leather whip instead of a velvet one, his back would be a bloody mess.

But worse than the shame, he felt again a powerful confusion. Liara and Ivrian—somehow, in some impossible manner, he felt sure they were one and the same. Yet, in personality they were utterly different.

Now Fafhrd spoke of ghosts.

"Vlana?" the Mouser said without looking at his friend. He unfastened his weapons belt and hung it over the back of the only chair.

The bed creaked as Fafhrd shifted his weight and leaned back against the wall again. "She was waiting for me in an alley when I left Laurian."

The Mouser whirled. "Sadaster's wife? Is that where you've been these past two days?"

Fafhrd snapped his fingers, or rather tried to snap them. For a moment, he stared at his thumb. A second time he tried and achieved a faint pop. "Snatched me right out of the air, she did. She's got Sadaster's power, you know. At least she did." Fafhrd took another drink before adding morosely, "She's dead."

Abruptly, Fafhrd lurched off the bed and across the room to the table. Knocking the empty wine bottle aside, he poured water from a pitcher into a basin and splashed his face. "Malygris killed her," he said bitterly, "and I couldn't stop him." Gritting his teeth, he pounded one fist on the table. The basin jumped, spilling water over its side, and the pitcher teetered dangerously before righting itself.

The Mouser moved softly away from the table and into a corner near the bed, giving his friend a respectful space. A wise man didn't crowd Fafhrd when such dark moods were upon him. Without comment, he noted the huge new sword sheathed and leaning nearby. No doubt that, too, had a part in Fafhrd's story, and he would unfold the tale in time.

Then he would tell all he knew and suspected of the Dark Butterfly and the House of Night Cries, yes, even of how her doorman had pitched him insensate into the street when Liara had finished her vile humiliations and subtle tortures. He would tell even that and risk Fafhrd's scorn or laughter.

Rubbing his stubbled chin, he eyed Fafhrd warily and watched him tremble with silent, barely controlled anger. While he waited for Fafhrd to resume the story, his mind worked. Vlana's ghost. Ivrian and Liara. More mysteries to trouble him. Mysteries upon mysteries.

And all Sheelba had sent them to do was find one wizard.

The Mouser's mouth slowly gaped. "Oh, gods," he murmured, suddenly filled with a dreadful realization. He uttered another low, horror-filled curse. "Mog's black soul! Fafhrd, look at me!" He waited until the Northerner turned. "Did Malygris cast some great magic last night? Something to affect the entire city?"

Fafhrd frowned in puzzlement.

The Mouser smashed one fist against a palm, ignoring Fafhrd now. "It had to be magic! Nothing else could explain the madness! And everyone touched by it . . . !" He stared wide-eyed at Fafhrd again as he thought of Malygris's wasting spell flashing like some invisible lightning bolt among last night's unsuspecting celebrants.

"The fog!" he whispered, thinking hard, remembering how it rolled so unnaturally through the streets.

"Laurian controlled the fog," Fafhrd offered, seeming to shake off his drunken state. "She used it somehow to find Malygris."

"Laurian?" the Mouser questioned. That didn't make sense. "Why would Laurian . . ."

He didn't get a chance to finish.

The door smashed open. Corporal Scarface leaped into the room, sword drawn. More soldiers filled the corridor beyond the threshold. "Now you little runt, I've trapped you!" Scarface froze in mid-threat and stared up at Fafhrd's seven-foot height and at the pitcher hurtling down toward his head.

"I don't think you've met my partner," the Mouser said as the pitcher shattered on Scarface's helmet, showering him with water and ceramic fragments. With a loud groan, the corporal sank to his knees.

"Next!" Fafhrd cried, seizing the basin and flinging its contents at the soldiers who pushed through the door. Then he flung the basin, itself.

A pair of soldiers charged through, stepping on their corporal in the zeal to tackle Fafhrd. One hit him high, the other low, and the giant went down with a thunderous crash.

Cursing, Scarface struggled up. Still gripping his sword, he scowled as he turned toward the Mouser. Another pair of soldiers rushed in to back him up.

Backed against the wall, the Mouser grabbed for Fafhrd's sword and dragged it free of its sheath. Beautifully polished, the naked blade gleamed. But the Mouser hesitated. It felt like a gross weight in his hand, and it was nearly as long as he was tall. "What the hell do I do with this thing?" he shouted.

Gripping the hilt in both hands, he swung the sword in a broad swishing arc, forcing Scarface and his men to retreat a step. Wildly, he swung it again, carving an invisible deadly line in the air to keep his attackers at bay.

With a loud growl, Fafhrd flung off the pair that had tackled him and rose to his feet. Yet another soldier charged at him. Side-stepping, Fafhrd stuck out a foot. With a startled yowl, that one flew through the air and out the open window above Bones Alley. A predictably short scream followed him.

A sword flashed down at Fafhrd. Dancing away, the Northerner snatched the Mouser's weapons belt from the back of the chair where it hung, and hurled the chair. He whipped free the Mouser's rapier. "What am I supposed to do with this toothpick?" he shouted across the room to his partner. "Why don't you get a real sword?"

"You lack the skill and finesse to appreciate what you hold," the Mouser shot back. He continued to swing Fafhrd's heavy blade in the widest possible arc as Scarface and another soldier tried to close with him.

Fafhrd made an exaggerated lunge and nicked his opponent's shoulder, drawing a small neat trickle of blood. Wide-eyed, the surprised soldier touched his wound and stared at the blood that came away on his hand.

"Bah! He didn't even fall down!" Fafhrd called to his embattled comrade as he scowled at the Mouser's weapon. In truth, it appeared tiny in his great fist. "This thing's far too dainty for me.

Here's a man's weapon!" So saying, he snatched up the table with
one hand. Holding it shield-like, he screamed a blood-curdling
battlecry and charged the wounded soldier, knocking him and two
others back through the door and into the hallway beyond. "Come,
Mouser!" he shouted, laughing. "I'll clear a path to the bar!"

Sprawled on the corridor's floor, the three soldiers and two
more saw the mocking flame-haired giant standing over them
brandishing table in one hand and unlikely sword in the other.
Scrambling up, they nearly tripped on each other as they fled
toward the stairs.

Fafhrd laughed again and flung the table after them. He
called again to the Mouser on the far side of the room. "Would
you stop dawdling?"

"A moment more of this excellent exercise," the Mouser answered, puffing as he held off the two remaining attackers. "It's
having some salutary effect on my mood."

Just then, Scarface's partner stepped too close. The Mouser
brought his foot up in a sharp kick. Clutching his groin with
one hand, the soldier dropped his sword and sagged to his knees.
"Yes," the Mouser said, "I'm feeling much better now."

A startled Scarface unwisely glanced at his collapsed and
groaning comrade. The Mouser's powerful swing, barely under
his control, whistled toward the corporal's head. The big sword's
point cut through the leather chin strap of Scarface's helmet,
and cut a deep gash in his unblemished cheek. Blood gushed.
Scarface shrieked with pain, clapping one hand to his face as he
leaped back.

"Now you'll have a fine matched set," the Mouser said with a
smirk.

A hoarse cry bubbled up in Scarface's throat, and he grasped
his sword in both hands for a final, hysterical charge. Before he
could rush forward, Fafhrd appeared behind him, lifted the
helmet from the corporal's head, and slammed the rapier's
pommel against an unprotected skull.

"You're an impatient lout," the Mouser pouted.

"Just like your namesake," Fafhrd scolded, "you play too much with your food."

The Mouser snatched back his rapier and handed the great sword to Fafhrd. "I wasn't going to eat him," he said defensively as he reclaimed his weapons belt with Catsclaw from the room's wreckage.

A low groan drew his attention to the soldier that lay on the floor with his hands still tucked between his thighs. Bending over the man, the Mouser murmured, "I feel compelled to apologize for that. Most men would rather be run through."

Biting his lip, eyes squeezed shut with pain, the poor man managed to nod agreement.

Fafhrd leaned in the doorway with one eye to the corridor beyond. "The boot is mightier than the sword," the Mouser whispered as he joined him there.

"He'll sing his love songs in a new octave surely," Fafhrd said.

They crept down the corridor toward the stairs, Fafhrd leading the way. At the top step, they paused.

A half dozen soldiers waited at the bottom, swords drawn, tense, steeled for combat. Sweat gleamed on their faces; fear shone in their eyes. Nervously, they stared upward.

The Mouser and Fafhrd exchanged glances. Seizing the bannister with one hand, the Mouser screamed a battlecry. His gray cloak spread like a bird's wings as he vaulted the rail. Fafhrd roared. Carving the air with his great sword, he ran down the stairs like a fire-haired madman.

The soldiers screamed. Weapons clattered to the floor. Booted feet caused a thunder as six terrified men ran over each other, pushing and shoving to get to the door and away from the flying imp and the charging giant. Fafhrd chased them as far as the threshold. His mocking laughter chased them up the street.

The Mouser sheathed his rapier as Fafhrd turned back toward him. "You ogre," he said with a mock-frown to his partner. "I

think they wet their trousers." He picked up an overturned wine
bottle from the floor and shook it. Finding a swallow remaining,
he put the bottle to his lips, drained it, and wiped his mouth.

"Thirsty work terrorizing helpless soldiers?" Fafhrd replied as
he sheathed his own sword.

A smile turned up the corners of the Gray Mouser's lips. "I
noticed the vintage," he said, dropping the empty vessel. It shattered at his feet. "Tovilyis. It would have been a crime not to
finish it."

A groan drew their attention to the bar. Cherig One-hand
struggled drunkenly to sit up. His arms thrashed at the air, and
one leg twitched. Then with an awkward cry of surprise, he fell
off the bar's narrow surface, disappearing behind it.

The Mouser hurried to help his fat landlord, as did Fafhrd.
Together, they pulled him up, walked him to a stool, and
propped him against the wall.

With bleary red eyes, Cherig studied both their faces, seeming
not to recognize them. Then, he clapped Fafhrd's shoulder. "Oh,
it's you, Fafhrd," he mumbled, his words slurring. He shook a
finger under the Northerner's nose. "You better be careful. Some
of the Overlord's men have been asking about that gray partner
of yours, and if you ask me, I think they're watching the place."

"I'll warn him," Fafhrd said, waving a hand under his nose to
disperse the foul odor of Cherig's breath.

"You do that," Cherig answered, nodding. He closed his eyes
and slid sideways off the stool, his back still to the wall. A loud
snore escaped his parting lips as his jaw sagged.

"He must have had an interesting night," Fafhrd commented.

The Mouser looked at him sharply. "You don't know?"

Fafhrd shook his head. "The party was over when I came
home. Now tell me what you did to raise the ire of the constab-
ulary."

It took only a few moments for the Mouser to explain his capture outside the Tower of Koh-Vombi and his subsequent escape from Rokkarsh's dungeon into the tunnels below the city. Of the Temple of Hates and its conversion into a sanctuary for homeless victims of Malygris's curse, he told more, giving details of his meetings with Demptha Negatarth and his daughter, Jesane. Lastly, his mood turning darker, he told of Demptha's disappearance.

"Demptha has a jeweler's shop just north of the Street of the Gods," the Mouser said. "If you're not too sotted from all that wine, I want to go there."

Fafhrd wiped a hand over his brow. "Exercise has a way of clearing the head," he said.

A muffled crash followed by a loud groan and a curse sounded from upstairs. The voice was plainly that of the scarfaced corporal.

"Now might be a good time to seek your shop," Fafhrd suggested.

"It would be more fun to stay and bash him again," the Mouser muttered, but he led the way from the Silver Eel into Dim Lane.

At the corner of Cheap Street, they encountered a lone pedestrian. Hurrying along hunched over in a hooded cloak, the man nearly ran into Fafhrd. Glancing up suddenly, he gave a sharp gasp and stepped back. His right hand flew out from under the cloak, and a slender knife flashed. Beneath the hood, fearful eyes snapped wide.

For a moment, the man stared at the pair. Then, putting the knife back under his cloak, he murmured a hasty apology, ran to the far side of the street and continued on his way.

"What was that all about?" Fafhrd asked, scratching his chin as he stared after the pedestrian. Then he swept his gaze up and down the street. "Where is everyone? It's morning, and the street is virtually empty!"

"Did you see how his hand trembled?" the Mouser commented in a low voice. He drew his own cloak closer about his shoulders. "Scarface's soldiers were afraid, too."

"Of course they were afraid!" Fafhrd laughed. "Are we not a fearsome pair? Why, all by itself that dusky face of yours could scare . . . !"

The Mouser jabbed an elbow against Fafhrd's hip. "Do not besmirch my porcelain beauty," he warned with mock-gravity. He turned serious once more. "They badly outnumbered us. But if those soldiers were already afraid, before even knocking at our door, no wonder we defeated them easily."

"Afraid! Afraid!" Fafhrd said testily. "Afraid of what?"

Stepping slowly into the center of the street, the Gray Mouser gazed up and down it. Cheap Street at this time of morning should have been busy with early shoppers, merchants on the way to their businesses, delivery carts laden with fresh wares.

Not so much as a dog prowled through the gutters.

As he turned back toward his partner, from the corner of his eye the Mouser noted a window directly above them. Its shutter hung slightly open; a nervous pair of eyes peered down at them, drawn perhaps by their voices.

Fafhrd followed the Mouser's gaze. Putting on a big smile, he raised a hand and wiggled his fingers at the peeper.

White fingers curled around the shutter's edge and drew it quietly closed.

Staring at the closed shutter, the Mouser sniffed the air. "You don't feel it?" he whispered to his partner. "Something intangible, indefinable, like a cold breath on the back of your neck?" He paused and swallowed. Once before, he had felt fear such as this, but stronger—in the tunnels under Lankhmar. "A strange wind is blowing, Fafhrd."

The Northerner frowned. "I don't feel any wind," he said. "Nor this fear you speak of, whatever it is."

"Do you not feel it, my stubborn friend?" the Mouser said, starting northward up the street. "Then tell me truly why I found you deep in your second bottle before the sun was even over the rooftops?"

Quickly overtaking the Mouser, Fafhrd started to protest. Instead, he fell silent, and his face took on an expression as grim as his companion's, and his eyes began to minutely search the alley entrances and shadowed places as they made their way.

From Dim Lane to Craft Street they encountered no more than five people. None spoke or offered any greeting. Averting their eyes, those citizens hurried past clutching parcels or purses or daggers concealed beneath their cloaks.

At the Craft Street intersection only two merchants had opened their shops. One of them stood in the doorway, glaring suspiciously up and down the road. In one hand he gripped a wooden mallet that might have been a tool of his trade.

On the Street of Thinkers, the university bells tolled, calling students to study. Today, the bells carried a lonely quality and their summons went unheeded.

The Street of Silk Merchants normally bustled with trade even at the earliest hours. It was totally empty. Shop doors remained closed, windows shuttered.

"If Laurian cast a powerful spell last night," the Mouser said, "I think every citizen must have felt it. Something's left them cowed and hiding in their homes."

Fafhrd put a hand to his mouth and coughed, a soft explosion that rose from deep in his lungs. "If you're right," he said, wiping a trace of spittle from his lips, "then this is a city of the damned."

The Mouser stared at his partner, and he paled. "Malygris's curse," he said with a sudden dreadful understanding. "It may have touched every person touched by Laurian's magic."

A look of infinite sadness settled upon Fafhrd's face. "I wonder if she knew what she did?" He shook his head forcefully. "I can't believe she would doom so many innocents."

Gray-gloved hands curled into fists at the Mouser's sides. "I wonder if Laurian is responsible at all," he said tersely. "Or Malygris, for that matter."

"Malygris killed Laurian last night," Fafhrd snapped. "He's no innocent."

The Mouser only half-listened as, privately, he dealt with a bitter realization. Magic had compelled him to seek out the Dark Butterfly and suffer her humiliations. He felt sure of that, but the surety no longer brought any consolation. Rather, it brought danger, threat, and uncertainty. Would he, too, now fall victim to a horrible, wasting sickness?

"I don't know what that wizard is," the Mouser muttered, "but I swear, Fafhrd, there's some greater mystery here that we've not yet touched upon."

The same hushed quiet filled the Street of the Gods, but on this most major of major thoroughfares, braver souls ventured. The clip-clop of a horse caused Fafhrd and the Mouser to turn and watch as a black carriage, its small drapes drawn to conceal the occupant, passed them by. The driver kept his gaze straight ahead, studiously ignoring them.

At the Temple of Mog, a squad of armed priests stood guard by the entrance and along the surrounding wall, a clear reminder of their battle with the priests of Aarth and the violence that had taken place only days before. They glared with dark suspicion at the few citizens wandering among the open shops and businesses.

Only one block northward, however, Temple Street appeared abandoned. The south side of the street consisted of temple walls and back gates, but small closely crowded shops lined the opposite side. With no good idea exactly where Demptha's business stood, the Mouser scratched his chin and wondered which way to go. He chose the riverward direction and began scrutinizing the merchants' signs carefully.

Finally, he stopped and peered upward at an elaborately painted sign. Portrayed upon it in vibrant colors was a wild peacock, its tail feathers displayed, an emerald clutched in one talon, a ruby in the other. "*The Bird of Jewels,* from the Lankhmaran tarot," the Mouser said, putting his hand upon the door. "I should have expected it."

Fafhrd put a hand on his companion's arm. "Can you be sure you have the right shop?"

The Mouser nodded. "I recognize the style of his art." The door swung open at his touch. "Unlocked," he said with some surprise.

They slipped inside and hesitated while their eyes adjusted to the gloom. A large worktable with various tools for gem-cutting and delicate metal-shaping scattered upon it occupied most of the visible interior. Several cupboards and empty display cases stood against a wall. A fine layer of dust covered everything.

"Demptha?" the Mouser called softly. Then louder, "Demptha?"

Fafhrd pointed to a curtained doorway at the rear of the shop. With the tip of one finger, he pushed back the edge and peeked through. He beckoned for the Mouser to follow.

The rear room was larger, but empty of furniture. A few tools hung on pegs on the walls, and an empty chest stood with its lid open. A broken chair leaned in one corner. In another corner a narrow wooden staircase led to an attic.

With one hand on Catsclaw's hilt, the Mouser crept up the stairs. Carefully, he eased up the horizontal door. "Mog's blood!" he exclaimed. "Fafhrd, come see this!"

The Northerner climbed the stairs while the Mouser waited open-mouthed at the top. With only his head and shoulders above the attic floor, Fafhrd gave a low whistle.

It was hardly an attic at all. Plush scarlet carpets covered the floor. Paintings done by Demptha's hand adorned the wall. A gold samovar stood close by. Another large table dominated the center of the room. Upon it an array of flasks and alembics glimmered in the light from a pair of candles. A deck of cards lay scattered between the candles.

The bookshelves that covered the wall behind the table revealed an impressive collection of volumes.

"I suspect this is Demptha's *real* work room," the Mouser commented.

A barely audible groan quivered up from the shadows behind the table.

"Demptha?" Taking a tighter grip on his dagger, the Mouser seized one of the candles and moved around the table. Fafhrd came around the other side.

The light fell on a lined and wrinkled face, on a mass of gray hair, and shriveled breasts. Horror and revulsion gripped the Mouser at this unexpected sight, for in that aged visage he recognized another. "Jesane!" he exclaimed, dropping to his knees.

Fafhrd raised an eyebrow. "The daughter?"

Jesane rolled rheumy eyes toward the Mouser. Then her gaze shifted to a book that lay open on the floor just beyond her reach. She strained for it, but the Mouser gathered her up in a cradling embrace. She felt brittle in his arms, this woman who had saved his life, like old parchment.

"What happened to you?" the Mouser cried as he brushed strands of hair from her brow. He searched that face for traces of her former beauty, recalled the sparkle in those once-bright eyes, the strength and vitality of a once-supple body that he had desired. "By all the gods, what happened?"

Jesane's mouth trembled and opened. A thin string of spittle hung suspended between her cracked lips. A brown tongue licked it weakly away. "Shadowland," she whispered, her eyes widening at some horror. She tried to roll free of the Mouser's embrace, tried to reach with twig-like fingers for the book on the floor. "Shadowland is here!"

A dry rattle issued from her throat, and she went limp.

"Dead," the Mouser said, his voice heavy with sadness as he laid her gently down. He picked up the fallen book, intending only to place it on the table. But the distinctive calligraphy caught his eye. He lingered over the page where the book was opened.

But before he could read a word, the page exploded in violent flame. The flash singed the Mouser's eyebrows and, but for his glove, would have burned his hand. Instinctively, he dropped the book with a howl.

With unnatural speed, the flames devoured the book and spread to the thick carpet. A streamer of fire shot across the floor straight for the bookshelves.

"No!" Fafhrd shouted, leaping up. He snatched volumes off the shelves, attempting to save them, but each one burst into new flame in his grasp.

The Mouser pulled him away.

"What a loss!" Fafhrd cried. "All that knowledge!"

"We've got to get out of here!" the Mouser insisted, shielding his face from the heat. "This whole place is going to burn!"

They ran down the stairs and out into the street. They didn't stop there. Neither wanted to be found lingering around a sudden fire when soldiers were already seeking the Mouser. They ducked around the next corner. Emerging onto the Street of the Gods, they headed toward the river.

Ahead, drifting over the southwestern rooftops, a column of black smoke climbed into the blue sky. Fafhrd eyed it with a strange expression, then began walking faster and faster. Finally he ran with the Mouser pursuing.

Still a block from this second fire, Fafhrd stopped. "Sadaster's estate," he said, nodding toward the crackling flames. "Another library destroyed."

The Mouser let go a long sigh. The streets were no longer deserted. People thronged the way, watching the great house burn. A water-line had formed, not to douse the flames engulfing Sadaster's house, but to protect the buildings around it. Fortunately, the estates in this part of town were well-spaced. There was little chance this fire would spread.

"I wish you could have seen it," Fafhrd whispered. "Such a collection of books."

"Nothing like a fire to draw a crowd," the Mouser muttered. He turned away from the inferno to witness the column of smoke rising over Temple Street.

Let Fafhrd mourn the books. He would mourn Jesane.

SEVENTEEN

WIZARD'S RAGE

S quads of soldiers came racing down Nun Street, drawn by
the crackling flames that engulfed Sadaster's estate.
Mindful of the Mouser's status as a wanted man, Fafhrd
caught his partner's elbow and quickly pushed him into the
thick of the spectators.

The Mouser understood and drew his hood closer about his
face. Without drawing attention to themselves, they slipped
through the crowd into a narrow, serpentine alley and quick-
footed away from the scene, emerging some blocks eastward in
Crypt Court.

Tall ramshackle apartment buildings, mostly abandoned, rose
on all sides of the square. The structures were among the oldest in
Lankhmar, and they showed it, leaning at crazy angles on their
ancient, eroded foundations. Sunlight streamed through holes in
the roofs, through cracked and weathered walls.

Only the poorest and most desperate Lankhmarans, those at
the very nadir of their luck, came here to live. The individual
apartments were no more than tiny, cheerless cells—hence the
name, *Crypt Court.* The floorings were treacherously rotten and
the windows shutterless. A good wind could raise a creaking and
a groaning from the wooden beams and set the structures to
swaying.

Such was the nature of Lankhmar that its worst tenements stood side by side with its wealthiest neighborhoods, connected sometimes by no more than a narrow road or a few alleyways.

At the center of the court a small cracked fountain gurgled softly. Water from a ceramic pipe trickled into a round pool whose bottom was covered with a mossy, dark green growth. Pushing his cloak back over his shoulders, Fafhrd dipped a hand into the water, and wiped his face and neck. Though he declined to say so to the Mouser, a dull ache banged at the back of his head from the wine he had drunk.

Even here a smell of smoke hung in the air, evoking memories of Sadaster's fantastic library, of Laurian, of sweet Sameel and the joy she had given him. He grieved for those books and grieved anew for the ladies. The thought of their bodies burning in that holocaust angered and sickened him.

"I can't get over the way Jesane looked," the Mouser said wearily as he stretched his legs out before him and sat on the fountain's low stone wall. Pursing his lips thoughtfully, he cradled his chin in one palm. His face took on a troubled, faraway look.

"Laurian had the same look when she died," Fafhrd said quietly. "At the end, she seemed to age rapidly, and her beauty faded like a rose in a . . ."—he hesitated before finishing his remark—". . . in a fire."

The Mouser drew his legs up and leaned on his knees. "Nuulpha said that Jesane was older than she looked. Demptha, too."

Unconsciously, Fafhrd mirrored the Mouser's posture, leaning his elbows on his knees, cradling his chin as he stared at the cobbled court. "In our dream," he said at last, "Sadaster used enchantment to keep Laurian young."

The Mouser looked up sharply. "You never cease to amaze me, my friend," he said. "You've done what I could not—fit together two pieces of the puzzle."

Fafhrd brightened at the compliment, then frowned. "What puzzle?"

Unexpectedly, the Mouser barked a short laugh and gave an exaggerated shrug. "I don't know!" he said. "But can it be coincidence that two women we know are dead under arcane circumstances, and that both were preserving their beauty against all nature?"

Fafhrd scratched the new copper-colored beard on his cheeks. He hadn't shaved for days now, and the short growth itched. "What has any of that to do with the reason we are here, namely Malygris?"

"I don't know!" the Mouser said again, waving his hands irritably as he rose to his feet. Abruptly he froze in mid-gesture. "Or maybe I do know. To strike at Laurian's husband, Malygris created his thrice-cursed curse. Jesane and her father worked to bring some comfort to innocent victims of that curse."

"That's pretty thin," Fafhrd scoffed.

"Perhaps," the Gray Mouser admitted. "But there's one thing I know well enough." Forcing a grin, he put a hand to his stomach. "I'm so hungry I could eat a Quarmallian ox."

Fafhrd raised an eyebrow and glanced at the empty dwellings that surrounded them. "You'd better keep that face of yours out of sight," he said, rising to his feet. "I'll find breakfast. You see if you can find us a room around here."

Scratching his head, the Mouser turned in a slow circle. "Can we afford this neighborhood?" he asked.

Fafhrd patted his purse. "It's in our price range," he answered. "I wasn't fool enough to leave Sadaster's house without a few choice baubles."

"Well if price is no object," the Mouser said with a dainty curtsey, "I'll find your Lordship a rathole with a view."

"I'll settle for a solid floor."

Fafhrd adjusted the hood of his cloak to conceal his face as he started back through the alley to Nun Street. The smell of smoke hung in the air as he reached the thoroughfare, and to the north a black plume rose into the blue sky.

At first he considered joining the crowd he knew would be gathered to watch the fire. There would be plenty of pockets to pick and purse strings to cut. However, the Thieves' Guild would no doubt have agents working the same crowd, and though he longed for an excuse to tangle with that group again, now was not the time.

He worked his way west, keeping to narrow roads and back streets, until he came to the river. A pair of barges, majestically graceful for their cumbersome size and design, sailed past with pennons streaming in the wind, headed for Lankhmar's southern lands. A few fishing boats, trawling close to the shores, bounced on the barges' powerful wakes.

Standing in the dusty, rutted track that paralleled the river, Fafhrd scanned the banks with an intense gaze, noting an old woman with her basket of laundry, a fisherman half asleep over a cane pole, a trio of young boys skipping stones. For a moment, he envied them their simple carefree lives.

But they weren't really carefree, he reminded himself. If he had learned nothing else he knew this, that everyone struggled. The old woman probably worked to support herself. The fisherman waited patiently for the fish that would feed his family. The children—perhaps they wondered where they would sleep next, and would they be safe?

He looked at them again, those citizens of Lankhmar, willing himself to see past the surface, through the illusion. They were poor; their clothes gave that away. They were brave, too; they went about their tasks and their lives, while others in the city hid from the madness that pervaded the city.

He wondered what ghosts they carried around.

Stepping off the road, he followed the grassy bank until he reached the old woman's side. Her back was bent and arched as she leaned over the water. The knobby ridges of her spine showed right through the threadbare black dress she wore. A frayed brown ribbon wound through her gray hair and held it in a knot on top of her head, exposing the deep wrinkles carved into her bird-like neck and high-cheeked face.

As Fafhrd's shadow fell across the water, she froze. Then, tossing a sopping wad of cloth into the basket at her side, she sat stiffly back on her heels and looked up wordlessly. Her eyes, though they contained a certain fear, revealed more—a deep resignation, perhaps even boredom, that let her face death, if such this giant represented, with an almost imperious dignity.

"Don't worry, grandmother," Fafhrd said as he reached into his purse. He pulled out a necklace of amethysts and silver beads, thinking of Sameel and Laurian, from whose room he had taken it. Kneeling down, he spread the precious ornament upon the wet clothes and forced a smile. Briefly, he touched her shoulder. Then he concealed the necklace beneath a damp fold. "Something for a rainy day."

The old woman gazed suspiciously at her mysterious benefactor for a long moment before her eyes flickered to the basket. Fafhrd rose quietly and moved back to the road, feeling a rare satisfaction. He thought Laurian would be pleased, too. He shot a final glance back over his shoulder—and paused.

For an instant, as she rose half crouched over her basket, her black dress hanging on her frail form like an old loose robe, she reminded him of someone else. He recalled another thin figure draped in black—the fisherman, poling his skiff across the river late at night, the pilot who, in a stranger form, had sailed upon a sea of fog through his dreams.

He had been looking for that figure, he realized, as he scanned the riverbanks again. Instead, he had found the old woman, so thin and gray, at the end of her days. Repressing a shiver as he watched her from a distance, he wondered, was this an omen of his own demise?

The old woman rearranged the items in her basket. Kneeling down again, she took another garment and dipped it in the river. Gathering it wet, she scrubbed it determinedly between her gnarly knuckles, her face stern, almost impassive, as she returned to her common task.

Fafhrd lifted his head and drew a deep breath. If she was an omen, she also represented a lesson. Life, however short, went on. He felt a slight tightening in his chest, the threat of a cough, a barely perceptible weakness, but he chuckled to himself. Despite her newly gained wealth, the old woman went on with her job. He also had a job to do, a task to complete.

And suddenly he knew how he would do it.

Turning, he began to whistle as he walked toward the wharves. The morning sun warmed his face, and the sweet smell that rose off the water refreshed his spirit. Even the breeze that played in the ropes and cables of the ships at dock, and the lapping of the waves that set the boards to creaking, sounded like music—the music of life.

If the merchants at the heart of Lankhmar were too timid to venture out and open their shops, not so the common laborers who worked the riverfront. A line of sweaty, bare-chested workmen loaded barrels aboard a waiting bireme. A captain called commands to his crew. A teary-eyed girl, blond hair sparkling in the sunlight, blue cloak stirring about her like gossamer in the wind, waved a hanky at her sweetheart.

A half block eastward from the wharves on curvy Eel Street, Fafhrd used a thin gold ring to purchase a quantity of hot, buttered fish, which the pinch-faced old merchant carefully rolled in the stout, broad mint leaves that grew south of Lankhmar. At another shop across the road he paid several tik-pennies for two loaves of bread and a round of pale cheese. For another tik-penny, the proprietor's wife offered him a worn cloth sack to carry his purchases.

At yet another shop he bought an earthen jug and several beans of precious gahvey. Back at the wharves, he lingered for a final time inside a shop that sold ships' supplies, purchasing two pitch torches, an oil lamp, and a tinder box.

With his shopping in the sack slung over his shoulder, he made his way back to Crypt Court. The Mouser hailed him with a wave from a third-floor window.

Fafhrd beckoned his companion to join him by the fountain, where he spread out his feast. The fish, though cool, still smelled with a mouth-watering richness as he set them on the fountain's low wall. Next, he gathered handfuls of dry grass that grew between the court's flagstones and added bits of old twigs and rotten splinters of wood that he found in the shadows of the buildings. Using the tinderbox, he soon had a small fire going.

"You're in a good mood," the Mouser noted as he reached Fafhrd's side.

"I feel good," Fafhrd answered as he filled the jug he'd bought with water from the fountain. He placed it in the flames to boil and gestured toward the sack. "Carve us some cheese and slice the bread."

Lifting the cheese close to his hawkish nose, the Mouser inhaled deeply and let go a noisy sigh. Catsclaw came out of its sheath. Carving a thin slice, the Mouser popped it into his mouth, closed his eyes, and sighed again. Then, noticing Fafhrd's actions, his jaw gaped.

"Is that gahvey?" he asked eagerly.

Fafhrd nodded as he ground the precious black beans vigorously between his palms and sprinkled them into the jug of water. "Did you find us an apartment?"

"With a solid floor, as your Lordship requested," he said, carving a slice of bread. "But watch the stairs as you go up, and don't put any weight at all on the bannisters."

Leaning their backs against the fountain wall, they ate, savoring the minty butter-flavored fish, the strong cheese, and the fresh bread. When the gahvey was ready, they pulled it from the fire with gloved fingers and waited for it to cool sufficiently. They drank, passing the jar between them.

"We're not alone," Fafhrd whispered suddenly as he cast a subtle glance toward an upper-level window where a small face had appeared briefly and quickly disappeared.

"They're quick," the Mouser said, sipping the gahvey. "I noticed them earlier. I believe we've discovered where the city's street urchins spend their nights."

With a bite of bread at his lips, Fafhrd hesitated. He'd spent his own youth in the comparative luxury afforded by his mother's high station in the Cold Wastes. As the leader of the Snow Clan, and a Snow Witch herself, her tent had never lacked for heat, nor furs to wear, nor food to eat. In his own distant land he was practically a prince.

Slowly he lowered the morsel from his mouth and placed it beside the remains of their meal. There was still some fish left, some bread, and plenty of cheese. Taking his own dagger, he carved the cheese and bread into neat slices and arranged it all along the fountain's wall.

"What are you doing?" the Mouser asked, setting the gahvey jar aside and reaching for another bite of fish.

Fafhrd rapped the Mouser's knuckles with the flat of the dagger's blade. "A good deed," he explained. "You've stuffed yourself enough. A fat partner will be useless to me later."

The Mouser stuck out his tongue. Then patting his stomach, he released a loud belch in Fafhrd's direction. "Speaking of useless," he said, pointing to his companion's other purchases, "why buy torches? The lantern will serve us well and safely come nightfall, but an unshielded firestick could send this entire court up in flames. And between us, I've seen enough fire for one day."

"The lantern's to light our newfound nest," Fafhrd said. "The torches are for another purpose." Without offering further explanation, he drained the last of the gahvey and rose to his feet.

"I propose to sleep," he announced, stretching. "I think we have a long night ahead of us."

Still seated, the Mouser leaned back on his hands and regarded Fafhrd queerly. "I think you have some plan stewing in that fine brain of yours," he said.

"Leave the leftovers for the children," Fafhrd continued as if the Mouser had not spoken. Leaning over the fountain, he filled the jar with water. "And light the lantern now before I douse our little fire. There's oil enough in it to last."

Rising slowly, the Mouser shrugged. "Well if we feed them a little now, maybe they won't try to knock us in the head while we sleep." Selecting a small burning twig from the fire, he touched it to the lantern's wick and lowered the perforated metal shield over the flame.

Fafhrd upended the jar. A loud hissing and sputtering followed as fire and water met. A cloud of steam and smoke boiled upward, and the air smelled of ash.

Again, Fafhrd thought of the splendid books in Sadaster's library, all lost to flames, and once more he grieved. But when melancholy threatened to descend upon him, he fought it off with a little song.

"Now I've had my bread,
And I'm very well fed,
So off to bed, sing hey!
Lay down my head,
Sleep like the dead—
It's sundown, end of the day!"

With the fire extinguished and the lantern lit, they made their way out of the sunlight and into the gloom of the ramshackle building the Mouser had chosen for them. The wooden stairs creaked and shivered under their weight as they climbed to a third-floor apartment.

"Don't touch the bannister," the Mouser warned, his voice automatically dropping to a whisper. He placed his palm on the once-ornate support to show how loose and rotten it had become.

"The finest suite in Lankhmar," Fafhrd said, frowning as he followed his partner into their rooms. Just past the threshold, a man-sized hole perforated the floor. Pausing, he peered down into the dirty rooms below, then stepped carefully around it, feeling the boards give menacingly beneath his every step. "I hope the rats appreciate such luxury."

The window allowed a commanding view of the court below. A pair of old shutters were pushed open and back against the outer wall. Seizing the right shutter by its latch, he eased it back and forth, testing its old hinges. Metal protested noisily, then old wood sighed. The shutter came loose at the top and leaned outward away from Fafhrd's grasp. Its own weight too much, it pulled loose from the bottom and tumbled to the ground.

"I swear I can't take you anyplace," the Mouser said, placing the lantern in one corner on the floor and setting down the bag that contained the torches. "What will the landlord say?"

Fafhrd removed his sword, then spread his cloak upon the dusty floor. "Wake me if he wants to lodge a complaint," he said, curling up. Hugging the sheathed blade to his chest, he closed his eyes without another word, leaving the Mouser standing with hands on his hips, gaping open-mouthed.

Fafhrd woke drenched in sweat. Slowly, he sat up and wiped a hand over his face. Saturated with perspiration, his garments clung to him. The cloak on which he slept showed a clear, damp outline of his body. He didn't feel warm or feverish, but he shifted position, moving closer to the window.

The last colors of twilight lingered in the west as night moved in from the east. A strange sky, he thought, observing the mottled shades of gray, deep blues, and black. A bruised sky. A flock of blackbirds winged slowly, gracefully, overhead. Fafhrd watched them pass out of sight.

A soft evening breeze blew across the rooftops. It kissed his face and dried his sweat as he drew a deep breath of fresh air.

Long shadows filled the court below. He gazed toward the fountain. Not a single crumb of the food left there remained. Smiling to himself, he scanned the darkened windows and doors of the apartments opposite him. Far down the way, a small head lingered watchfully low in the corner of a third-floor shutterless square.

How many, he wondered. How many children—orphans and runaways—called these treacherous structures home? He felt the shiver of the wind through the old boards, the ever-so-slight swaying in the beams and timbers. A rare wave of pity swept over him, and he wished that he'd had more food to leave.

He, himself, had never known an orphan's existence.

Not so for his partner, he thought as he gazed across the darkening room. The Mouser slept sitting up in a corner, his back against the wall, feet crossed like an eastern philosopher, chin resting on his chest, arms hanging lank at his sides. The low flame of the lantern perched on the rickety table nearby downlit his somber, sleeping features.

The Mouser never talked at all about his early youth. He had never known his parents. He might have been the son of some starving whore that couldn't afford to keep him, or the secret cast-off shame of some noblewoman or queen. He didn't know his land of origin, or even if he had ever had a proper name. Like a small, ferocious animal he had fought and scrapped for every bite of food, for every moment of his cruel existence until the herb-wizard, Glavas Rho, stumbling upon the little savage in the alleys of Lankhmar and seeing some spark in the boy, took him in, educated him, and gave him a taste for the finer things civilization offered.

Noting the sky's deepening color, Fafhrd rose slowly to his feet, careful not to make the old boards creak and thus disturb his friend. Retrieving his cloak, he fastened it about his shoulders, then chose a torch from the pair he had purchased earlier. Lastly, he fastened his sword in place on his hip and crept soundlessly to the apartment door. Pausing, he looked back.

The Mouser had not stirred. His slender chest rose and fell in a soft, even sleep-rhythm. His gray partner would be angry to wake and find himself alone, Fafhrd knew, but this one battle he felt he must fight alone. Only he, not the Mouser, had been touched by Malygris's curse. He would not risk exposing his good friend to the magical forces he intended to challenge this night.

He crept carefully down the stairs in utter darkness, feeling his way, testing every step lest his weight plunge him through some rotten wood. At the bottom, he paused in the doorway and gazed out over the courtyard. A pair of small shadows sat on a nearby stoop. Swift and alert as mice, they vanished inside as Fafhrd stepped into the open.

Feeling inside his purse, which was still full of Laurian's jewelry, he found a bracelet. Blood-red garnets depending from silver links glimmered darkly in the pale starlight that reached into the court. Fafhrd crossed the expanse and placed it on the very stoop where the children had sat.

"Take this bauble to Fisret the Fence on the Street of Honest Men," he whispered into the black opening of a doorway. "The profit should feed you all for a week if you spend wisely." He paused, listening, but expecting no answer. He had no doubt, though, that the children heard him. Finally he added, "Tell the old rat-face that Fafhrd of the Red Hair, to whom he owes a thousand favors, sent you. That will guarantee a fair-value trade."

He turned from the stoop, expecting no thanks. Such children as these trusted no one outside of their small band, least of

all a huge adult of uncertain intentions with a sword longer than
the tallest of them. He strode away, but after a few paces, glanced
back over his shoulder and grinned as a tiny hand on a skinny
arm shot out and snatched the treasure.

"You're welcome," Fafhrd murmured.

Clutching his unlit torch, he left Crypt Court, feeling his
way through alleys so narrow the walls brushed his shoulders.
The sun had little chance to bake the ground in such close passages. Slime and filth mucked his boots. Wrinkling his nose
against the pungent odors of mud and slop-jar leavings, he
draped the hem of his cloak over one arm to avoid soiling it.

Like a fleet shadow, he crossed Nun Street, deftly avoiding
the street lanterns and a patrol of soldiers marching south in
tight formation. He watched their backs until they were out of
sight, wondering what business they were about. Then, once
more keeping to the alleys and back streets, he made his way
past homes and apartments, shops and warehouses until he
stood on the shore of the River Hlal.

A cool breeze kissed his face, and the lapping of little waves
sounded like soft music. The dark water glimmered and gleamed
under the rich spangle of stars that filled Lankhmar's sky. Fafhrd
drew a deep breath and let it out slowly, appreciating the serene
beauty, tasting for just a brief moment the unending vastness of
life represented by the river and the heavens.

After a moment, he began to wander the bank. He gathered
pieces of driftwood, tore up small handfuls of dry grass and
piled them together. With his sharp eyes he searched the water's
edge for the whitest, smoothest stones. Carefully, he rinsed them
clean of any mud. Upon each stone he blew a stream of breath,
and when he had enough, he built a small, crude pyramid beside his pile of grass and driftwood.

Rummaging in his purse, digging past Laurian's jewels, he
found the tinder box he had purchased earlier that day and set
to work over the grass and driftwood. When the grass at last

took fire, he seized the pitch torch, which he had set aside, and lit it. He forced the end into the ground so that it stood beside his pyramid.

In his circle of light, Fafhrd knelt down and drew out his dagger. Extending his left arm over the pyramid, he drew the razor sharp blade across his flesh. A thin red stream splashed upon the white stones.

"Kos," he whispered, murmuring a prayer to that grim northern god of his ancestors as he watched his red essence seep over and around the stones. "I seldom call your name except for the most blasphemous of reasons. But taste the blood of your wayward son upon this small altar and hear me now. Reach out from the silence of the Icy Wastes, place your hoary hand in my enemy's back, and compel him to me."

He bent closer over the makeshift altar as a few more drops of blood splattered the stones. His green eyes glittered, and his copper curls shone like liquid gold in the firelight. "Cold Kos," he urged, "do this—and the next three virgins I take, I'll deflower in your name."

A sharp wind gusted at his back. The torch and the small campfire fluttered wildly. A thin spray lifted from the river, dampening his neck, and a veil of dust swept upward from the grassy bank to roll inland.

Through that veil of dust a cloaked form stood suddenly revealed.

"Your frozen god can't help you, barbarian," the figure hissed. With one hand it pushed back a concealing hood. Firelight gleamed on a bald head, in small spidery eyes.

A hideous smile turned up the corners of Fafhrd's lips. Rising calmly, he tossed back the edge of his cloak to reveal Graywand. He wrapped his fingers slowly, deliberately around its hilt, not defensively, not out of surprise. From that cool gesture issued a deadly threat and promise of battle.

"Truly the gods move in mysterious ways," Fafhrd said in a grim voice, "Kos is generous to have delivered you up so quickly." Touching the wound on the back of his sword arm with two fingers, he drew a pair of red streaks on each cheek, his gaze never leaving Malygris's face.

"Pathetic dog," the wizard said. "I've watched you all night and day and into this night again, since the moment you left Laurian's side, waited to punish you for daring to defile my true love!"

"As you have dared to defile the memory of my one true love!" Fafhrd shot back angrily. "I realized today. It isn't Vlana's ghost that haunts me through the city streets, but a damnable trick of your illusions!"

"Fool, and ranting fool!" Malygris answered bitterly. A hand thrust from under the folds of the wizard's cloak. In response, the small campfire flared. Tongues of flame shot outward, catching in the grass, burning with unnatural fury. A hot, crackling ring swiftly encircled Fafhrd.

Waves of heat whipped at Fafhrd. For a reflexive instant, he threw up an arm to shield his eyes. Then grinning, he lowered his arm and drew Graywand from its sheath. The red light shimmered on the impressive length of steel.

"Spare me your cheap mirages," Fafhrd sneered, ignoring the circle of fire that drew ever tighter about him. He snatched up the torch standing at his side where he'd planted it in the earth. "Have some real fire," he said, flinging it.

The pitch torch *whooshed* through the night like a blazing missile, propelled by Fafhrd's might. A startled Malygris stared in wide-eyed disbelief, seemingly transfixed. At the last possible instant, voicing a small cry, he ducked and leaped aside. His foot caught in the grass, and as he tumbled backward, his cloak parted to reveal one arm bound tightly against his body. His face wrinkled in pain.

"So I did mark you," Fafhrd gloated, remembering that he'd hurled a stone and struck the wizard's elbow at their first meeting. "Well, I'll carve a deeper mark and rid Lankhmar of a rabid rat." Clutching Graywand in both hands, he swung the blade high. "Now a nightmare ends," he hissed.

Suddenly the world tilted. The ground began to spin. Earth and sky traded places and traded again. Fafhrd lurched backward, fighting for balance like a man on the deck of a tempest-tossed ship. He spun about, fell, landed on his back barely clinging to his sword as he cried out in rage and fear.

"Mock my power now, Barbarian." Malygris's voice laughed in his ears, but the wizard could not be seen. "You cannot even stand."

In a dim and desperate corner of his brain, Fafhrd realized that all he saw was still just illusion. He struggled to rise and toppled sideways again as the earth shifted under him and the sky whirled. He squeezed his eyes shut, hoping that would end the deception, but Malygris's power seared deeper into his mind. Though he fought disorientation, all his senses betrayed him. Still struggling, he opened his eyes again.

A ring of wizards surrounded him, all wearing the angry face of Malygris.

"I found you naked in her house," the wizards accused in chorus. "Tell me that you never touched her, and I'll kill you quickly."

"I can see you're beside yourself at the thought," Fafhrd answered sarcastically. By force of will he fought to his knees. Gripping Graywand in both hands, he plunged it deep into the earth and clung. At least it was some small anchor, some point of reference, in this dizzying madness.

Instantly the world turned upside-down, and he screamed, expecting to find himself dangling from his sword's hilt. Instead, his posture relative to the weapon remained the same. With some relief, he stared at the ring of wizards. Which was the real one? How could he tell? Were any of them real?

A horrible thought struck him. The real Malygris, made invisible to him by illusion, might at this very moment be sneaking up on his back side. Clinging to Graywand with one hand, he grabbed his dagger and swung it in a wild arc as he tried to look around.

Malygris laughed again. "I can make this torment last all night," the wizard said. "Tell me! Did you touch Laurian?"

"How long will your torment last," Fafhrd shot back, "if I refuse to answer?" Again the world tilted. Desperately, he flung his arms around Graywand, his anchor, and tried to drive the illusion from his mind. "She chose Sadaster over you. What if she chose me over you, as well? What if she chose a thousand men over you?"

The images of Malygris threw back their heads and howled.

"I could tell you what an idiot you've been," Fafhrd muttered under his breath, feeling a growing sickness in his stomach. "Were I not about to lose my lunch."

"Laurian!"

The wizard's outcry startled Fafhrd. Even in his state he heard the anguish and despair in that tortured shriek, and he wondered if, in some black corner of Malygris's evil heart, the wizard had, indeed, not merely coveted and desired Sadaster's wife, but loved her.

Fafhrd swallowed. Steeling his courage, he gripped Graywand's hilt and carefully levered himself off his knees. At first he crouched experimentally with his legs on either side of the sword. Then he stood precariously, not daring to let go.

"What kind of love," he said, his voice turning cold with contempt, "drives a man to murder? To lay a curse, not just upon his enemy, but upon uncounted innocent lives?"

Red anger flashed suddenly in the eyes of Malygris's images. "What do I care for innocent lives?" he shouted bitterly. "A spell got out of hand, that's all. To win Laurian's hand, I would burn Lankhmar to the ground!"

Fafhrd swallowed again. He thought of Vlana, his one true love, and a memory of her dark hair and bright eyes flashed softly through his mind. He smiled, recalling how he had climbed a high tree to catch his first sight of her as she danced in a tent for the men of his village.

His mother, Mor, had sought to keep him from that show and from the beautiful culture dancer. So Fafhrd and Vlana ran away from the show, from family, from the Cold Wastes—and from Mor, who in her anger and jealousy tried to kill them both with her ice magic.

Fafhrd shook his head. His mother, for all her faults, had been a good teacher, and her last lesson came home to him, suddenly clear.

It wasn't love that drove Malygris—only jealousy that had festered, poisoned, and turned into something monstrous.

"I touched her," Fafhrd said grimly. "I topped her like a great ram. I rocked her bed until the walls shook with the force of our lust, and still she called out, 'More! More!'"

The wizards howled again. They flung out their good arms, and bolts of blue lightning lanced toward Fafhrd, burning him with furious cobalt energy.

But Fafhrd didn't burn, for these were the old, weaker illusions. "'Fafhrd! Fafhrd!' she cried. And once, 'Oh my poor Sadaster!'" He continued, mocking the wizard now, determined to cut Malygris deeper with words than any sword ever would. "Never once did she murmur your name."

For a moment the spinning slowed, and the world resumed its natural positioning. A single wizard stood before Fafhrd again, turmoil written in the wretched expression he wore. Malygris stared at the ground, his eyes filled with visions of lost opportunity and lost hope.

Fafhrd saw his chance. He still held his dagger. It sprouted from his fist like a steel thorn. Fighting through the after-effects of his disorientation, he drew back and threw the blade with all his strength.

Barely in time, Malygris recovered himself and twisted away. Instead of his heart, the dagger sank into his already injured arm, biting through the bandages deep into muscle and bone. His high-pitched scream rang with shock and pain.

Fafhrd ripped his sword from the ground, determined to finish this confrontation. "One drop of your heart's blood," he said through clenched teeth. "Small payment for the suffering you've brought." He charged.

Graywand writhed in Fafhrd's grip, transforming itself into a ruby-eyed, tongue-lashing serpent. It coiled around Fafhrd's wrist and sank fangs deep into his bicep.

It was only an illusion, but the unexpectedness of it, coupled with Fafhrd's utter revulsion for snakes, proved an effective distraction.

Malygris ran.

EIGHTEEN
FESTIVAL'S END

Wrapped in his cloak, the Gray Mouser skulked through the shadows by the rutted road that ran parallel to the river. His keen eyes searched the riverbank. He sniffed the air. He listened, but except for the tranquil purling of that black ribbon of water, the night kept its silence.

Thin lips moved in a soundless curse.

Bad enough that Fafhrd had attempted to sneak past a sleeping Mouser without waking him. The Mouser's ego still smarted at that insult. Why, not so much as a rat, nay a roach on the floor, could slip by without stirring the Mouser, so lightly did he sleep!

But to actually have lost the great log-foot in the winding alleys east of Nun Street!

A brow furrowed under a gray hood, and one gray-gloved fist ground against a gloved palm. Disgusted with himself, the Mouser shook his head and prayed to Mog that Fafhrd hadn't purposefully given him the slip. He imagined the arrogant lummox crouching behind some barrel, chuckling to himself, then darting right into the shadows when the Mouser went left.

The Mouser knew he'd never hear the end of it, nor live down the shame if his partner had, indeed, tricked him.

Maybe he should have just stayed behind and spared himself potential embarrassment.

He scowled at another thought. What if Fafhrd was just sneaking out for some woman or a taste of the grape? Why partner or no partner, the Mouser would crown that splendid red head with the nearest wine-pot!

The thought of wine made him thirsty. Licking dry lips, he glided through thick grass down the riverbank's gentle slope to the river's edge. Bending low, he put his fingers into the softly flowing water. Its strange warmth surprised him. Marveling, he drew his hand out and thrust it back in again, sending small ripples dancing into the darkness.

Blood warm, he thought morbidly. With a curious trepidation, he raised his wet fingers and put them in his mouth. Only water. He chided himself for an overly imaginative fool. Cupping one palm, he took a deeper drink and wiped his hand on his cloak as he rose.

Far down the shore the faint light of a campfire glimmered. Gypsies, he expected. Still, lacking any other sense of Fafhrd's direction, he crept toward that flickering glow.

The fire reminded him sadly of Demptha's great burned library and the blaze at Sadaster's estate. So many books—so much knowledge lost. His heart ached at the loss, and his chest swelled with anger.

Yet what was to be gained by anger alone? Once again, he put his mind to work searching for answers to questions he could barely form, convinced that Malygris alone was no longer their only foe. *Sadaster and Demptha,* he murmured to himself.

What was the connection?

Concealed by the grass and the darkness, a narrow drainage ditch crossed the Mouser's path, carrying sewage and run-off from the edge of the city to the river. The Mouser's next step landed several inches lower than anticipated, and his foot slipped in a black slime. The world tilted, and the sky spun sharply clockwise. Choking back an outcry, the Mouser toppled side-ways with a muted splash.

Muttering curses, he dragged himself up and scrambled out of the ditch. A miasma swam in his nostrils. Mud covered his garments, saturated them. Disgust wrinkling his face, he shook black filth from his hands and fingers. "Capricious gods!" he grumbled as he bent down and wiped his hands in the grass. Unsatisfied, he went back to the river's shore and plunged them in the water.

But nothing could be done about his clothes. He sniffed himself and nearly gagged on the stench. Boots, trousers, sleeves, cloak—he took a mental inventory and cursed again. "What a world," he groused. "What a fine, pungent perfume for a dainty fellow like me!"

Muffled voices, born over the water, drew the Mouser's attention from his smelly plight. He turned his head toward the distant campfire again, slowly rising. Now he spied a second, smaller flame. A torch, perhaps?

He chewed his lower lip, listening, and his eyes narrowed suddenly. Despite the distance and the sound-distorting effect of the river, one of those voices carried a familiar note.

Forgetting his condition, he began to run. The sloping ground dipped and rolled under his feet. His sheathed sword slapped his leg, and his hood fell away from his face. In the dark-ness he stumbled, caught his balance, and kept running toward the campfire and the voices, which now were shouts, and one of them unmistakably belonged to Fafhrd!

Cast by the campfire, elongated shadows shifted and stirred over the dark sward. At the heart of those shadows, Fafhrd spun and danced like a drunken fool with arms outstretched, hands grasping at the air, head thrown back with a drunkard's fascina-tion for the stars.

With a natural caution, the Mouser stopped just beyond the reach of the light and crouched in the grass. Only an idiot rushed headlong into a fight without assessing the situation, and he considered himself no idiot.

But was this a fight? Though he had clearly heard two voices before, he saw no foe. Fafhrd shouted and cursed, and as the Mouser watched, the Northerner flung himself on the ground, twitching and kicking.

In horror, the Mouser cursed caution and prepared to rush to Fafhrd's side.

Before he could move, a chilling laugh rang out. "I can make this torment last all night," a voice said. "Tell me! Did you touch Laurian?"

The Mouser flattened himself in the grass, his gaze searching. At the very eastern edge of the campfire's glow, barely visible in the night, a figure stood with grim expression and bitter eyes, one arm extended, fingers clutching air in a menacing gesture.

Malygris!

The Mouser knew the wizard instantly and without doubt. Breath caught in his throat, and excitement quickened his heart. Here at last was their foe!

The wizard took a single step toward Fafhrd, crossing the tenuous border of darkness to stand just within the light of the campfire. His skin gleamed silver and orange, and the glow filled his angry gaze, lending it a queer quality.

The Mouser almost gasped aloud, recalling an image of Malygris that Sheelba had conjured from a campfire in the dark of night. For an instant, image and man made a perfect match, right down to the arrogant pose.

Then Malygris moved again and the match shattered. For one thing, the man was clothed in rags, and the Mouser noted the way he held an injured arm.

Fafhrd thrust his huge sword into the ground. Using it like a crutch, he attempted to rise and made it to his knees. "How long will your torment last?" he shouted in answer.

The Mouser ceased to listen. He rolled away from the edge of the light into deeper darkness. When he thought himself safely invisible, he rose and circled around behind Malygris, putting himself between the wizard and the city.

Fafhrd continued to shout, and his gaze darted off at strange angles as he reacted to things the Mouser couldn't see. Yet the Northerner climbed unsteadily to his feet and leaned on the sword.

Achieving the position he preferred, the Mouser drew his slender blade and crept down the easy slope, his boots making no sound in the soft grass and spongy earth. Malygris's broad back offered itself. If Fafhrd held the wizard's attention just a little longer, Scalpel would draw the precious, needed drop of heart-blood. Then let Sheelba work his magic and end this nightmare!

The wizard howled with a soul-deep pain and anger that froze the Mouser in his tracks before he could strike the fatal thrust. Then, clutching suddenly at that injured arm, Malygris howled a second time.

The Mouser saw his chance. Raising his sword, he rushed forward.

"Small payment for the suffering you've brought," Fafhrd cried grimly.

So suddenly did Malygris spin about that the Mouser was caught off-guard. The wizard ran straight into him, barely avoiding the rapier's deadly point. The impact whirled the Mouser about, and he crashed to the ground on his rump.

For a brief moment, Malygris loomed above him, an expression of dark rage on his face. The Mouser caught a glimpse of a dagger sprouting from the injured arm and a black, spreading smear on the sleeve. Blood!

The sight reminded him of his purpose. Clumsily, he thrust upward with his sword.

Growling like a cornered animal, the wizard disappeared before the Mouser's open eyes. The Mouser leaped to his feet again. Swinging his thin sword like a whip, he slashed desperately at the air where his foe had been.

A huge shadow fell over the earth as a figure blotted out the fire's glow. "My dagger for an appetizer!" Fafhrd roared fiercely. "Here comes the banquet!"

His great sword whistled down at the Mouser's head. In astonishment, the Mouser danced lithely back, and his rapier came up not to meet the larger blade, but at an angle to deflect it.

"There you are!" he cried, wondering how Malygris had come by his partner's weapon, for it was the wizard who attacked him, and there was no sign of Fafhrd. He eyed the massive sword, which looked improbably heavy in Malygris's thinly gnarled hands. "I see you're ready to dance. How fortunate for you there's still a place on my card!"

The Mouser lunged forward in a straight thrust, bending his back knee almost to the earth to come under the great sword. With surprising speed, the larger sword smashed downward, blocking his effort, turning his point aside with such force the Mouser barely kept his grip.

Yet keep it he did. With a flick of his wrist, he slashed his sword point at his opponent's hand, hoping to disarm with a cut. But Malygris moved marginally faster and turned the blow on the great sword's tangs.

Undaunted, the Mouser attacked. With three swift, skipping steps he drove the wizard toward the river. Malygris retreated adroitly, dodging the first thrust, ducking the second, turning the third away with the flat of his sword.

Then the Mouser's eyes widened in surprise. The wizard— brazen fool!—attacked him straight on! The great sword whirled in his hands, becoming a dazzling blur that gleamed red and gold in the firelight. The Mouser scrambled back from a fierce attack, pressed to defend himself against a blade that could smash his own narrow weapon into pieces.

The great sword sang down toward his head again. With delicate artistry, the Mouser's Scalpel flashed out and kissed it away. At the same time, the Mouser danced in close. Catching the front of Malygris's tunic in his empty hand, he attempted to head-butt his foe.

A massive hand came up and caught his face. Steel fingers squeezed. The Mouser felt himself lifted and flung bodily through the air. Managing to roll on the soft ground, he came up in a ready crouch with a greater respect for his enemy.

Malygris advanced, then stopped with a sour expression on his face. Reaching up, he pinched his nostrils shut. "Piss and spit, man!" he cursed in a loud nasal voice. "Your stench is worse than your swordplay! Did you shit your pants in fear of me?"

Stunned by this pronouncement, the Mouser sniffed himself. He coughed at the assault on his sensibilities. The smell of the ditch still clung. "It's a fair effluvia," he answered defensively. "Five silver smerduks an ounce, and all the rage with the dandies in the palace." He blinked, welcoming a chance to get his breath before the fight resumed. "How came you by my partner's sword?"

Malygris's right eyebrow shot up. "I was about to ask how you come by that toothpick the Gray Mouser calls a weapon. Or how you suddenly happen to speak with his same smirking, half-witted sarcasm?"

"Half-witted . . . ?" With narrowing eyes, the Mouser took a tighter grip on the hilt of his sword. "Well, this is certainly my very sword, Scalpel. But I shall be happy to give you a little of it."

His foe took a defensive posture. "Then mine is the more generous nature, for this is my sword, Graywand, and you shall have half its length!"

Yet no sooner had the wizard completed his boast than he fell back in a sudden fit of coughing. Gripped in both hands, the great sword wavered uncertainly. And though he struggled to keep his gaze upon the Mouser, the wizard's eyes widened with a quiet inner fear. He coughed harder, a deep wracking sound that issued from the depths of his lungs, and a thin scarlet spittle stained the corner of his lip.

Slowly, the Gray Mouser lowered his sword. A chill of understanding and subtle horror passed through him. "And how is it," he said in a low voice, "that you cough with the same resonant note as Fafhrd Red-Hair did early this morning and again in his sleep this early evening?"

Malygris's eyes flashed even through the sickness that filled them. "Play me no more games, madman! I am Fafhrd Red-Hair!"

"I know," the Mouser said softly, sheathing his sword. "And do you not recognize your own blood-and-oath bound friend?"

The point of the great sword dipped to the ground. Fafhrd, wrapped in the illusory appearance of Malygris, stared strangely. "Mouser?" he said.

The air around Fafhrd trembled as with heat-shimmer. Malygris, his angry demeanor, his rags and all melted away like vapor, leaving the tall copper-haired Northerner in his place. For a long moment, he gaped at the Mouser. Then his open mouth closed, and he leaned wearily on the sword he called Graywand.

"I thought you were Malygris," he said, shaking his huge head in confusion. Then his voice turned bitter as he wiped his lip and shot a look toward the city. "He fooled us with another of his damned illusions to make good his escape."

"He worked his magic on us both," the Mouser admitted. "To my eyes you were the image of him. Only the sound of your coughing stayed my hand, else I would have run you through."

The rightward corner of Fafhrd's mouth curled upward in a grin or a sneer. "Spoken boldly, for a man dumped on his rump in the combat. I would surely have taken your head had I not noted the familiar tenor of your boasting. Only that stayed my hand, that and your gut-churning stench, which would keep any man at a distance." He waved a hand under his nose and rolled his eyes in a mock-faint. "Your smell surpasses . . ."

The Mouser interrupted him. "It's Malygris's curse, isn't it?" he said. "It's touched you, too." He bit his lip. A band tightened around his chest, and breath failed him for a moment as he regarded the only man he had ever deigned to call *friend*.

Then something exploded inside him. He stamped his foot in the grass and smashed his fists on his thighs. "Did you think you could keep it secret?" he raged. "Why didn't you tell me?"

His shouts rolled over the water, and the night carried his accusing words far up and down the river banks. He didn't care who heard; Malygris was gone, escaped, and out of the Mouser's thoughts completely. Fafhrd alone mattered.

Not Malygris, not all of Lankhmar, not Sheelba. Only Fafhrd.

"How would I have profited by telling you?" Fafhrd answered with a restrained tension that betrayed his own turmoil. "The only thing you can do is what we've tried and failed so far to do—kill the creator of this dismal curse and take a drop of his heart's blood to the one who can effect a cure."

"And you thought you could do that best by sneaking off without me?" The Mouser shook his fists at the sky. Half-blinded by anger and a sense of betrayal he knew in his heart to be misplaced, he seized up the burning torch and hurled it toward the river, then scattered the campfire with a sweeping kick. Hot ash and sparks spiraled around him and upward into the dark night. "We are partners, Fafhrd—or we are nothing!"

Fafhrd coughed again and hung his head. From deep-shadowed eyes made strange by the remaining pieces of fireglow he fixed the Mouser with a hard look. He put one hand on his chest as if to measure his own heartbeat.

"This is no way for a man to die," he said, his voice little more than a whisper. "I feel it eating at me inside, like a tiny worm whose appetite is endless." He extended one hand toward his partner. "My grip is weaker. My breath is shorter. I don't have Sadaster's magic to stave off the outward symptoms, nor his blindness to what is really happening." He swallowed. "I left you behind to spare you this."

"You can't spare me!" The Mouser fairly screamed at his friend. "The risk is already before me. Did Sheelba not transport me as he did you? Did Laurian's ill-considered spell not drive me to . . ."

Abruptly he shut up, and just as abruptly he mastered all his rage and fear. Such an emotional outburst shamed him. Fafhrd needed his friendship and his swordarm—not anger that should rightly be directed at their enemy.

Reaching over a shoulder, he felt his upper back where the red welts of Liara's velvet whip still stung his flesh. "Well, never mind what it drove me to," he said at last, forcing a little chuckle as he went to Fafhrd's side, "though you'd love to hear the tale."

Frowning, Fafhrd backed off a step and held up a hand. "I face a horrible enough end," he warned. "I beg you, come no closer lest I choke on your reek!"

A grin broke over the Mouser's face and he flung his arms wide. "Then let it be a mercy killing!" he cried.

With that, he leaped upon Fafhrd, wrapping arms and legs about his partner's torso, clinging and laughing and waggling his head under Fafhrd's nose while the Northerner made all manner of gagging and retching noises and tried to wrestle free.

Finally they fell upon the ground, and Fafhrd lay still, eyes wide and staring, tongue lolling out the side of his mouth—a morbidly funny impersonation of death.

The Mouser straddled Fafhrd's chest. "Now my stink is all over you," he announced victoriously.

Fafhrd's eyes snapped closed; his head rolled limply to the side. "The curse in my body is bowing and scraping in the presence of a more potent and horrible force," he whispered.

"Maybe I can drive it out completely," the Mouser suggested. Making a wad of the muddiest part of his cloak, he pressed it to Fafhrd's nose.

Fafhrd's gag this time was genuine. With bunching muscles, he flung his partner off and got to his feet. "Physician, the cure is worse than the disease." He snatched up his sword from where it had fallen and pushed the blade into the sheath on his belt.

The Mouser picked himself up from the grass, straightened his cloak on his shoulders, and turned serious once more. With a grim note he answered, "Then together let's seek out the recommended medicine."

By unspoken agreement they turned away from the river and strode up the shallow slope toward the city. After only a few paces, they stopped again. Something gleamed in the grass. Bending down, Fafhrd retrieved his dagger. He held it up. The remaining light from the scattered campfire shone on the wetly incarnadined blade.

Fafhrd growled low in his throat, then opened his mouth and drew the blade over his tongue and licked the blood away. "It's only from his arm," he said sternly, "yet it may have an effect."

The Mouser nodded. "If only to make you hungry for the more potent stuff."

Once again they took to the alleyways and backstreets of nighted Lankhmar. Hooded, with hands on their weapon hilts, they kept to the shadows and sought the empty ways with Crypt Court their destination, there to consider the next course of action. Moving soundlessly past darkened shops and old, rat-infested tenements, they came finally to the warehouses and towering silos that bordered Grain Street.

"We're not returning to Crypt Court," the Mouser announced suddenly. With a pinched look and a furrowed brow, he led the way into the broad open lane, forsaking the gloomy alleys, and headed northward at a rapid pace. "We're going to the Festival District, and to the House of Night Cries."

Fafhrd grimaced. "Surely, Mouser, we face more important tasks than the slaking of your perverted lusts."

The Mouser barely listened. His mind worked furiously as he turned a corner and started down Barter Street, which would take them to the Garden of Dark Delights and thence to Face-of-the-Moon Street. It all had begun in the Festival District, beneath its streets in the Temple of Hates. There Malygris had concocted the evil spell that Sheelba and Demptha Negatarth both said should have been beyond his meager conjurer's skill.

Who, then, had aided him?

Ivrian. The name rang in his head like the bitter pealing of a broken bell. He no longer thought of her as Liara, for he had no doubt that she was, indeed, Ivrian, whom he had once called his true love.

Affection and desire had blinded him to any part she played in this mysterious adventure. But Fafhrd's illness and the desperateness of the situation now opened his eyes. More than a year ago he had seen Ivrian dead, her corpse chewed to bloody ruin by rats, then consumed by fire.

Yet she lived!

Malygris and Ivrian—he did not yet know the connection, but he felt intuitively there must be one.

Just so, he knew that Sadaster and Demptha Negatarth shared a connection—the spells they used to keep wife and daughter young beyond their years.

Convinced they were pieces of the same puzzle, he quickened his step. The answers lay with Ivrian!

"Here's another piece of the puzzle for you," Fafhrd said when the Mouser had explained his reasoning. He grabbed his gray comrade's arm and jerked him to a halt in the middle of the street. Raising one arm, he pointed down a narrow sidestreet.

Vlana, or her ghost, beckoned to them from the shadows. A milky nimbus of unnatural light surrounded her form. She swayed her hips to some unheard music, and her arms undulated with fluid, serpentine motions. Black hair swept about her kohl-eyed face, stirred and lifted by a wind neither Fafhrd nor the Mouser felt.

Some pain seemed to stab at Fafhrd's heart. Clutching his chest, he lurched toward her like a man entranced. "Vlana!" he cried. "True love!"

The Mouser caught a piece of Fafhrd's cloak and jerked. A loud gasping, gagging noise issued from Fafhrd's throat as the clasp unexpectedly choked him. Like a man snapped rudely awake, he stopped and spun about.

"Don't look at her!" the Mouser shouted. Catching hold of Fafhrd's arms, he gave him a shake. "Don't you see? She only means to delay us!" He looked up into Fafhrd's eyes. Then, jaw slack with new revelation, he stepped back and slapped his forehead.

"That's what they are supposed to do," he cried, shaking Fafhrd again. "Vlana and Ivrian have done nothing but delay us and prevent us from looking for Malygris."

Fafhrd mumbled as he looked back over his shoulder to the dancing Vlana. "I thought she was one of Malygris's illusions," he admitted. "But I'm not sure!" His voice rose, thick with emotion. "I let her die, Mouser. I let the rats and the fire eat her ivory flesh side by side with your own Ivrian!"

"And someone cruelly uses the guilt we feel," the Mouser answered in a voice turned cold, "to turn us from our real task—finding Malygris." He, too, stared with Fafhrd down the sidestreet. Vlana stood still now, dancing no more, an accusing look upon her pale face.

The Mouser's voice softened somewhat. "I tell you, Fafhrd, she is no more than a decoy. Run off and chase her through the night if you must. But I will not be turned aside."

The Northerner hung his head, and with his eyes squeezed tightly shut, pushed past the Mouser. His feet shuffled in the road for a few steps, then moved with determination. Breathing a sigh of relief, the Mouser took his place at Fafhrd's side, and they continued on to the Festival District.

But he couldn't resist a final glance over his shoulder. Vlana, or whatever she was, had disappeared.

A few blocks further, and they reached the edge of the Festival District. The streets, which should have yet been crowded with celebrants, merchants and entertainers, instead were quiet, nearly empty. A now familiar pallid fear marked the faces of the few pedestrians they encountered. Shops were closed. The kiosks had been taken down. The taverns remained open, but the busiest hosted only a squad of off-duty soldiers, and the noise that issued even from that seemed muted and nervous.

The magic that had compelled such a carnal frenzy the night before had exacted a toll of suspicion and uncertainty from the citizens. Many had stayed home tonight; some had left the city early to return to their farms and villages.

A man suddenly leaped from behind a rain barrel to block their path. Round, wide eyes filled with the light of madness glared at them from a sallow, too-thin face. His wild hair jutted from his head at all angles, and clothes that once were finely made hung on him in tatters.

"Good sirs, don't go any further!" came a sibilant whisper. The man paused and shot fearful looks over his bony shoulders before turning back to Fafhrd and the Mouser. "There's plague in the district! Plague!" He hesitated again, then thrust a hand forward. Keeping his voice low, he added, "That'll be a tikpenny for the warning."

"We know," Fafhrd answered. Delicately, he put his hand to his mouth and gave a sharp cough, then another.

The beggar's eyes grew even wider, and his knees began to shake. When Fafhrd coughed a third time, he turned and fled down the street, disappearing around a corner.

"That didn't sound like a very genuine cough," the Mouser commented.

"I didn't feel like parting with a tik-penny," Fafhrd said with a wry wink and a shrug.

Skirting the edge of the Garden of Dark Delights, they came to Face-of-the-Moon Street. The Mouser proceeded Fafhrd up the pebbled walkway, past the elaborate lawn sculptures, and up the marble steps. Small oil lamps suspended on bronze pegs burned on either side of the door tonight, their flames shielded by glass globes.

"Stand here," the Mouser said, positioning Fafhrd against the wall where he'd be just out of sight when the door opened. "When I hook the fish, you net him."

Seizing the brass knocker, the Mouser slammed it twice against the plate. In a moment, the door opened. The Mouser pushed back his hood and smiled at the hugely muscled, bald warrior that served the house as guardian and doorman.

"Good evening, you over-grown jackass. Remember me?"

The doorman growled. "Yes, little man. I threw you out on your drunken head last night."

He reached for the Mouser with large, grasping hands. When the Mouser backed up a step, the doorman followed. Fafhrd tapped him on the shoulder and, when he turned, smashed his own huge fist against the doorman's jaw.

The doorman's eyes glazed, but his lips parted in a weak grin. "Thank you, sir. May I have another?" Half-heartedly, he raised a fist to strike back, but Fafhrd's blow had achieved its purpose. The Mouser dropped to his hands and knees behind the door-man's legs, and Fafhrd gave a push. Over the doorman went into the bushes beside the high marble steps.

"A mightier blow I couldn't have delivered myself," the Mouser said, brushing his hands. "Now for Ivrian and a few answers!"

Yet before they could enter the house, a startled gasp spun them about. At the gateway to the marbled path, wrapped in a walking cloak, Ivrian stood still as a deer and stared nervously at them both. Then she bolted back into the street.

Fafhrd and the Gray Mouser bounded down the steps in pursuit, reaching the street just in time to see the girl dash into the Garden of Dark Delights. They charged after her. A flash of a heel led them through the shadows; a swish of a cloak drew them deeper still into the park.

Abruptly, Fafhrd grabbed the Mouser's arm and jerked him to a halt. "You know I'm not a cautious man by nature," he whispered, peering around. "But this situation, in the parlance of my distant northern cousins, stinks."

A familiar voice called out from behind them. "The only stink here," it said, "clings to the two of you!"

Fafhrd whirled, the great sword he called Graywand sweeping from its sheath in one smooth motion.

The Mouser held up a hand. "Captain!" he cried in greeting as he turned.

"I was having a drink at a tavern," Nuulpha said. The faint moonlight glinted on his corporal's helmet as he pushed back his hood. "I thought I saw you skulking past, so I followed."

"How fares that fat, spend-thrift wife of yours?" Fafhrd asked, sheathing his blade again.

"Not well," Nuulpha answered, his voice dropping a note. "Though I speak roughly of her sometimes, she is the reason I serve Demptha Negatarth—in hope of a cure. She too suffers from Malygris's curse."

"Forgive me," Fafhrd said quickly. "I intended no cruelty."

Nuulpha shrugged. Unfastening his chin strap, he removed his helmet and wiped a hand through his damp black hair. "It's no matter . . ." he said. Then he screamed.

Before their eyes, his helmet transformed into a spitting black cat. Fangs sank deep into Nuulpha's hand; the beast wrapped itself ferociously around his arm and with razor-sharp talons raked his flesh to red ribbons. Not all his efforts could shake the creature loose.

"Wizard!" Fafhrd shouted, whipping out his sword again.

Once more the earth began to buck and shake, to lift and roll in wave after wave, and to spin like a child's top. With an awkward and frustrated cry, the Northerner fell and thrashed on the ground. The Mouser, too, toppled helplessly sideways.

"Time to die, fools!" Malygris called. "Time for all to die— you, me, Lankhmar itself. Laurian is lost, so let all be lost!"

The Mouser twisted his head up from the grass and tried to gaze around. Malygris was somewhere close to judge by his voice. Yet, the wizard cloaked himself with still another damned illusion, rendering himself invisible. He twisted his head the other way. Fafhrd and Nuulpha kicked and struggled and twitched to no avail. The cat, at least, was gone. That too had only been an illusion.

A deranged voice boomed in the Mouser's ear. "Hear the death-cry of an entire city!"

Immediately the ground turned solid again. The Mouser found himself standing in the middle of a street. Flames leaped up from scores of buildings. The dead lay piled in the gutters and ditches. A cart trundled toward him, stacked with bodies. As it went by, he stared at the pale, horror-stricken faces, the bloody lips and the ruptured eyes. The driver coughed so severely he could barely work the reins and guide his draft-ox.

A trio of wild-eyed men bearing torches dashed past him. "Plague!" they screamed. "Plague!" Kicking open the door of a house, they proceeded to set fire to the interior.

"No!" shrieked an old woman. In her arms she cradled a small boy. The child lay limply in her arms, weakly coughing. A thin red film trickled from its lips and down its chin as the Mouser stood helplessly by.

"It's everything we have!" the old woman cried.

One of the men swung his torch, knocking her into the street. The cart rolled heedlessly across her back, crushing woman and child.

The Mouser fought down his revulsion and gathered his strength. "Illusion!" he cried, squeezing his eyes shut. "It's not real! None of it's real!"

Abruptly he was in the park again, sprawled on the grass, staring up at the sky through the thick trees.

"Isn't it?" Malygris's voice said coldly. "Listen carefully, little one. Listen to the groans of fear that come even now from the other side of the garden walls; now a cry goes up through the city, becomes a chorus; the despairing wails begin to mount."

The Mouser listened, and true enough he thought he heard, like a distant wind, the voices of terror, a lamentation rising in the night.

"Show yourself, coward!" Fafhrd said as he rose uncertainly to his feet. "Let me put another dagger in you."

"I have already won our duel, barbarian," Malygris answered. "I see the streaming mark of my curse upon you."

Fafhrd gave a stricken look and wiped the back of one hand across his mouth. It came away with a red smear.

Farther down the walkway, the darkness flickered in a peculiar manner, as if the wind had rippled a black curtain and parted it. Malygris's thin, bald form appeared, his arms folded into ragged bloodstained sleeves, his eyes burning with madness.

"Perhaps you'd like a preview of things to come," he said, his wild gaze fixed on Fafhrd.

A violent coughing wracked Fafhrd's mighty frame, bending him double as he clutched his chest and throat. His hair turned thin, lost its luster, and began to fall out. He spit blood into his hands; crimson spotted his lips and chin, the front of his tunic.

Dark circles formed around his eyes, and the flesh began to hang upon his cheekbones.

Weakened legs gave way beneath him, and he fell gasping for air with spasming lungs. His musculature dissolved away until his bones began to show through bloodless flesh and his ribs showed right through his garments until he appeared little more than a pitifully thrashing skeleton with a veil of parchment draped over it.

A desperate mewling issued from Fafhrd's dehydrated lips, and he raised a supplicating hand toward the Mouser.

"Stop it!" the Mouser cried. In horror he watched as Fafhrd's bloody teeth dropped out of his head. Drawing his dagger, Catsclaw, he prepared to throw, but suddenly there were three images of Malygris, then six, then nine, then more than the Mouser could count, all arrayed before him like an impossible, ragged army.

He screamed in frustration. Scooping up a handful of pebbles from the walkway, he flung them. Every image of Malygris reacted exactly the same, raising one arm to shield a laughing face.

"This is how it will be for you, defiler!" Malygris said to Fafhrd, his eyes blazing, his voice an angry hiss. "But you'll die slowly, over weeks, perhaps months. Your flesh will rot and drip from your bones. Just as it was with Sadaster. You'll curse the day you came between me and Laurian!"

Through a gumless slash of a mouth, Fafhrd managed to answer, "You're insane."

Balancing his dagger carefully by the point, the Mouser folded his legs and sat down on the ground. His eyes narrowed to small slits; he calmed his breathing and let his racing heart slow. *It's all illusion*, he reminded himself. Fafhrd was not really dying at his feet. Nor did his enemy stand before him in scores.

He had been the pupil and ward of Glavas Rho. The herb-wizard had raised him through boyhood and taught him a thing or two about magic. A simpler form of magic, to be sure, but the

Mouser had paid attention to his studies. A discerning eye, he knew, could tell the real from the false.

"Yes, insane!" Malygris agreed. "You destroyed the most precious jewel in Nehwon, my Laurian. Now I will have my revenge!" The wizard barked a short, ugly laugh. "Just imagine when your heart stops, barbarian!"

Fafhrd's bulging eyes snapped wider. A choked gasp of pain forced its way sharply from his lips as he clutched his shrunken chest.

The Mouser remained calm. Subtly, he snatched another pebble and flicked it toward one of the images of Malygris. When it failed to react, he hid a smile. *False*, he judged. So the unreal images only reacted when the real wizard moved.

"You killed Laurian," Fafhrd croaked. Somehow, as if he too were managing to fight the illusions, he struggled to his hands and knees. "You wrapped your own hands around her silken neck, because she hated you with all her heart! You are the murderer—and the fool."

The Mouser flicked pebbles at three more images, eliminating them in his mind. When he found one that reacted, then his dagger would fly.

"I could have won her," Malygris raged. The images shook their fists at Fafhrd. "But Sadaster stole her from me and dragged her to this cursed city. Sadaster and Lankhmar poisoned her heart against me. Now see how they are punished!"

Malygris thrust his good arm upward, and his fingers strained toward the sky.

High above the treetops, a thin red glow appeared. A ribbon of bloody hue wafted as if on a wind, furling and unfurling on itself, floating gracefully like a thin kite. Yet through the pretty light it radiated an evil, a soul-shriveling vileness of dark and vast power.

The Mouser stared. The ribbon descended through the trees to swirl a few times about Malygris's upraised hand. It moved then to Fafhrd, but as if with some arcanely primitive power of recognition, it turned away.

Despite himself, the Mouser's heart quailed. That tenuous scarlet veil swept across the lawn. Too late, he leaped to his feet. The red horror poured into his nostrils, into his mouth as he gave an involuntary cry.

In the moment that it touched him, entered him, *infected him,* he felt a hunger deeper and blacker than anything his mind had ever conceived, a starving void, a ravening gulf, greedy in its need. It swallowed him like a morsel, *devoured* him.

Then it spit him out again like chewed gristle and moved on.

The Mouser shivered with fear even as he fought to remain calm. A barely perceptible weakness burrowed in his muscles; he felt it like the tiniest tear in his soul through which his life-force leaked away.

Forgotten in the conflict, Nuulpha rose suddenly from the ground as the red ribbon coiled serpent-like about his throat. If Nuulpha noticed at all, though, he gave no sign of it. And un-coiling, the ribbon rose away from him and faded. Was Nuulpha, then, already infected as well?

The corporal thrust a hand under his crimson cloak and into a vest pocket on his jerkin. "They are mere swordsmen, fool," he said coldly. Only the voice was not that of Nuulpha! The air seemed to ripple around him like water. *Illusions and illusions!* The image of Nuulpha melted. In his place stood Demptha Negatarth. "And your fight is here."

Out of that vest pocket came a deck of cards. Demptha Negatarth bent them sharply in his fingers and scattered them through the air.

"You swore not to interfere!" the images of Malygris screamed.

"I swore not to warn Sadaster," Demptha Negatarth answered. "And I've paid the price. Your damned curse is beyond your control. It destroyed my daughter, and now it's poisoned me. I'll see you dead for it, and pour your heartblood myself into a vessel for these adventurers."

Demptha's tarot cards flew with unnatural accuracy. Touched by the cards, the images of Malygris vanished, leaving only a single image—Malygris, himself.

Seething with rage, the wizard extended his good arm toward Demptha. But before he could cast any spell one of the fluttering cards landed on his outstretched hand.

Immediately, the painting on the card came to frightening life. A glittering bird, seemingly formed all of crystal and jewels, sank talons into Malygris's flesh. Shimmering wings with razor-sharp facets beat furiously at his face, and an emerald beak flashed at his eyes.

Malygris screamed in pain and terror, and the bird grew larger. Now its wings beat the air. Malygris swung his arms wildly, trying to fight free as the creature struggled to lift him bodily into the air.

Above him, the red ribbon appeared again, glowing a deeper, uglier shade, pulsing and throbbing with unholy life. Lengthening and lengthening, it wrapped around Malygris and the bird both, muffling the wizard's screams and the bird's angry caws, extinguishing them.

Around and around the ribbon flashed until it was no longer a ribbon at all, but a huge ball, a bubble of blackly crimson hue through which only the vaguest shadows of Malygris and the bird could be seen still locked in combat.

"What enchantment is this?" Fafhrd asked, rising and backing away from the bubble until he stood at the Mouser's side. Free from Malygris's power, he looked himself again.

"Not mine," answered Demptha Negatarth with bitterness and puzzlement.

Then from out of the shrubbery another figure emerged.

"Ivrian!" the Mouser cried.

She paid him no attention, but ran straight to the bubble of red light. Without thinking, the Mouser leaped to intercept her, but his hands closed only on a string of pearls around her neck before she entered that evil glow.

Flying through the air, Fafhrd hit him from the side, his arms locking tight about the Mouser's waist as they fell to the ground in a tangled heap. "Ivrian!" the Mouser cried again.

Within that luminous orb, a winsome silhouette seemed to turn his way.

Slowly, the orb sank into the earth, taking wizard and bird and girl. Its bloody light faded, too, leaving them in darkness and a chilling quiet.

The Mouser stared forlornly at the place where the orb had been. On the grass nearby a few pearls glimmered. He opened his fist. On his palm lay a few more pearls, and a few strands of soft blond hair.

Fafhrd began to speak. "Mouser . . . ?"

In the distance, Aarth's great bell began to peel, and the sound of it froze them. Twelve times it rang, then a pause and an extra final note that vibrated across the city.

"Midnight," Demptha Negatarth whispered, "and Festival's end."

NINETEEN

SHADOWLAND

The Mouser spun toward Demptha Negatarth. "What did he mean, you swore not to interfere?"

Demptha frowned as he hung his old head. He looked pathetically small suddenly in the too-large corporal's uniform he wore. Slowly, stiffly, he bent and retrieved the helmet that lay on the ground nearby.

"Nuulpha!" he called loudly, straightening. "Nuulpha!" Then, licking his lower lip, he finally met the Mouser's hard stare. "When Jesane was four summers old she developed a blood disease. My magic couldn't help her, but Malygris had a spell. He came to me in the night and offered it. Not only could it halt the effects of aging—you saw that in your dream of Laurian—but used in another manner, it could hold back death indefinitely."

"Wizards are stingy with their secrets," Fafhrd said scornfully. "He just gave you this powerful enchantment?"

Demptha Negatarth shook his head. "We bargained. He gave me the spell to save my daughter's life. In exchange, I swore never to interfere in any of his undertakings. I knew it was a promise I would one day regret. Malygris was never to be trusted, and even then I suspected his hatred for Sadaster, who was my friend. But to save Jesane's life, I dealt with the devil when he appeared on my doorstep."

The Mouser bent to collect one of Ivrian's fallen pearls from the grass. "Why didn't you ask Sadaster for the spell?" he questioned.

Demptha's frown deepened. "When Jesane was out of danger, I went to Sadaster, driven by a sense of guilt that I had bargained with his enemy, and he received me cordially. I meant to keep my word to Malygris, I told him, but as a gesture of regret, and in a spirit of atonement, I offered to share this new bit of arcana with him." He gave a short, bitter laugh. "What a joke on me it was—and a shock to my host—to learn that the spell was one of Sadaster's most closely guarded secrets. Not so closely guarded, however, that Malygris had not been able to steal it."

"There at least is the connection I sought," the Mouser mused as he pushed the pearl down inside his right glove. "It must have been Sadaster's spell . . ."—he looked at Demptha—"that very spell in the book that exploded in my hand and set fire to your library."

Fafhrd coughed unpleasantly into his fist, nodding. "I'll wager there was another copy of that same spell in Sadaster's library, which also burned."

Nuulpha came charging up the pebbled walkway, clad only in a loincloth, a soft tunic, and his boots with a brown nondescript cloak thrown around his shoulders. In his arms, he carried a bundle of clothes. "I heard your call," he said to Demptha, and the two men began exchanging clothes.

"My powers are not what they used to be," Demptha explained with some embarrassment as he disrobed. "Dressing in Nuulpha's garments reinforced the illusion that I was Nuulpha. I could never have gotten that close to Malygris, otherwise."

Nuulpha looked to the Mouser as he took his red corporal's cloak from Demptha and put the brown one around the older man. "There were two more fires yesterday. The Patriarch's private library in the Temple of Aarth burned. And Rokkarsh's private rooms in the Rainbow Palace—both small fires and quickly contained." He wriggled into blue pantaloons, and stomped into his boots again, then strapped on the sword belt Demptha had borrowed.

Dressed in simple brown robes, Demptha put on a troubled scowl as he looked at the Mouser. "Another connection there?"

The Mouser pulled up his hood, feeling the need to cloak his face from the others. The tiny weakness growing inside him, Malygris's curse, scared him more than he wanted the others to know. He listened to Fafhrd's ragged cough again and tried to steel himself against his fear.

"We're playing some game," he said at last, "without knowing the rules and without all the pieces. But at last I know where we'll find the answers. When Malygris's curse touched me I felt something powerful, something Malygris could not possibly have created or conjured, something far beyond his ability. Something old—a terror I've experienced only once before."

"In the tunnels?" Nuulpha whispered in a dry, nervous voice. The Mouser nodded.

"Tunnels?" Fafhrd noted with distasteful grimace. "That red ball of light took Malygris under the ground."

"It surprised him as much as us," Demptha said. "He looked frightened."

"Ivrian, on the other hand," the Mouser replied bitterly, "ran to it eagerly." He stamped his foot on the spot where she had stood in that eerie crimson glow. "Wherever Malygris went, we are dead men if we don't follow, Fafhrd. His curse is upon us both."

Demptha stepped closer to the Mouser. "I'm also infected now, and I'll go with you, for I know those tunnels as well as Jesane knew them. Nuulpha, though, is untouched by this damned curse." He turned to the man who, though a soldier in service to the Overlord, had served him so well and faithfully. "Go home to your wife, Nuulpha. She needs you in her final hours."

Nuulpha's expression hardened. He drew his sword half out of its sheath as he appealed to Demptha. "These good men say a drop of blood from the wizard's heart can save her. Let my blade draw that drop and more."

Fafhrd touched Nuulpha's hand and pushed the sword back into its sheath. "I was not with my Vlana when she died," he said, "and I've never yet forgiven myself. If Malygris's hard heart can be pierced, we'll draw the medicine ourselves. Listen to Demptha."

Moving apart from the others, the Mouser kept silent. He too had been absent at that moment when Ivrian and Vlana died, and that guilt also ate at his soul. Only now he found that Ivrian lived, or a cruel version of her. How did he feel about her now? What had happened to his love?

He felt the hot sting of tears in his eyes and pulled his hood closer about his face. How could a man stand such confusion?

"Go home, Nuulpha," he said at last, his voice cracking with emotion. "Go home to your wife."

A conflicted look darkened the corporal's features, but he relinquished the grip on his sword's hilt. Shoulders sagging, he said to Demptha, "You've been like a father to me." He squeezed the old man's arm, unable to say more. The graveled path crunched under his boots as he turned and strode away.

Demptha sighed as he watched the corporal depart. "He's been like a son," he said quietly when only the Mouser and Fafhrd could hear. "I don't believe he ever realized that Jesane loved him."

"His wife is truly ill?" Fafhrd asked.

"Near death," Demptha affirmed.

"All the more reason to act swiftly," the Mouser said, "while the hot anger in our hearts shields us against the fear of what we must do."

Despite his paleness, Fafhrd grinned at Demptha. "The Mouser makes his prettiest speeches when he's mad." He threw back his head and laughed.

The streets of the Festival District were virtually empty. Even the taverns had shut up their doors and windows. Through the cracks of the shutters, muted lamplight filtered, and sometimes a silhouetted face peered suspiciously out.

A few blocks away, perhaps in the neighboring Plaza District, someone wandered through the streets calling, "Plague! Plague!" And from another voice farther away came the same cry. The echoes of those voices bouncing among the buildings conspired to trick the ears, and in the black hour after midnight it seemed that some unholy chorus was at work.

Leaving the taverns of the Festival District behind, Demptha Negatarth set a determined pace on the road that ran in the shadow of the Great Marsh Wall. On one side of the street, warehouses loomed, seemingly at unnatural angles, as if the earth had somehow tilted under them, and slanted rooftops seemed on the verge of sliding off the walls that supported them. Their windows, like square black eyes, seemed to watch the street and the odd trio that passed by, and huge doors gaped like black mouths.

Every shape and sight possessed an ominous air on this morbid night, and every slightest sound seemed a warning cry. The capricious wind felt like an unexpected breath on the back of the neck or the side of the face, and the smell of death hung over all like a tenuous perfume.

Thick clouds raced across the sky like massive phantoms, bringing an unseasonable chill, sending dust from the streets swirling.

High on the great wall's rampart, a nervous guard shouted down for them to identify themselves.

Fafhrd responded with a rude gesture. "Identify this!" he called back.

At last they reached a familiar warehouse. The Mouser ran ahead of Demptha, down the narrow alleyway, and tugged open the door. With one hand on Graywand, Fafhrd slipped past the Mouser and entered the warehouse first. Following, Demptha stepped on the Mouser's foot.

A sharp breath hissed between the Mouser's lips as he bit back a curse.

"Sorry," Demptha whispered.

The Mouser continued to mutter under his breath as he pulled the door closed and slid home a wooden bolt. Now they were sealed inside. Little relief or consolation in that, however. The darkness inside the structure felt more imposing, more impenetrable, than the darkness in the streets.

"Over here," Demptha called.

Tugging on Fafhrd's sleeve, the Mouser limped to the corn crib that concealed Demptha's personal staircase to the underworld. He well remembered the last time he used that stair and recalled the horrible screaming, the numbing fear, the empty room, and a lot of vanished sick people.

"What happened in the Temple of Hates?" he asked abruptly as he balanced with his booted toes on the very edge of the first step. "What became of Mish and all your sick patients?"

"I don't know," came Demptha's pensive answer. "I left Jesane in charge while I stepped out for some air." He paused as if wondering whether to say more. At last he continued. "Strangest thing," he muttered, his voice dropping with a mixture of embarrassment and shame. "As it had so many nights of late, a heavy fog rolled in. Yet, this one seemed to bring with it peculiar thoughts and odd stirrings. An old whore came walking down the road in the midst of it. The lowest class of street-walker, working late I suppose. Suddenly I was diddling her on the very doorstep of the Rat God's temple!"

"Laurian's handiwork again," Fafhrd said with a sad shake of his head. Abruptly he changed the subject as he peered into the black stairwell. "You know I'm not a superstitious man, Mouser. But if your plan is to descend into this hole without any kind of light, I'd like a few moments to change your mind."

"Feel around in the corner near your foot, Fafhrd," Demptha instructed. "You should find an old lantern, battered and rusted, as if it had been discarded and forgotten years ago. But if you shake it, you'll find the reservoir still contains a small amount of oil."

Fafhrd crouched low and explored the corner of the crib with a broad sweep of his hand, encountering the lantern lying on its side. Holding it close to his ear, he shook it and smiled at the sloshing sound it made.

"How do you expect to fire the wick?" the Mouser asked.

Demptha Negatarth gave a low, mocking chuckle. "As some wise friend once said, wizards are stingy with their secrets."

A small flame sprang suddenly from the lantern's wick. An orange glow lit up Fafhrd's startled face. Hiding his own surprise, the Mouser blinked at the sudden light. Though it was hard to be sure, he thought he saw a tiny rain of fine black powder above the wick before Demptha withdrew his hand.

"A mere trick of prestidigitation," he scoffed, assuming a professional disinterest, though in truth he was considerably impressed.

"Your friend asked for light," Demptha replied with the slightest of smiles. "Not miracles."

Seizing the lantern by its bail, the Mouser turned the wick as high as it would go and lowered the glass shield around it. Then, drawing slender Scalpel from its sheath, he led the way down the narrow steps.

Demptha followed, and Fafhrd brought up the rear. The Northerner's great body nearly filled the tiny tunnel at the bottom. He bent low, and still his head brushed the ceiling. He thumped the close walls on either side with his fists.

"A worm burrowing through the earth has more room," he grumbled.

"But it lacks your charm and good nature," the Mouser said impatiently as he lifted the light high and started forward.

"Not to mention my good looks," Fafhrd shot back.

"The tunnels below Lankhmar are not always so cramped," Demptha explained as he gave Fafhrd's arm a sympathetic pat. "Some, however, are worse."

They stopped talking then. Their small light quivered, intimidated by the blackness ahead, but the Mouser pricked the dark with the point of his rapier and pushed it back with each nervously determined step. He felt the weight of Ivrian's pearl on the back of his right hand where he had thrust it under his glove and thought of her down here somewhere with Malygris— and with something still more dreadful.

The tunnel merged into another, then another. At last Fafhrd could stand straight as he walked. He gave a soft cough, stifling it as best he could with his hand. "Were I not already at Death's door," he whispered, "the quailing in my heart would send me clawing right up to the surface world again."

The Mouser said nothing. The same crushing fear that had filled these passages before still permeated them. He could barely breathe, for the choking hand of it held him by the throat. Only the thought of Ivrian drew him on.

The softest weeping rose from Demptha. "My poor Jesane," he murmured. "Even with her brave heart, she must have run from this terror, abandoning her charges."

"It caught up with her," the Mouser said, tight-lipped.

Against the strangling dark, they pressed on. Demptha's weeping ceased as they emerged into a cavern. "Is this the way to the Temple of Hates?" the Mouser asked doubtfully, for it lacked the look of the cavern that led to that place.

Demptha moved past the Mouser, turning his gaze toward the high ceiling, then all around as he walked to the very edge of the lantern's light and touched a stalagmite that stood twice his height. He shook his head. "This is wrong," he said, and a new fear shadowed his face as he turned back toward the light. "Yet it can't be. We came the proper route."

"What is this mist rising from the ground?" Fafhrd said apprehensively.

The Mouser fairly jumped as he glanced downward at a creeping vapor that curled around his boots. Everywhere he looked, as far as the lantern let him see, a fine cold smaze seeped up through the cavern floor and filtered into the air, diffusing the quality of the lantern's light, leeching away the faint warmth it offered.

The very walls seemed to retreat into the deepening darkness. The ceiling, too, arched away from vision. Still the vapor rose, growing thicker, hiding the floor and the tops of their feet, climbing their ankles and shin-bones.

The Mouser shivered as he lifted the lantern higher. "I think the way lies there," he said, pointing to the rightward side of the cavern with his sword. "I'm sure I saw the opening of another tunnel."

Every sense screamed to turn away, but the Mouser fixed his gaze ahead, and his comrades followed. *Could this be one of Malygris's illusions?* he briefly wondered. Then he dismissed that consideration. Their true foe, he felt sure, remained unknown—and unnamed.

To his small relief the passage on the far side of the cavern lay exactly where he thought it should. Yet, as he shone the lantern's light upon its threshold, he hesitated, alerted by a shadow.

An emaciated figure lurched from the tunnel into the cavern. Bulging, jaundiced eyes glared with a horrible light from a thinly bearded face.

"Mish!" Demptha Negatarth cried over the Mouser's shoulder as he recognized his missing friend, and the Mouser also gaped with surprise—a mistake.

With a sweep of his arm, Mish knocked the Mouser's sword away. A hand of astonishing strength seized the Mouser's tunic and flung him crashing to the rocky ground. His head struck against a towering stalagmite, filling his eyes with sparks of colored fire. The lantern rattled loudly and rolled to a stop against a jutting stone; the wick hissed; veiled beneath cold white vapor, the quivering flame threatened to go out.

"Turn away!" Mish howled at the Mouser. Then his unnatural gaze locked on Demptha Negatarth. His hands shot out. Catching the old wizard by the throat, he squeezed. "Ten more!" he cried.

Fafhrd leaped around Demptha, who stood in his way. Graywand whisked from its sheath as he moved, and the blade flashed.

Mish screamed. Stumbling back, he held up the twin stumps of severed arms and stared. Again he screamed, and the sound of his pain echoed desperately against the walls of earth and stone.

Demptha screamed, too, and fell to the ground, wrestling with the hands that still stubbornly tried to throttle him.

Fafhrd struck again. Swinging with all his fear-driven might, he sliced off Mish's head and sent it smashing against the same stalagmite where the Mouser struggled to sit up. It landed in his gray-clad lap between his very knees.

A sound of repulsion gurgled in the Mouser's throat. Hurling the head away, he scrambled to save the lantern.

Mish's corpse fell. It kept on falling, as if the mist were water, and a feathery white wave closed over it. Ripping free the hands that gripped him, Demptha dropped them into the unnatural stuff, and they too sank away as if into a rippling lake.

Rising with the lantern in one hand, his sword in the other, the Mouser walked cautiously to the spot and poked the rapier into it. The point scraped on solid stone. Licking his lips, looking to his comrades, he stamped his feet upon the place.

"Dance this way with that light," Fafhrd said, "and look at this." He held Graywand's broad blade to the amber glow. It gleamed cleanly. "No blood."

"Whatever that was," the Mouser said to Demptha, "it wasn't Mish." Yet in his heart, he wasn't so sure. He couldn't discount the radical change in Ivrian, once his true love.

Entering the new tunnel, the Mouser steeled himself against the terror that permeated this strange labyrinth. Once again the stone walls pressed close, and the ceiling slanted gradually lower and lower. The mist thickened as they advanced, and the small lantern became virtually useless. Unable to see more than a few feet ahead, the Mouser waved his sword before him, tapping first one wall and then the other.

Suddenly metal rang on metal. The Mouser felt a shock rise up through his sword and into his arm. Barely keeping a grip on his weapon's hilt, he leaped back, colliding with an unwary Demptha. "Fall back! Fall back!" he cried. Shoving the lantern into Demptha's hands, he drew his dagger, Catsclaw.

A figure brandishing shield and a long dirk rushed screaming out of the fog at the Mouser. Behind that ferocious warrior, from the narrow tunnel, came four more, similarly armed. Blocking the dirk's thrust with Scalpel, he brought his foot up against the nearest shield and kicked the closest foe back into his companions.

The Mouser's eyes snapped wide. He recognized the face that appeared just over that shield rim. "The Ilthmarts!" he shouted. "The dead Ilthmarts!"

"Ilthmarts behind us, too!" Fafhrd answered grimly. "Five more!" There was no room in the tunnel for Graywand. He drew his dagger, instead. Bellowing a mighty roar, he charged straight into the five, slashing with the thin blade and smashing with his fists, using his huge body to clear a retreat back into the larger cavern.

Pushing Demptha Negatarth before him, the Mouser leaped past Fafhrd's victims before they could stir to their feet. "Out! Out!" he shouted at the wizard. "And take care to guard that light!"

A booming laugh filled the cavern as Fafhrd emerged and freed Graywand. Thrusting Demptha aside, he called to his partner as the Mouser emerged. "Hah, a good battle is a cure for the numbing fear-stink that fills this blasted maze!"

"Personally, I'm insulted," the Mouser answered diffidently. "Ilthmarts—and Ilthmarts we've already beaten."

Fafhrd laughed again and twirled Graywand in a showy one-handed arc as he fell back into a defensive posture. "It would be rude of me to point out that Laurian's magic defeated them when they had us cornered like a pair of rats."

"A treacherous slander!" the Mouser scoffed. "She merely interfered while I was catching my second wind."

A host of battlecries sounded, and the Ilthmart warriors charged into the cavern. Fafhrd met the first one, knocking him aside with a ringing blow on a shield. The second warrior tripped over the first, smacking his chin on the rocky floor. The third leaped screaming over the first two. With a dancer's grace, the Mouser dropped to one knee and thrust upward, piercing flesh with Scalpel's point.

The fourth and fifth squeezed out behind the third. Both charged the Mouser. The rapier edge of Catsclaw swept in a sidewise arc, slipping beneath a shield to slice a muscled thigh before the Mouser rolled aside and jumped to his feet.

The rest of the Ilthmarts rushed clumsily from the narrow tunnel, pushing and shoving each other as they emerged. "Eight more!" they shouted. "Eight more for the Shadowland!"

"These fools can't count!" Fafhrd laughed as he waded into them, swinging left and right with Graywand. "We are but three!"

A dirk flashed through the air toward the Mouser. With a flick of his blade, he batted it aside in mid-flight, and with an advancing lunge, pushed his point through the throat of the thrower.

"Seven more!"

The odd count caught the Mouser's attention. Whirling about, he spied the Ilthmart that had voiced it. That warrior loomed over a cowering Demptha, dirk upraised, prepared to strike a death blow.

"No!" the Mouser shouted, too far away to help.

But Demptha did not cower. He merely stooped to set the lantern safely aside. Even as the Ilthmart stabbed downward, Demptha reached into his left sleeve. Out came a packet. Black powder showered over the Ilthmart. Bright star-like sparks flared, and a hideous scream tore through the cavern. Shield, dirk, clothes, and Ilthmart all burst into white flame.

Shielding his eyes against the sudden painful brightness and the crackling heat, the Mouser ran to Demptha's side and pulled him up. "Stay behind me!" he ordered.

On the distant side of the cavern, partially obscured by the gray vapor, a silhouetted Fafhrd gave a forceful shout. Graywand's blade and elaborate hilt sparkled like blue lightning as he cleaved an arc through the air and drove the sword through the final Ilthmart's shoulder and deep into his torso, carving the man nearly in half.

For a moment, the two combatants stood as if frozen, still as statues, a captured tableau of desperation and death. Then the Ilthmart corpse slipped free of the great blade and fell out of sight under the mist.

For a moment more, Fafhrd remained unmoving. Finally, he lowered his sword and leaned heavily on it. A wracking cough shook his great form.

Before the Mouser could run to his friend, the burning Ilthmart, now the major source of light, screamed his last scream and fell face-forward into the thick mist, sinking into it just as Mish had done. A crushing blackness once more filled the cavern with nothing more than the lantern's small flame to hold it back. In the renewed dark, the Mouser rubbed a gloved fist over his eyes, unable to see. "Fafhrd!" he called.

"I'm here," Fafhrd answered, emerging from the mist into the small light of the lantern as Demptha raised it. A dark smear of blood stained his mouth and chin.

"You're wounded!" Demptha cried.

Fafhrd allowed a humorless smirk. "Not by any Ilthmart blade," he answered.

None of their foes remained. All the fallen had vanished, swallowed by the fleecy white river that flowed over the cavern floor.

Filled with concern for Fafhrd, the Mouser stared at his friend, sickened with worry at sight of the blood on those lips. He thought of suggesting a respite, a brief chance to let Fafhrd recover. Fafhrd would take it as an insult, so instead he stalled.

His quiet voice reverberated with surreal effect from the stone walls. "What means this count?" he wondered aloud. "Ten more, eight more, seven more."

"Aye," Fafhrd murmured. "And what happened to nine?"

The Mouser stomped carefully over the area of battle. No bodies. No trace even of the shields and dirks. "How do ten dead men rise up and fight again, Fafhrd?"

Fafhrd fixed the Mouser with a gaze. His green eyes burned suddenly like those of a cat. "How is it, Mouser, that Vlana and Ivrian have risen up to haunt us?"

The lantern flame shivered suddenly in Demptha's hand as he turned. "How indeed," he whispered, pointing to the tunnel entrance.

Jesane floated there, her bare feet seeming to stand upon the misty sea. Tendrils of white vapor stirred modestly about her pale naked body, veiling her face as she tempted them with a dark-eyed look.

"I warned you," she whispered. Though her lips moved, her voice didn't seem to come from her, but unnaturally from the cavern itself. "Shadowland has come to the City of a Thousand Smokes—and you have come to Shadowland." Raising a slender arm, she crooked a finger and floated backward into the mouth of the tunnel, her gaze locking with her father's.

"Now I know our enemy," Demptha Negatarth said without taking his eyes from Jesane. "I know my sin." Without a glance at his comrades, he followed after his daughter, taking the lantern with him.

As darkness closed around them, the Mouser gripped Fafhrd's brawny arm. "I've sometimes thought that we are two halves of one soul, Fafhrd," he said as he stared after the disappearing light. "If we lose that one soul tonight, know that I think well of you."

Fafhrd nodded, sheathing Graywand and drawing his dagger once again. "Some few have joked that a certain pair of thieves were ill-met that night long ago in Lankhmar when they collided under a bridge on Gold Street. I have never thought so."

The time for sentiment was ended. The Mouser swallowed and peered down the tunnel after Demptha and Jesane, who could no longer be seen. The lantern gave only the dimmest glow from far ahead. Sheathing Scalpel but keeping Catsclaw in hand, he entered the passage a second time with Fafhrd right behind and Jesane's words in his mind.

Shadowland has come to the City of a Thousand Smokes.

In the world of Nehwon lay two great poles. In the far west lay Godsland, and all the gods, known and unknown, dwelled there, seldom venturing from that paradise. In the far east lay Nehwon's opposite pole, Shadowland—the land of the dead.

The soft whisper of Jesane's eerie voice drifted back to him. "Five more," she murmured with a dreamlike weariness.

What happened to six? the Mouser wondered, waving a hand to part the mist that swirled before his eyes. *Six what? Five what?*

Abruptly the tunnel ended. The Mouser stepped out warily, not into another tunnel or a larger cavern, but onto a vast and sprawling plain. A white sea of feathery vapor stretched as far as the eye could see, while overhead in a black velvet sky, stars as sharp and bright as diamonds glittered.

No familiar constellations, the Mouser noted, studying that awesome heaven. He directed his gaze farther afield, seeking the lantern's light. Hand in hand now, father and daughter stood patiently, as if waiting.

"In a dream," Fafhrd said as if to himself, "I've been here before." Stretching out an arm, he pointed. "A barge will come from there. I know it."

Indeed, a second faint light appeared in the distance. Slowly it approached, but smoothly, growing subtly brighter. Out of the blackness sailed a fantastic barge of black wood and gold fittings. A simple lantern fixed to its prow lit the way across the foggy sea.

Upon that barge sat an elaborate throne of the same black wood marked with gold and silver inlay, cushioned with fine pillows. Upon that lustrous seat a tall figure sat with casual posture, his features concealed under a hood and behind a shining black mask.

The barge stopped. Jesane floated up to the deck to stand before the seated figure. Her father clambered up the side, climbed over the ebony rail and remained there.

Without sail or oar, with no sound of water or wind, the barge turned toward Fafhrd and the Mouser.

For perhaps the first time in his life, the Mouser gave thanks for his short stature, for the fog rose up to his thighs and hid the trembling in his knees. Fafhrd stirred uneasily beside him. His friend had exchanged his dagger once again for the greater comfort, not to mention reach, of Graywand.

The barge drifted to an easy stop.

"Only four more," Jesane said to the figure on the throne. "A child comes, Pilsh her name."

Nodding, the seated figure rose and walked gracefully to the barge's fore. Involuntarily, the Mouser flung up an arm, averting his gaze from the evil eyes that stared from behind that glittering mask.

"No, little man," said a voice that came from behind that mask. "I am beyond mortal concepts of good and evil."

Fafhrd did not look away, but lifted his chin defiantly to meet the creature's stare. "Then who are you?" he shouted. "Where is Malygris?"

"Fafhrd, son of Mor and Nalgron," the figure answered. "We have fought before, you and I. And though it was only a game— no serious duel—you did well." He looked from Fafhrd to the Mouser and back again. "In truth, you both have done well, each playing your part."

"Answer my question," Fafhrd demanded.

Leaning over the barge's rail, the figure bowed ever so slightly. "Do you not recognize me?" A black-gloved finger rose to touch the mask. A light seemed to brighten around the creature's face.

"The ferry-man!" Fafhrd cried, recoiling. "The pilot in my dream!"

Simultaneously, the Mouser cried. "Rokkarsh!"

The two friends looked at each other stupidly.

The masked figure laughed and the sound of it boomed across his Shadowland. "Death has many faces," he said.

Demptha Negatarth climbed over the side of the barge and came to stand beside the Mouser. "He is Death of Nehwon," the wizard said.

Death of Nehwon gave a small shrug. "Only a minor Death in the cosmic scheme of things," he said modestly. "But as with all other Deaths in all the worlds and dimensions, I serve a purpose."

Abruptly, Death of Nehwon held up a hand. Fathomless eyes closed behind a mask that was only a mask again. "A fisherman, Massek by name," he intoned. Then those horribly vast eyes opened again. "Now only two remain, and soon this play will end."

Death of Nehwon stretched out his hand to the sky.

A red light appeared in the heavens. Softly glowing, it sank from the firmament, wafting with a strangely lazy motion, and the Mouser knew it for Malygris's hideous ribbon of evil. Lower and lower it drifted, touching the misty sea near the barge, disappearing into it only to rise again.

With it rose a huge obloid, an egg whose white shell was laced with red streaks and veins of pulsing scarlet.

Death of Nehwon waved his hand. The ribbon fluttered away and disappeared. At the same time, cracks formed on the egg's surface, widening, deepening, filling the air with a sound like thunder. Suddenly it exploded, showering fragments into the air. They did not fall again.

On the remaining piece of shell, Malygris stood, confused and trembling. His gaze darted in nervous fear as he tried to discern his tormentors, gauge his situation. Biting his lip, he stared at last toward the ominous, masked barge-master.

"Here is a man who dared to affront me," Death of Nehwon said.

"There were others," Demptha Negatarth interrupted, finding his voice. He stepped toward the barge, craning his neck toward the ruler of Shadowland. "Sadaster, Aarth's Patriarch, Rokkarsh, myself!"

Death of Nehwon might have smiled behind that mask as he looked down upon Demptha. "Confession is good for the soul, is it not, mortal?"

Cowed by the sarcasm, Demptha hung his head and stepped back.

A sneering voice continued as Death of Nehwon stabbed a finger at Malygris. "In his jealousy and madness, this fool reached beyond his meager talents, creating a spell to strike at his enemy. So he thought. In truth, he unleashed a mindless force and destroyed hundreds of lives."

Death of Nehwon paused and looked down upon the three men before him. "I took no interest in that. All mortals die in their time, and I am the Keeper of the Schedule."

The Mouser raised his fist. He had worked hard to piece the puzzle together, and he had no intention of being grandstanded, not even by such a being as he stood before.

"But there was another spell, wasn't there?" he called. "One you couldn't ignore. A secret that Sadaster possessed, and a secret that Malygris stole from him. A spell that Demptha bargained for with Malygris."

Death of Nehwon nodded appreciatively. "You are shrewd for a mortal," he complimented. "I see why Fate has set her mark on you. But hear the rest of the story." He glanced toward Demptha. "Then a decision must be made."

"Well, tell it quickly," Fafhrd shouted. "Though you claim you've no interest in it, Malygris's curse works in my body, and I may shortly puke on the front of your fine boat."

Did a low chuckle issue from behind that mask? The Mouser could not tell.

"The rest is simple enough," Death of Nehwon said. "Or should I say, human enough. As your gray friend has figured out, Sadaster's spell not only erased the tracks of time from Laurian's lovely face, it held back the years."

"It held back death," the Mouser said. "It kept you at bay."

Death of Nehwon scoffed. "Oh, pish. Perhaps you are not so shrewd after all. Everyone's name is written in a book of my keeping, and every time is appointed. The life given each man is finite. Yet with this spell of Sadaster's, some few took time that didn't belong to them."

"And thus shortened the time of other innocents?" Demptha murmured, shame-faced. "I didn't know."

"Each man has an apportioned share of time. To add more to his own share meant diminishing someone else's—thus upsetting my precious schedule," said Death of Nehwon coldly.

"That I could not ignore. Selfish men stole time that rightfully belonged to others. Sadaster prolonged his own life and looks, as well as Laurian's. Jealousy drove Malygris to the same sin."

"And Aarth's Patriarch," the Mouser interrupted. "How does he fit into this?"

Death of Nehwon laughed. "The Patriarch, through his own magic, learned of Malygris's plan to kill Sadaster. Malygris bought his silence with the secret of prolonging life. The Patriarch, mortal fool that he was, then curried favor with the Overlord Rokkarsh by sharing it with him. Nor would it have ended there. Rokkarsh intended to share it with several of his nearest noble relatives."

A sigh came from behind the mask. "Their vanity earned them my annoyance. Now their souls are waiting table in the banquet halls of Hell."

"But I used the spell, too," Demptha said. "Why am I alive when Jesane is dead?"

"Your daughter is dead because her time expired years ago. When I extended my kingdom into Lankhmar's underworld, I found her with others whose time had expired in the place you call the Temple of Hates. I reached out my hand and claimed them. Surprisingly, Jesane slipped through my fingers for a few desperate moments, long enough to try to warn you." He inclined his head toward her. "Now as it happens, I look with favor on such devotion and courage. It pleases me, and I've made her my handmaiden."

Malygris took a sudden step forward, and the shell upon which he stood cracked loudly under his feet, causing him to retreat to his original place as all attention turned upon him. He wore a look of dawning terror. "Your schedule? Your kingdom? Who are you, monster? What is this dreary place?"

As if stirred by a wind, the mist swirled on the surface of the white sea. Forms and figures rose up with the mist, pale shapes, some with familiar faces. There was Mish again, whole with his arms and head. And Gamron with his Ilthmarts. A blond girl-child with bright eyes and a straw poppet in her arms.

"Sameel," Fafhrd whispered, his gaze fastening on a beautiful young woman who stood shyly apart from the other figures.

Scores, hundreds, perhaps more walked out of the fog and stood silently by as if to give witness. These were the ones from whom time and life had been stolen. Here also were the victims of Malygris's jealous evil.

The wizard gave a shrill scream, as if at last he understood, and the sound filled the Mouser with an icy satisfaction.

Death of Nehwon spoke again. "Only you, Demptha Negatarth, of those who possessed Sadaster's spell, used it for no selfish end. You wear the wrinkles you have earned and stoop beneath your properly accumulated years. Only for your daughter's benefit did you employ this insulting magic." He nodded ever so slightly, briefly closing his eyes as he did so. "I forgive you," he pronounced.

Jesane leaned close to Death of Nehwon, and the two appeared to confer. A moment later, she floated down from the barge and stood beside her father. Taking his hand in hers, she looked up to her master.

"Still, a price must be paid," Death of Nehwon proclaimed. "Two deaths yet remain before this play is ended. The despicable Malygris is but one."

Malygris clutched a fist to his heart, and a panicked gleam lit his eyes.

Demptha looked to his daughter, and tears sparkled on his old cheeks. "The other?" he asked.

Thick whips of mist lashed over the sides of the barge, seizing Death of Nehwon, hardening instantly to ice. The very air around him froze, cocooning him in a glacial prison. More mist spiraled up from the shallow sea and froze, burying the barge under a crushing glacial mass.

"I spit upon your hidden face!" Malygris shouted defiantly. The shell shattered, loud as thunder beneath his running footsteps. "And piss upon your timetable; you'll not find my name written there, today or ever!"

The Mouser's blood rushed suddenly, and so did he to overtake the fleeing wizard. He had not come through so much, so far, to this strange court to lose his prey now. "Then I'll write it there, myself," he cried in challenge, brandishing Scalpel. "Stand still, Inkwell, and let me dip my pen."

A loud roar stopped the Mouser in his tracks. A serpent's head large as an elephant's, surged up from the mist on a green stalk of a neck. A red mouth gaped horribly, exposing white rapier teeth that dripped a milky venom. Yellow eyes burned. With dreadful speed, it lunged.

The Mouser dove into the thick mist. Submerged, but on solid substance, he rolled swiftly over and thrust upward with his blade, feeling the point bite into scaled flesh and carve a long scratch. He didn't need to see through the gray blanket, however, to know he did no serious damage. He scrambled up and shot a frantic look for the creature. It glared, undulating on its long neck and yawning to show its teeth again.

Now he got a good look at it, and his heart nearly stopped in his chest. A sea serpent from the Great Inner Sea. Not one, but two! Beyond it, he spied a wake, a subtle parting of the mist, and barely visible as it swam, a second reptilian form with hungry eyes fixed on him.

The Mouser called his partner's name. When no answer came, he risked a glance over his shoulder. A sickening sight greeted him.

A mighty eagle clung to Fafhrd's face, its pinions beating, its talons buried deep in the Northerner's eye sockets. Blood and humor gushed, and Fafhrd's mouth hung open in a strangely voiceless scream as he thrashed and tried to fight the raptor off.

O grisly hell! Ignoring his own peril, the Mouser spun about, preparing to run to the aid of his friend.

Then, in mid-step, he paused, and his lips curled back in an almost feral snarl. A bitter suspicion filled him. No mere bird could ever score such a victory upon mighty Fafhrd. Nor could sea serpents swim in that which was not truly a sea.

He spun again. "Malygris!" he shouted, ignoring the toothy monster that lunged at him. "My pen still needs a dipping!" He leaped away from the serpent's mouth. Though he swore it was only another of the wizard's illusions, why take chances? Dashing around it, leaping over the back of the second swimming monster, he overtook his foe.

The look on Malygris's face as he whirled about was barely human. "Fire!" he hissed.

As the Mouser raised his sword to strike, the steel burst into flame. In a heartbeat he knew it for yet another damned illusion, but instinctively he dropped his weapon. Cursing, he hurled himself forward, arms grasping. His hands, though, closed on nothing. Malygris faded into nothingness, and a harsh, mocking laughter filled the Mouser's ears.

Then, another laugh rose over that, softer, pitched higher, yet somehow mad, more femininely savage.

Malygris became suddenly visible once more, and another figure, as well, blocking his way. Mist and darkness parted like curtains to reveal an ornate sarcophagus that gleamed like silver. Intricate latches, fashioned like hands and fingers, snapped eerily open. A long black crack appeared, widened, and the thing began to open.

A dark-haired woman, swathed in white linen, smiled a red-lipped smile as she emerged from that box.

On the verge of fleeing again, Malygris hesitated, then gasped. "Laurian?"

The woman held out her arms. "You've wanted me so long," she whispered. "Now I've come for you." She reached for him, and reached, her arms growing longer, unnaturally long, her fingers stretching, becoming claws. With a shriek, she flung herself upon the wizard. Her arms encircled him like ropes, her nails tore bloody grooves in his flesh. Her legs entangled him, as well, tripping him, bearing him down as her teeth sought his throat.

"No!" the wizard cried, a sound of pure despair.

The thing that was Laurian laughed. "Tell me how you love me!"

They both disappeared under the misty waves. For a moment a turbulent froth churned over the spot, then all became tranquil. For a seeming long time, the Mouser stared in uncertain worry until another, deeper laugh made him turn.

The Mouser blinked. There stood Fafhrd, whole and unbloodied, no sign of eagles or sea serpents. There was Scalpel, not dropped, but still in its sheath. And there before him, unruffled and calm, sat Death of Nehwon on his barge.

The Lord of Shadowland cast an amused glance toward Malygris where he yet stood on his arcane bit of shell. But now the wizard's eyes stared blankly, and if his face, once fearful, wore any expression at all, it was no more than a hint of sadness, or perhaps grief.

"The fool," Death of Nehwon murmured. "He thought his illusions could prevail over the stark reality I represent. Now his power is turned against him; he stands helpless in a hell of his own manufacture."

The Mouser rubbed a weary hand across his eyes. "I thought he'd nearly escaped us again."

Fafhrd leaned close and whispered, "I thought an eagle ate your civilized eyes."

So they had shared illusions. Had any time passed at all, the Mouser wondered? Though he recalled running and leaping and chasing, he seemed in fact not to have moved.

Demptha Negatarth drew his daughter closer. He seemed untouched or unaffected by what had just transpired. "You said another," he quietly reminded their host. "One more yet to die. I must know."

"Sabash, wife of Nuulpha."

Demptha looked as if he'd been struck a blow. "No!" he cried angrily. "She has no part in this! Let her live!"

Death of Nehwon said nothing, just stared down upon him. All around the souls of the dead waited and watched.

Demptha lifted his head as a sudden calm descended upon him. He took his daughter's hand again. "The price is mine to pay. Take whatever time I have left and give it to Sabash. Spare her a while longer."

An approving nod from Death of Nehwon. "You have made the right decision and thereby earned yourself a place, not in hell, but in the pleasure halls of my own palace." A black-gloved hand pointed into the distance. Through the mist appeared the vague outline of a distant structure, elaborate with its minarets and spires and turreted towers. "Your daughter will show you the way."

Demptha cast a final glance at Fafhrd and the Mouser. "Live well and long, young heroes," he said. Then mist swirled around father and daughter, urging them on their journey. Three paces, and they began to fade from the Mouser's sight. Ten paces, and they were gone forever.

Death leaned on the rail of his barge. When he spoke, did the Mouser imagine it, or was there a note of weariness in his voice?

"The final deed is yours, Gray Mouser," he said. "Fate has declared that your dagger, Catsclaw, shall draw the heartblood Sheelba requires to save his life and yours."

The Mouser heard the voice of Death, and yet his thoughts turned elsewhere, to hell and pleasure halls.

"Hurry," Death of Nehwon urged. "Lest I pick up my book and find your names on tomorrow's page."

The Mouser swallowed. "Where is Ivrian?" he demanded. "I want to see her. And Fafhrd's Vlana, too."

The black hand of Nehwon's Death tightened on the barge's rail. "Like the soldiers I commanded with Rokkarsh's face, the women were but tools to delay and slow you, to occupy your thoughts and muddle your minds. Else with your cleverness you might have found Malygris too quickly. Like Fate, Sheelba chose his henchmen well." Death of Nehwon relaxed then and shrugged. "But for your hard work, I will reward you. Turn around."

The Mouser and Fafhrd exchanged looks, then slowly turned.

"Hello, my love," Vlana said. She held out her hand as Fafhrd reached to embrace her. "You may not touch me. For sins of my past, that was decreed before this began."

"Vlana!" Fafhrd cried. Despite her words, he started toward her with outstretched arms. But a force closed about him and prevented him from moving. "I love you, woman," he said finally. "My heart hasn't forgotten you."

The Mouser merely stared at Ivrian. He sheathed the dagger and sword he held and with gloved fingers he made a pass at his eyes. The hard cruelty of Liara was gone from her face, and she stood before him purely, as his One True Love. "I'm not allowed to embrace you, either, am I?" he said.

"No, my little Mouse," she said with soft affection, using his boyhood name. "I am stripped again of the flesh I wore, and shortly my merciful master will strip me of the memories of the things he made me do to you."

"I love you," he whispered, extending his fingertips toward her, though he knew she wouldn't return his touch. "Forever."

"In Shadowland," she answered, "forever is a long, long time. Farewell. I loved you, too."

The Death of Nehwon interrupted any further love-making. "Now let them go," he said to Fafhrd and the Mouser. "They too have earned honored places in my halls."

Putting a hand to his mouth, Fafhrd gave an uneasy cough. "Save a place for me, Vlana," he said.

The mist shifted suddenly, and their true loves vanished, leaving an emptiness in the Mouser's heart that made him cry out with pain. Pushing the fingers of his right hand down inside his left glove, he drew out the large pearl he had saved from Ivrian's broken necklace. In nearly the same motion, he ripped free the leather thong that bound back his thick black hair.

As if reading his intention, Fafhrd moved to stop him. "Not your sling!" the Northerner hissed.

But not even Fafhrd was fast enough to stop him. Setting the pearl in the tiny pouch, the Mouser launched it with all his pent-up fury. "Monster!" he screamed.

The pearl streaked upward and smashed into powder against the black mask of Nehwon's Death. The looming figure said nothing, nor did he react at all.

Trembling with rage, the Mouser clenched his fists and glared at Shadowland's lord. The white stain on that mask did nothing to assuage his hurt. Jerking Catsclaw from its sheath once again, he turned toward the insensate Malygris. When Fafhrd caught his arm, he pulled free.

Not as Sheelba's hireling, but as an aggrieved and half-maddened victim, he stood before the wizard and raised the fateful blade. It bothered him not at all that Malygris stood helpless, only that he stood entranced and unfeeling. "I wish you could feel this!" he whispered to the wizard as he prepared to strike.

The Mouser drew back to drive the blade deep. Then to his shock and startlement, Malygris's eyes snapped wide. An angry fire flared in those black pupils. With one hand, he caught the Mouser's wrist, stopping the thrust, while his other hand closed on the Mouser's windpipe and exerted a fierce strength. His yellow-toothed mouth opened. "Did you think I would meekly take your steel? Even Death's power cannot long restrain me!"

"Take it any way you like," the Mouser grunted, recovering his wits. "Just take it!"

He twisted away from Malygris, breaking the grip on his throat, but before he could free his trapped wrist, the wizard leaped upon him, bearing him off-balance. A rain of fists fell on his head and face, teeth bit his neck and scalp, thumbs dug into his eyes. "If one more must die tonight," Malygris roared, "the name will not be mine!"

Through the ringing and the rush of blood in his ears, the Mouser heard Fafhrd's voice. "Hold on, Gray Mouser! I'll strike . . . !" Then a paroxysm of coughing stilled the Northerner's speech.

The bitter sound steeled the Mouser's resolve. With a cold determination, he flung Malygris away. The wizard tumbled head over heels and smashed to the ground, disappearing under the mist. The Mouser followed, finding Catsclaw still in his hand. He knew unerringly where his foe lay, and this time, he allowed for no chance. He didn't need, nor even want, to see beneath the blanketing mist.

All was silence now, silence and cold dampness, save for the heat of his anger, the steam of his perspiration, the rasp of his breath. No witticism, no challenge, no triumphant cry formed in his mouth. Indeed, there was nothing more to say, only an ending to make of it all.

Straddling Malygris's chest, he used his knees to pin the wizard's arms. He squeezed his eyes shut. The point of his blade seemed to find its own way, to press against Malygris's chest, to angle itself properly downward toward a frantically beating heart, furiously beating, desperately.

Malygris drew a breath. "Please . . . !"

The Mouser shut his ears. With a grunt, he leaned on Catsclaw, driving it deep. The breath sighed from Malygris's lips, a short, soft song of release, and perhaps—did the Mouser, out of some unwarranted sense of guilt, imagine it?—relief. The wizard's chest sank, and his whole form seemed to grow smaller between the Mouser's knees.

At last, the Mouser found his voice. "Damn you," he said, no witticism, no challenge, no triumphant cry, just a fervent wish. "Damn you to hell."

Death of Nehwon laughed.

The chill mist of Shadowland swirled, filling the Mouser's eyes, obscuring the great barge and its master. The souls of the dead seemed to blow apart like smoke in a wind. Fafhrd cried the Mouser's name.

The Mouser barely heard, nor could he answer, and soon Fafhrd stopped calling. All was silence and mist.

And cold—the mist was so cold.

TWENTY

HEROES' REPOSE

The Mouser hung suspended in a misty limbo, an impossible neverland without time or sensation, dimension or vista. A death-like chill rimed his senses. He saw nothing but gray vapor, heard no sound, smelled only the anaesthetic dampness, felt nothing but the cold.

Only one other thing touched his awareness—Malygris's curse. Like a sharp-toothed worm, it ate at his vitals with a voracious, desperate hunger. He felt it working faster, devouring him, as if it knew with some vague, obscene intelligence that its time was running out.

A soft wind blew through the void, tearing and scattering the fog. Pieces of mist ripped away and formed little whirling dervishes; thin vaporous wisps darted about briefly, like forlorn ghosts reluctant to quit a haunting. The rest of the fog rippled and fluttered like an unnatural veil as it slowly dissolved.

The world of Nehwon resolved itself under the Mouser's feet. Like a man waking from a long dream, he looked around. A veritable sea of tall grass waved before him. The stars—all his precious, familiar constellations—peppered the night sky. A deeply velvet, cobalt shimmer on the eastern horizon heralded the approach of dawn.

To his right, in the distance, he spied the yellow winking and twinkling of glow-wasps. Equally distant to his left stood the long black silhouette of Lankhmar's walls.

Fafhrd spoke from behind him. "Dare we believe that we stand in the Great Salt Marsh?"

The Mouser didn't answer. He raised one incarnadined hand before his eyes. In the starlight, dripping Catsclaw glistened wetly in his fist. His once-gray glove, his sleeve, were black and sticky. Blood spotted his tunic, his trousers, and his cloak. A streak of moisture slowly dried on his left cheek.

A scream boiled up from deep inside. He fought to suppress it, but it rose, forced itself up to his lips. Still he resisted, muttering, "No! No!" The scream would not be denied.

Throat raw, he sank to his knees in the spongy marsh soil, vaguely aware of Fafhrd's comforting hands on his shoulders. In his mind he saw Malygris's horror-stricken face at the moment of death, and he saw his own hand drenched in the wizard's blood. Revulsion filled him, that he had killed a helpless man, even one such as Malygris, who couldn't act to defend himself.

Yet, as he wept, he knew his tears were not for Malygris. "Ivrian," he whispered. "Ivrian!" Death had torn her from his side yet again. To see her, to hold her, and to lose her all over! How could a heart bear that?

Fafhrd pulled away, wracked by a fit of coughing. As if cold water had been thrown on the Mouser, he jumped to his feet. The Northerner stood a few paces off, bent double, hands braced weakly on knees. A thin black phlegm trailed from his lips to the grass.

With a handful of his gray cloak, the Mouser wiped Fafhrd's mouth. "You know I'm not a superstitious man," Fafhrd muttered.

"Of course not," the Mouser answered as he wiped the rest of his partner's sweating face. His own concerns thrust aside, he repressed a shiver of fear as he cared for his friend. Fafhrd burned with fever; his garments were soaked with perspiration, and a constant, unceasing quiver shook that massive frame. "You're a paragon of enlightened civilization," he added.

Fafhrd swallowed, unable to rise from his bent posture. "If you're going to insult me," he said, his voice little more than a croak, "then we'll part company right here."

"Don't even think of leaving me, Fafhrd Red-Hair," the Mouser answered bluntly, and the thought raced through his mind, *what would I do without half my soul?*

"You know I'm not a superstitious man," Fafhrd repeated as he pushed one hand into the purse on his belt. "But if I had a tik-penny, I'd buy a favor from the gods." He drew out a handful of glimmering rings and necklaces. "I don't think there's any luck in a dead woman's treasure."

"Then buy your favor with that," the Mouser said grimly.

Fafhrd's fist tightened about the jewels, and he closed his eyes in prayer. Stiffly, painfully, he straightened. Opening his eyes, he drew back his left arm, turned toward the cobalt glow of the approaching sun, and let fly. The weird pre-dawn light caught the gems and bits of gold and silver as they arced high above the marsh. For an instant, the air flashed and sparkled.

If the gems fell to earth, or if some divine hand snatched them in mid-flight, the Mouser could not swear, for something else distracted him. Against that strange velvet blueness, he spied a distant silhouette, a vague half-glimpsed shape, there for a moment, then gone. Yet his heart leaped with hope.

Still clutching bloody Catsclaw, he put his clean arm around Fafhrd. "Come on," he urged, supporting his friend. "Come on, walk with me."

"Where?" Fafhrd asked, drawing himself erect, doing his best to hide the pain on his pale face.

"Toward the sun," the Mouser said, starting off with one eye on his partner.

"Why didn't you just say you wanted the jewels before I threw them away?" Fafhrd grumbled. "You'll never find them in this grass."

"To hell with the jewels," the Mouser snapped as they moved forward.

Fafhrd snorted indignantly. "I don't want any more favors from that quarter."

Despite himself, the Mouser smiled. There was the Fafhrd he loved best, quick-witted and spirited in the face of disaster. He fairly ran, skipping a few paces ahead of his partner as he pushed his way through the tall grass. Up a small, rolling rise they made their way with the Mouser hugging the bloody dagger protectively to his chest.

"There it is!" the Mouser called back to Fafhrd. "I knew I saw it!" Staring up the rise, he cupped one hand to his mouth and called, "Sheelba! Sheelba, you transfigured, green-blooded, black-hearted, wizard-spawned accident of your mother! We're here!"

Sheelba's black hut perched on its stilted legs at the dawn-lit summit. The wind that shivered over the marsh rustled its grass-thatched roof and teased the flap of cloth that covered its squat doorway. Nothing else moved around the hut. No lamp or candlelight shone from within.

A black circle on the earth near the hut marked where a fire once had burned. The ashes, however, were long dead and cold. "Sheelba?" the Mouser called again, eliciting no answer. He exchanged a nervous look with Fafhrd, then turned cautiously toward the ladder that rose to the hut's entrance and put one hand on the rung.

The hut gave a quiver. The Mouser snatched his hand away in shock and surprise. The rung was warm, pulsing! And though it looked like bamboo wood, it felt like. . . . Something else.

Sheelba's hut was alive.

"Problem?" Fafhrd asked quietly from the dead ashes of the old fire.

"No problem," the Mouser answered nervously. "None at all." He stared up at the black doorway again, and now it looked to him like a mouth, and the flap curling in the breeze so much like a tongue licking its lips in anticipation of a morsel.

Determinedly, the Mouser shot out his hand, grasped a ladder rung, and began to climb. "I'll bite you right back," he promised under his breath.

"What's that?" Fafhrd called.

The Mouser didn't answer. He climbed to the doorway, which was just a doorway after all, and pushed back the cloth covering, which was thankfully just a cloth covering. Or so it seemed. How could he be sure, after this adventure, that anything was really what it seemed anymore?

The cloth fell behind him as he rose to stand on the thinly carpeted floor. He had expected darkness, but the moment he stepped upon the rugs, a perfect crystal ball mounted upon an elaborately worked gold pedestal ignited with a soft white glow.

At a glance, the Mouser appraised the pedestal's potential value, estimated its weight, and judged the chances of carrying it off. Then he chided himself. Now was not the time for such thoughts.

The interior of the hut was a single circular space. A large chair and foot cushion dominated one area. A table with a silver tea samovar and a small cup stood beside it. A shelf of books and scrolls occupied another area. A pallet of braided rushes and blankets served for a simple bed. The rest of the space was given over to trunks, and racks of herbs, strange bottles, old candle stubs, and a surprisingly massive worktable draped with a plain white cloth.

The worktable caught the Mouser's attention. Upon it, a flask lay overturned amid the shards of a broken alembic, and the candles on either end of the table had burned completely down into their holders.

In the center of the workspace stood a wide crystal crucible that gleamed and glittered as if it had been cut and hollowed from one half of an impossibly large diamond. The light from the crystal ball burned on its facets and cast rainbow images all across the workspace and around the hut. The Mouser's jaw dropped as he beheld it. With an awesome reverence, he crept across the carpets toward the beautiful vessel, one hand extended, not to steal it, but just for the joy and honor of touching so great a rarity.

Yet halfway across the room, he froze. Just below the edge of the table's drapery, he spied a booted foot and a tiny fraction of a black robe's hem.

"What a dump," Fafhrd commented, poking his head through the doorway from the ladder and looking around.

"Take a closer look," the Mouser suggested as he eased cautiously behind the worktable. He caught his breath. Cursing, he dropped to his knees.

A figure in black robes and a hood lay face down, partially concealed by the table drapery, as if he had grasped it as he fell and dragged some of it with him. The Mouser had no doubt that it was Sheelba. He grasped the wizard by the shoulders and turned him over, surprised by the slight weight and the brittle bone of the body inside the robes.

A raspy whisper issued from within the hood, as a skeletally thin hand reached trembling up to draw the hood even closer and so conceal whatever was within. "Wizard-spawned accident of my mother?" Sheelba rasped.

The Mouser shrugged, greatly relieved to find the wizard alive. "Rhetorical excess," he said.

Fafhrd bent over the Mouser to peer down at Sheelba. The rainbows from the diamond crucible filled his eyes and hid the worry in them. "Let's get him to his bed."

Sheelba raised a hand and grasped at the table drapery. "No," he insisted. His words came haltingly, painfully through lips as dry as parchment. "I smell the blood of our enemy on you. Help me up, that we might end this nightmare." Before he could say more, he gave a sigh. His fingers relaxed their grip in the drapery, and his hand slipped to the floor.

"Sheelba?" the Mouser said. No answer came from within the black hood. Over his shoulder, he spoke to Fafhrd. "The samovar has water or tea. Fill the cup and bring it."

Sheelba stirred again even as Fafhrd moved. "Water be damned," he murmured. "I've lain here for days too weak to move. Bring wine from the black trunk with the copper hinges. Bring the jug." This time, he grasped the Mouser's tunic. "Get me on my feet, Gray One."

The Mouser slipped his clean arm under the wizard's shoulders. Sheelba weighed so little he had no trouble lifting him up. Fafhrd stood ready with the jug in one hand, the small cup in the other. "A cupful first," he said, holding it close to Sheelba's lips and tipping it. "The jug if you keep it down."

But Sheelba did no more than wet his lips before he pushed Fafhrd away. He leaned upon the worktable, his hands on either side of the crucible. Fiery rainbows danced on the thinly translucent skin that stretched over his knuckles. Even the faceless darkness within his hood began to fill with color. "I feared you would not succeed in time," he said. "But you have—barely. The ingredients are mixed. Add Malygris's blood to the potion, and your victory is complete."

For the first time, the Mouser bent over the crucible and saw that it contained a still, clear liquid. For a moment, he stared in small confusion, a slight vertigo clawing at his senses. Then he gasped.

The rainbow light that danced about the room came not from the interplay of the crystal ball's glow on the facets of the crucible, but from some strange energies contained within that liquid, energies that swam and swirled languidly, directionless, through a watery suspension.

Half-entranced by the sight, the Mouser raised Catsclaw and his bloody hand over the vessel. All that he had done, all that he and Fafhrd had endured in Lankhmar, had come to this. He saw his own hand rising as if pulled by a string. He saw himself as a puppet, manipulated by another hand greater and more powerful than his own.

And he resented it.

"Plunge it in!" Sheelba rasped. Bony fingers closed around the Mouser's arm and sought weakly to force it downward. "Plunge it in, and save us all!"

The Mouser's jaw knotted, and he gnashed his teeth in anger. The blood on his hand—it stank in his nostrils! Not innocent blood, by any means. Malygris, the jealous and insane fool, had intended to kill, and kill he did. But was he, too, no more than a puppet, playing a part dictated to him, dancing on strings pulled by some greater power?

The Mouser did not doubt it, and the hand that held bloody Catsclaw trembled with rage.

Then Fafhrd doubled over in a fit of coughing. One hand clutching at the edge of the table drapery, he stumbled back. The liquid in the crucible splashed violently. The crucible itself threatened to tip and spill its life-saving contents. Sheelba made a grab for the vessel, but the Mouser brushed his hands aside and caught the rim and saved the potion himself.

Fafhrd's spasm passed, leaving him gasping for breath and pale of face. Wiping a hand over his lips, he looked with fearless eyes toward his partner.

The Mouser nodded to himself as much as to Fafhrd. Then unseen by the others, he rolled his dark and angry eyes toward the roof and beyond. *Well-played, you puppet-masters,* he thought. *Well-played. To save Fafhrd I'll dance your jig.*

With that, he plunged Catsclaw into the liquid.

The rainbow energies, directionless before as they swam, surged around the blade, entwined around it like fiery serpents.

The blood diffused into the liquid, and for a brief moment, the liquid turned scarlet, and the rainbows faded away as if some battle had been lost.

But the scarlet faded in turn, and from within the red water the rainbows rose again. They danced upon the dagger blade, climbed it, licked the blood from the Mouser's hand and sleeve, growing as they fed until bands of colored fire encircled the Gray Mouser.

A spark leaped from those bands, then another, each touching Sheelba and Fafhrd, and the arcanely heatless flames spiraled around and around them. Within those bands, Fafhrd straightened; he drew back his shoulders, and lifted his head, and when he looked across the room at the Mouser, all pain was gone from his bright green eyes.

Within his own body, the Gray Mouser felt a sharp-toothed worm die. For the life of him, though, and for the lives he had won, he could not rejoice. Even as vitality and renewed life flowed back into his frame, his thoughts turned to Ivrian. Ivrian, who was dead. He felt her absence and the distance between them like a horrible, heart-breaking gulf.

He opened his eyes again. Fafhrd stood at the hut's doorway staring outward. "Come and see this," he said quietly to the Mouser.

"Go on," Sheelba urged. In one hand, he held the jug Fafhrd had fetched. With the other, he lifted the lid of the trunk where he kept his wine. "I have a much better vintage than this, and we have much to celebrate."

"We have nothing to celebrate," the Mouser said bitterly. "But bring your wine. I need a drink."

The Mouser went to the doorway and pushed aside the covering. Fafhrd was already climbing down the ladder, but he kept his gaze toward Lankhmar's distant walls as he descended.

The Mouser leaned in the doorway, beholding a sight like none he had ever seen. Nor would he ever, he knew, see another like it.

Arching across the walls, the spires, and minarets of Nehwon's most ancient and mysterious city, a shimmering aurora blazed against the star-speckled heaven, neatly dividing the black of night in the west from the creeping light of dawn. Brighter, far more spectacular than the northern lights of Fafhrd's cold homeland, more awesome than any common rainbow, it floated in the air like a burning promise that Malygris's curse was forever ended.

A tear rolled down the Gray Mouser's cheek. One tear for all the dead. For Jesane and Demptha Negatarth. For Sadaster and Laurian. For a little blond girl with a straw poppet. For his beloved Ivrian.

He brushed the tear away before Sheelba could see it as he felt the wizard come up behind him. "You used me," he said coldly. "Death used me."

"Nor is that the end of it," Sheelba answered, not without some sympathy in his voice. "Death is only Death after all, and is used in turn by greater powers. That's what truly frightens you. You think you have glimpsed those greater powers."

"Is nothing we do of our own choosing?" the Mouser demanded. "Are we just pawns advanced or sacrificed at Fate's whim?"

"Climb down," Sheelba suggested patiently. He sloshed the bottle of wine he held. "We can all use a drink."

The Mouser obeyed. Weary in body and spirit, he went to Fafhrd's side. It was where he belonged, where he was meant to be. Fafhrd, the other half of his soul, for whom he would do anything, risk anything.

But did he belong at Fafhrd's side because he chose to be there? Did he have any say at all in where he went, what he did, who he called friend?

He looked at Fafhrd with blackly resentful eyes.

"I'm thinking of Vlana," Fafhrd whispered, not noticing the hate-filled look of his partner. "The night she first came to Cold

Corner with a troupe of actors and dancers, an aurora hung like a curtain in the sky. We joked once that it was the curtain going up on the stage-play that our lives together would make." He paused, though his gaze continued fixed on the blazing vision over Lankhmar. "In my homeland, auroras are considered omens. I've sometimes wondered if the aurora that burned that night over my love-making with Vlana was for good or ill."

The hate and anger faded from the Mouser's face. "I know you're not a superstitious man . . ." he said.

"I'm not!" Fafhrd interrupted defensively.

"Then forget omens," the Mouser said. "Just cling to Vlana's memory. Hold tight to it, Fafhrd. Keep it like a treasure, or the gods will steal it away from you." He cast his gaze upward.

No sky had ever been more beautiful, or seemed to him more alien. Through that shimmering curtain that hung high above the world like the drapery of some cosmic proscenium he glimpsed subtle shadows and a hint of puppeteers' strings.

"Drink," Sheelba said, wiping the back of his hand over the lower part of his unseen face as he passed the bottle of wine to Fafhrd. "The gods never give thanks to mortals. Such is not the nature of the world. But if it means anything, I thank you."

Fafhrd took a long pull from the bottle and swallowed noisily. "Only three words mean more," he said, passing the bottle to the Mouser.

Sheelba folded his hands inside his sleeves. "And they are?"

"I love you," the Mouser answered somberly. Closing his eyes, he conjured the face of his one true love and drank a deep, final toast to her. "At least I had the chance to apologize and ask Ivrian's forgiveness for not being at her side when she died."

Fafhrd nodded gravely. "And I had the same chance with Vlana. Perhaps I can at last let go of that guilt and pain."

Sheelba took the bottle back from the Mouser and stoppered it. "There is another price you'll have to pay for that pain-ease," the wizard said sadly. "Another day you will face Death of

Nehwon, and it must be as if for the first time. You'll see your women again and make your apologies."

Fafhrd scoffed. "No need to apologize twice to Vlana. We've made our peace." He put a hand on the Mouser's shoulder and gazed yet again at the dazzling aurora. In the distance, bells were pealing out from all the temples in Lankhmar. "We saved a city, Mouser," Fafhrd said. "Perhaps a world. Who knows how far Malygris's curse might eventually have reached. We've done good work."

The Mouser moved closer to Sheelba and rubbed a hand wearily over his eyes. "Fafhrd has a good heart," he whispered. "But he doesn't see. Malygris's curse was never out of control. It would have reached only as far as Death of Nehwon allowed it, or only as far as Death's master, Fate, would have allowed." He hugged himself against a cold that clung like a mist to his spirit and knew that he would never feel warm again. "But I see," he said. "I see."

"You see too much," Sheelba murmured softly, his voice hypnotic. "And though Fafhrd hides it, he sees as well and shares your resentment."

The Mouser rubbed his eyes again. His lids felt so heavy, and a growing numbness was spreading through his limbs. He turned to look at his partner. Fafhrd slowly slumped to the ground as he watched.

"I didn't see you drink," the Mouser said thickly. He groped for his sword, but couldn't seem to grasp Scalpel's oddly elusive hilt. "You bastard. What was in the bottle?"

"A draught of forgetfulness," Sheelba answered. His voice seemed to roll from some distant valley. It echoed and reverberated in the Mouser's ears as he felt himself sink to the ground. The grass felt so soft beneath him, so warm, so comfortable.

"Sleep," Sheelba intoned, "and wake again in the Elder Mountains, with Lord Hristo at your heels and saddlebags of treasure by your campfire."

"Don't," Fafhrd protested sleepily. "Don't make me forget Vlana."

"It's not fair," the Mouser said. "To have an adventure, and then forget it. What will we have learned from all this?"

"You've ended a plague, my heroes," Sheelba said. "No one but you two could have done that. If Fate has chosen you for her champions, it's because your skills and passions have made you worthy of her attention."

The Mouser's eyes closed. Still he heard Sheelba's voice in his ears, or perhaps in his mind. He tried to shut it out, but failed. He filled his thoughts with Ivrian's face, the memory of her touch. And more—he thought of Malygris, of Koh-Vombi, of a small gray cat on the rooftops of Lankhmar. All precious to him, every memory and detail. He clung to them ferociously, though they melted away one by one.

And through it all came Sheelba's voice, Sheelba, who he knew somehow he would meet again.

> *"Your adventure now is at a close;*
> *Sleep, heroes, in well-deserved repose.*
> *When you waken this bedevilment will seem*
> *But a vague, disturbing, half-remembered dream.*
> *With hearts unburdened by thoughts of Death and Fate,*
> *Find new trails to blaze, new seas to navigate.*
> *Rescue maidens! Sing! Drink! Enjoy!*
> *Life's a gift, and Nehwon is your toy!*
> *Solve her riddles, all her mystery,*
> *And burn your names in Lankhmar's history.*
> *Sleep now, Night's Black Agents, sleep,*
> *Our Knight and Knave of Swords—sleep.*
> *Your work is done, the tale is told,*
> *And lives are saved a hundred-fold.*
> *If only all man's plagues could be*
> *Such a neatly ended fantasy."*

THE END

ROBIN WAYNE BAILEY is the Nebula Award–nominated author of seventeen books, including the best-selling *Dragonkin* series, *Shadowdance*, and the *Frost* saga, among others. He's also published over one hundred short stories and edited two collections, including *Architects of Dreams: The SFWA Author Emeritus Anthology*.

Robin is a former president of the Science Fiction and Fantasy Writers of America. In 1996, he founded the Science Fiction and Fantasy Writers Hall of Fame with the help of James Gunn and the Center for the Study of Science Fiction, along with the Kansas City Science Fiction and Fantasy Society. In 2004, the SF Hall of Fame merged with Paul Allen's new Science Fiction Museum in Seattle, Washington. Robin continues to serve as ongoing chairman for the SF Hall of Fame's Induction Committee.

Robin lives in North Kansas City, Missouri. A bodybuilder and a martial artist, he studies Shotokan and Ryobu-kai karate, collects books, and loves old-time radio theater. Visit his website at robinwaynebailey.net.

The definitive graphic novel adaptation of
FAFHRD AND THE GRAY MOUSER

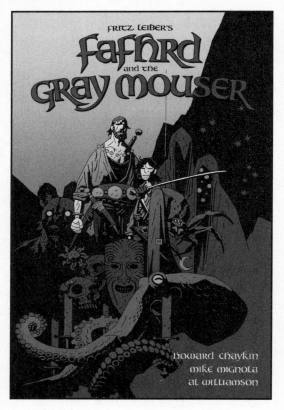

Discover the stories that defined the genre of sword & sorcery through the eyes of legendary comics writer Howard Chaykin and *Hellboy* creator Mike Mignola! Chaykin and Mignola's four-issue adaptation of *Fafhrd and the Gray Mouser*, long out of print, is collected here for the first time, with new cover art from Mignola.

ISBN 978-1-59307-713-6
$19.95
